WALKER BOOKS

SERIES: The Twilight Zone
TITLE: The Midnight Sun
CREATED BY: Rod Serling
ADAPTED BY: Mark Kneece
ILLUSTRATED BY: Anthony Spay
PB ISBN-13: 978-0-8027-9721-6
PB ISBN-10: 0-8027-9721-0
HC ISBN-13: 978-0-8027-9720-9
HC ISBN-10: 0-8027-9720-2
FORMAT: Paperback and hardcover graphic novel
TRIM: 6⅝ x 10
PB PRICE: $9.99 U.S./$11.00 Can.
HC PRICE: $16.99 U.S./$18.50 Can.
PUB DATE: June 2009
PAGE COUNT: 72
AGES: 12 and up
GRADES: 7 and up

CONTACT: Deb Shapiro
(646) 438-6070
deb.shapiro@bloomsburyusa.com

Please send us two copies of your review.
Walker Books
175 Fifth Avenue, 8th floor
New York, NY 10010

ROD SERLING worked as a writer and producer throughout his career in television and has won the most Emmy awards for dramatic writing in the history of television. He wrote more than seventy-five episodes of the *Twilight Zone* series, for which he won three of his Emmys. He was also the show's creator, host, and narrator.

MARK KNEECE cowrote a story in *Alien World* in 1987 for Pacific Comics and discovered a talent for comics writing. He has written stories for numerous comics, including *Batman: Legends of the Dark*. In 1993, he came to Savannah College of Art and Design and helped found the sequential art department. Since then, he has taught comics writing as a professor of sequential art. He lives in Savannah, Georgia.

ANTHONY SPAY graduated from Savannah College of Art and Design with an MFA in Sequential Art and has worked as a freelance illustrator for Devil's Due Publishing, Middlemind Games, and Knights Head Brewing. He is currently a staff illustrator for *Blitz* magazine. He lives in Philadelphia, Pennsylvania.

Marketing
- Full-color shelf talker available
- Ongoing national media pitch
- Ongoing targeted science fiction/fantasy graphic novel pitch
- Online promotions
- Targeted educational mailing to graphic novel big mouths/bloggers
- YA Galley List serv offering

Let us know your thoughts on this title!
Please e-mail your comments to:
deb.shapiro@bloomsburyusa.com

Published by Walker Books
175 Fifth Avenue, New York, NY 10010
www.walkerbooks.com

Rod Serling's iconic episodes enter the Graphic Novel Zone with an inventive new series

One of most groundbreaking shows in the history of television, *The Twilight Zone* has become a permanent fixture in pop culture. This graphic novel series reimagines the show's most enduring episodes, originally written by Serling himself, now adapted—from his original uncut scripts—for a new generation of fans.

In a time not unlike our own, two women are among the last people left behind in New York City, struggling to survive as the thermometer reaches an unbearable 120°. Almost overnight, modern-day conveniences become luxuries, and humans are pushed to their limits. As the climate grows more hostile, could these be the final days of life on Earth?

ROD SERLING's THE TWILIGHT ZONE

THE MIDNIGHT SUN

Adaptation from Rod Serling's original script by

MARK KNEECE

Illustrated by

ANTHONY SPAY

WALKER & COMPANY
NEW YORK

INTRODUCTION

There is a fifth dimension beyond that which is known to man. It is a dimension as vast as space and timeless as infinity. It is the middle ground between light and shadow, between science and superstition, and it lies between the pit of man's fears and the summit of his knowledge. This is the dimension of imagination. It is an area which we call the Twilight Zone.

America, between the 1950s and early 1960s, was itself in a sort of "twilight zone." Following the victories of World War II and the attending economic boom—but before the Civil Rights marches; the assassinations of John F. Kennedy, Martin Luther King, Jr., and Robert F. Kennedy; and the Vietnam War—we were wrapped in a gleaming package of shining chrome, white picket fences, and Hollywood glamour. But beneath this shimmering facade lay a turbulent core of racial inequality, sexual inequality, and the Cold War threat of nuclear attacks from the Soviet Union. We'd never been more affluent—or more frightened.

Enter Rodman Edward Serling of Binghamton, New York. Serling began writing in his teens for his high school newspaper; as a student at Antioch College, he was already selling scripts to radio programs. While serving as a paratrooper in the U.S. Army Eleventh Airborne (for which he earned a Purple Heart), he wrote for the Armed Services Radio. He went on to write for film and television, first in feature presentations for *Hallmark Hall of Fame* and *Playhouse 90*, including the lauded "Requiem for a Heavyweight," perhaps drawing inspiration from his own experiences as a Golden Gloves boxer. More than two hundred of his teleplays were produced. In all, his work would win not only the adoration of listeners and viewers but a host of prestigious awards, including a record-breaking six Emmy awards—two of them for his greatest achievement, *The Twilight Zone*.

The worlds and characters presented over the course of five seasons, beginning in October 1959, were like nothing audiences had seen before. Television, the new "must have" appliance for America's increasingly prosperous households, offered comedies such as *I Love Lucy* and *The Honeymooners*, news programs including Edward R. Murrow's *See It Now*, as well as Westerns, game shows, and soap operas. With a typewriter as his spade, Serling dug beneath the surface of the expected and planted the seeds of a more imaginative and thoughtful genre, writing more than half of the show's 156 episodes while producing and hosting all of them. He bravely took on themes of oppression, prejudice, and paranoia, all the while giving people what they needed at the end of the day: entertainment.

While he had his run-ins with censorship, Serling's clever use of other worlds and veiled scenarios generally protected him. As he explained, what he couldn't have a Republican or a Democrat espouse on the show, he could have an alien profess without offending the sponsors. This approach also allowed viewers to take away whatever message best suited them; the more reflective could consider the psychological and political implications, while others might be satisfied with simply enjoying the thrill of the surface story. So much more than mere science fiction or fantasy, Serling's scripts are parables that explore the multifaceted natures of hope, fear, humanity, loneliness, and self-delusion.

Half a century later, *The Twilight Zone* remains a part of our culture, routinely referenced in print and on television, having become a shorthand expression that succinctly describes the bizarre and unexpected. The original episodes are still aired on the SciFi Channel, both in late-night slots and as day-long marathons. The show was literally a Who's Who of Hollywood, helping to foster the careers of fledgling actors including Robert Redford, Ron Howard, Dennis Hopper, Charles Bronson, and William Shatner. It has also inspired countless authors and filmmakers, who have gone on to break through boundaries of their own.

In the fifty years since *The Twilight Zone* first aired, we've faced new enemies and have altered our definitions of happiness, but our core hopes and fears remain the same, as does our desire to be entertained. The stories are as compelling, and as telling, as ever. And now, in their newest incarnation, Serling's scripts serve as the basis for this graphic novel series, which honors the original text and even echoes the storyboarding of television, but offers a fresh interpretation, as seen through the eyes of a new generation of artists.

—Anna Marlis Burgard
Director of Industry Partnerships, Savannah College of Art and Design

You're traveling through
another dimension,
a dimension not only of sight and sound
but of mind;
a journey into a wondrous land
whose boundaries
are that of imagination.
That's the signpost up ahead—
your next stop,
the Twilight Zone!

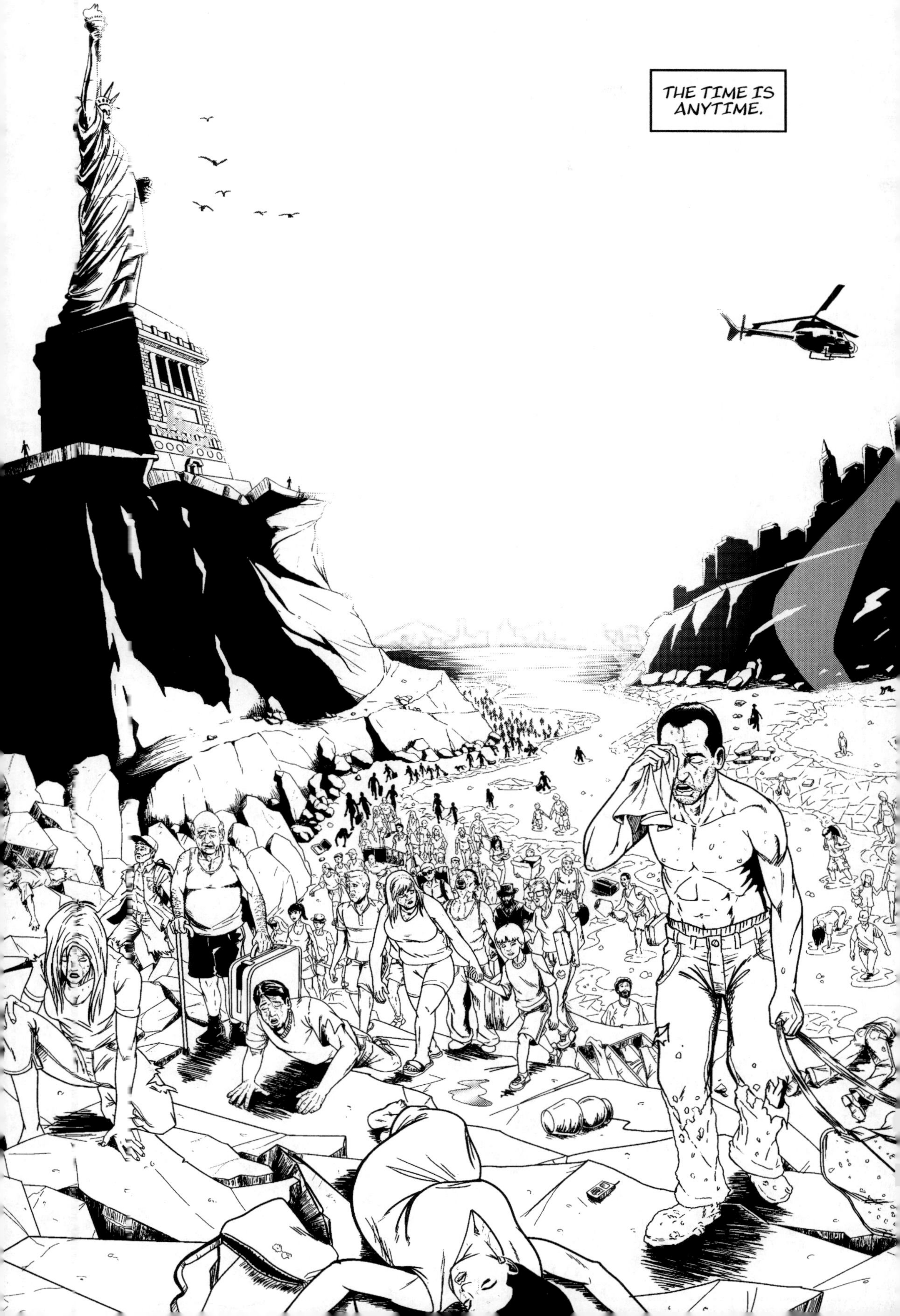
THE TIME IS ANYTIME.

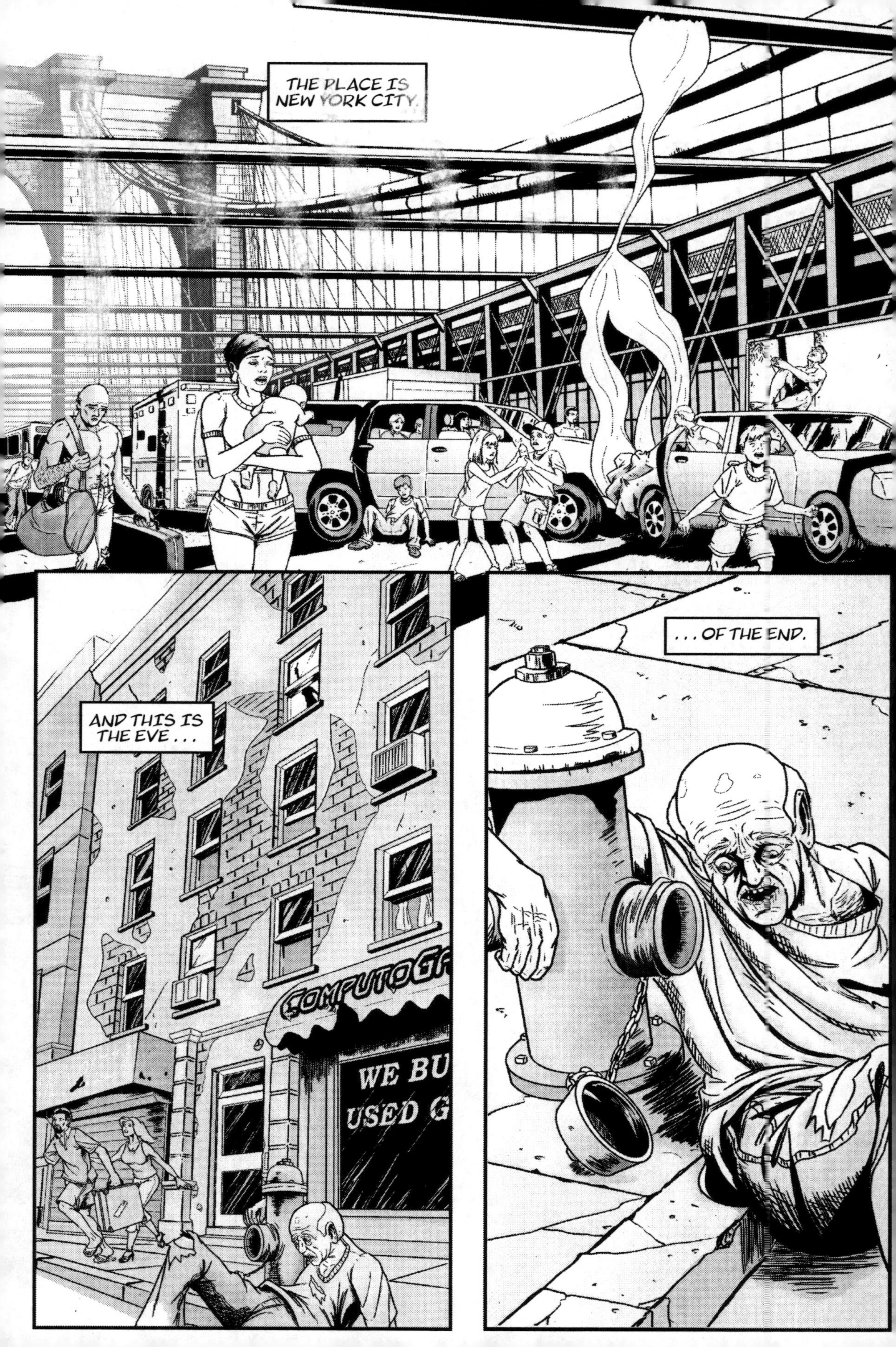
THE PLACE IS NEW YORK CITY.
AND THIS IS THE EVE . . .
COMPUTOGA
WE BU
USED G
. . . OF THE END.

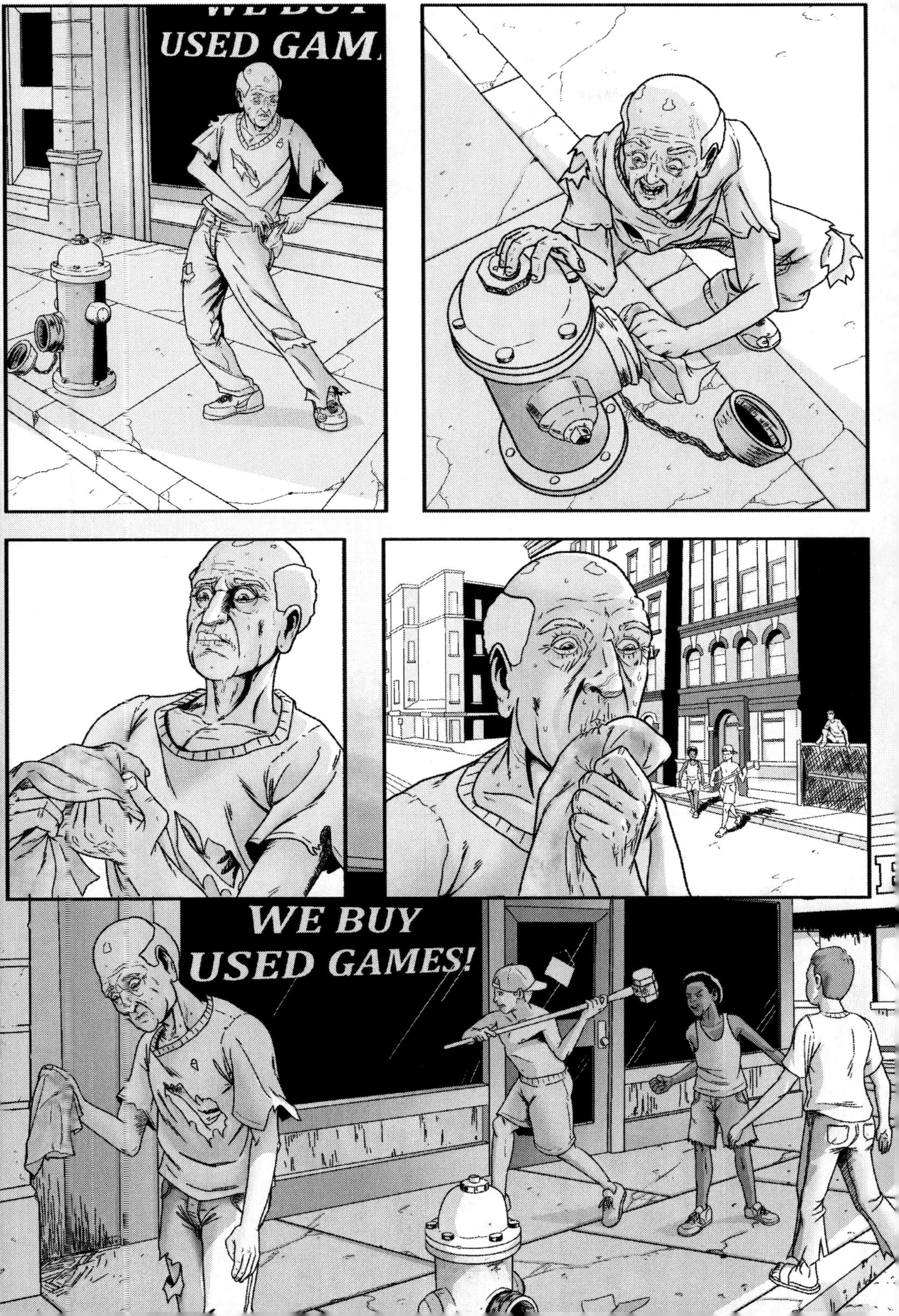
WE BUY
USED GAMES!

CRASH!

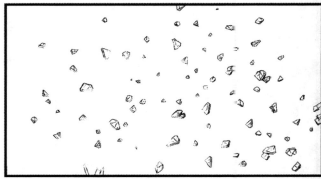

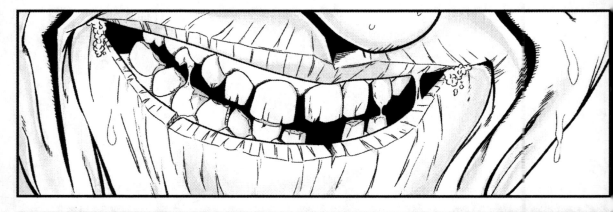

DIDJA REMEMBER TO GRAB THE BATTERIES? DIDJA? HUH?

HA HA HA HA HA HA!

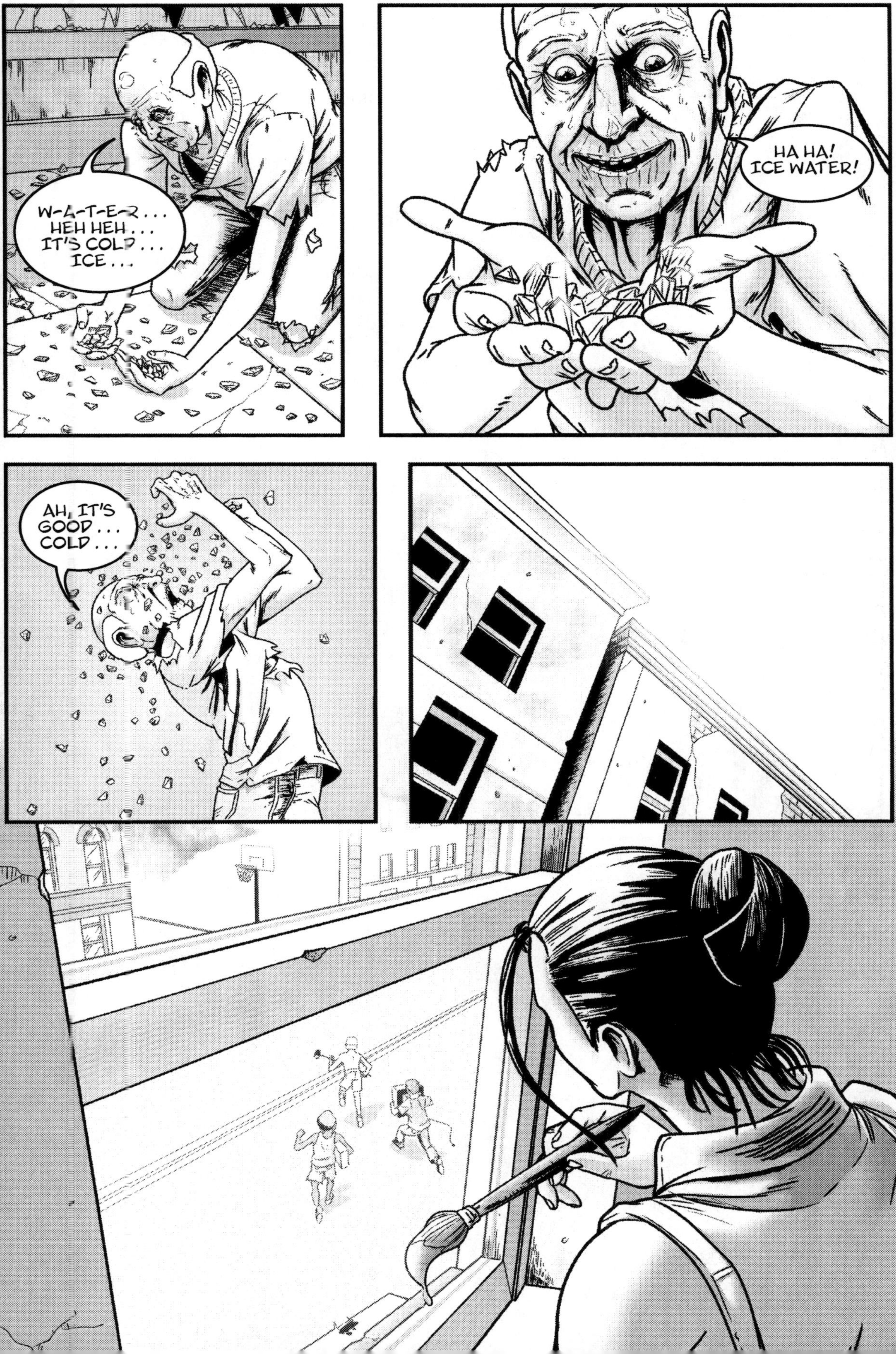
W-A-T-E-R . . .
HEH HEH . . .
IT'S COLD . . .
ICE . . .
HA HA!
ICE WATER!
AH, IT'S
GOOD . . .
COLD . . .

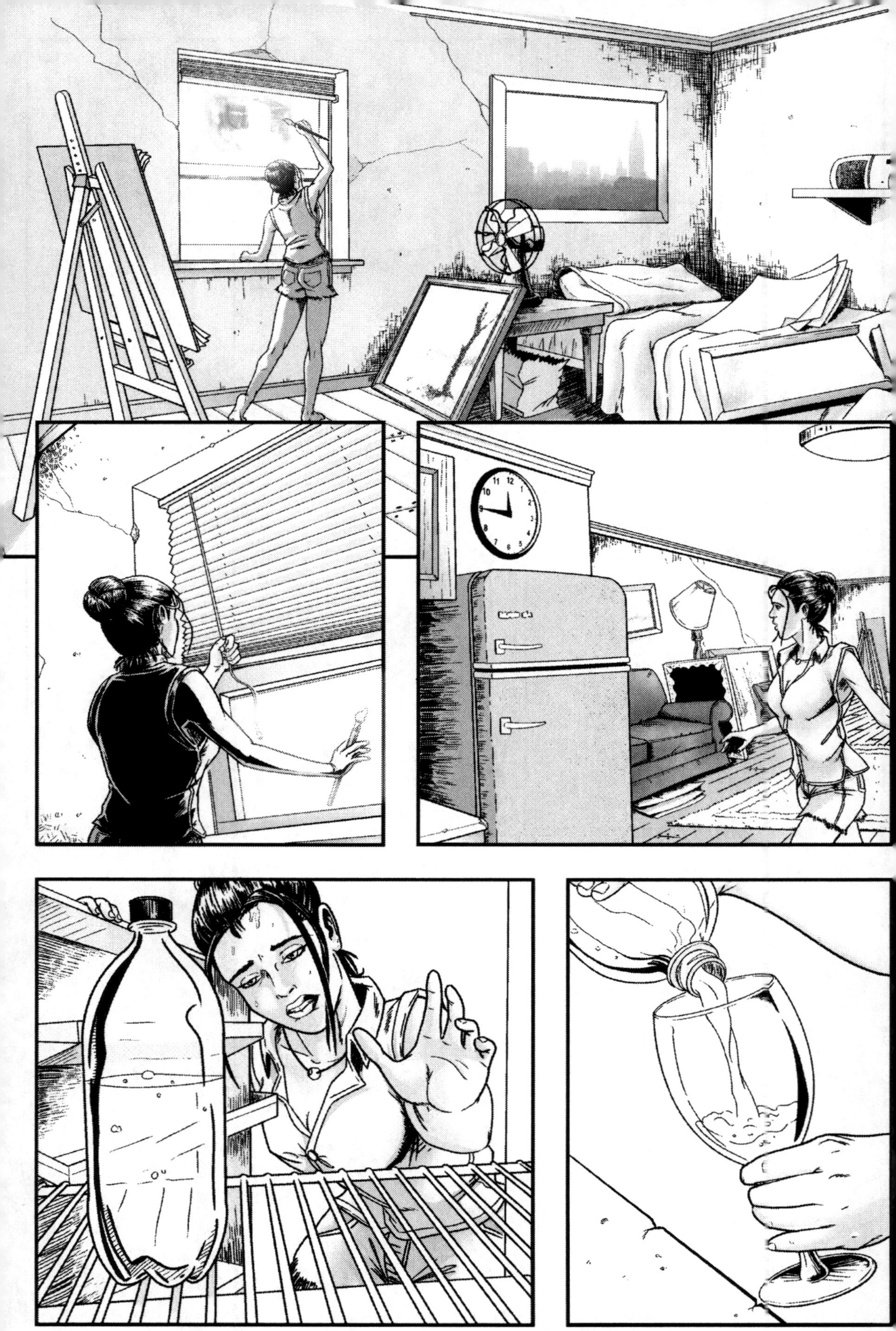

SUSIE! COME ON.

BUT I DON'T WANNA GO . . .

I DON'T WA–

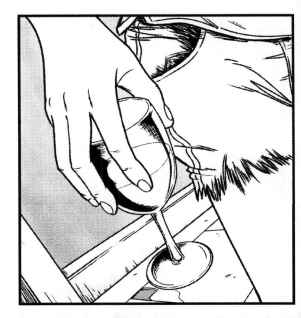

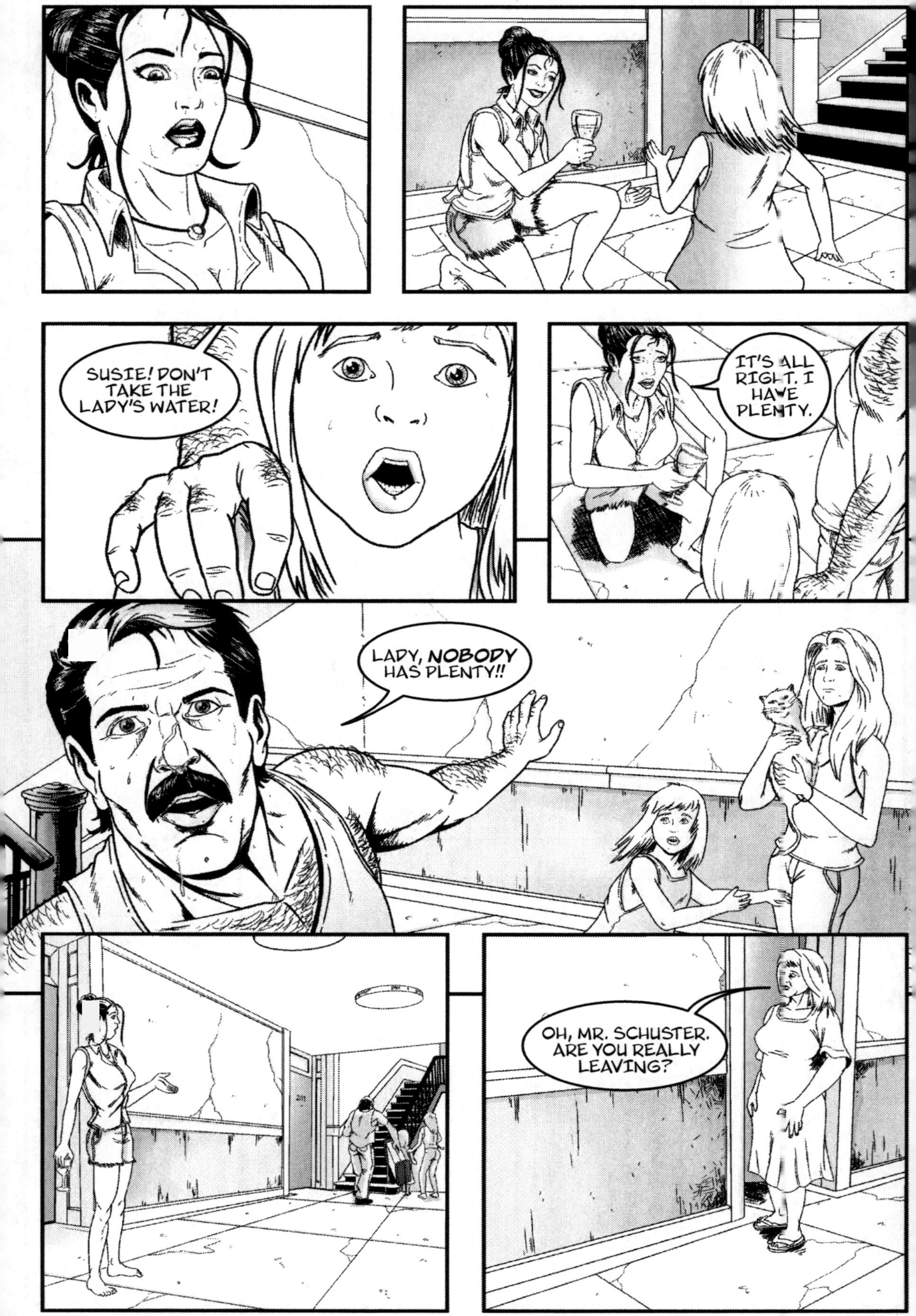
SUSIE! DON'T TAKE THE LADY'S WATER!
IT'S ALL RIGHT. I HAVE PLENTY.
LADY, **NOBODY** HAS PLENTY!!
OH, MR. SCHUSTER. ARE YOU REALLY LEAVING?

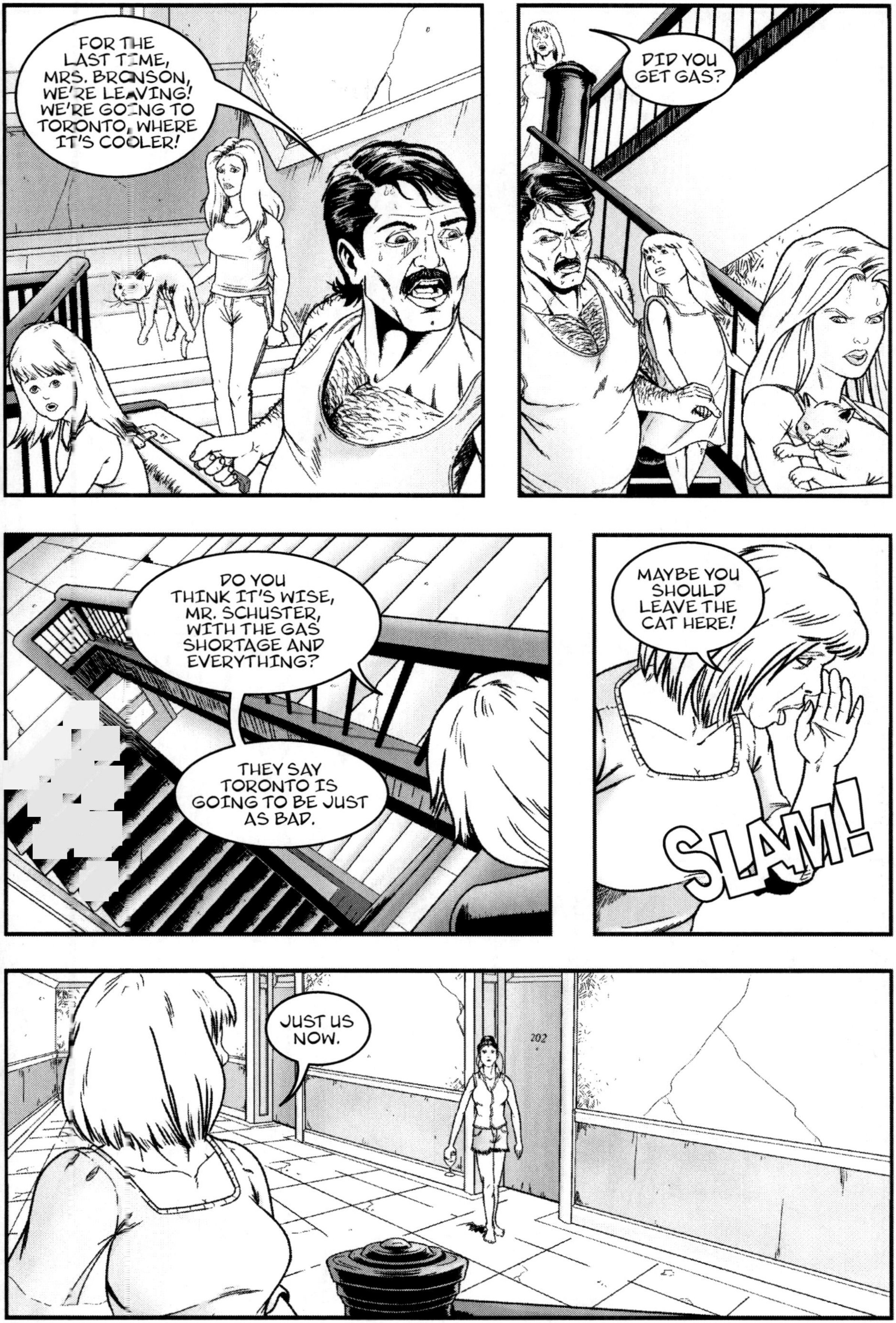
FOR THE LAST TIME, MRS. BRONSON, WE'RE LEAVING! WE'RE GOING TO TORONTO, WHERE IT'S COOLER!
DID YOU GET GAS?
DO YOU THINK IT'S WISE, MR. SCHUSTER, WITH THE GAS SHORTAGE AND EVERYTHING?
THEY SAY TORONTO IS GOING TO BE JUST AS BAD.
MAYBE YOU SHOULD LEAVE THE CAT HERE!
SLAM!
JUST US NOW.
202

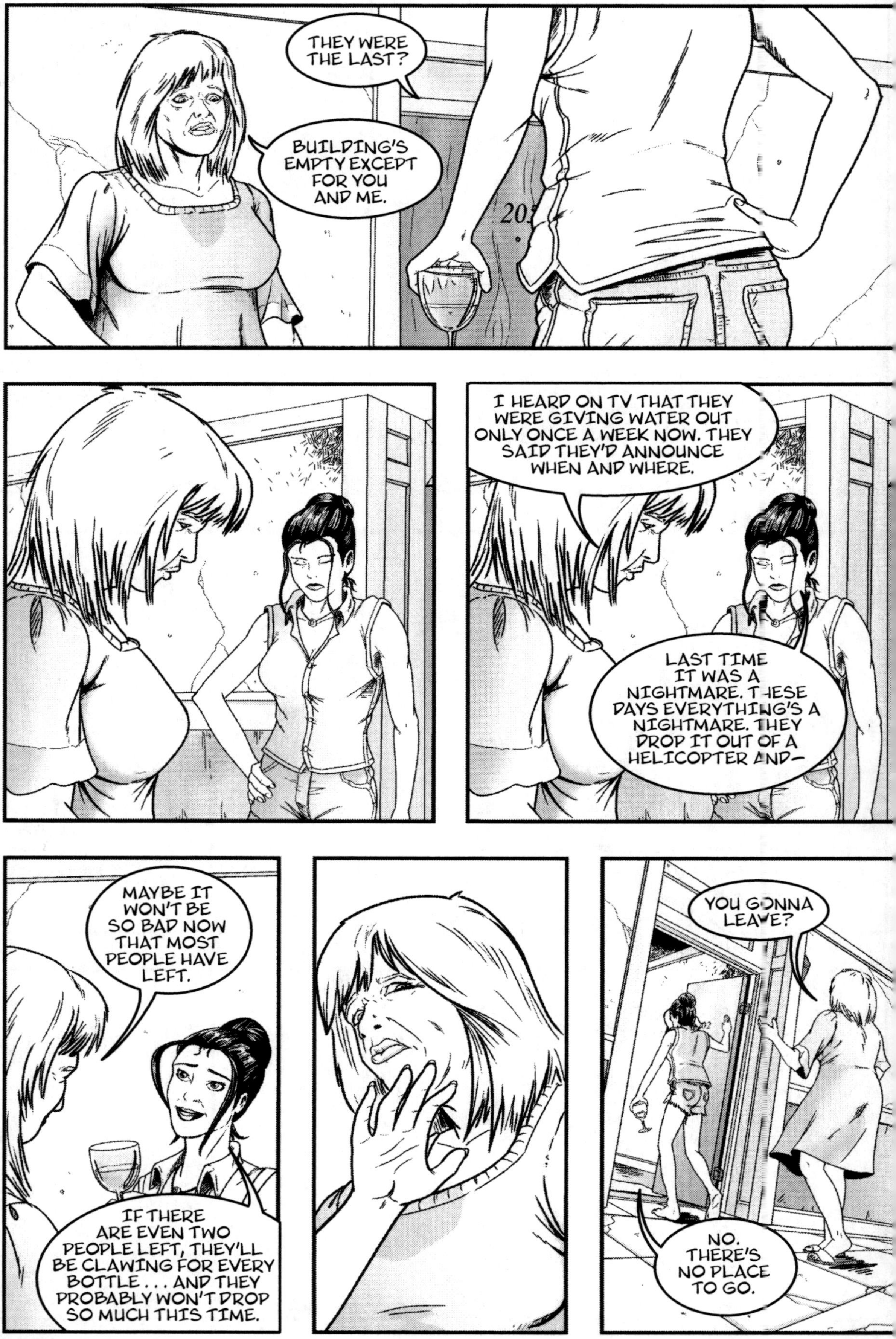
THEY WERE THE LAST?
BUILDING'S EMPTY EXCEPT FOR YOU AND ME.
202
I HEARD ON TV THAT THEY WERE GIVING WATER OUT ONLY ONCE A WEEK NOW. THEY SAID THEY'D ANNOUNCE WHEN AND WHERE.
LAST TIME IT WAS A NIGHTMARE. THESE DAYS EVERYTHING'S A NIGHTMARE. THEY DROP IT OUT OF A HELICOPTER AND—
MAYBE IT WON'T BE SO BAD NOW THAT MOST PEOPLE HAVE LEFT.
IF THERE ARE EVEN TWO PEOPLE LEFT, THEY'LL BE CLAWING FOR EVERY BOTTLE . . . AND THEY PROBABLY WON'T DROP SO MUCH THIS TIME.
YOU GONNA LEAVE?
NO. THERE'S NO PLACE TO GO.

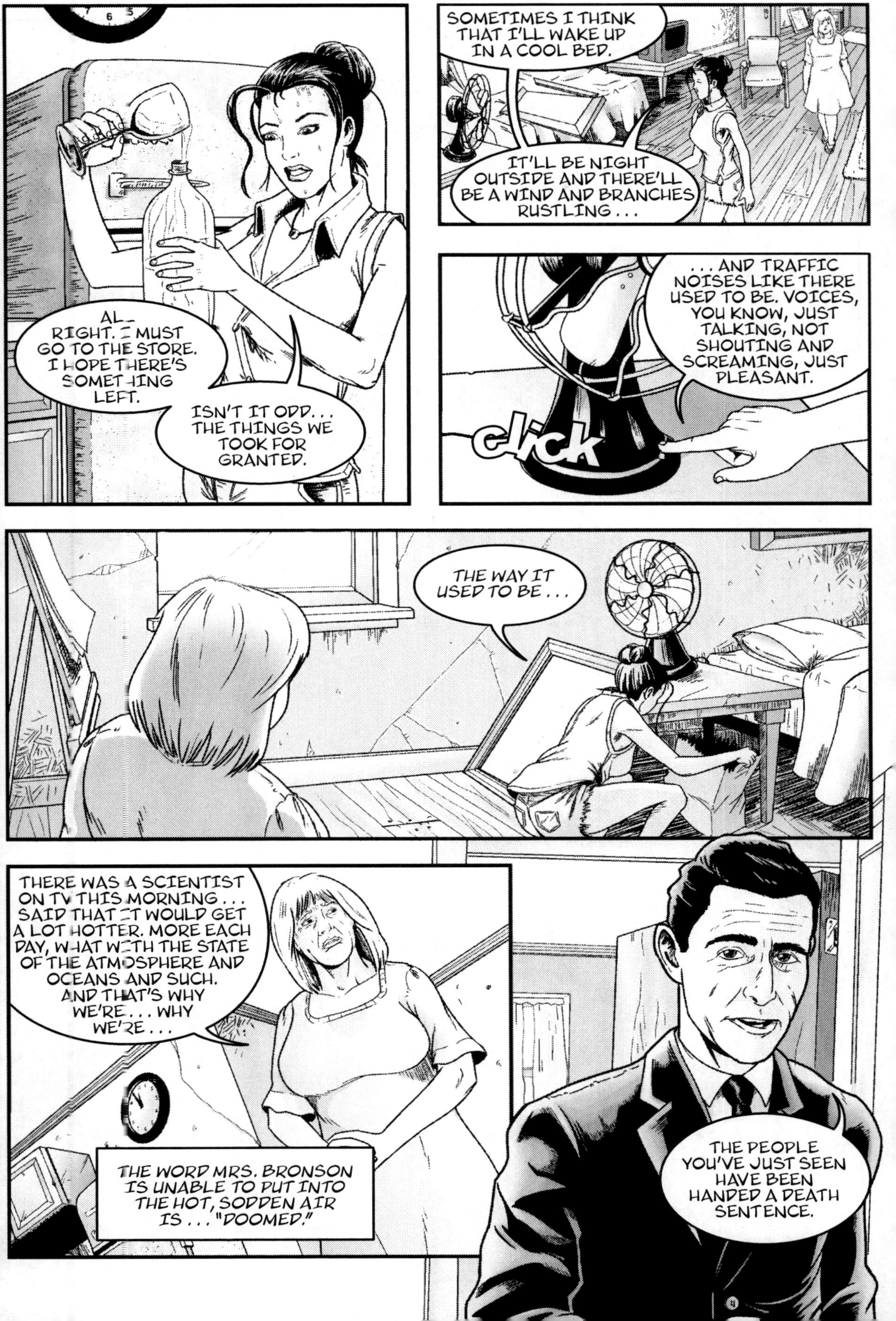
ALL RIGHT. I MUST GO TO THE STORE. I HOPE THERE'S SOMETHING LEFT.
ISN'T IT ODD . . . THE THINGS WE TOOK FOR GRANTED.
SOMETIMES I THINK THAT I'LL WAKE UP IN A COOL BED.
IT'LL BE NIGHT OUTSIDE AND THERE'LL BE A WIND AND BRANCHES RUSTLING . . .
. . . AND TRAFFIC NOISES LIKE THERE USED TO BE. VOICES, YOU KNOW, JUST TALKING, NOT SHOUTING AND SCREAMING, JUST PLEASANT.
CLICK
THE WAY IT USED TO BE . . .
THERE WAS A SCIENTIST ON TV THIS MORNING . . . SAID THAT IT WOULD GET A LOT HOTTER. MORE EACH DAY, WHAT WITH THE STATE OF THE ATMOSPHERE AND OCEANS AND SUCH. AND THAT'S WHY WE'RE . . . WHY WE'RE . . .
THE WORD MRS. BRONSON IS UNABLE TO PUT INTO THE HOT, SODDEN AIR IS . . . "DOOMED."
THE PEOPLE YOU'VE JUST SEEN HAVE BEEN HANDED A DEATH SENTENCE.

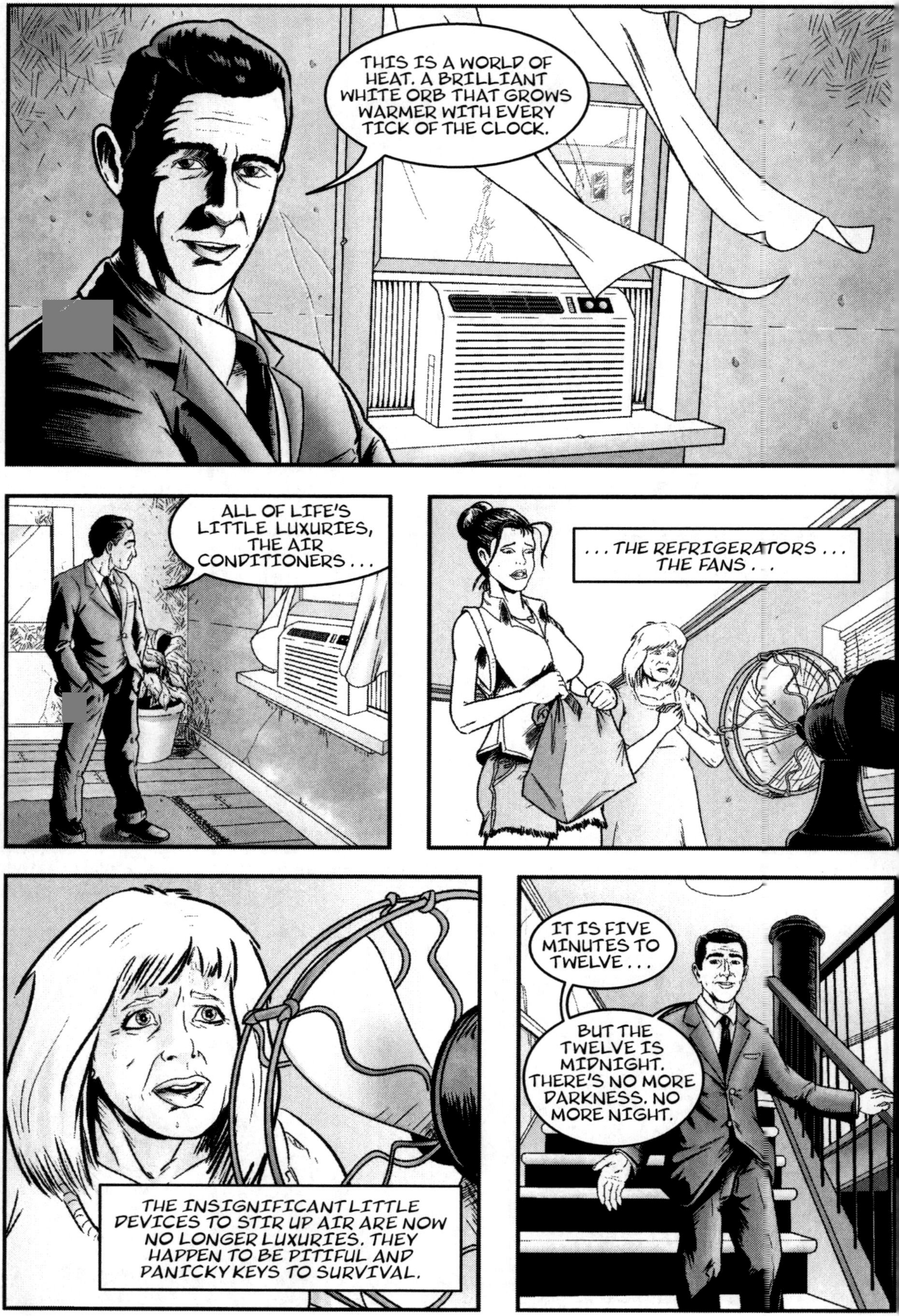
THIS IS A WORLD OF HEAT. A BRILLIANT WHITE ORB THAT GROWS WARMER WITH EVERY TICK OF THE CLOCK.
ALL OF LIFE'S LITTLE LUXURIES, THE AIR CONDITIONERS . . .
. . . THE REFRIGERATORS . . . THE FANS . . .
THE INSIGNIFICANT LITTLE DEVICES TO STIR UP AIR ARE NOW NO LONGER LUXURIES. THEY HAPPEN TO BE PITIFUL AND PANICKY KEYS TO SURVIVAL.
IT IS FIVE MINUTES TO TWELVE . . .
BUT THE TWELVE IS MIDNIGHT. THERE'S NO MORE DARKNESS. NO MORE NIGHT.

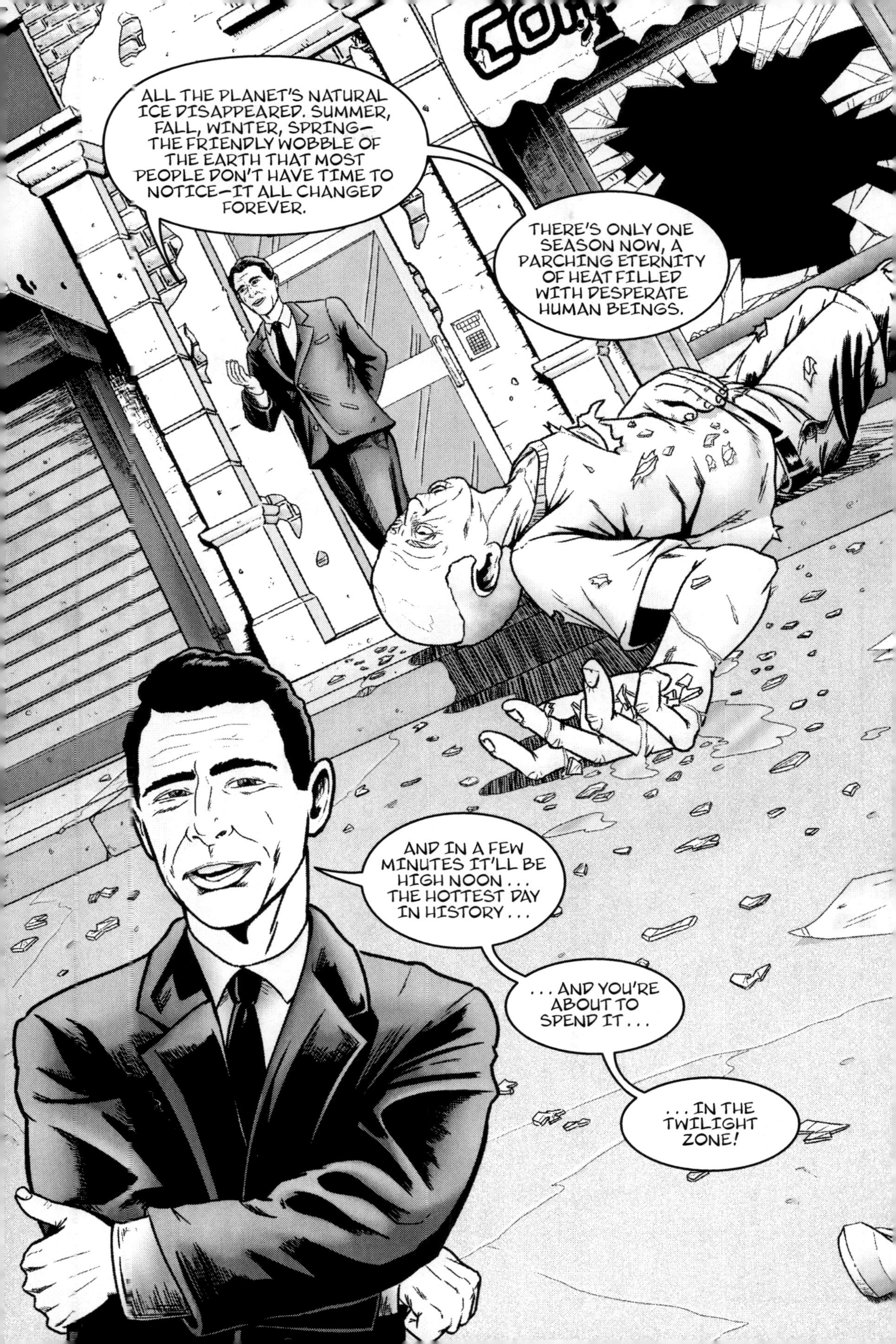
ALL THE PLANET'S NATURAL ICE DISAPPEARED. SUMMER, FALL, WINTER, SPRING—THE FRIENDLY WOBBLE OF THE EARTH THAT MOST PEOPLE DON'T HAVE TIME TO NOTICE—IT ALL CHANGED FOREVER.
THERE'S ONLY ONE SEASON NOW, A PARCHING ETERNITY OF HEAT FILLED WITH DESPERATE HUMAN BEINGS.
AND IN A FEW MINUTES IT'LL BE HIGH NOON . . . THE HOTTEST DAY IN HISTORY . . .
. . . AND YOU'RE ABOUT TO SPEND IT . . .
. . . IN THE TWILIGHT ZONE!

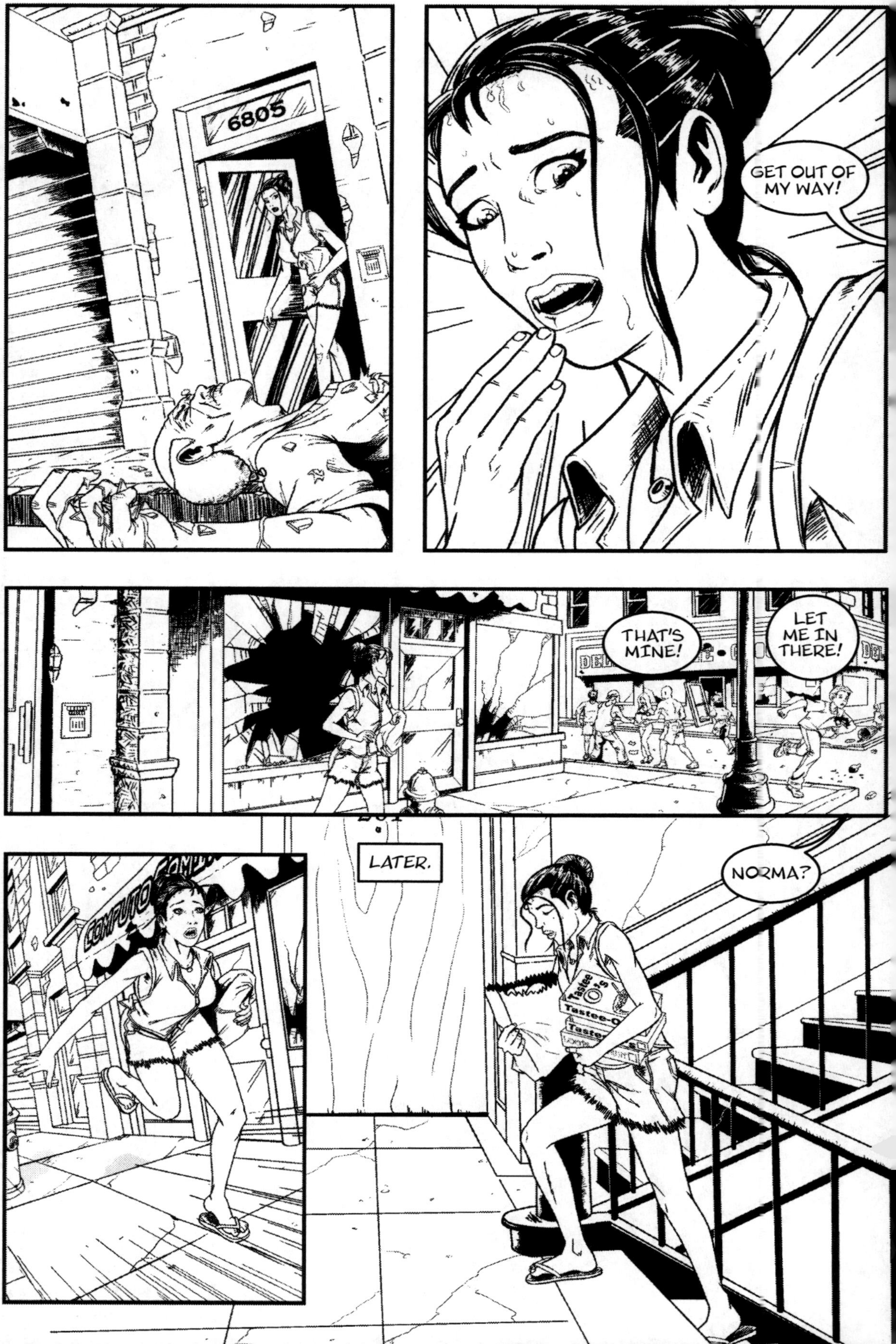
6805
GET OUT OF MY WAY!
THAT'S MINE!
LET ME IN THERE!
LATER.
NORMA?

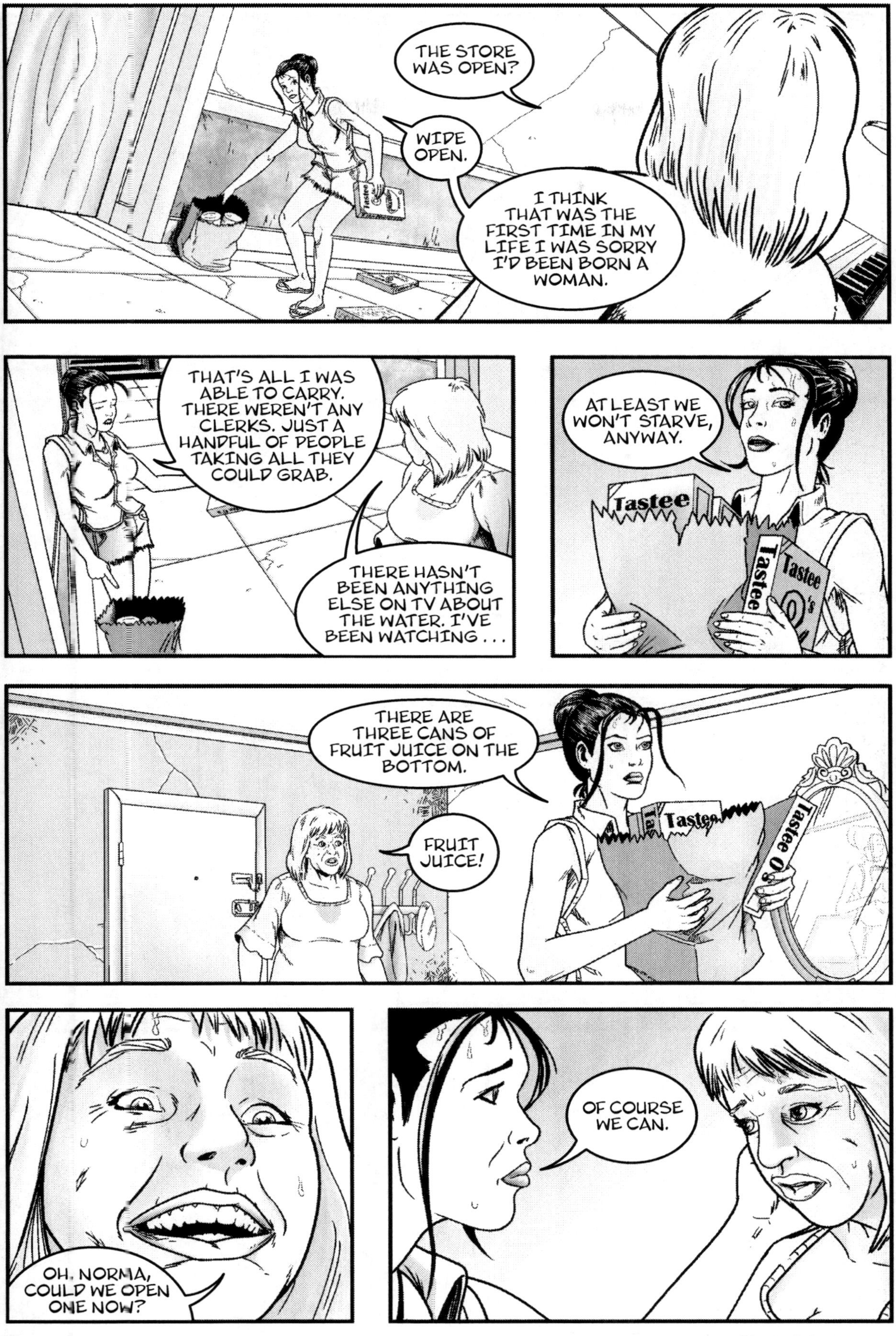
THE STORE WAS OPEN?
WIDE OPEN.
I THINK THAT WAS THE FIRST TIME IN MY LIFE I WAS SORRY I'D BEEN BORN A WOMAN.
THAT'S ALL I WAS ABLE TO CARRY. THERE WEREN'T ANY CLERKS. JUST A HANDFUL OF PEOPLE TAKING ALL THEY COULD GRAB.
THERE HASN'T BEEN ANYTHING ELSE ON TV ABOUT THE WATER. I'VE BEEN WATCHING . . .
AT LEAST WE WON'T STARVE, ANYWAY.
THERE ARE THREE CANS OF FRUIT JUICE ON THE BOTTOM.
FRUIT JUICE!
OH, NORMA, COULD WE OPEN ONE NOW?
OF COURSE WE CAN.

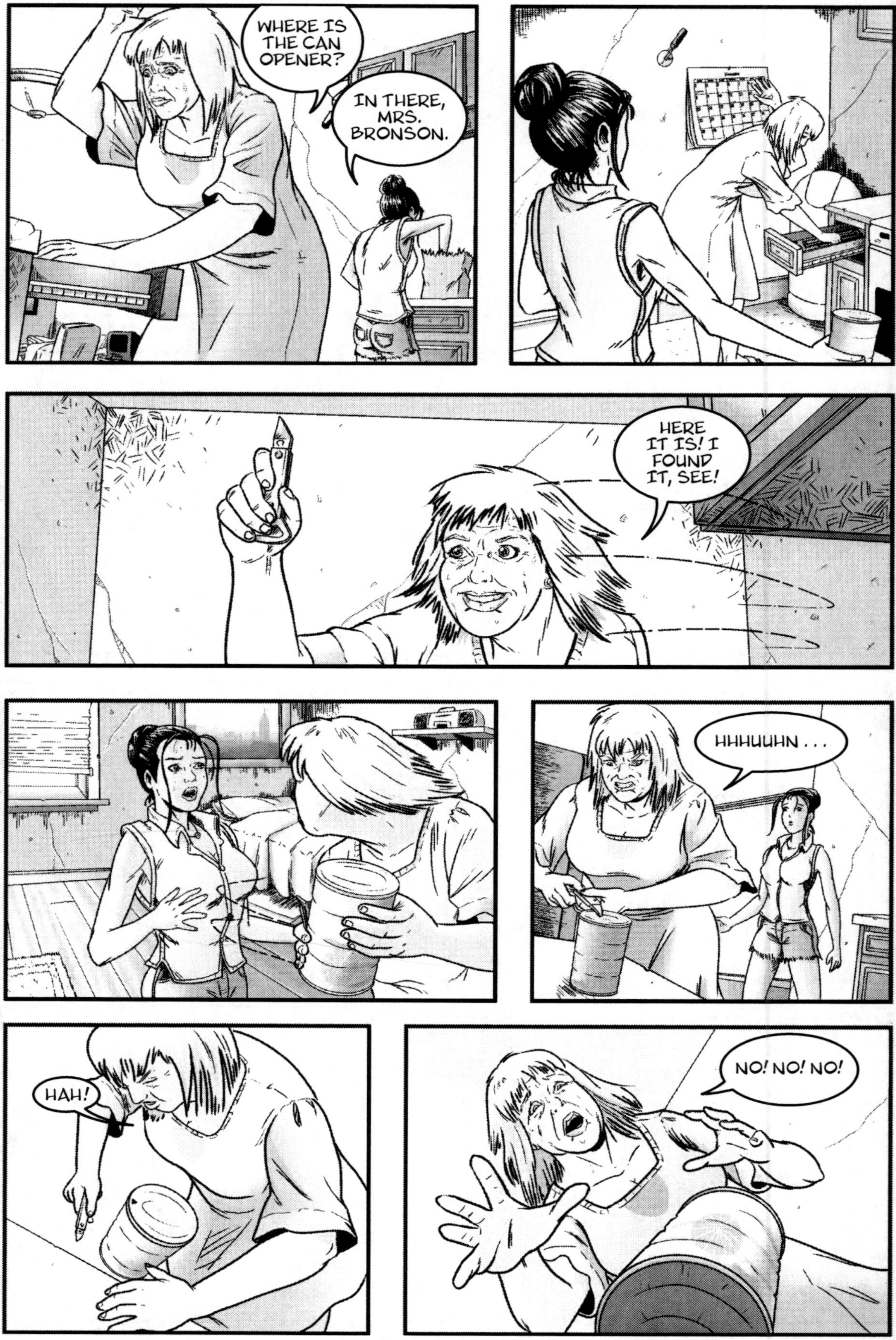
WHERE IS THE CAN OPENER?
IN THERE, MRS. BRONSON.
HERE IT IS! I FOUND IT, SEE!
HHHUUHN . . .
HAH!
NO! NO! NO!

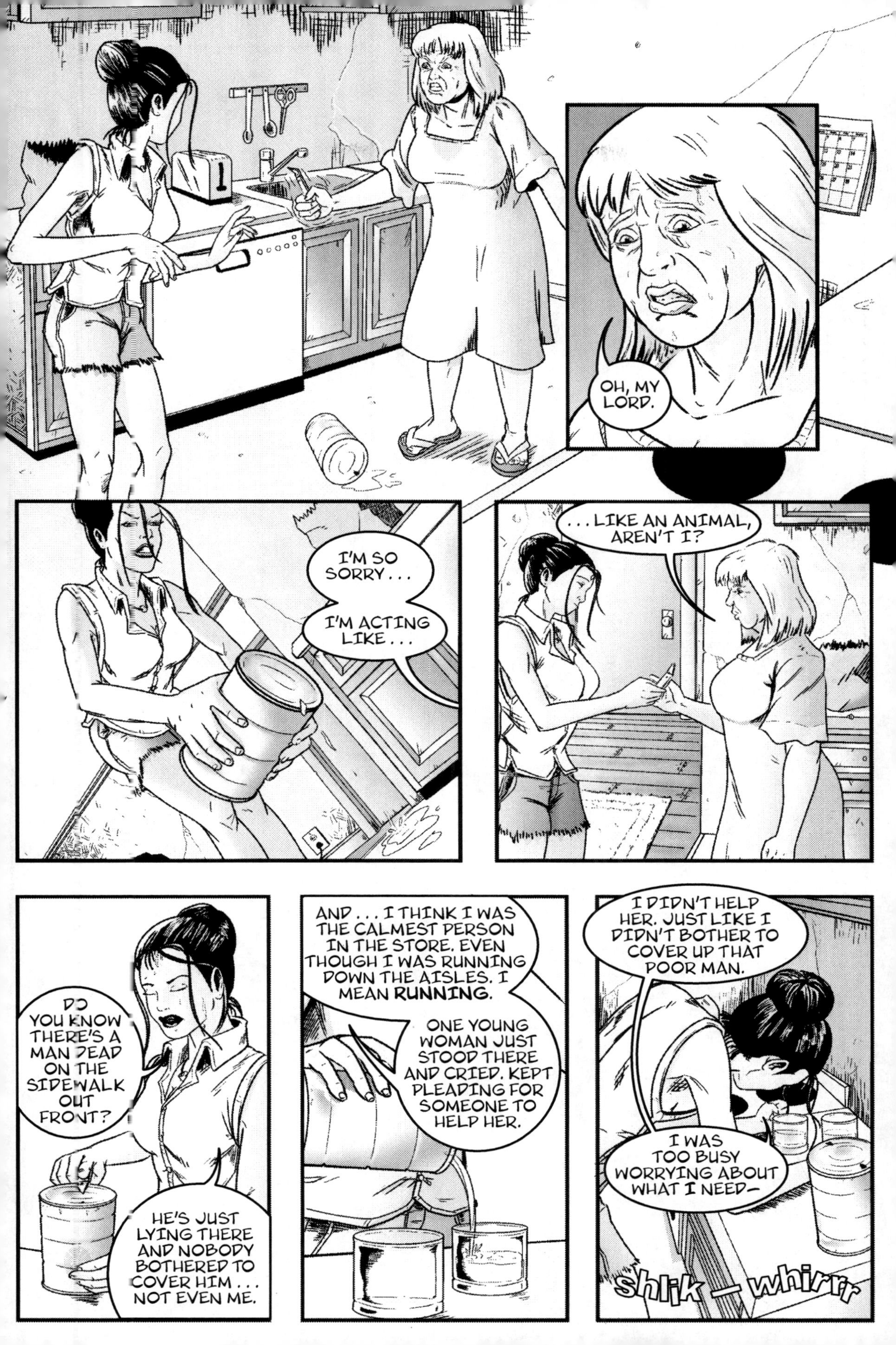
OH, MY LORD.
I'M SO SORRY . . .
I'M ACTING LIKE . . .
. . . LIKE AN ANIMAL, AREN'T I?
DO YOU KNOW THERE'S A MAN DEAD ON THE SIDEWALK OUT FRONT?
HE'S JUST LYING THERE AND NOBODY BOTHERED TO COVER HIM . . . NOT EVEN ME.
AND . . . I THINK I WAS THE CALMEST PERSON IN THE STORE. EVEN THOUGH I WAS RUNNING DOWN THE AISLES. I MEAN **RUNNING**.
ONE YOUNG WOMAN JUST STOOD THERE AND CRIED. KEPT PLEADING FOR SOMEONE TO HELP HER.
I DIDN'T HELP HER. JUST LIKE I DIDN'T BOTHER TO COVER UP THAT POOR MAN.
I WAS TOO BUSY WORRYING ABOUT WHAT **I** NEED—
shlik — whirrr

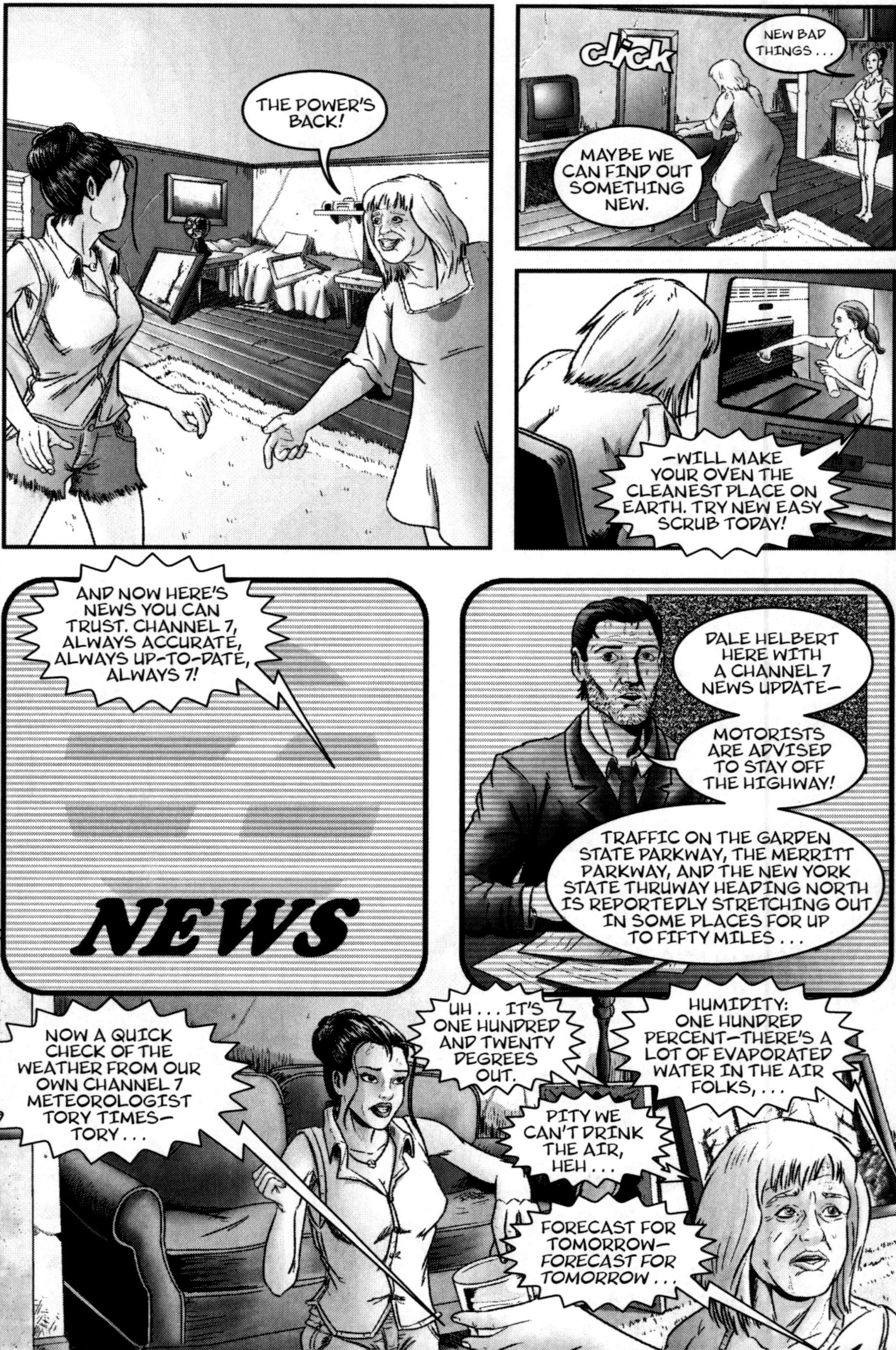
THE POWER'S BACK!
CLICK
NEW BAD THINGS . . .
MAYBE WE CAN FIND OUT SOMETHING NEW.
—WILL MAKE YOUR OVEN THE CLEANEST PLACE ON EARTH. TRY NEW EASY SCRUB TODAY!
AND NOW HERE'S NEWS YOU CAN TRUST. CHANNEL 7, ALWAYS ACCURATE, ALWAYS UP-TO-DATE, ALWAYS 7!
NEWS
DALE HELBERT HERE WITH A CHANNEL 7 NEWS UPDATE—
MOTORISTS ARE ADVISED TO STAY OFF THE HIGHWAY!
TRAFFIC ON THE GARDEN STATE PARKWAY, THE MERRITT PARKWAY, AND THE NEW YORK STATE THRUWAY HEADING NORTH IS REPORTEDLY STRETCHING OUT IN SOME PLACES FOR UP TO FIFTY MILES . . .
NOW A QUICK CHECK OF THE WEATHER FROM OUR OWN CHANNEL 7 METEOROLOGIST TORY TIMES— TORY . . .
UH . . . IT'S ONE HUNDRED AND TWENTY DEGREES OUT.
HUMIDITY: ONE HUNDRED PERCENT—THERE'S A LOT OF EVAPORATED WATER IN THE AIR FOLKS, . . .
PITY WE CAN'T DRINK THE AIR, HEH . . .
FORECAST FOR TOMORROW— FORECAST FOR TOMORROW . . .

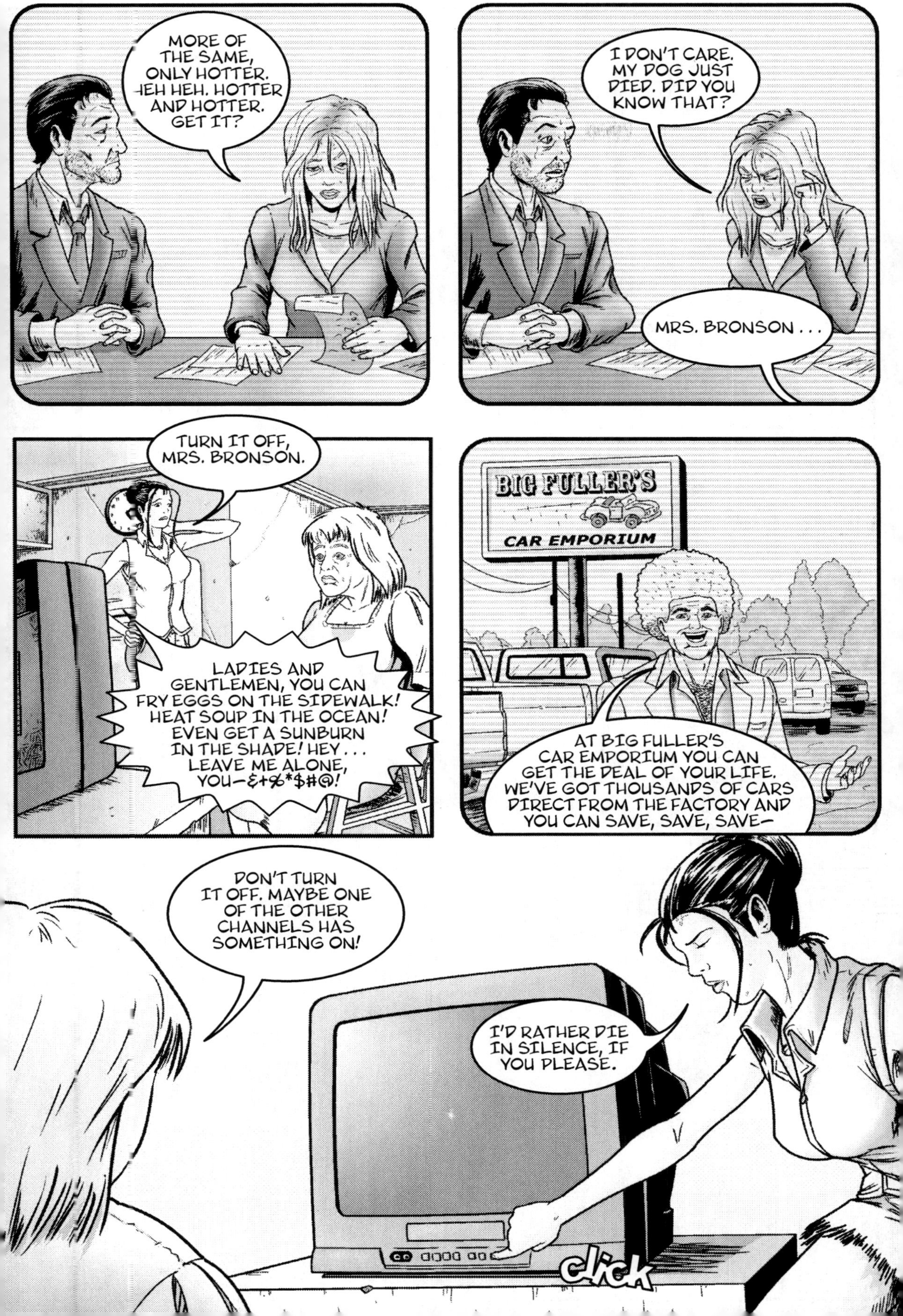
MORE OF THE SAME, ONLY HOTTER. HEH HEH. HOTTER AND HOTTER. GET IT?
I DON'T CARE. MY DOG JUST DIED. DID YOU KNOW THAT?
MRS. BRONSON . . .
TURN IT OFF, MRS. BRONSON.
LADIES AND GENTLEMEN, YOU CAN FRY EGGS ON THE SIDEWALK! HEAT SOUP IN THE OCEAN! EVEN GET A SUNBURN IN THE SHADE! HEY . . . LEAVE ME ALONE, YOU—&+%*$#@!
BIG FULLER'S
CAR EMPORIUM
AT BIG FULLER'S CAR EMPORIUM YOU CAN GET THE DEAL OF YOUR LIFE. WE'VE GOT THOUSANDS OF CARS DIRECT FROM THE FACTORY AND YOU CAN SAVE, SAVE, SAVE—
DON'T TURN IT OFF. MAYBE ONE OF THE OTHER CHANNELS HAS SOMETHING ON!
I'D RATHER DIE IN SILENCE, IF YOU PLEASE.
click

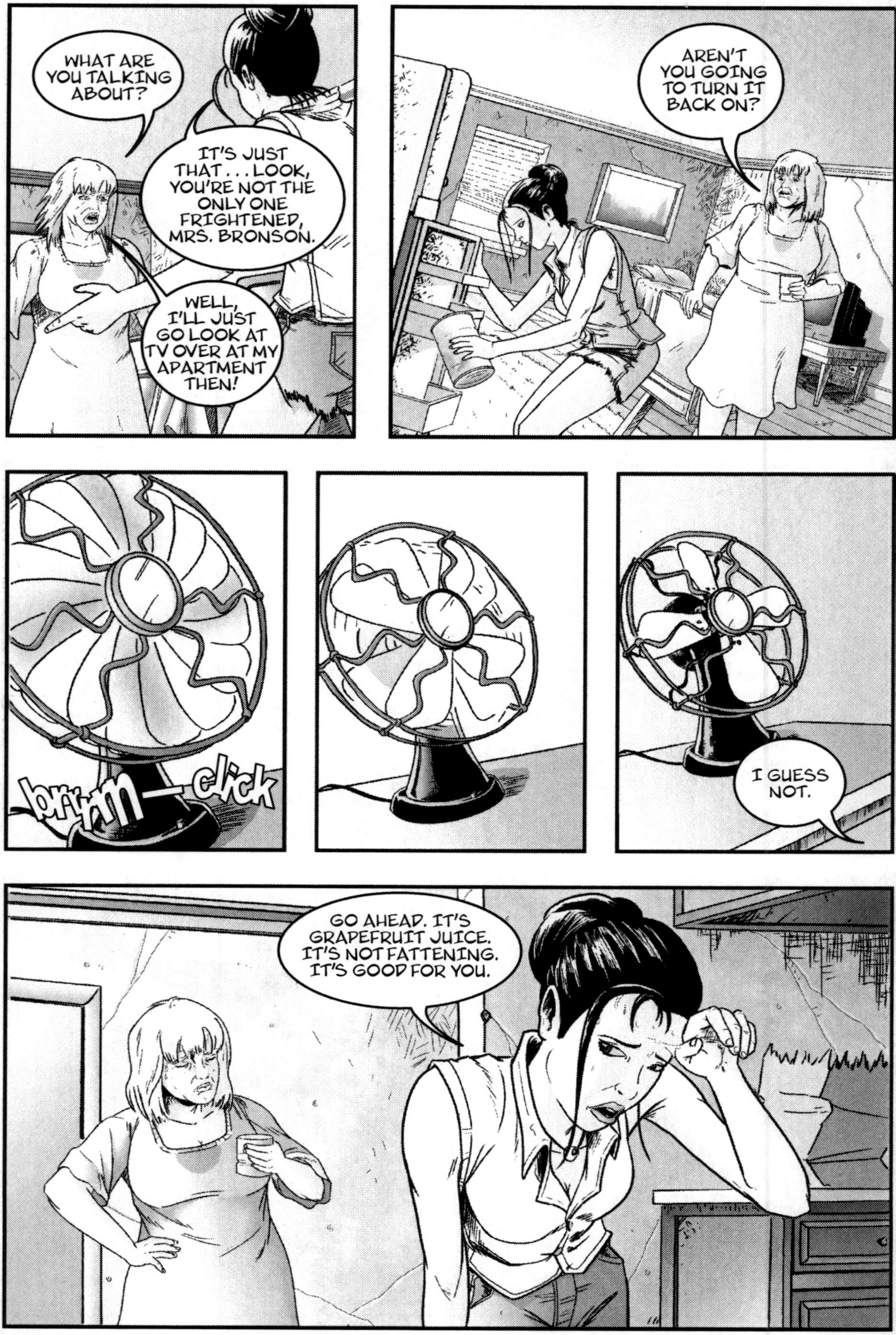
WHAT ARE YOU TALKING ABOUT?
IT'S JUST THAT . . . LOOK, YOU'RE NOT THE ONLY ONE FRIGHTENED, MRS. BRONSON.
WELL, I'LL JUST GO LOOK AT TV OVER AT MY APARTMENT THEN!
AREN'T YOU GOING TO TURN IT BACK ON?
brrrm—click
I GUESS NOT.
GO AHEAD. IT'S GRAPEFRUIT JUICE. IT'S NOT FATTENING. IT'S GOOD FOR YOU.

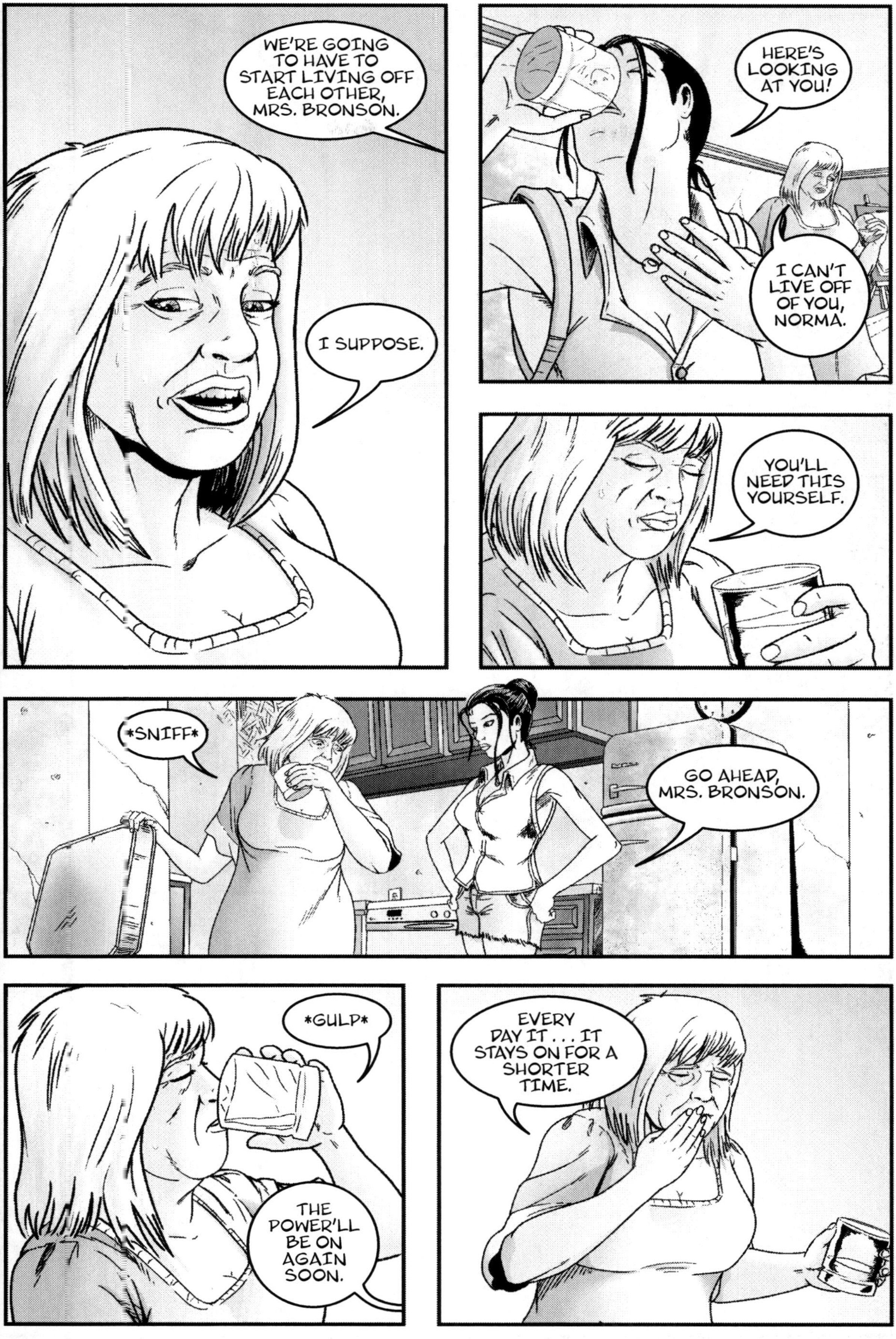
WE'RE GOING TO HAVE TO START LIVING OFF EACH OTHER, MRS. BRONSON.
I SUPPOSE.
HERE'S LOOKING AT YOU!
I CAN'T LIVE OFF OF YOU, NORMA.
YOU'LL NEED THIS YOURSELF.
SNIFF
GO AHEAD, MRS. BRONSON.
GULP
THE POWER'LL BE ON AGAIN SOON.
EVERY DAY IT . . . IT STAYS ON FOR A SHORTER TIME.

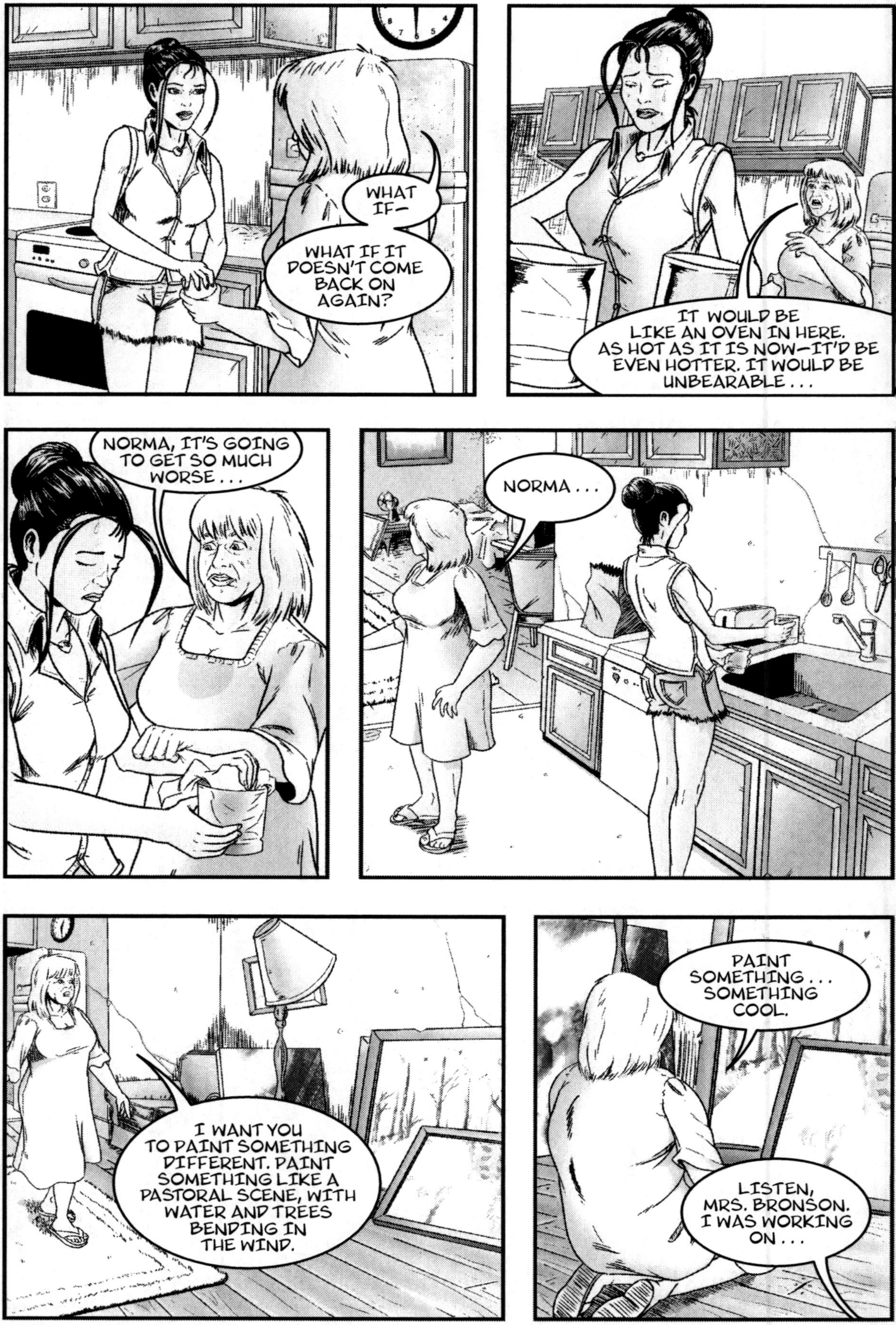
WHAT IF—
WHAT IF IT DOESN'T COME BACK ON AGAIN?
IT WOULD BE LIKE AN OVEN IN HERE. AS HOT AS IT IS NOW—IT'D BE EVEN HOTTER. IT WOULD BE UNBEARABLE . . .
NORMA, IT'S GOING TO GET SO MUCH WORSE . . .
NORMA . . .
I WANT YOU TO PAINT SOMETHING DIFFERENT. PAINT SOMETHING LIKE A PASTORAL SCENE, WITH WATER AND TREES BENDING IN THE WIND.
PAINT SOMETHING . . . SOMETHING COOL.
LISTEN, MRS. BRONSON. I WAS WORKING ON . . .

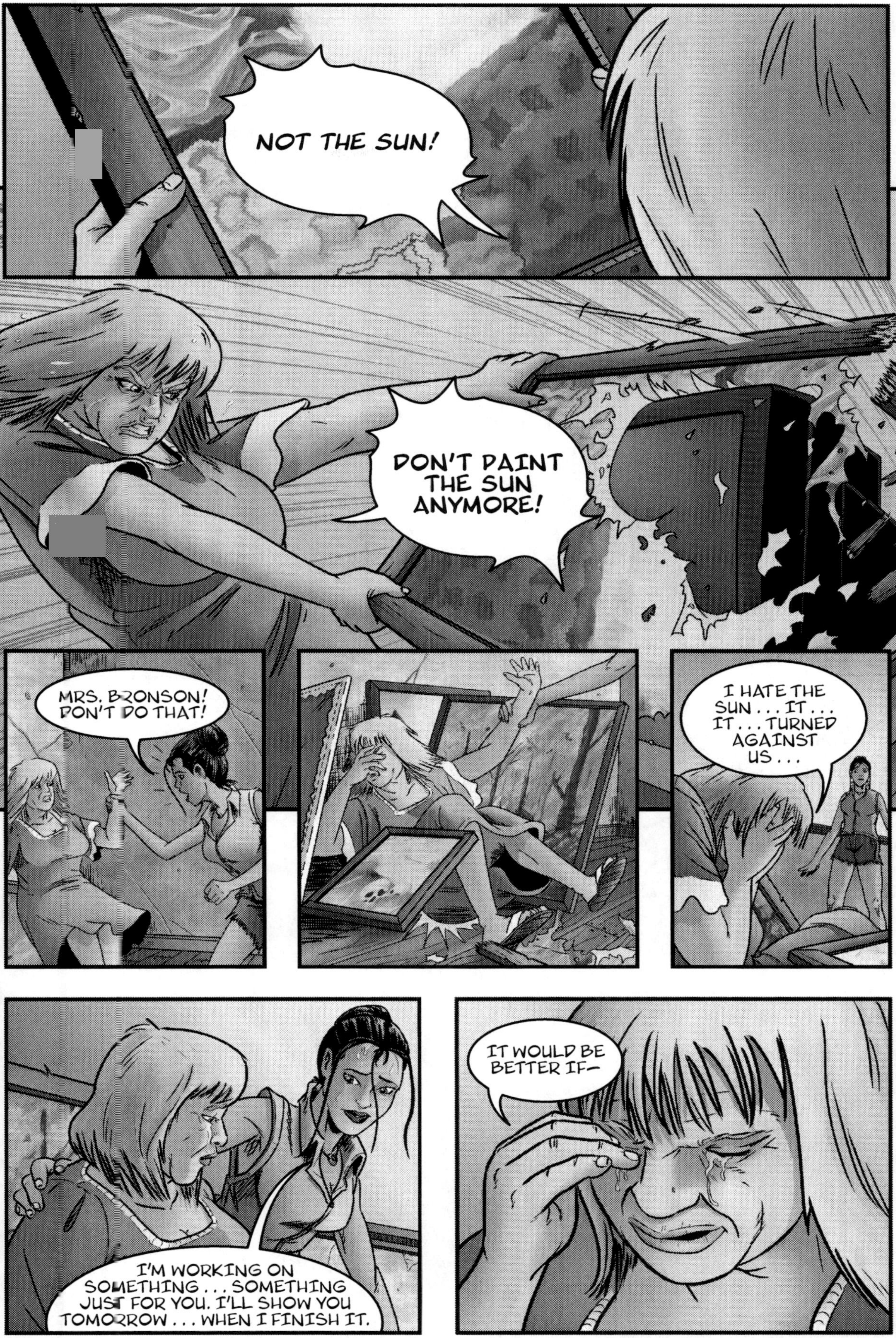
NOT THE SUN!
DON'T PAINT THE SUN ANYMORE!
MRS. BRONSON! DON'T DO THAT!
I HATE THE SUN . . . IT . . . IT . . . TURNED AGAINST US . . .
I'M WORKING ON SOMETHING . . . SOMETHING JUST FOR YOU. I'LL SHOW YOU TOMORROW . . . WHEN I FINISH IT.
IT WOULD BE BETTER IF—

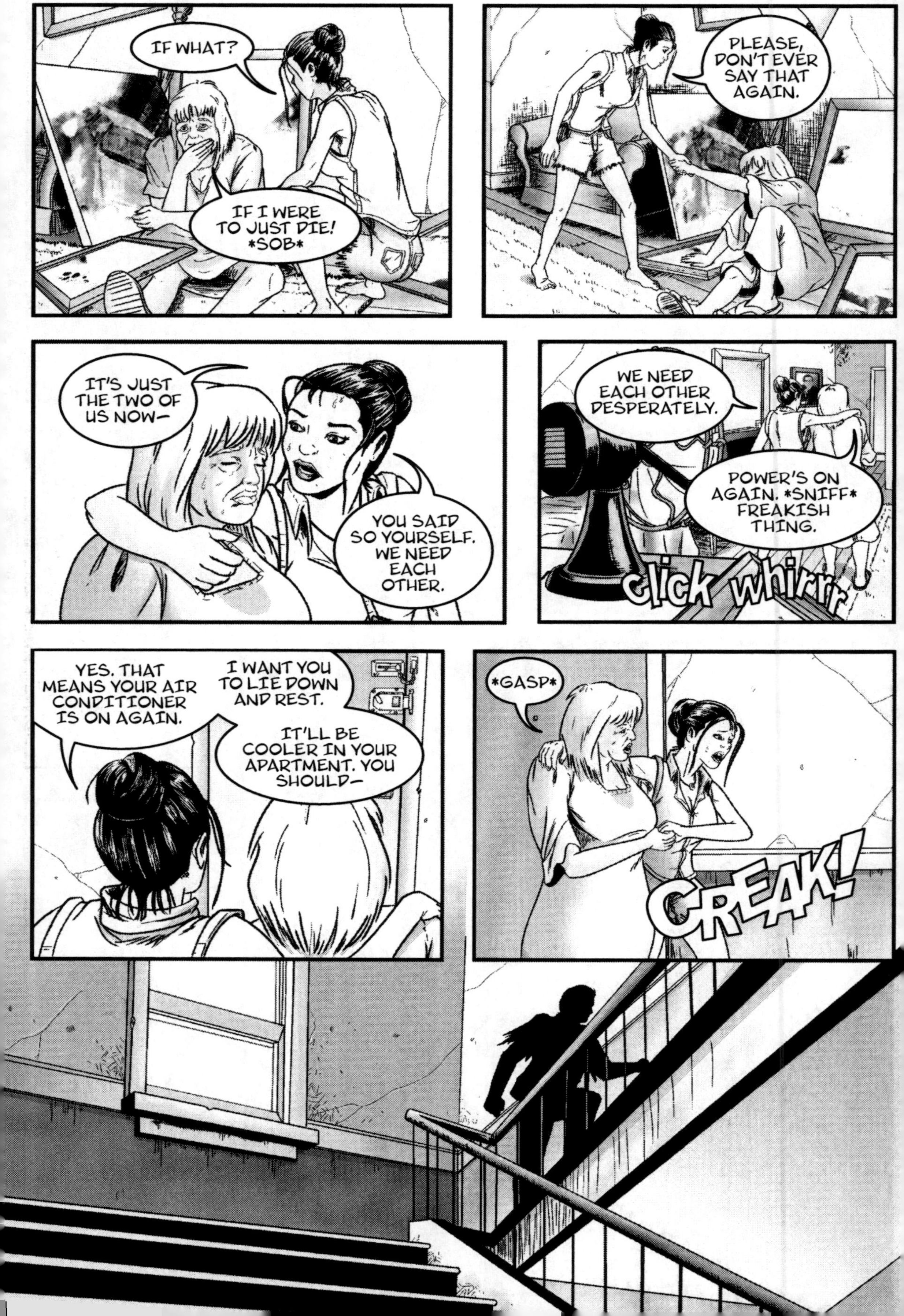
IF WHAT?
IF I WERE TO JUST DIE! *SOB*
PLEASE, DON'T EVER SAY THAT AGAIN.
IT'S JUST THE TWO OF US NOW—
YOU SAID SO YOURSELF. WE NEED EACH OTHER.
WE NEED EACH OTHER DESPERATELY.
POWER'S ON AGAIN. *SNIFF* FREAKISH THING.
click whirrr
YES. THAT MEANS YOUR AIR CONDITIONER IS ON AGAIN.
I WANT YOU TO LIE DOWN AND REST.
IT'LL BE COOLER IN YOUR APARTMENT. YOU SHOULD—
GASP
CREAK!

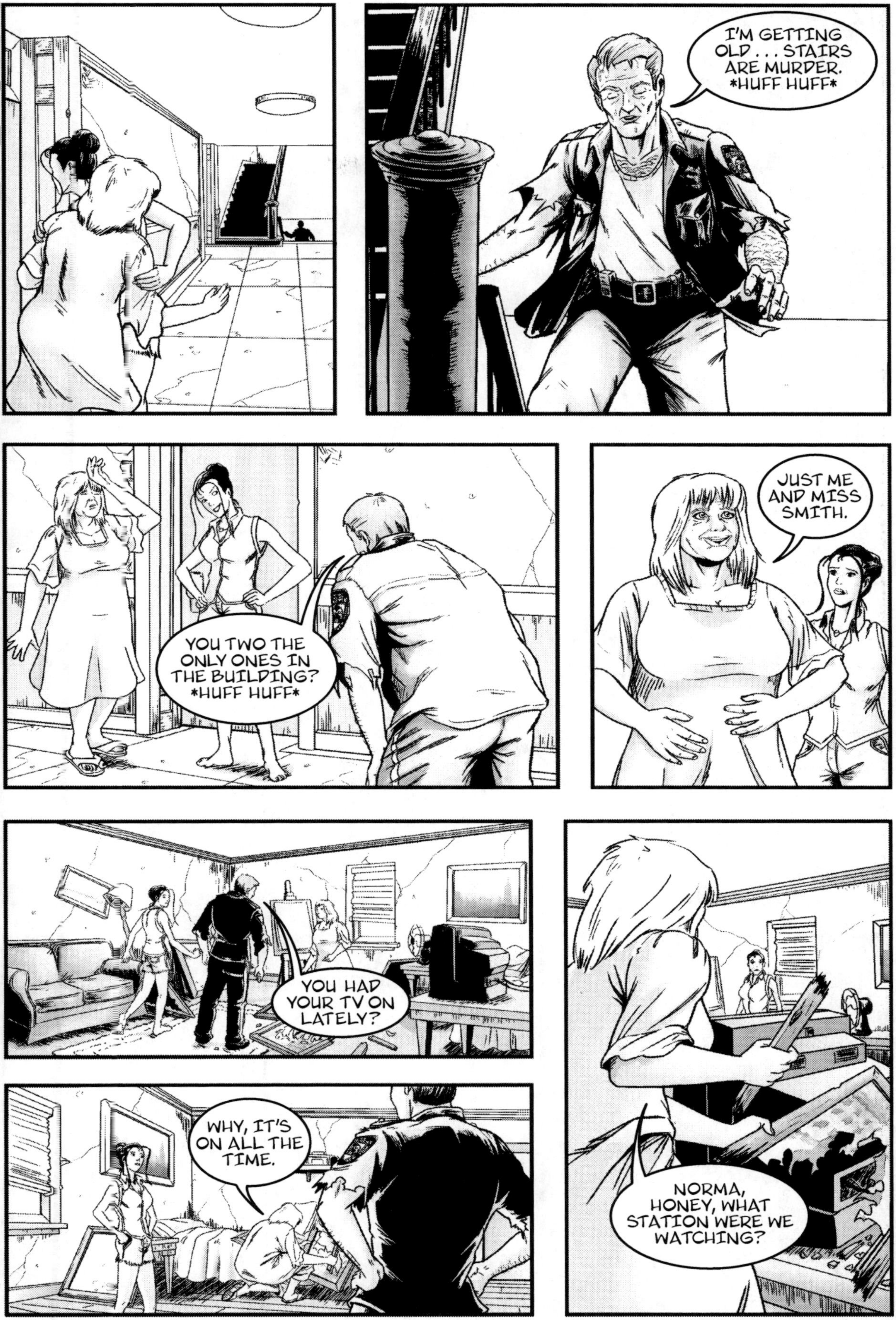
I'M GETTING OLD . . . STAIRS ARE MURDER. *HUFF HUFF*
YOU TWO THE ONLY ONES IN THE BUILDING? *HUFF HUFF*
JUST ME AND MISS SMITH.
YOU HAD YOUR TV ON LATELY?
WHY, IT'S ON ALL THE TIME.
NORMA, HONEY, WHAT STATION WERE WE WATCHING?

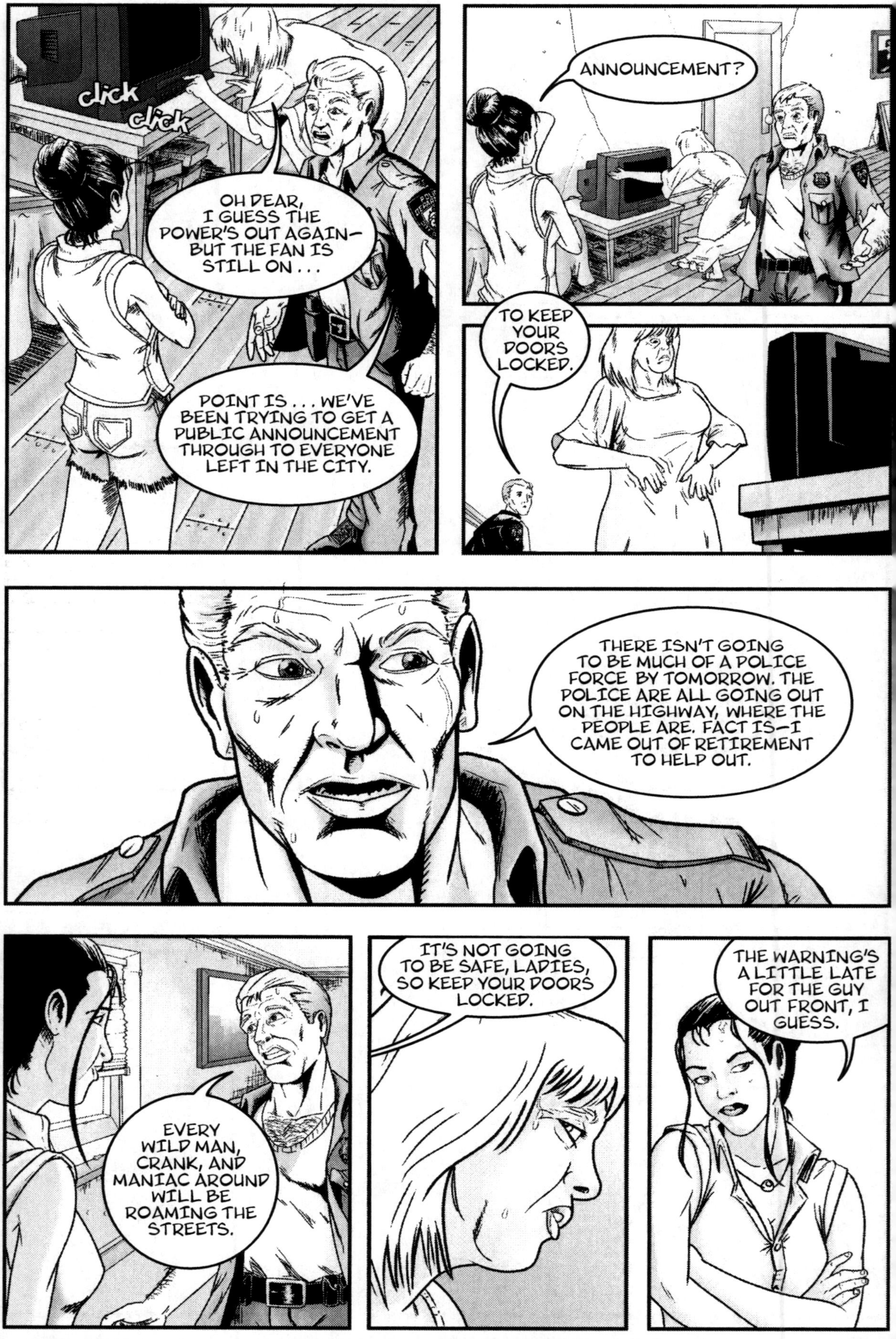
click
click
OH DEAR, I GUESS THE POWER'S OUT AGAIN—BUT THE FAN IS STILL ON . . .
POINT IS . . . WE'VE BEEN TRYING TO GET A PUBLIC ANNOUNCEMENT THROUGH TO EVERYONE LEFT IN THE CITY.
ANNOUNCEMENT?
TO KEEP YOUR DOORS LOCKED.
THERE ISN'T GOING TO BE MUCH OF A POLICE FORCE BY TOMORROW. THE POLICE ARE ALL GOING OUT ON THE HIGHWAY, WHERE THE PEOPLE ARE. FACT IS—I CAME OUT OF RETIREMENT TO HELP OUT.
EVERY WILD MAN, CRANK, AND MANIAC AROUND WILL BE ROAMING THE STREETS.
IT'S NOT GOING TO BE SAFE, LADIES, SO KEEP YOUR DOORS LOCKED.
THE WARNING'S A LITTLE LATE FOR THE GUY OUT FRONT, I GUESS.

YOU GOT A WEAPON IN HERE, MISS?

NO. NO, I DON'T.

I DON'T EITHER. I DON'T KNOW HOW TO SHOOT A GUN—

A KNIFE? SOMETHING TO PROTECT YOURSELF WITH, JUST IN CASE . . .

I BROKE MY KITCHEN KNIFE TRYING TO PRY OPEN THE WINDOW, BACK WHEN THIS ALL STARTED AND THE CENTRAL AIR WENT OUT.

NOW I'M GLAD I DIDN'T GET IT OPEN.

I DO HAVE A CAN OPENER.

WHY DID I GET VOTED OFF?! I HATE YOU ALL!

LIMITED POLICE PROTECTION...

click

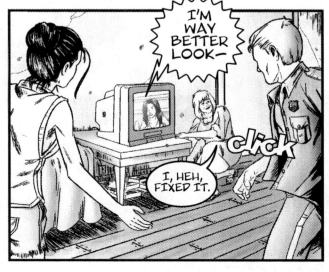

I'M WAY BETTER LOOK—

I, HEH, FIXED IT.

click

YOU BETTER HANG ON TO THIS.

IT'S ALL LOADED.

WE'LL SPLIT THINGS UP, NORMA. I'LL BE IN CHARGE OF KEEPING THE ROOF LOCKED...

THE SAFETY'S OFF. JUST PULL THE TRIGGER.

...AND YOU KEEP THE DOWNSTAIRS LOCKED.

GOOD LUCK TO YOU.

OFFICER—OFFICER, WHAT'S GOING TO HAPPEN TO US?

DON'T YOU KNOW, LADIES?

IT'S JUST GOING TO GET HOTTER AND HOTTER UNTIL IT'LL BE TOO HOT TO STAND IT.

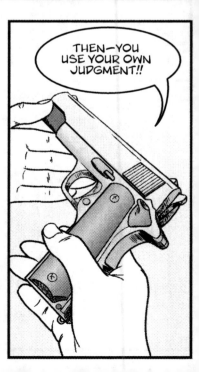

THEN—YOU USE YOUR OWN JUDGMENT!!

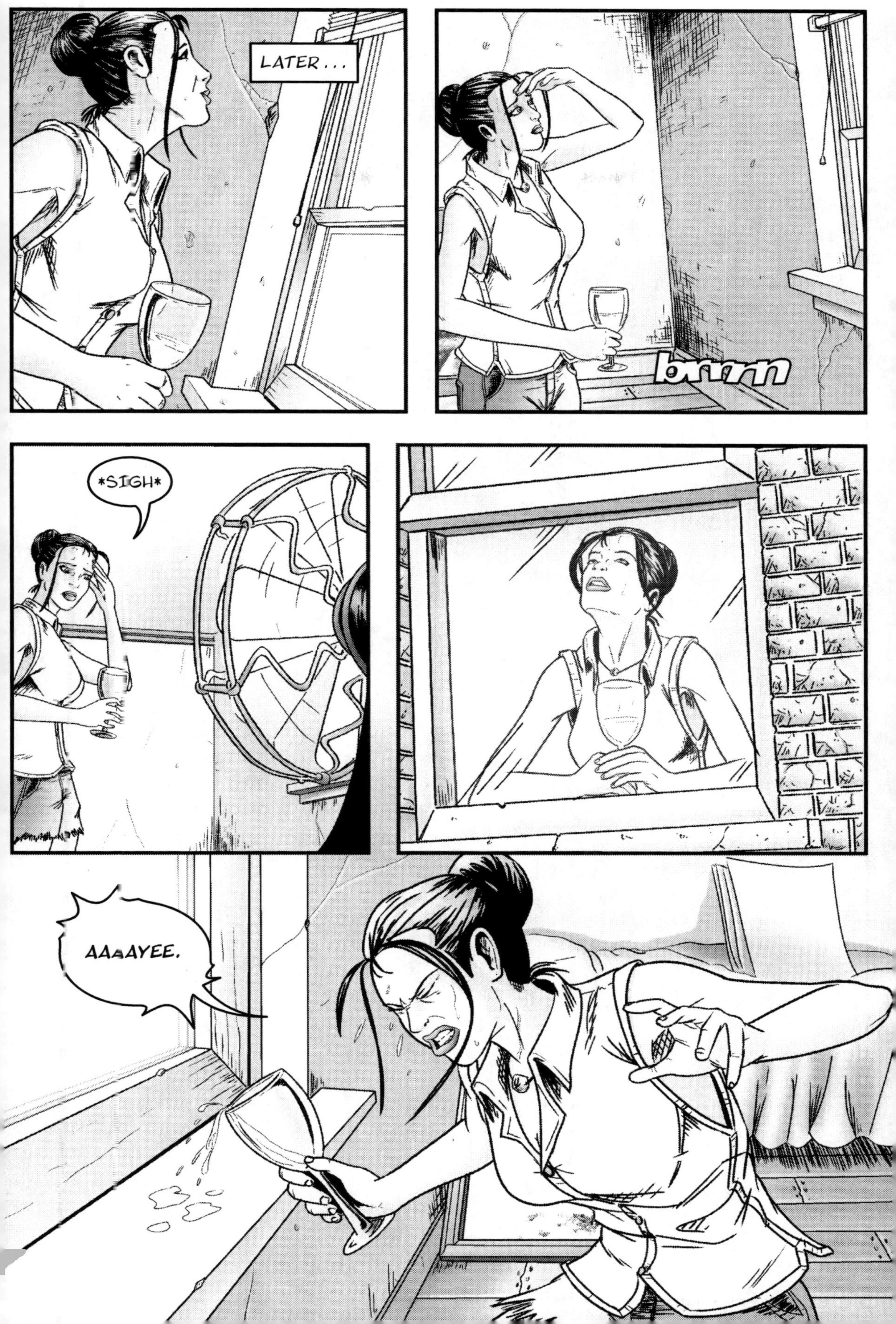
LATER . . .
brrrn
SIGH
AAAAAYEE.

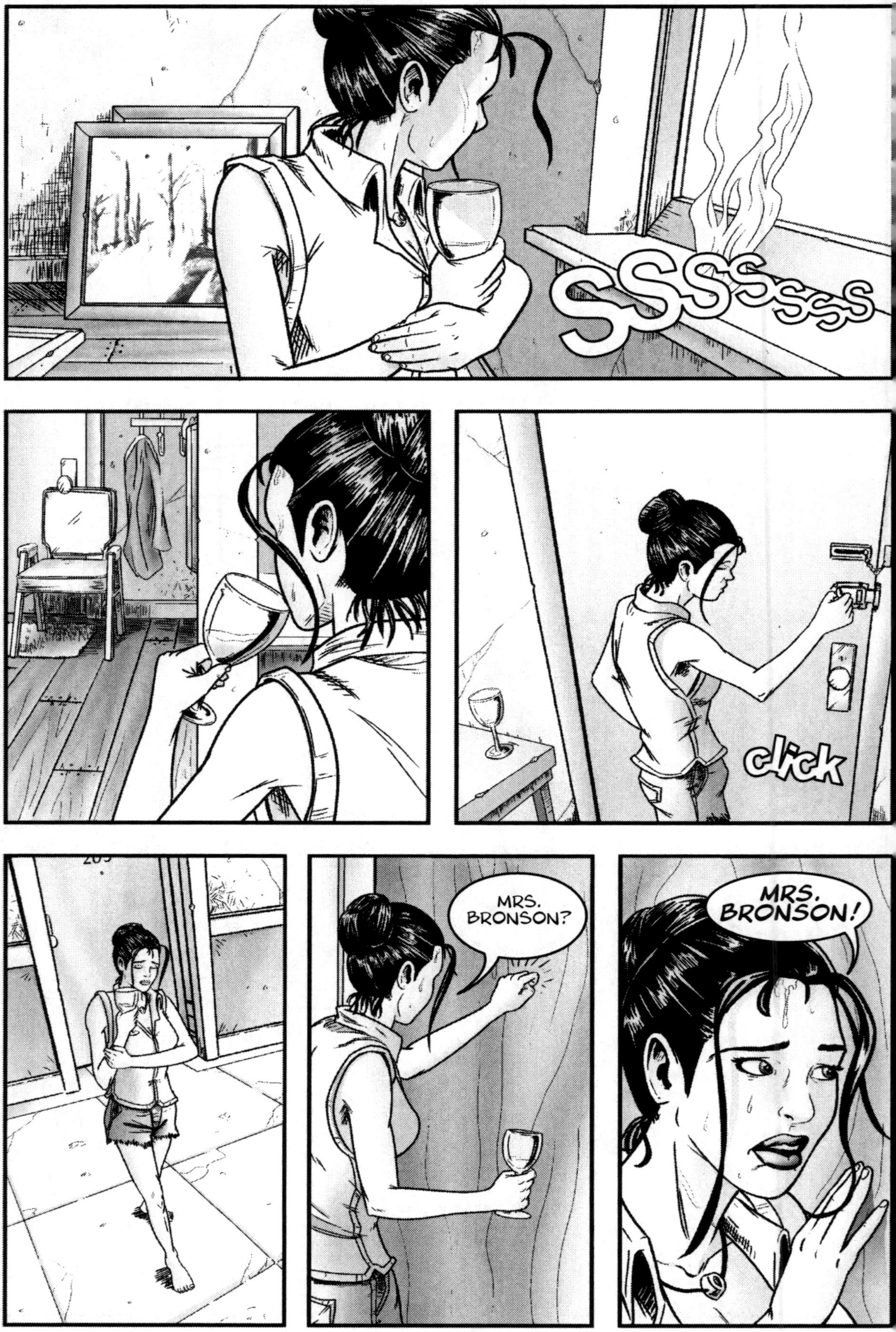
SSSssss
click
MRS. BRONSON?
MRS. BRONSON!

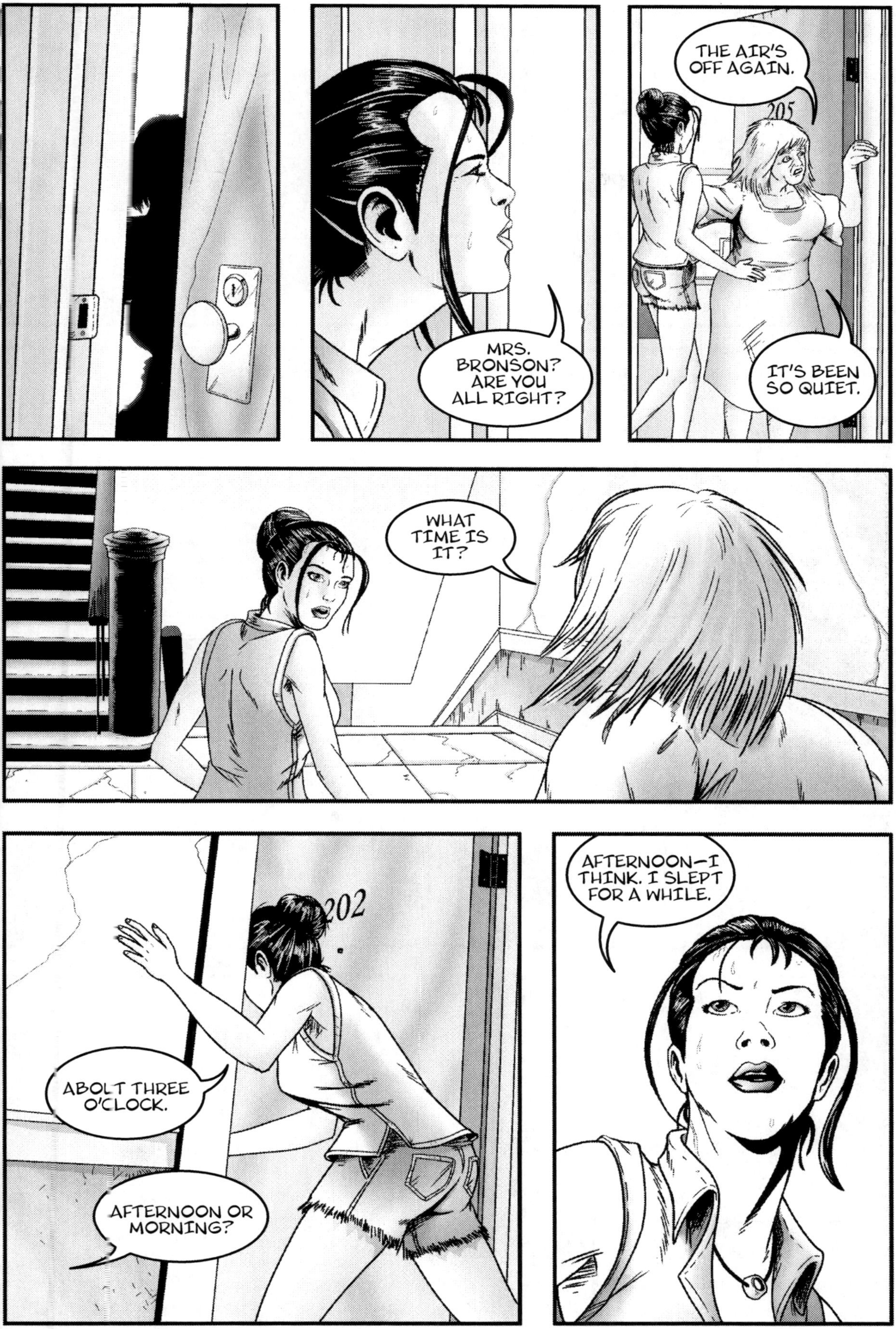
MRS. BRONSON? ARE YOU ALL RIGHT?
THE AIR'S OFF AGAIN.
205
IT'S BEEN SO QUIET.
WHAT TIME IS IT?
202
ABOLT THREE O'CLOCK.
AFTERNOON OR MORNING?
AFTERNOON—I THINK. I SLEPT FOR A WHILE.

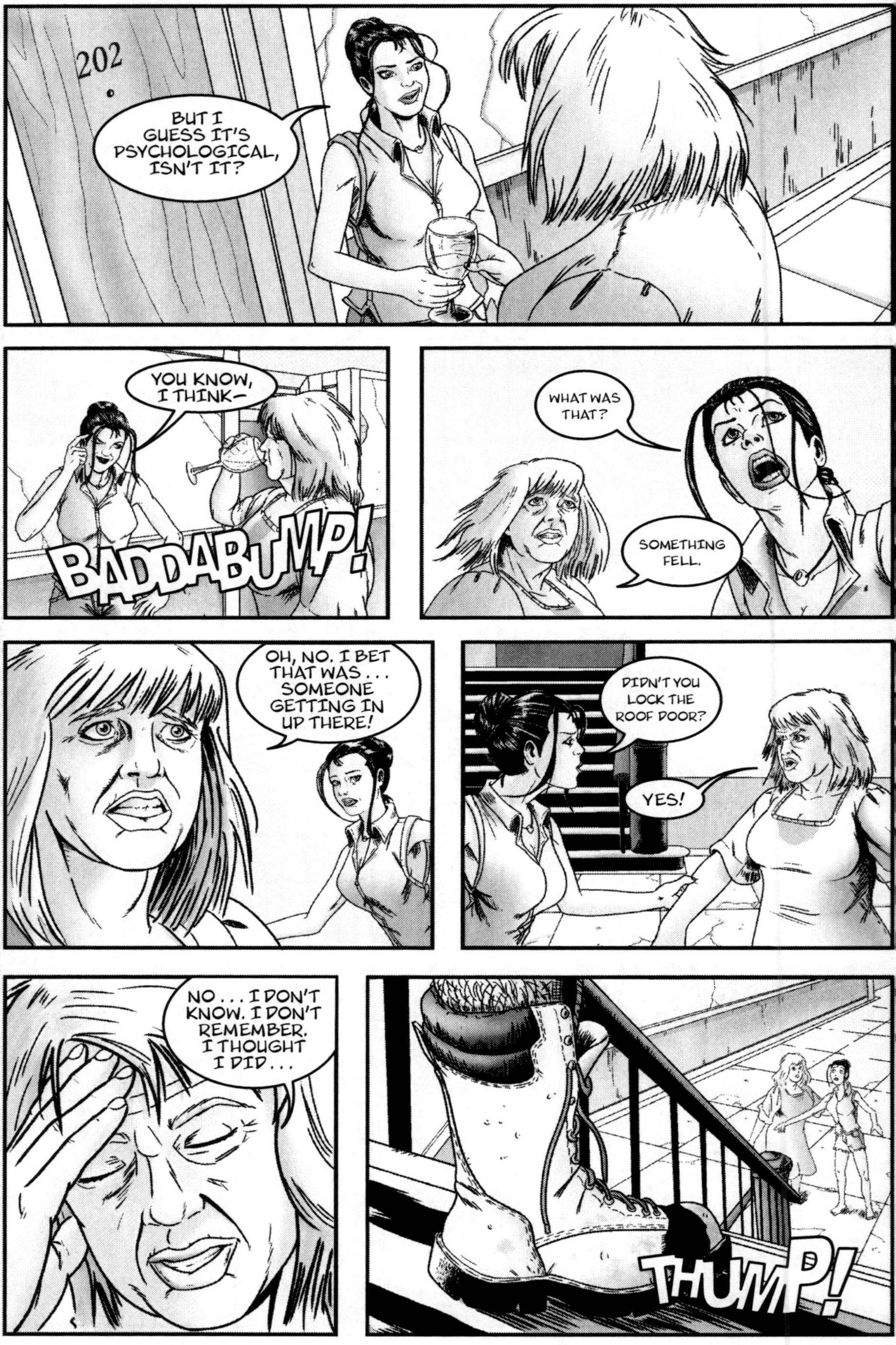
BUT I GUESS IT'S PSYCHOLOGICAL, ISN'T IT?
YOU KNOW, I THINK–
BADDABUMP!
WHAT WAS THAT?
SOMETHING FELL.
OH, NO. I BET THAT WAS . . . SOMEONE GETTING IN UP THERE!
DIDN'T YOU LOCK THE ROOF DOOR?
YES!
NO . . . I DON'T KNOW. I DON'T REMEMBER. I THOUGHT I DID . . .
THUMP!

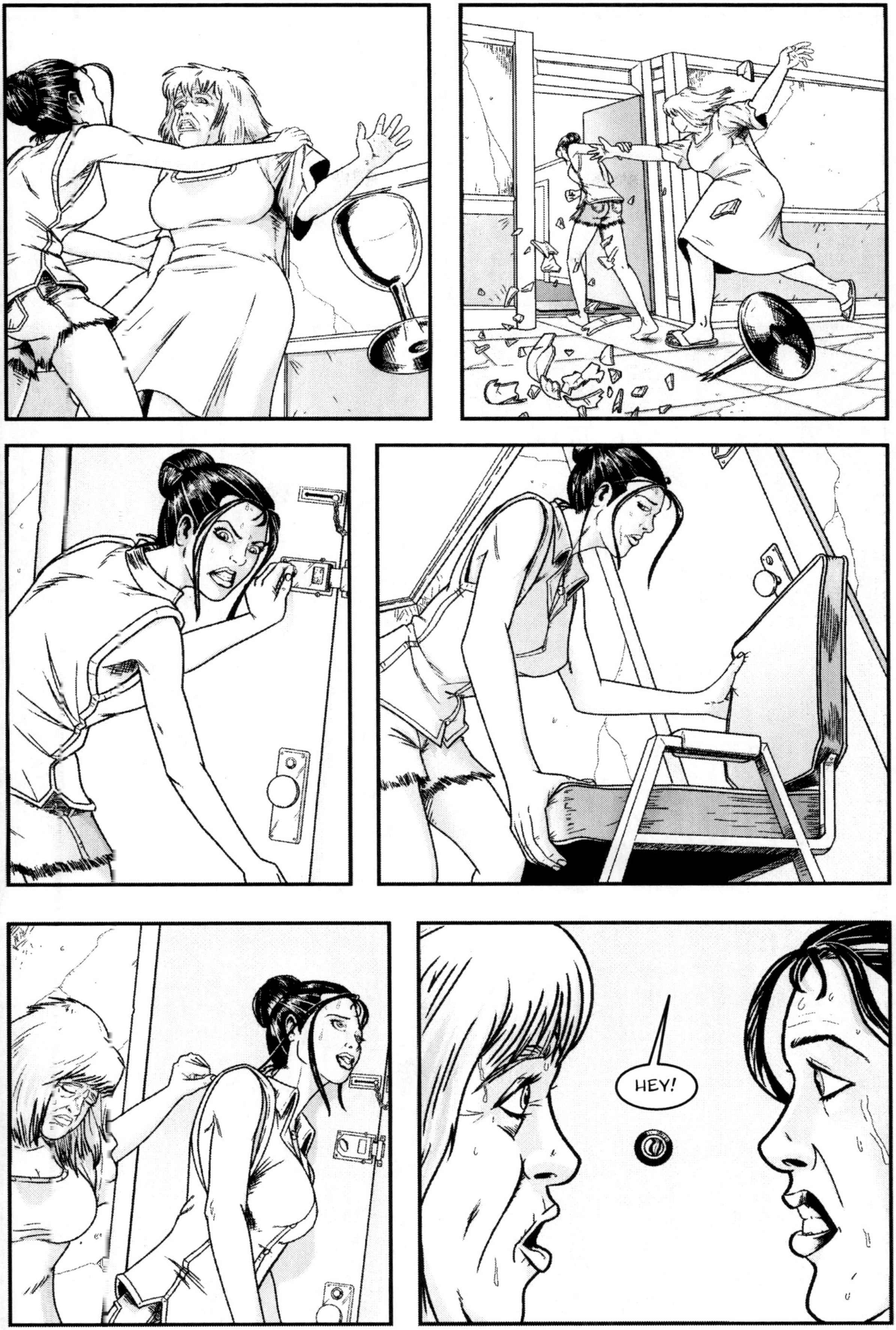
HEY!

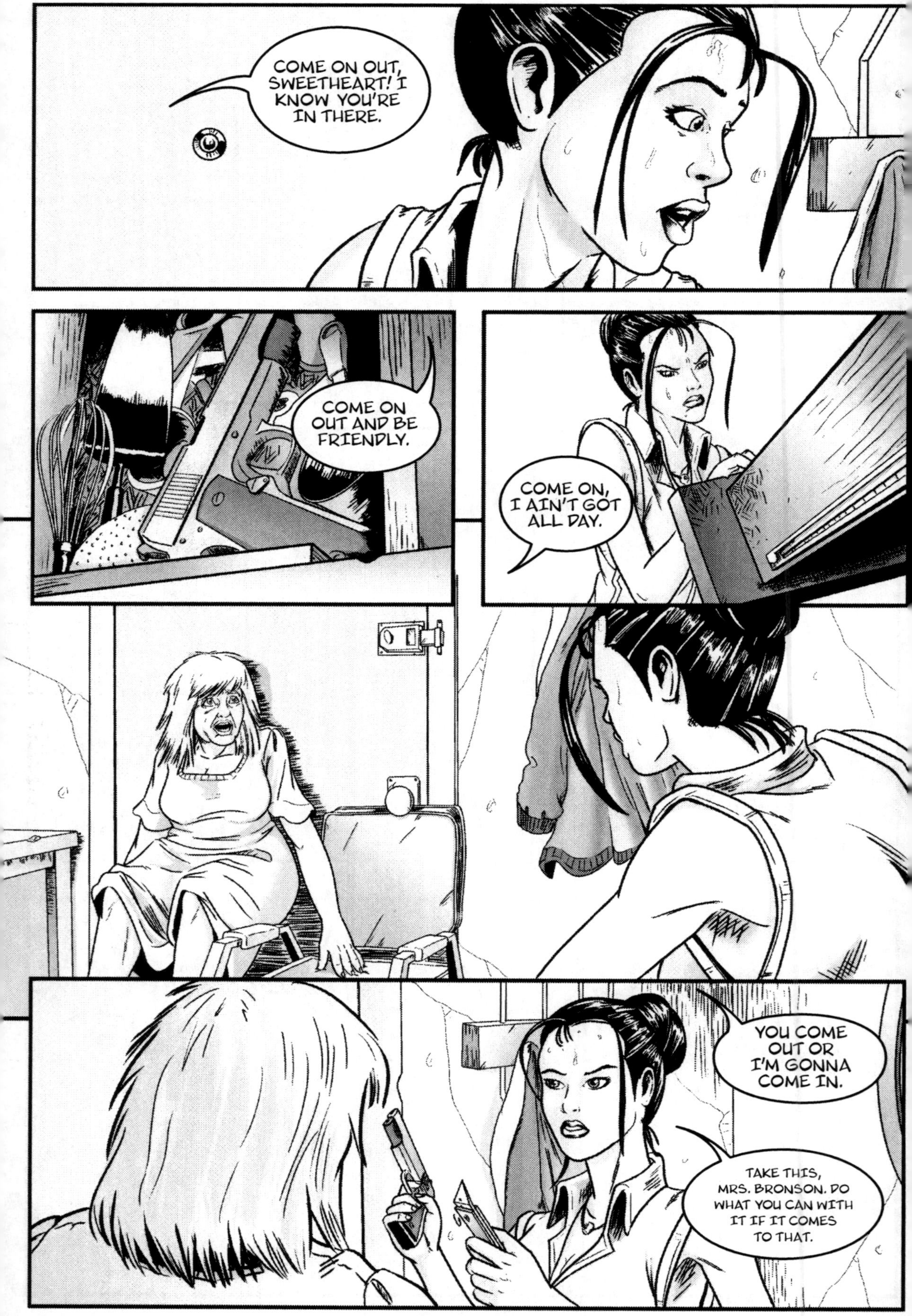
COME ON OUT, SWEETHEART! I KNOW YOU'RE IN THERE.
COME ON OUT AND BE FRIENDLY.
COME ON, I AIN'T GOT ALL DAY.
YOU COME OUT OR I'M GONNA COME IN.
TAKE THIS, MRS. BRONSON. DO WHAT YOU CAN WITH IT IF IT COMES TO THAT.

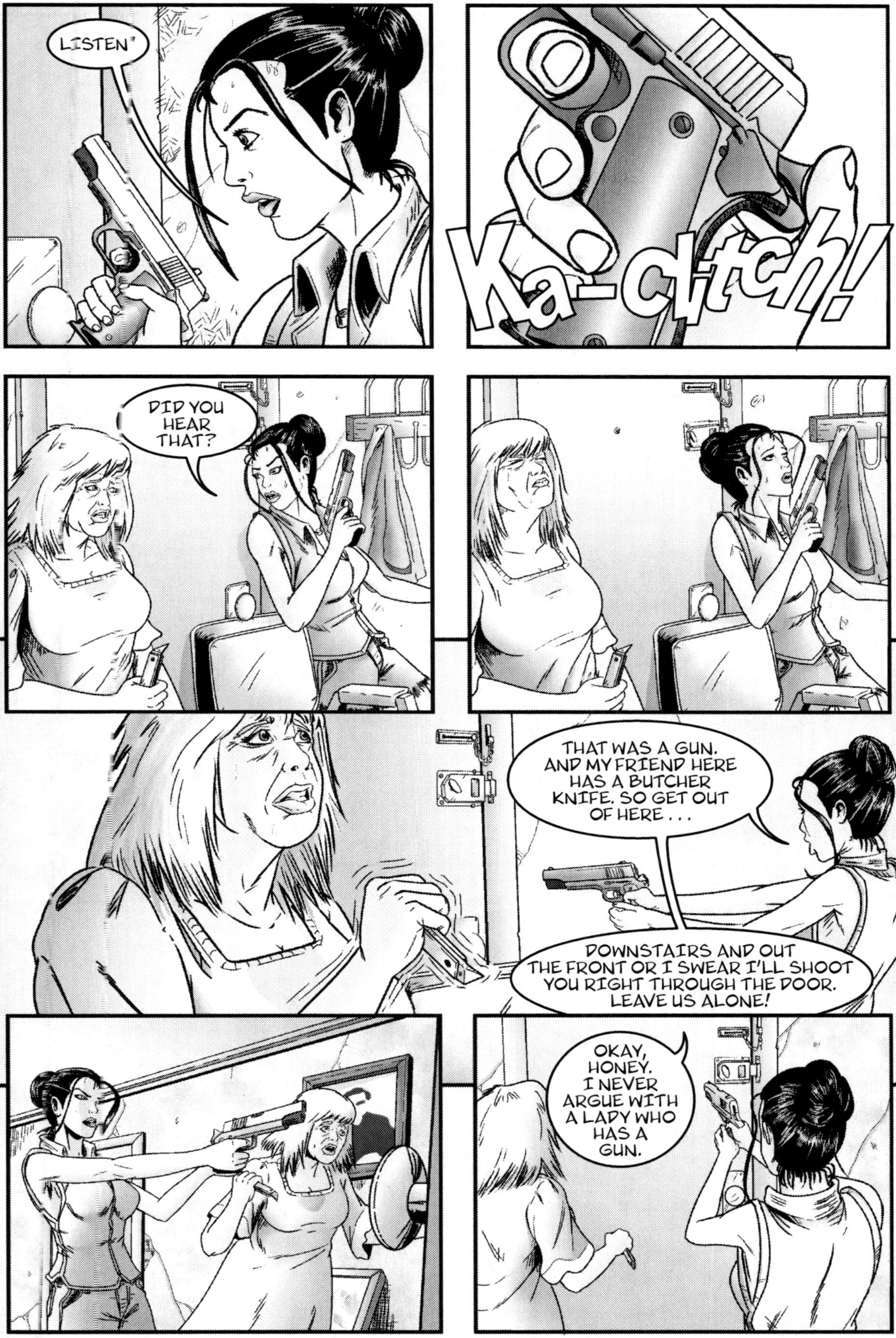

LISTEN'
Ka-clitch!
DID YOU HEAR THAT?
THAT WAS A GUN. AND MY FRIEND HERE HAS A BUTCHER KNIFE. SO GET OUT OF HERE . . .
DOWNSTAIRS AND OUT THE FRONT OR I SWEAR I'LL SHOOT YOU RIGHT THROUGH THE DOOR. LEAVE US ALONE!
OKAY, HONEY. I NEVER ARGUE WITH A LADY WHO HAS A GUN.

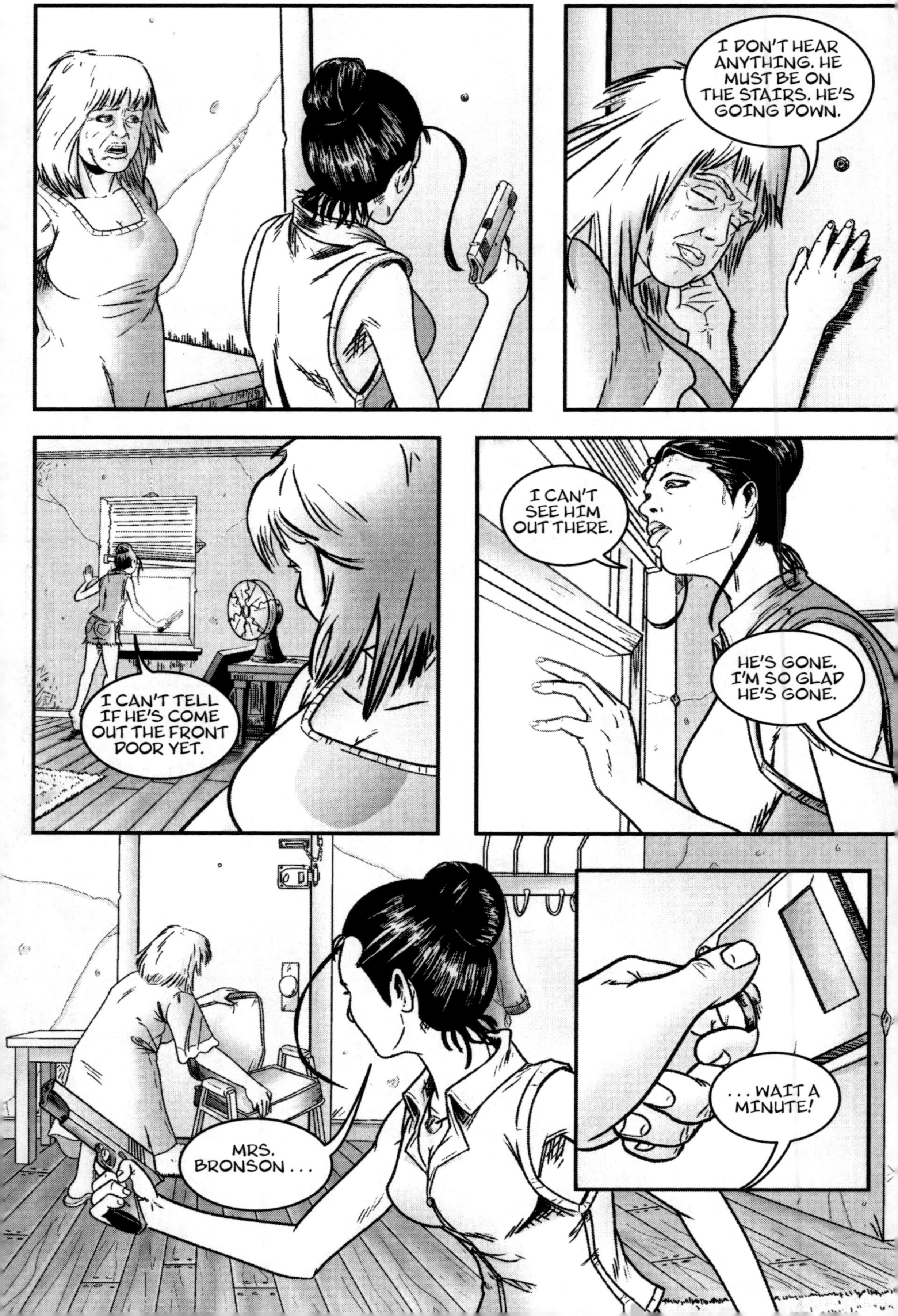
I DON'T HEAR ANYTHING. HE MUST BE ON THE STAIRS. HE'S GOING DOWN.
I CAN'T TELL IF HE'S COME OUT THE FRONT DOOR YET.
I CAN'T SEE HIM OUT THERE.
HE'S GONE. I'M SO GLAD HE'S GONE.
MRS. BRONSON . . .
. . . WAIT A MINUTE!

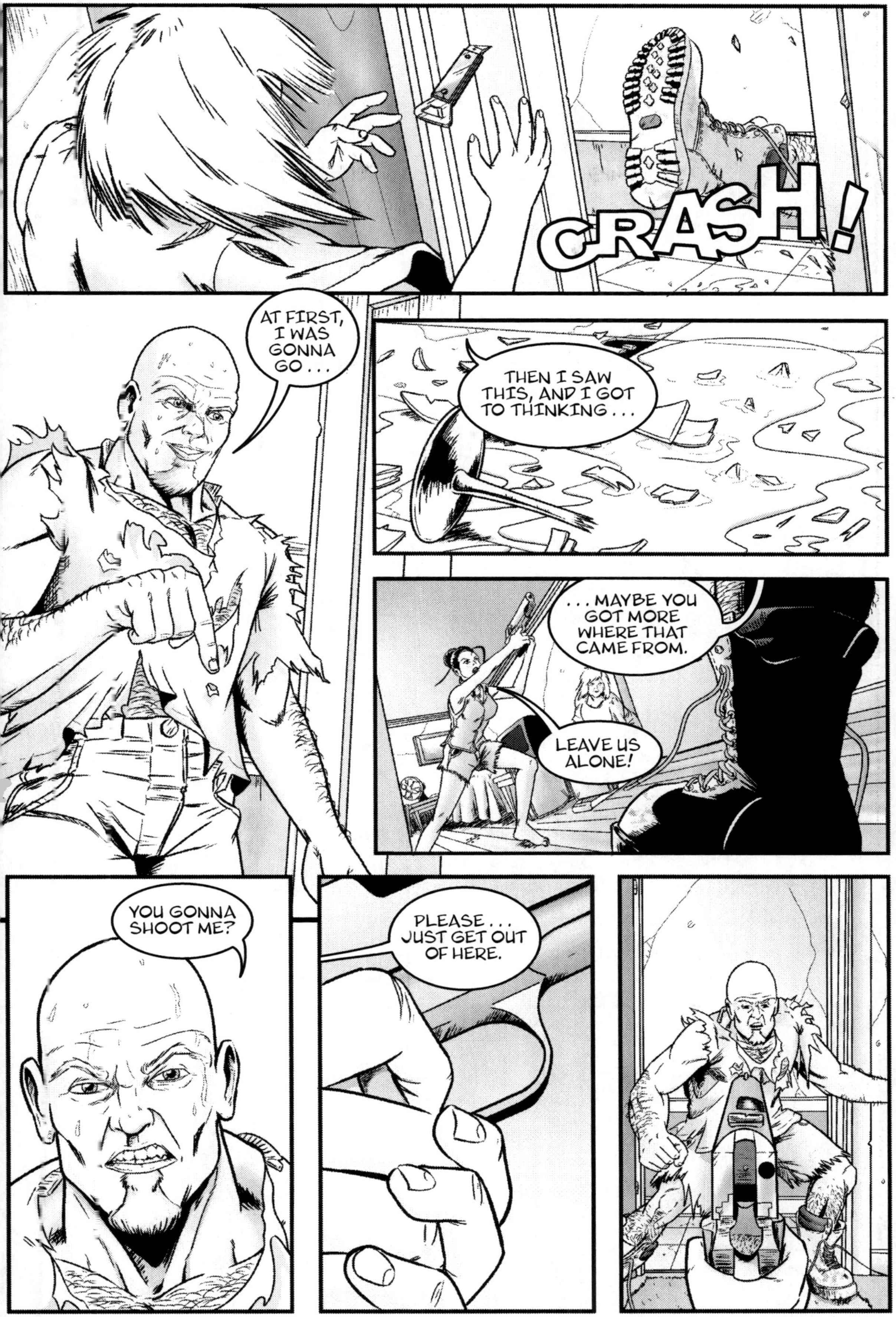
CRASH!
AT FIRST, I WAS GONNA GO . . .
THEN I SAW THIS, AND I GOT TO THINKING . . .
. . . MAYBE YOU GOT MORE WHERE THAT CAME FROM.
LEAVE US ALONE!
YOU GONNA SHOOT ME?
PLEASE . . . JUST GET OUT OF HERE.

LEAVE US ALONE!

MRS. BRONSON! NO! STAY AWAY!

GASP ... *GASP* ... *GASP* ... *GASP* ...

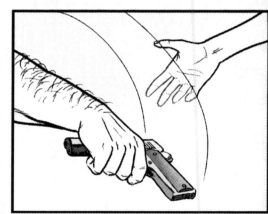

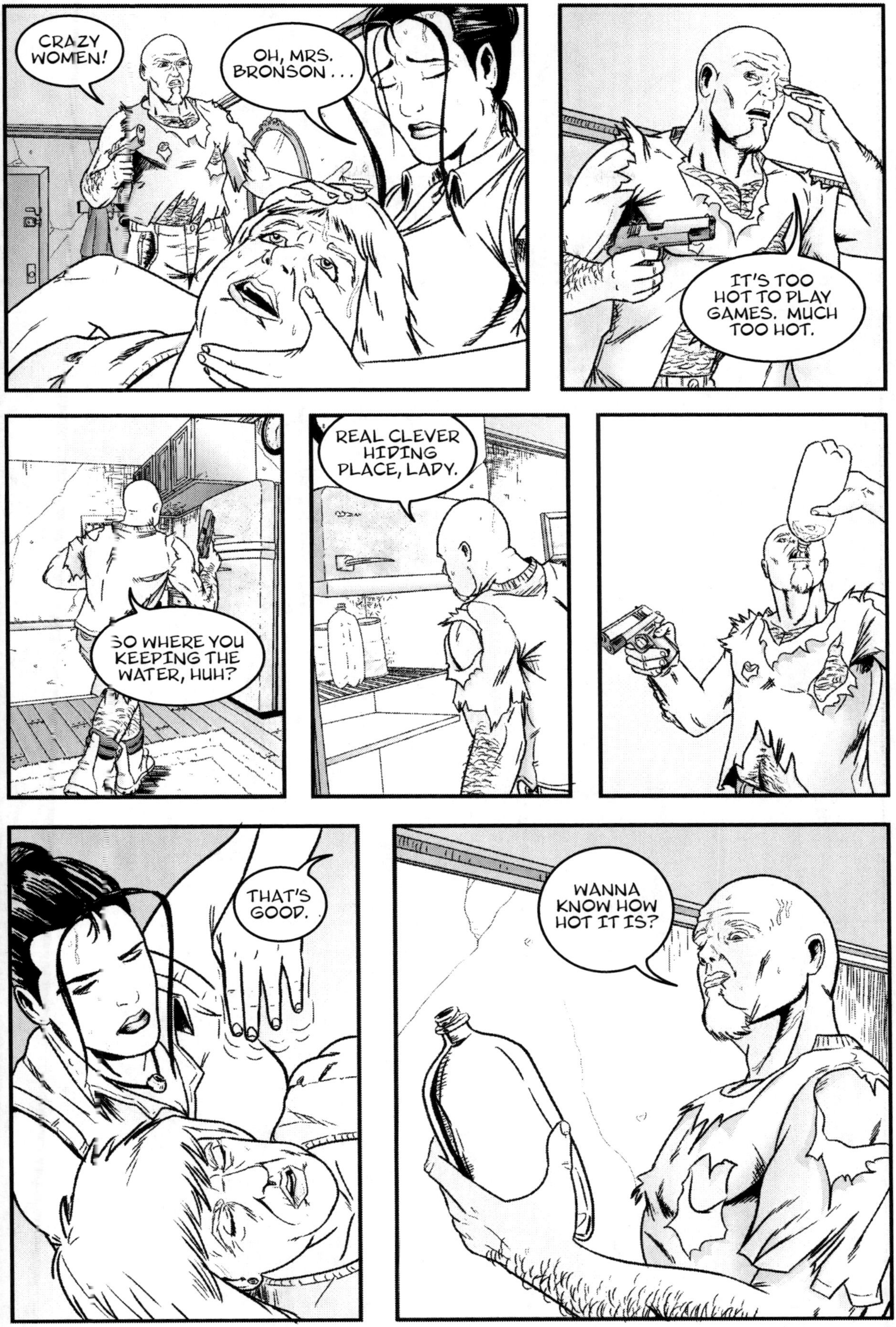
CRAZY WOMEN!
OH, MRS. BRONSON . . .
IT'S TOO HOT TO PLAY GAMES. MUCH TOO HOT.
SO WHERE YOU KEEPING THE WATER, HUH?
REAL CLEVER HIDING PLACE, LADY.
THAT'S GOOD.
WANNA KNOW HOW HOT IT IS?

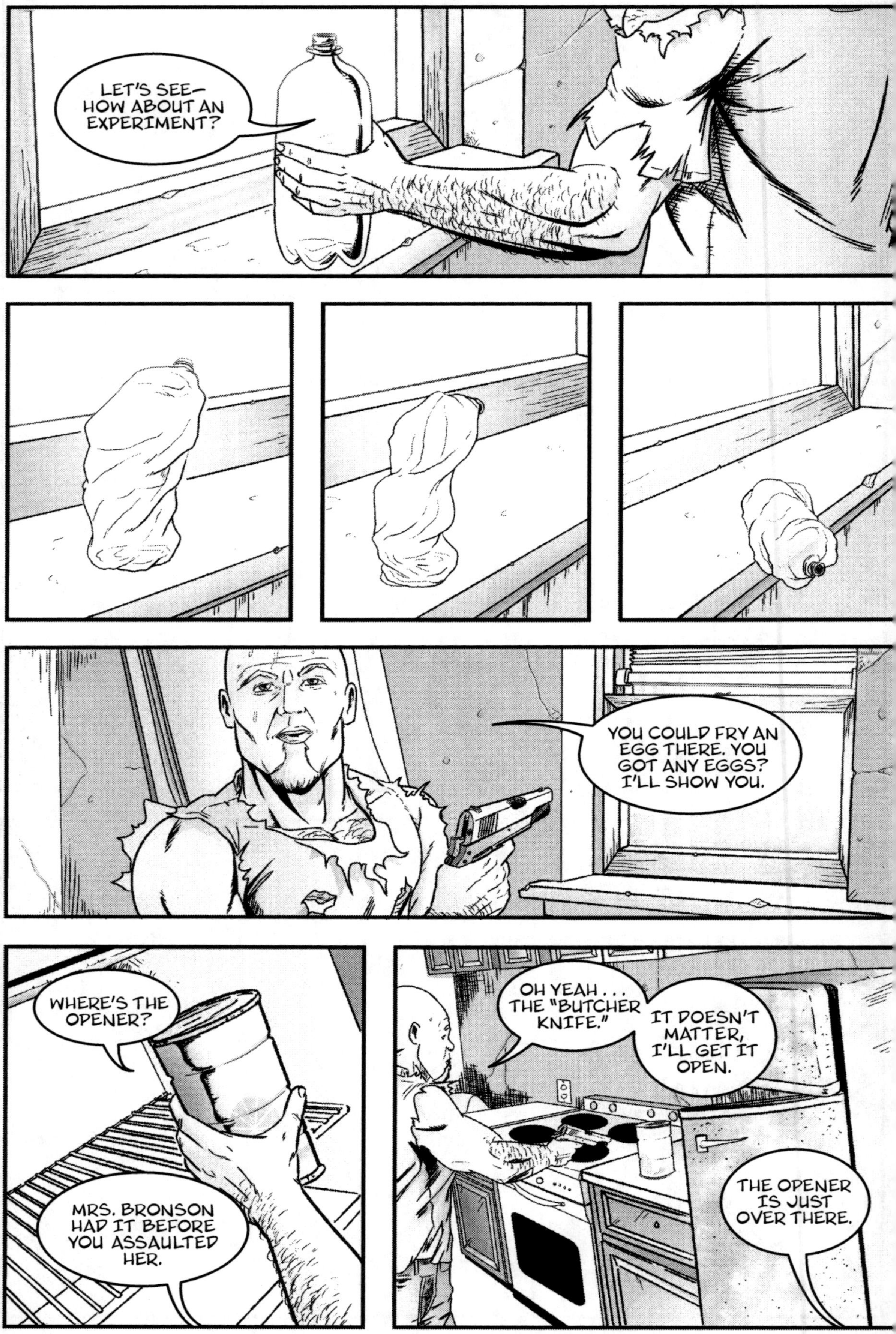
LET'S SEE— HOW ABOUT AN EXPERIMENT?
YOU COULD FRY AN EGG THERE. YOU GOT ANY EGGS? I'LL SHOW YOU.
WHERE'S THE OPENER?
MRS. BRONSON HAD IT BEFORE YOU ASSAULTED HER.
OH YEAH . . . THE "BUTCHER KNIFE."
IT DOESN'T MATTER, I'LL GET IT OPEN.
THE OPENER IS JUST OVER THERE.

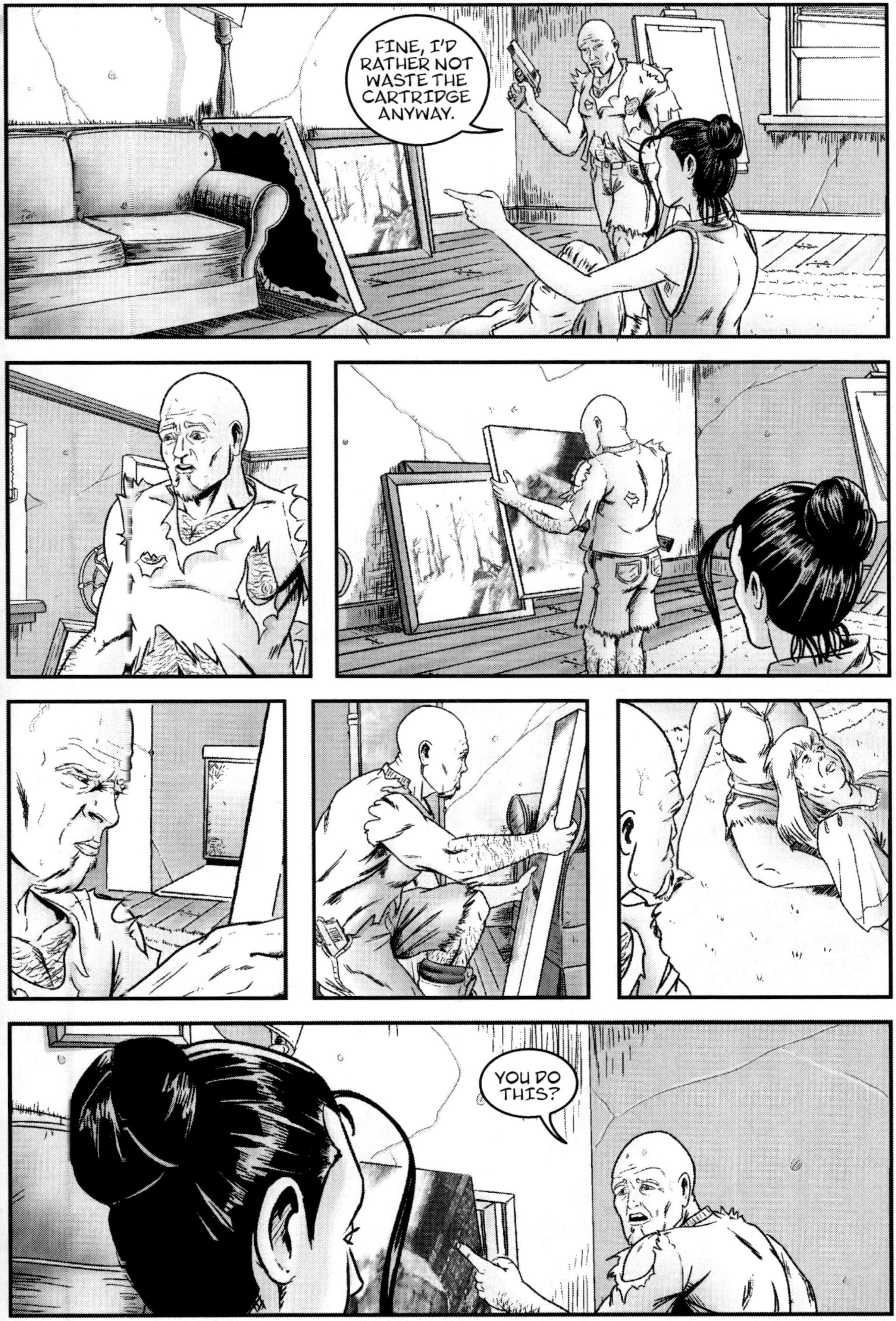
FINE, I'D RATHER NOT WASTE THE CARTRIDGE ANYWAY.
YOU DO THIS?

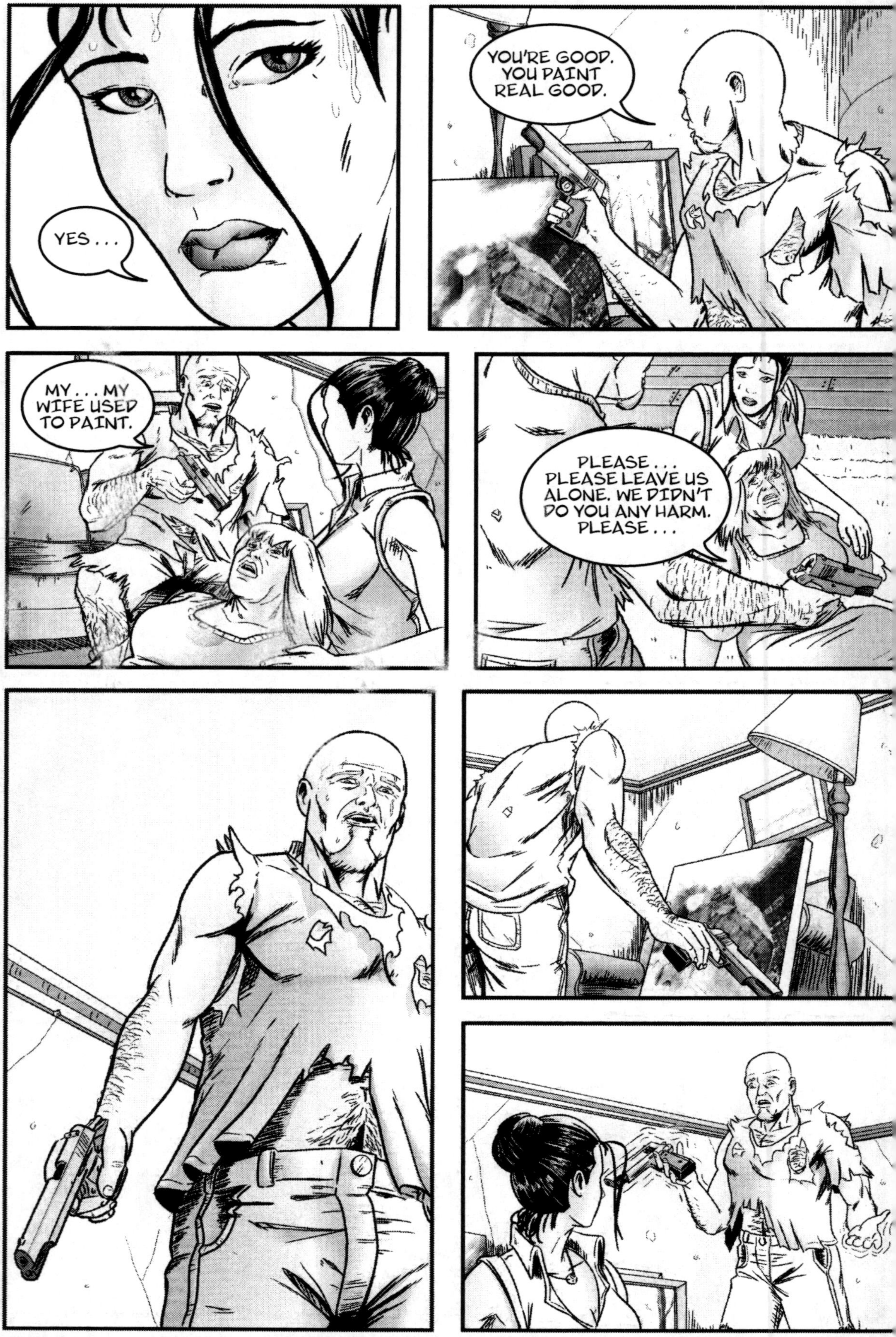
YES . . .
YOU'RE GOOD. YOU PAINT REAL GOOD.
MY . . . MY WIFE USED TO PAINT.
PLEASE . . . PLEASE LEAVE US ALONE. WE DIDN'T DO YOU ANY HARM. PLEASE . . .

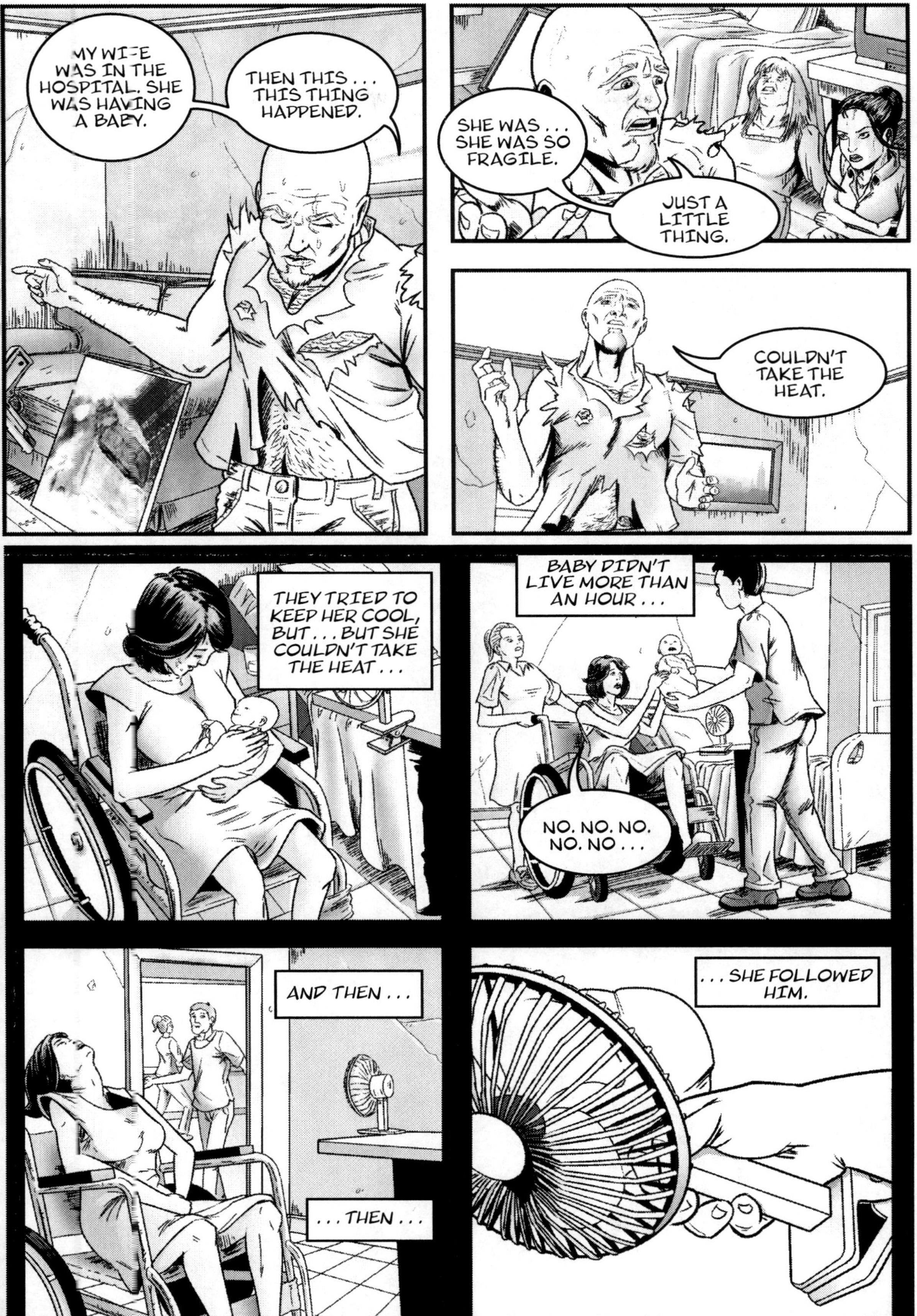
MY WIFE WAS IN THE HOSPITAL. SHE WAS HAVING A BABY.
THEN THIS . . . THIS THING HAPPENED.
SHE WAS . . . SHE WAS SO FRAGILE.
JUST A LITTLE THING.
COULDN'T TAKE THE HEAT.
THEY TRIED TO KEEP HER COOL, BUT . . . BUT SHE COULDN'T TAKE THE HEAT . . .
BABY DIDN'T LIVE MORE THAN AN HOUR . . .
NO. NO. NO. NO. NO . . .
AND THEN . . .
. . . THEN . . .
. . . SHE FOLLOWED HIM.

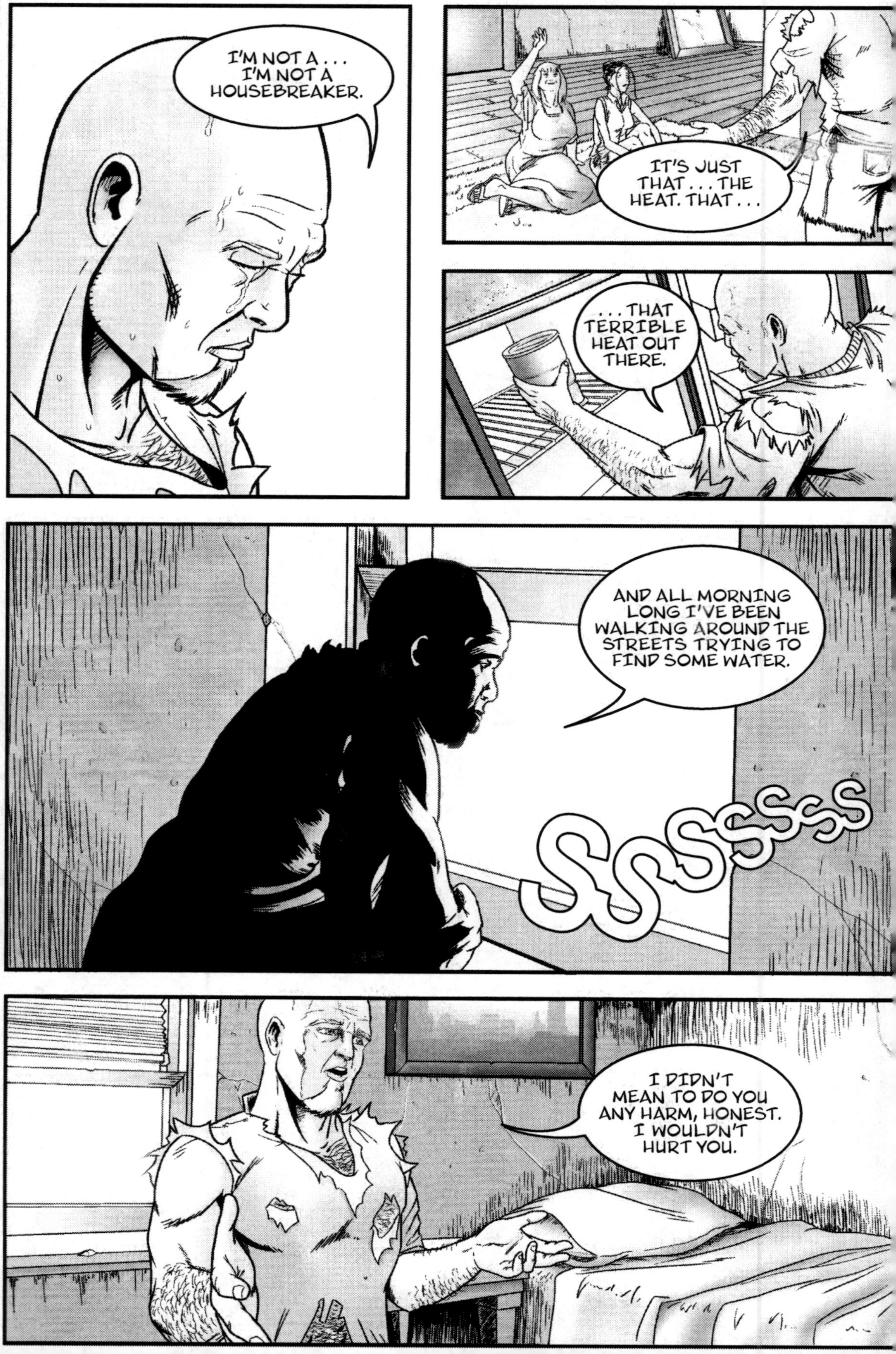
I'M NOT A . . . I'M NOT A HOUSEBREAKER.
IT'S JUST THAT . . . THE HEAT. THAT . . .
. . . THAT TERRIBLE HEAT OUT THERE.
AND ALL MORNING LONG I'VE BEEN WALKING AROUND THE STREETS TRYING TO FIND SOME WATER.
SSSSSSS
I DIDN'T MEAN TO DO YOU ANY HARM, HONEST. I WOULDN'T HURT YOU.

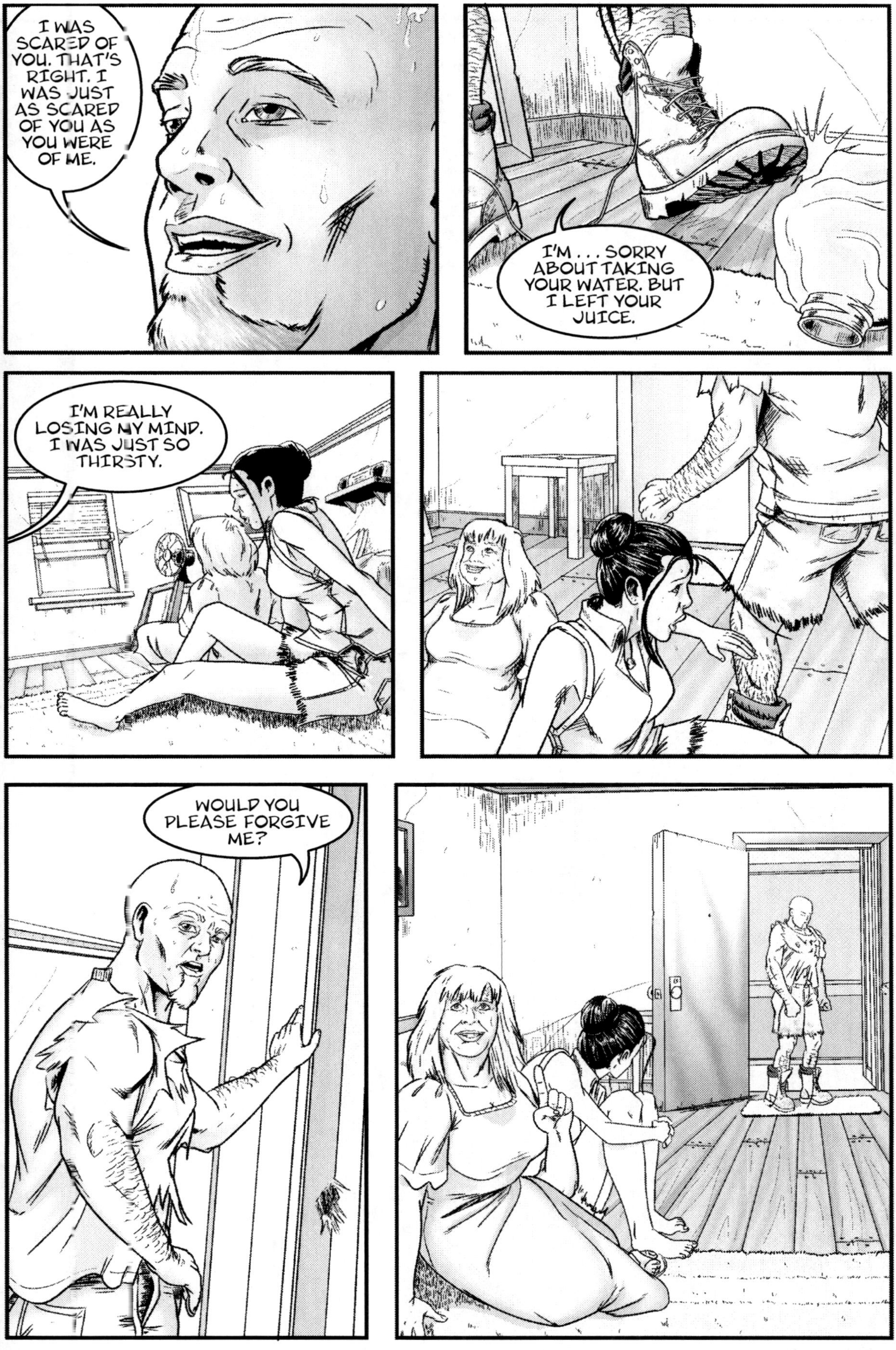
I WAS SCARED OF YOU. THAT'S RIGHT. I WAS JUST AS SCARED OF YOU AS YOU WERE OF ME.
I'M . . . SORRY ABOUT TAKING YOUR WATER. BUT I LEFT YOUR JUICE.
I'M REALLY LOSING MY MIND. I WAS JUST SO THIRSTY.
WOULD YOU PLEASE FORGIVE ME?

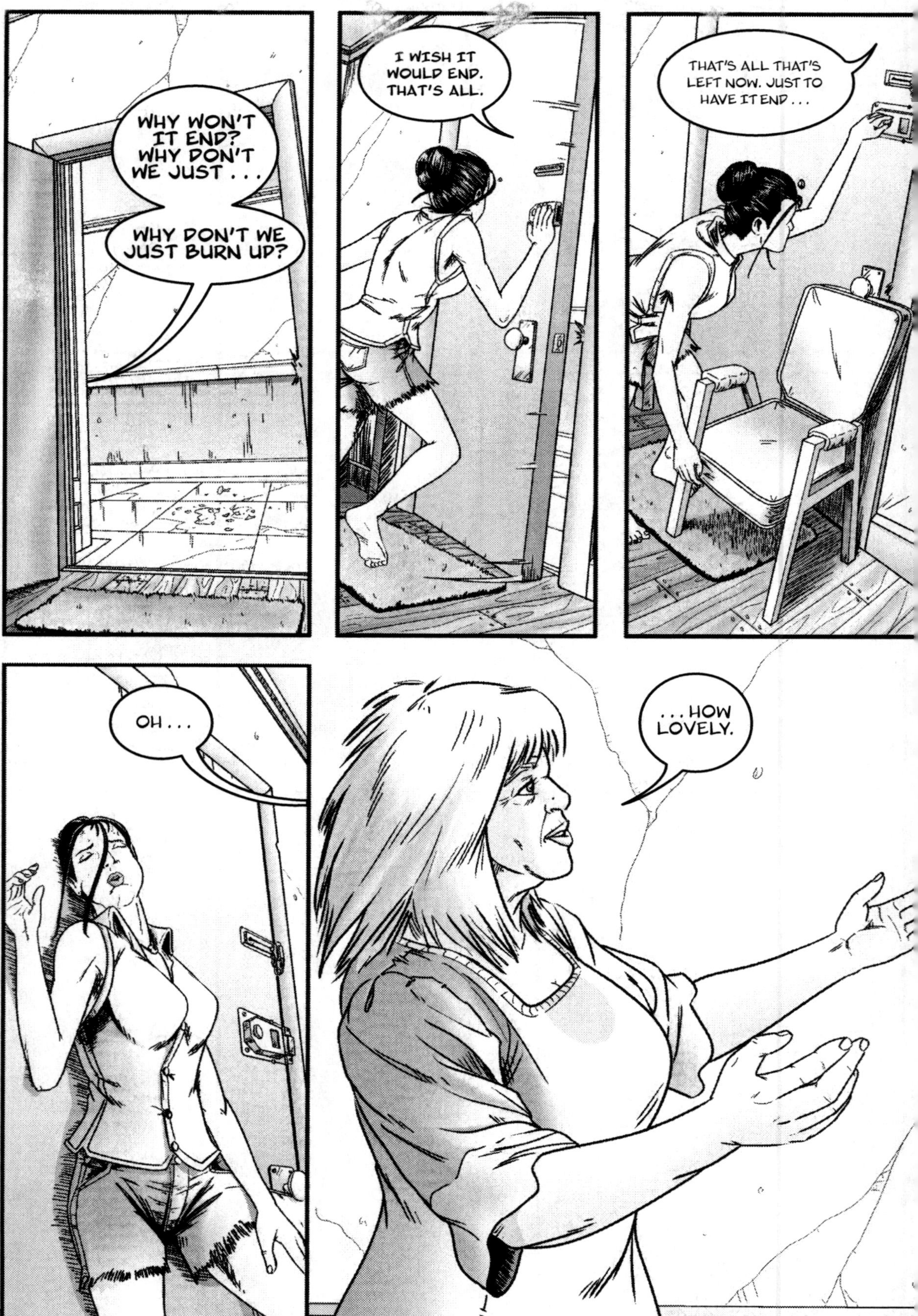
WHY WON'T IT END? WHY DON'T WE JUST . . .
WHY DON'T WE JUST BURN UP?
I WISH IT WOULD END. THAT'S ALL.
THAT'S ALL THAT'S LEFT NOW. JUST TO HAVE IT END . . .
OH . . .
. . . HOW LOVELY.

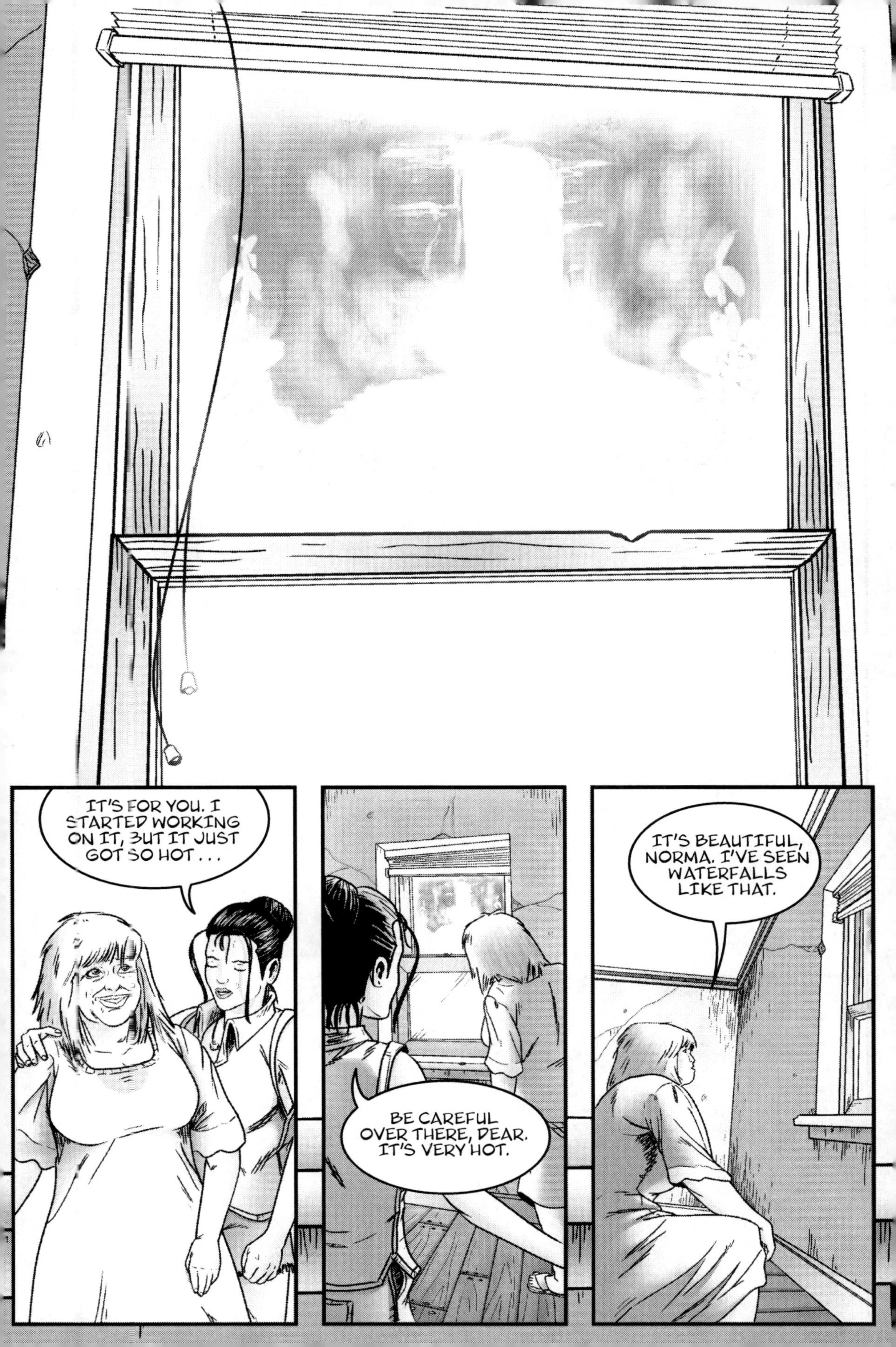
IT'S FOR YOU. I STARTED WORKING ON IT, BUT IT JUST GOT SO HOT . . .
BE CAREFUL OVER THERE, DEAR. IT'S VERY HOT.
IT'S BEAUTIFUL, NORMA. I'VE SEEN WATERFALLS LIKE THAT.

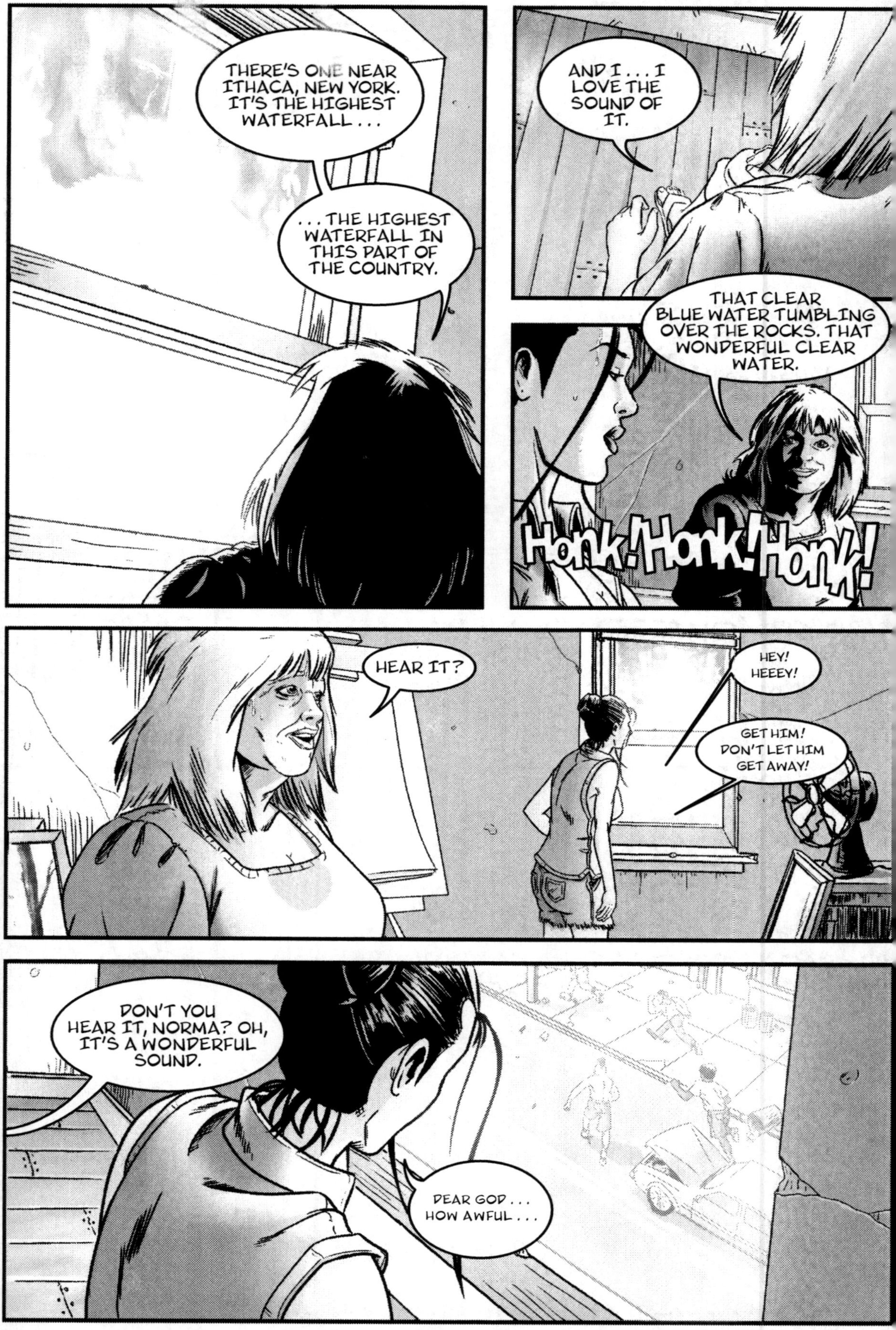
THERE'S ONE NEAR ITHACA, NEW YORK. IT'S THE HIGHEST WATERFALL . . .
. . . THE HIGHEST WATERFALL IN THIS PART OF THE COUNTRY.
AND I . . . I LOVE THE SOUND OF IT.
THAT CLEAR BLUE WATER TUMBLING OVER THE ROCKS. THAT WONDERFUL CLEAR WATER.
Honk! Honk! Honk!
HEAR IT?
HEY! HEEEY!
GET HIM! DON'T LET HIM GET AWAY!
DON'T YOU HEAR IT, NORMA? OH, IT'S A WONDERFUL SOUND.
DEAR GOD . . . HOW AWFUL . . .

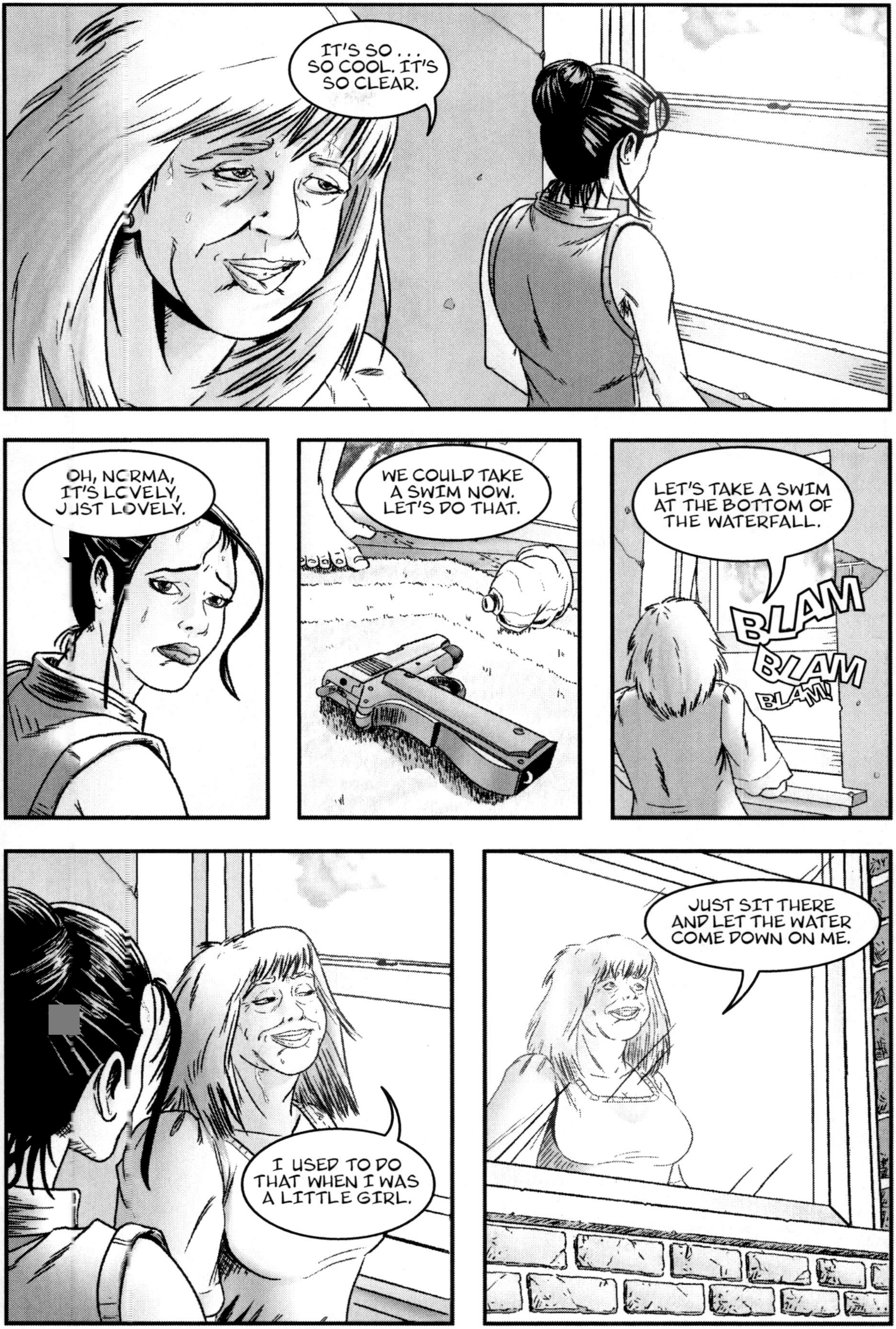
IT'S SO . . . SO COOL. IT'S SO CLEAR.
OH, NORMA, IT'S LOVELY, JUST LOVELY.
WE COULD TAKE A SWIM NOW. LET'S DO THAT.
LET'S TAKE A SWIM AT THE BOTTOM OF THE WATERFALL.
BLAM
BLAM
BLAM!
I USED TO DO THAT WHEN I WAS A LITTLE GIRL.
JUST SIT THERE AND LET THE WATER COME DOWN ON ME.

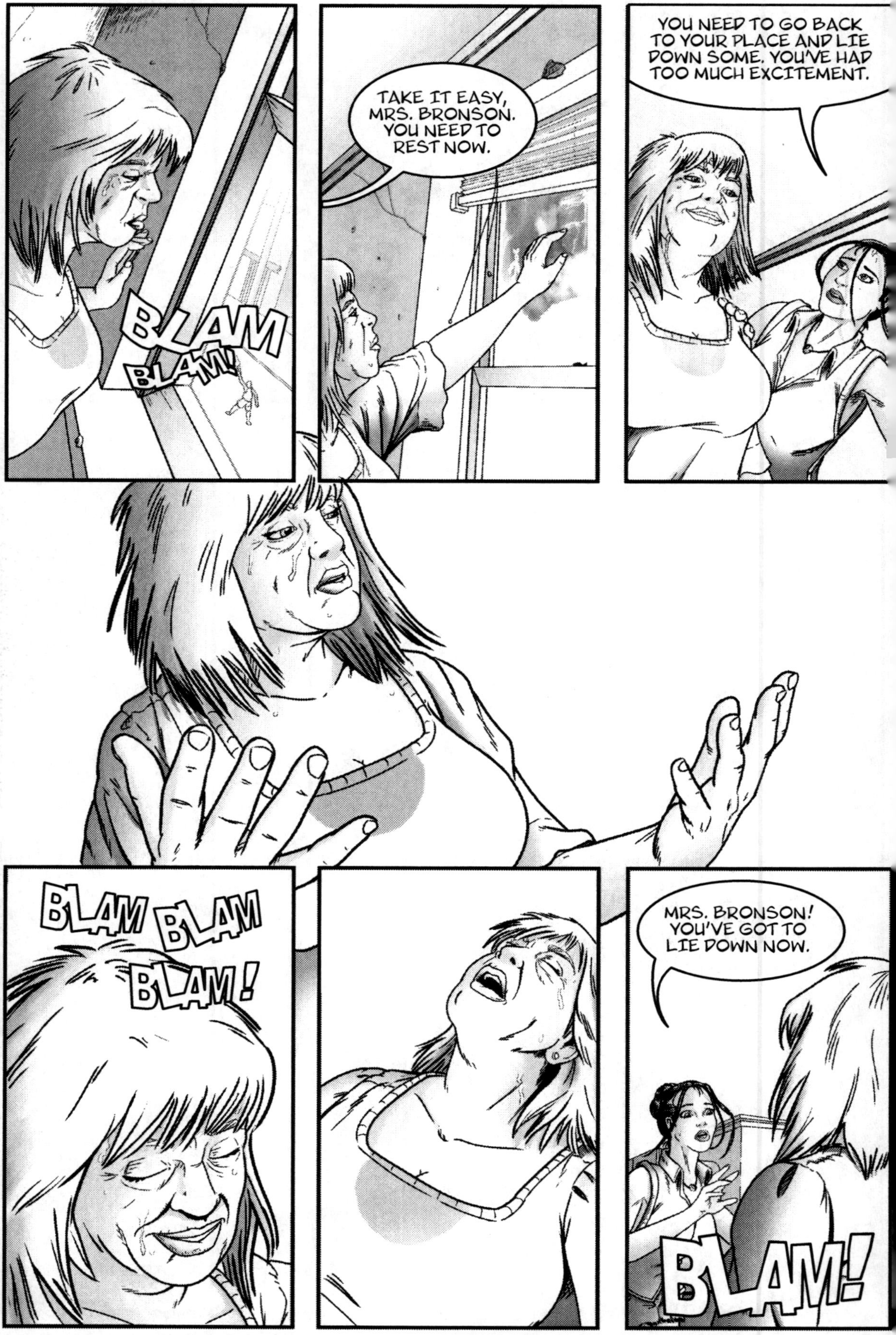
BLAM
BLAM!
TAKE IT EASY, MRS. BRONSON. YOU NEED TO REST NOW.
YOU NEED TO GO BACK TO YOUR PLACE AND LIE DOWN SOME. YOU'VE HAD TOO MUCH EXCITEMENT.
BLAM BLAM
BLAM!
MRS. BRONSON! YOU'VE GOT TO LIE DOWN NOW.
BLAM!

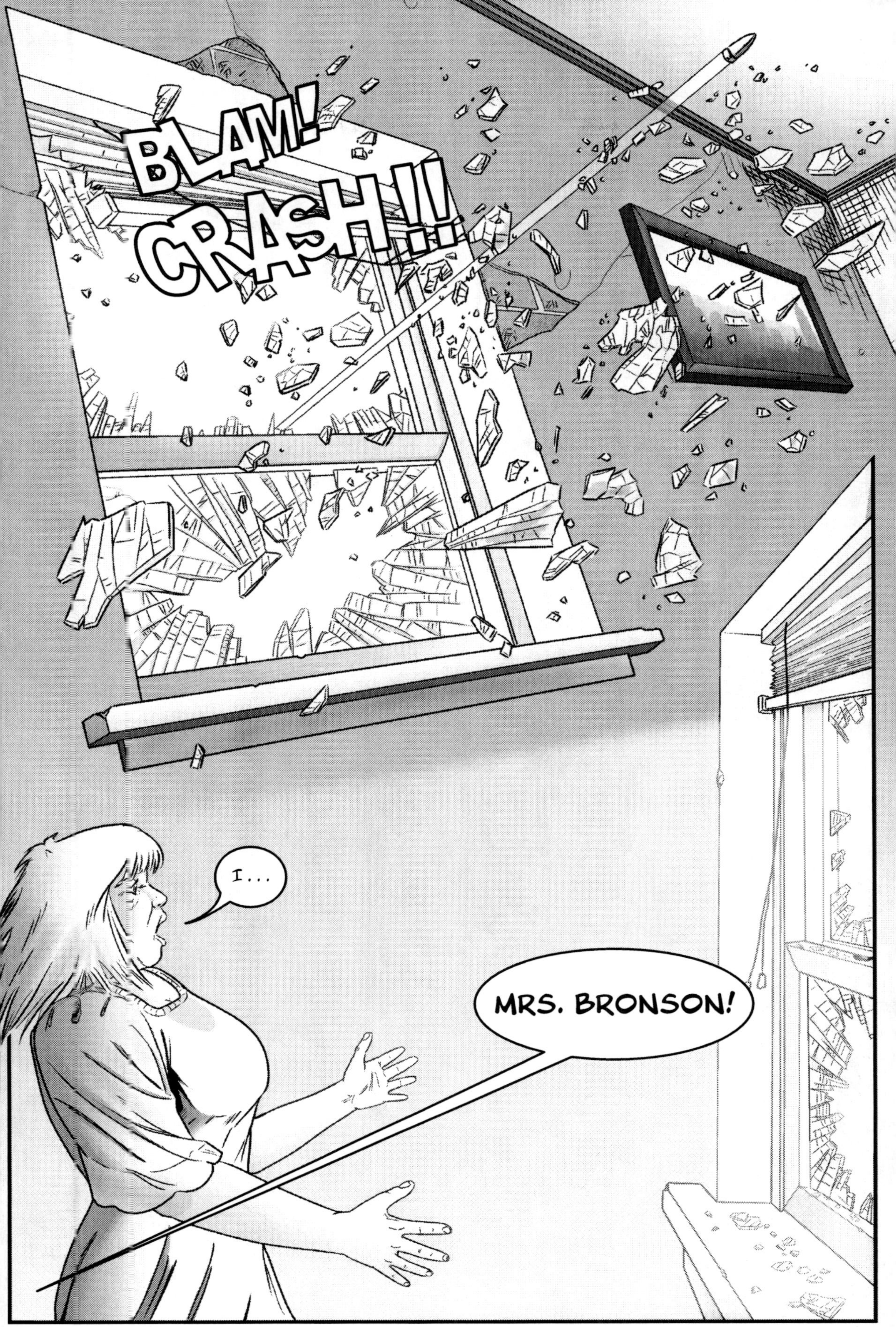
BLAM!
CRASH!!!
I...
MRS. BRONSON!

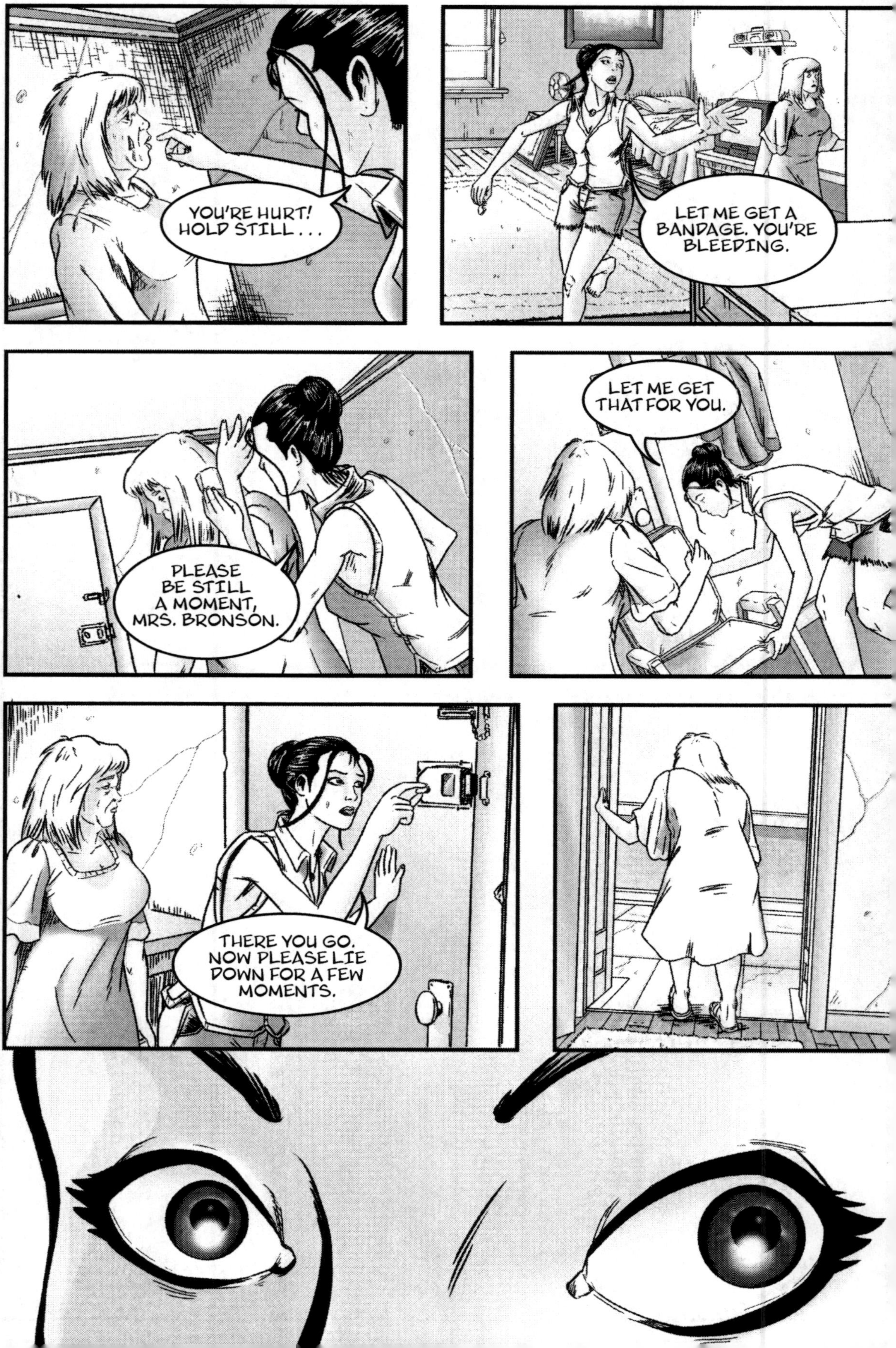
YOU'RE HURT! HOLD STILL . . .
LET ME GET A BANDAGE. YOU'RE BLEEDING.
PLEASE BE STILL A MOMENT, MRS. BRONSON.
LET ME GET THAT FOR YOU.
THERE YOU GO. NOW PLEASE LIE DOWN FOR A FEW MOMENTS.

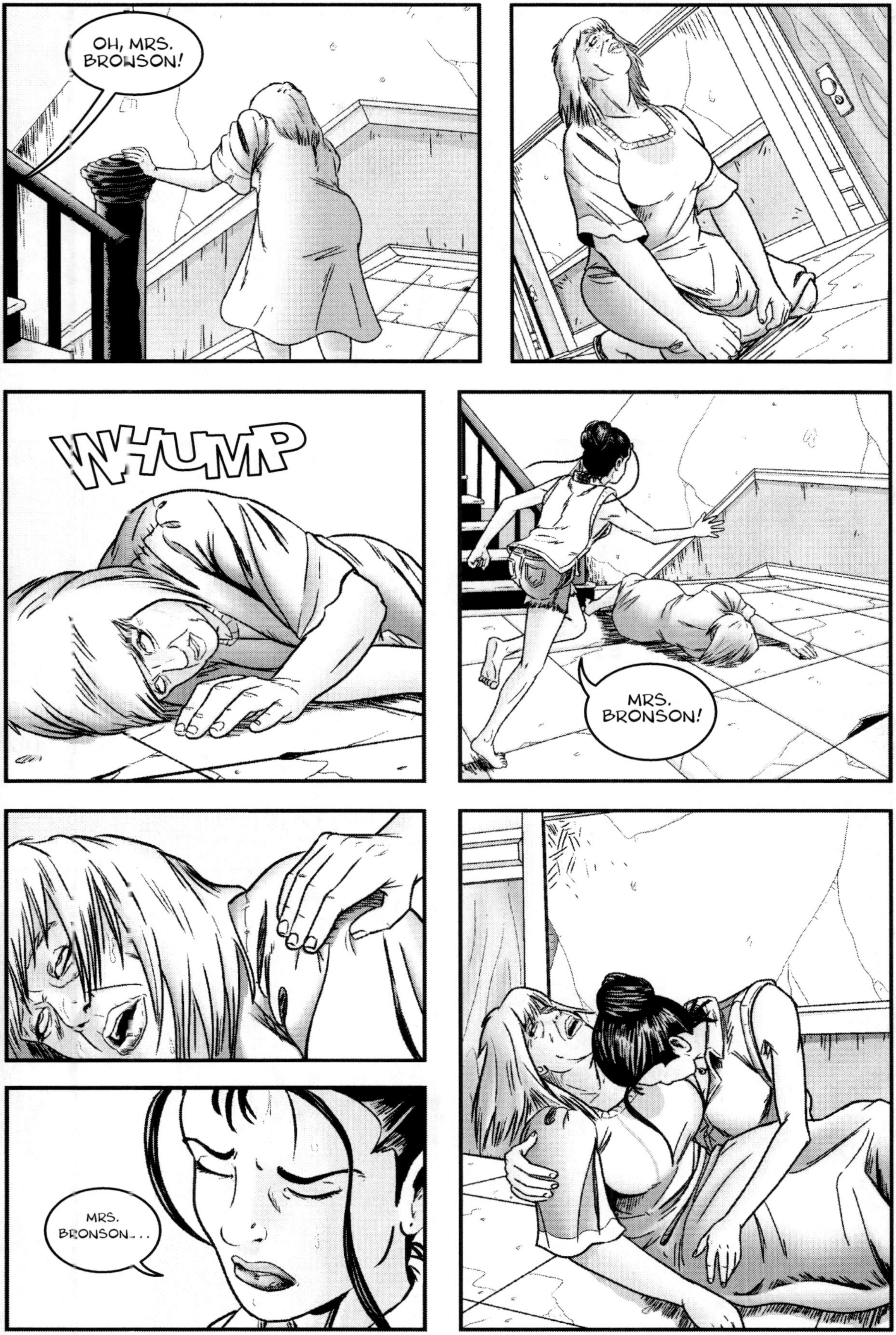
OH, MRS. BRONSON!
WHUMP
MRS. BRONSON!
MRS. BRONSON...

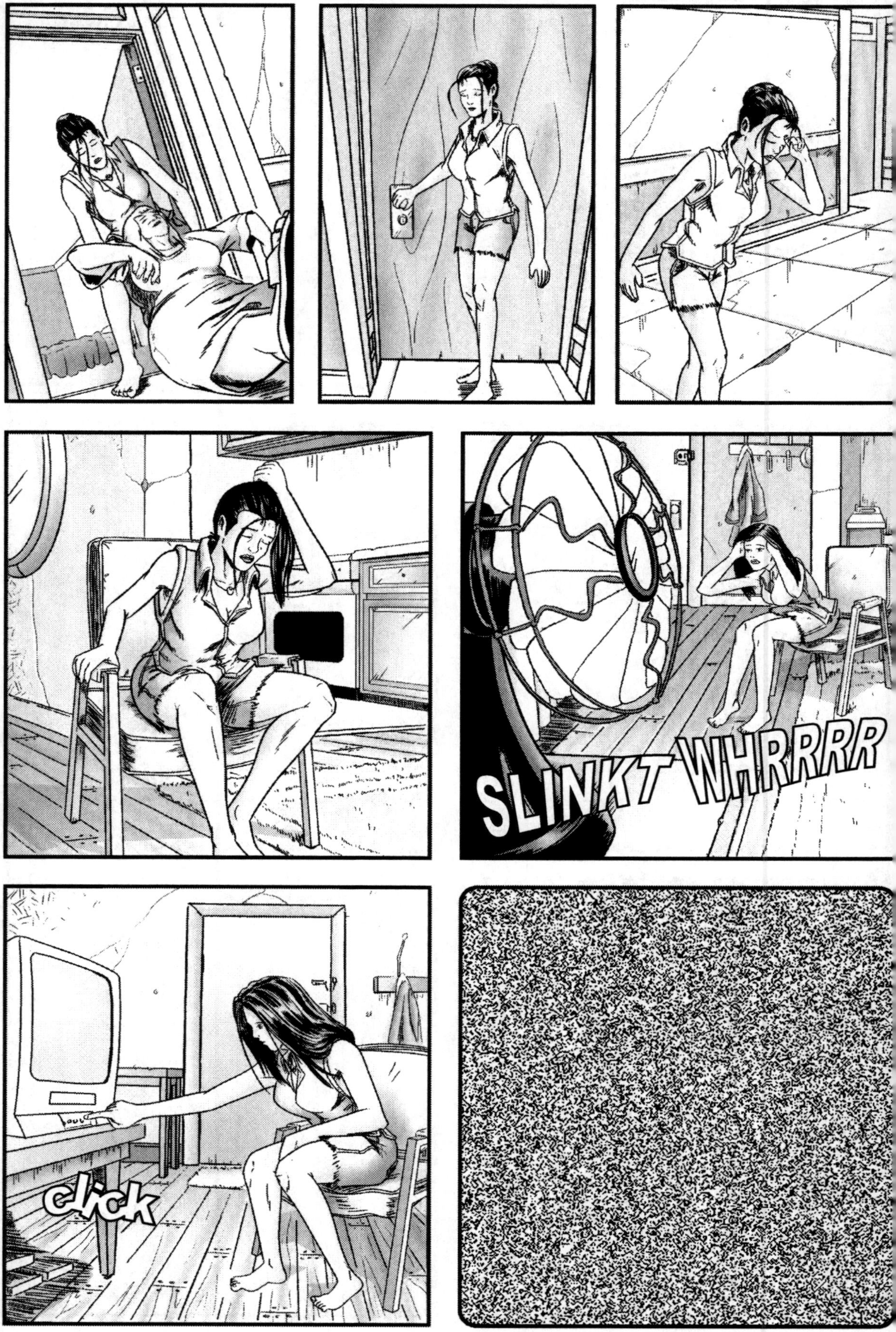
SLINKT WHRRRR
click

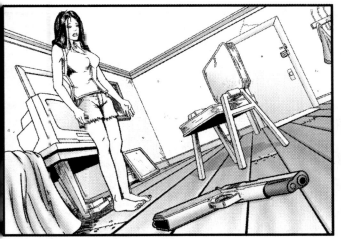

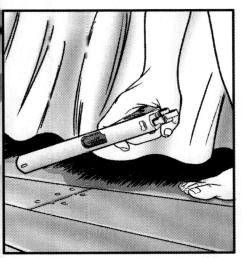

YAAAH!

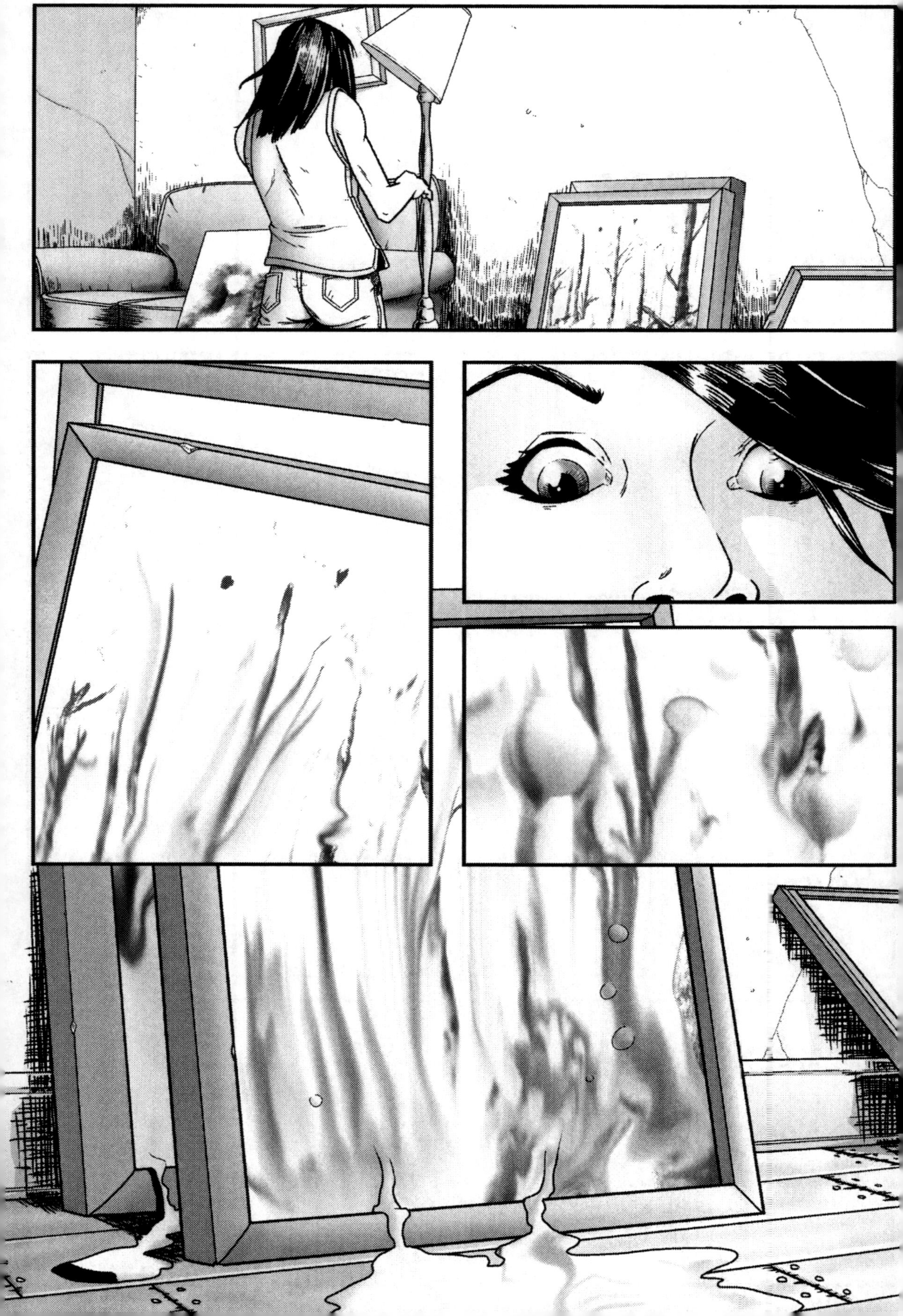

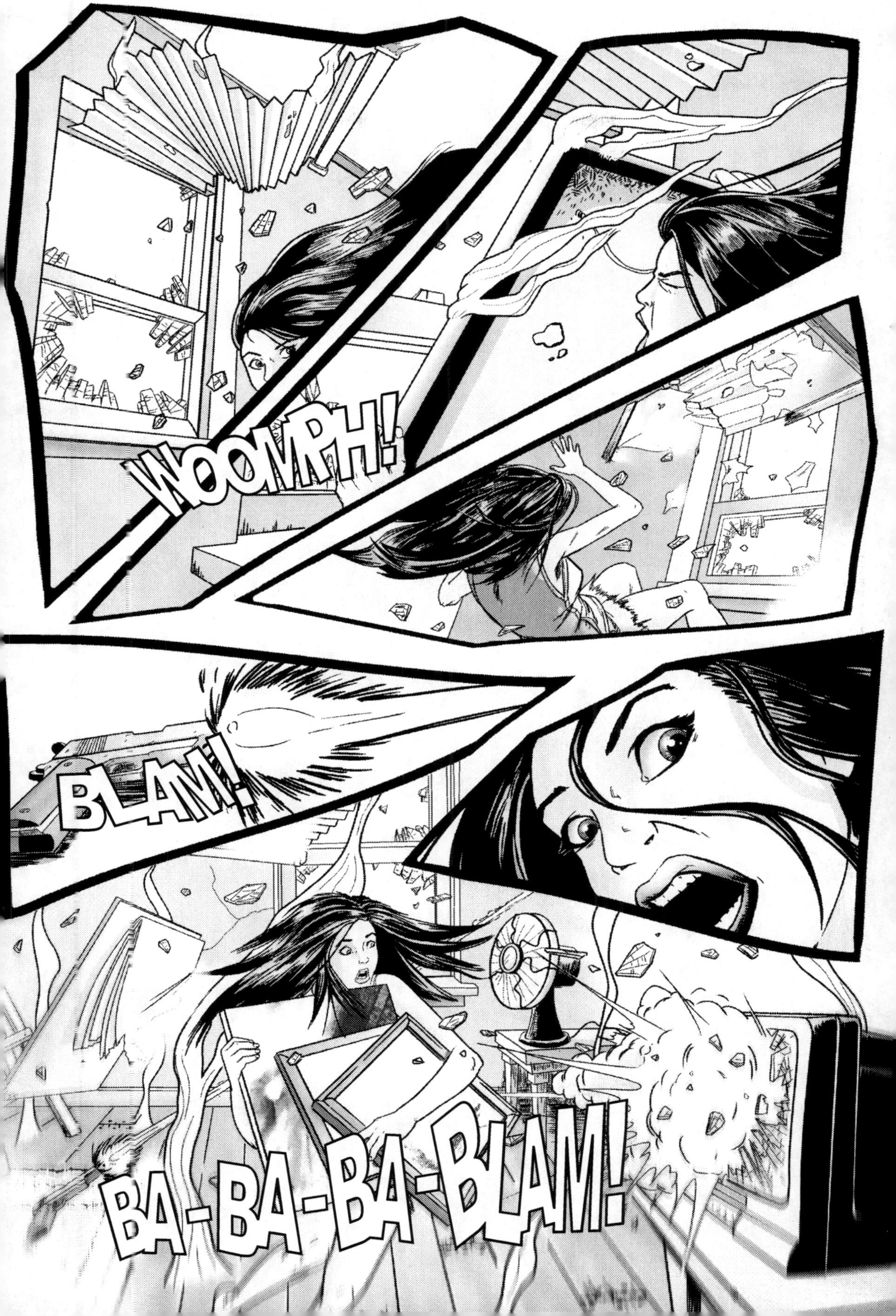
WOOMPH!
BLAM!
BA-BA-BA-BLAM!

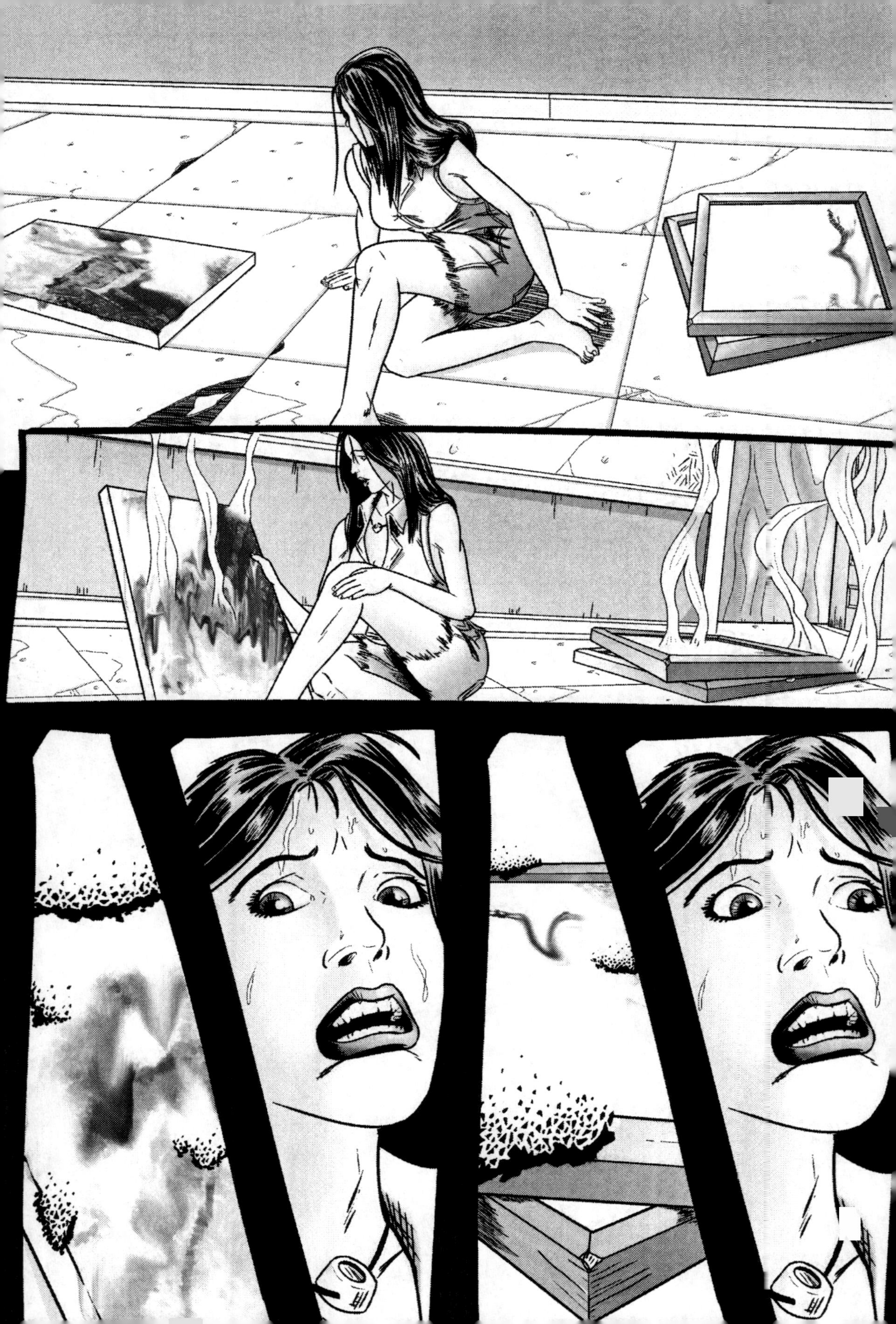

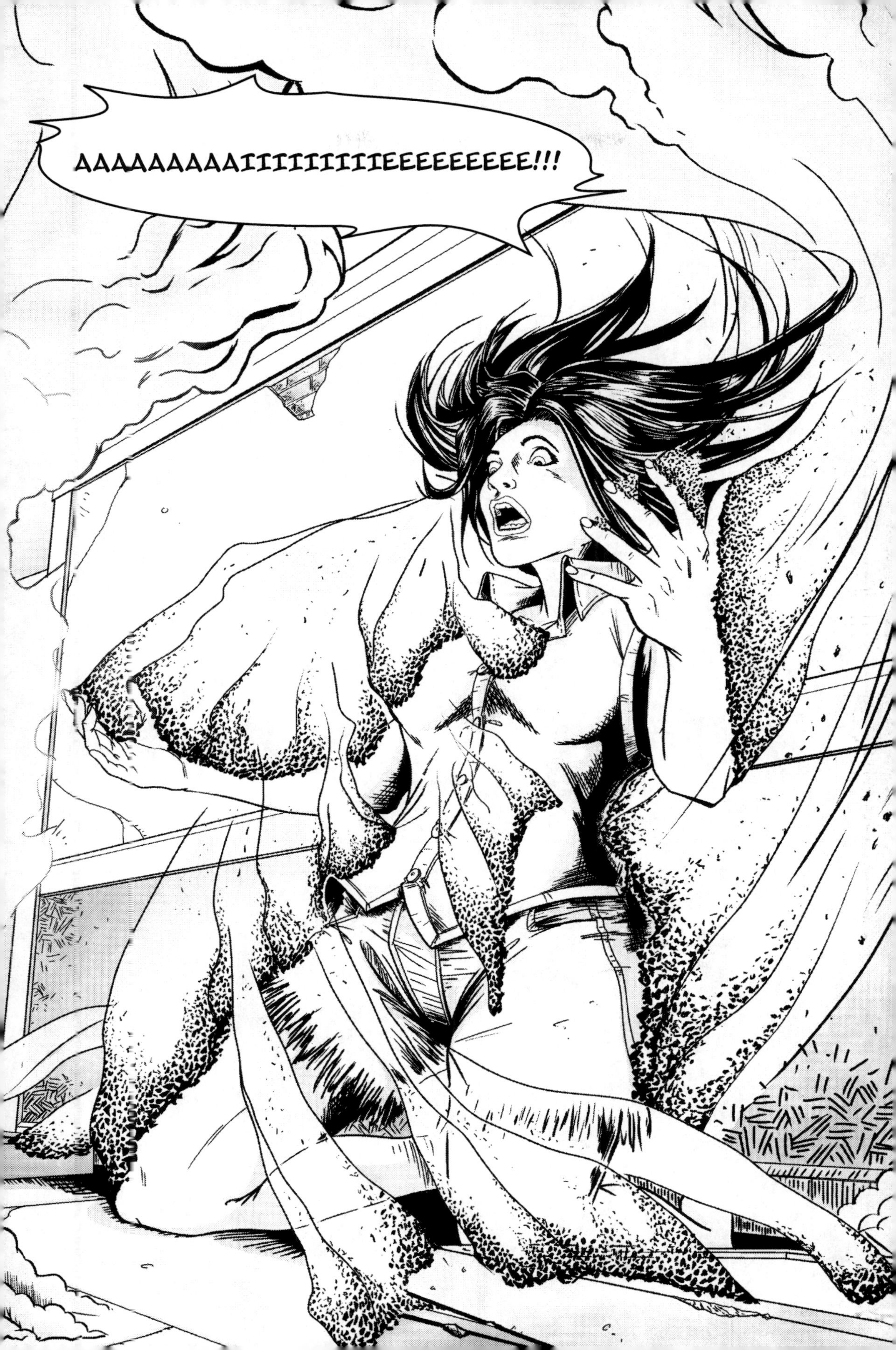
AAAAAAAAAIIIIIIIIIEEEEEEEEEE!!!

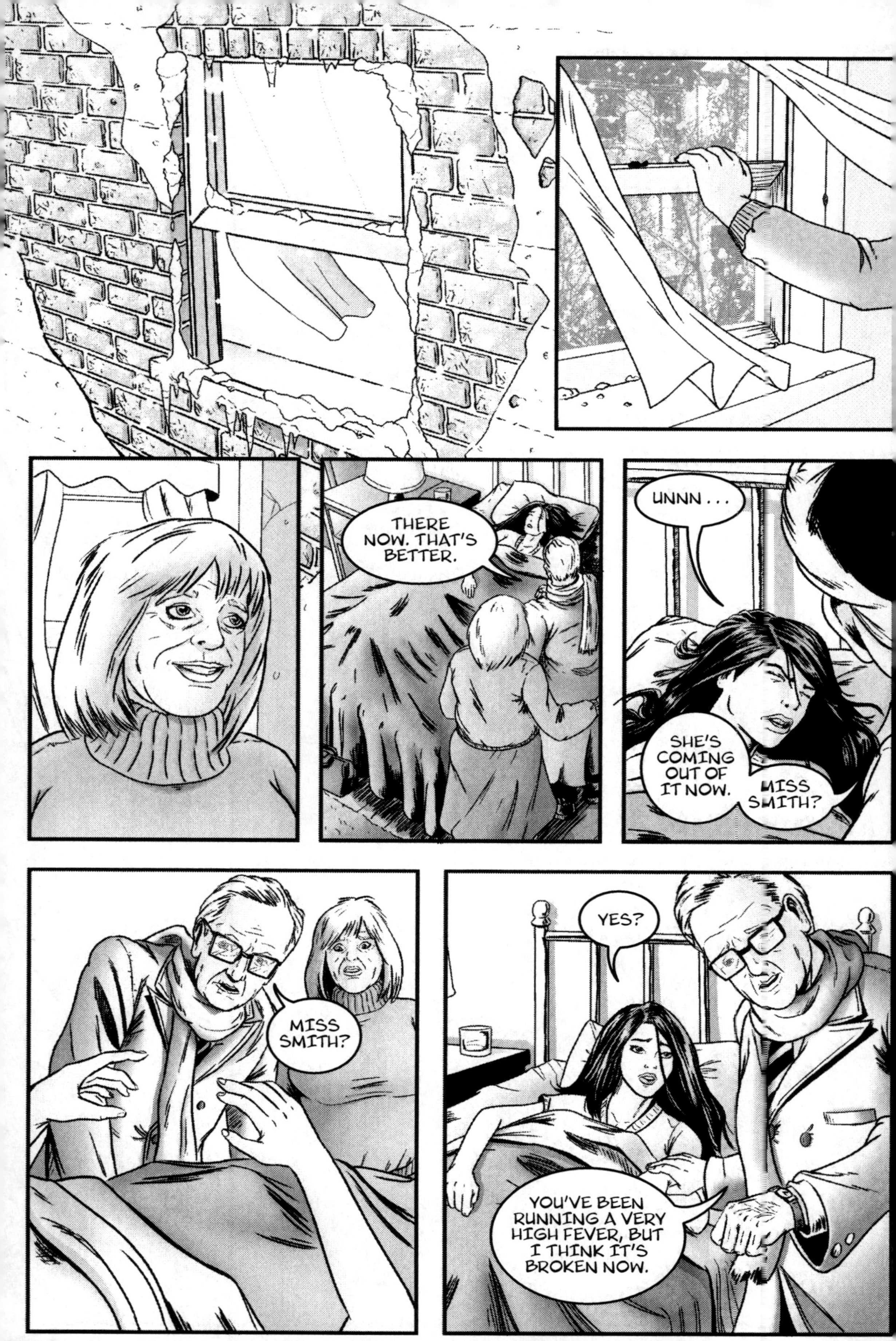
THERE NOW. THAT'S BETTER.
UNNN . . .
SHE'S COMING OUT OF IT NOW.
MISS SMITH?
MISS SMITH?
YES?
YOU'VE BEEN RUNNING A VERY HIGH FEVER, BUT I THINK IT'S BROKEN NOW.

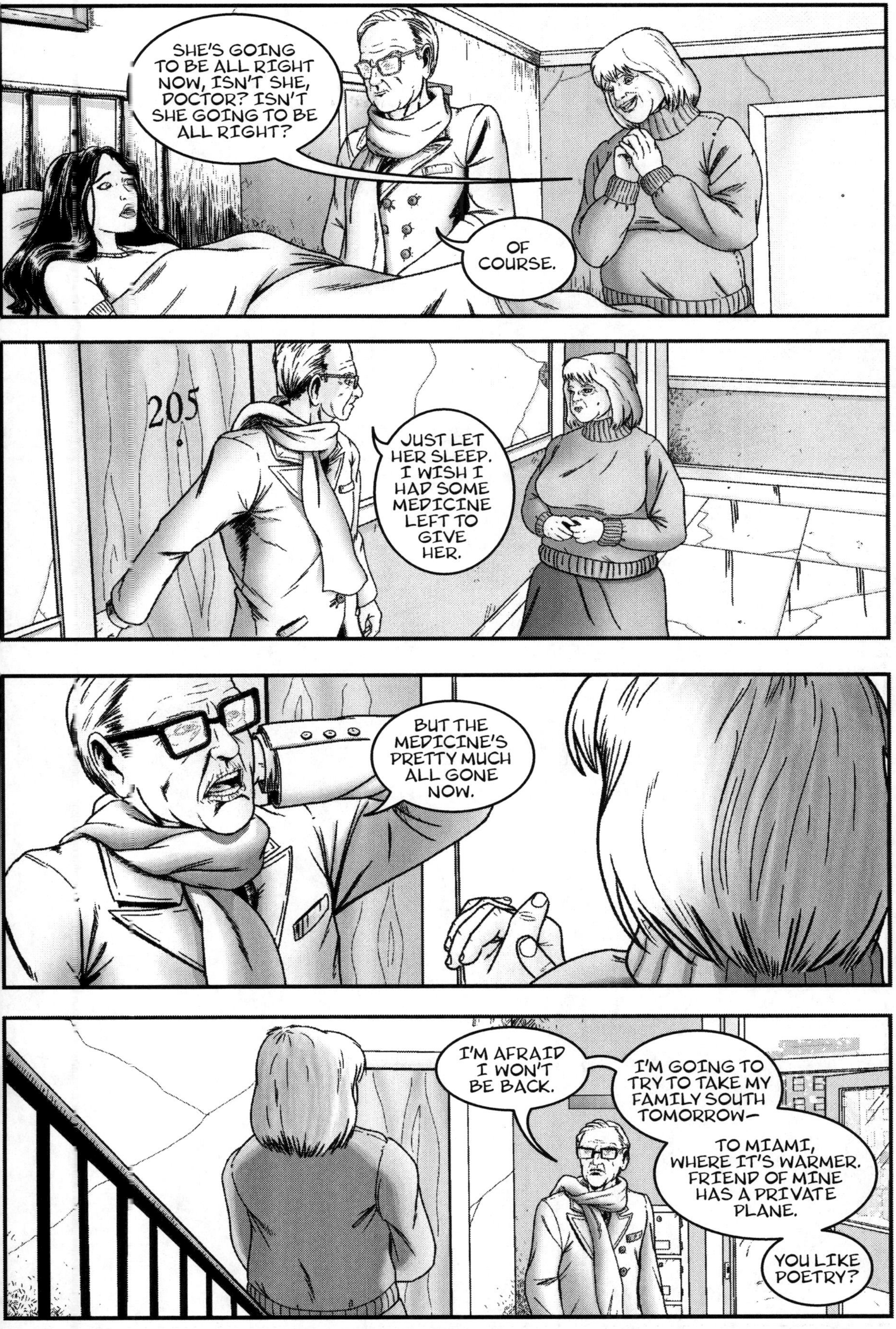
SHE'S GOING TO BE ALL RIGHT NOW, ISN'T SHE, DOCTOR? ISN'T SHE GOING TO BE ALL RIGHT?
OF COURSE.
205
JUST LET HER SLEEP. I WISH I HAD SOME MEDICINE LEFT TO GIVE HER.
BUT THE MEDICINE'S PRETTY MUCH ALL GONE NOW.
I'M AFRAID I WON'T BE BACK.
I'M GOING TO TRY TO TAKE MY FAMILY SOUTH TOMORROW—
TO MIAMI, WHERE IT'S WARMER. FRIEND OF MINE HAS A PRIVATE PLANE.
YOU LIKE POETRY?

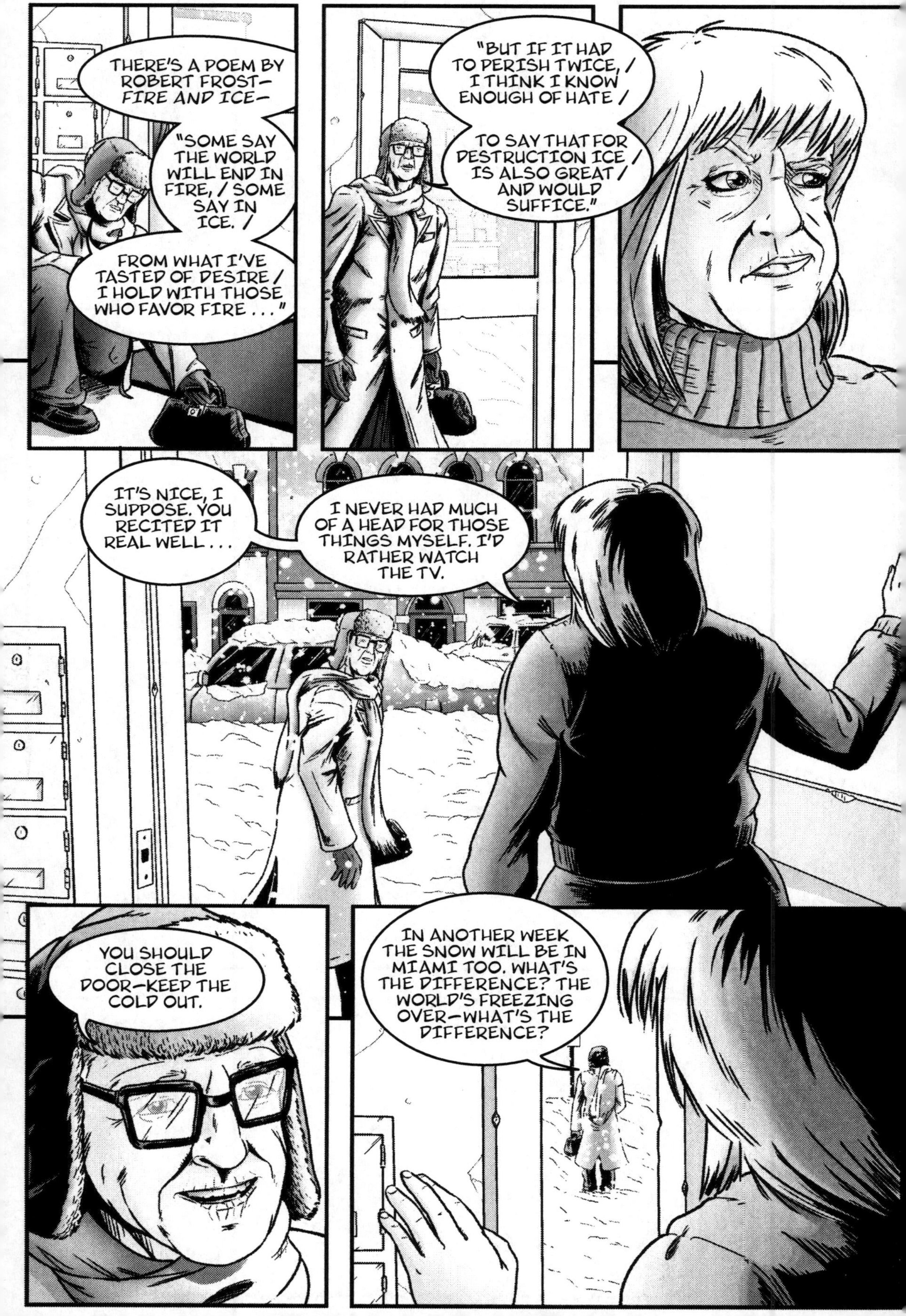
THERE'S A POEM BY ROBERT FROST— FIRE AND ICE—
"SOME SAY THE WORLD WILL END IN FIRE, / SOME SAY IN ICE. /
FROM WHAT I'VE TASTED OF DESIRE / I HOLD WITH THOSE WHO FAVOR FIRE . . ."
"BUT IF IT HAD TO PERISH TWICE, / I THINK I KNOW ENOUGH OF HATE /
TO SAY THAT FOR DESTRUCTION ICE / IS ALSO GREAT / AND WOULD SUFFICE."
IT'S NICE, I SUPPOSE. YOU RECITED IT REAL WELL . . .
I NEVER HAD MUCH OF A HEAD FOR THOSE THINGS MYSELF. I'D RATHER WATCH THE TV.
YOU SHOULD CLOSE THE DOOR—KEEP THE COLD OUT.
IN ANOTHER WEEK THE SNOW WILL BE IN MIAMI TOO. WHAT'S THE DIFFERENCE? THE WORLD'S FREEZING OVER—WHAT'S THE DIFFERENCE?

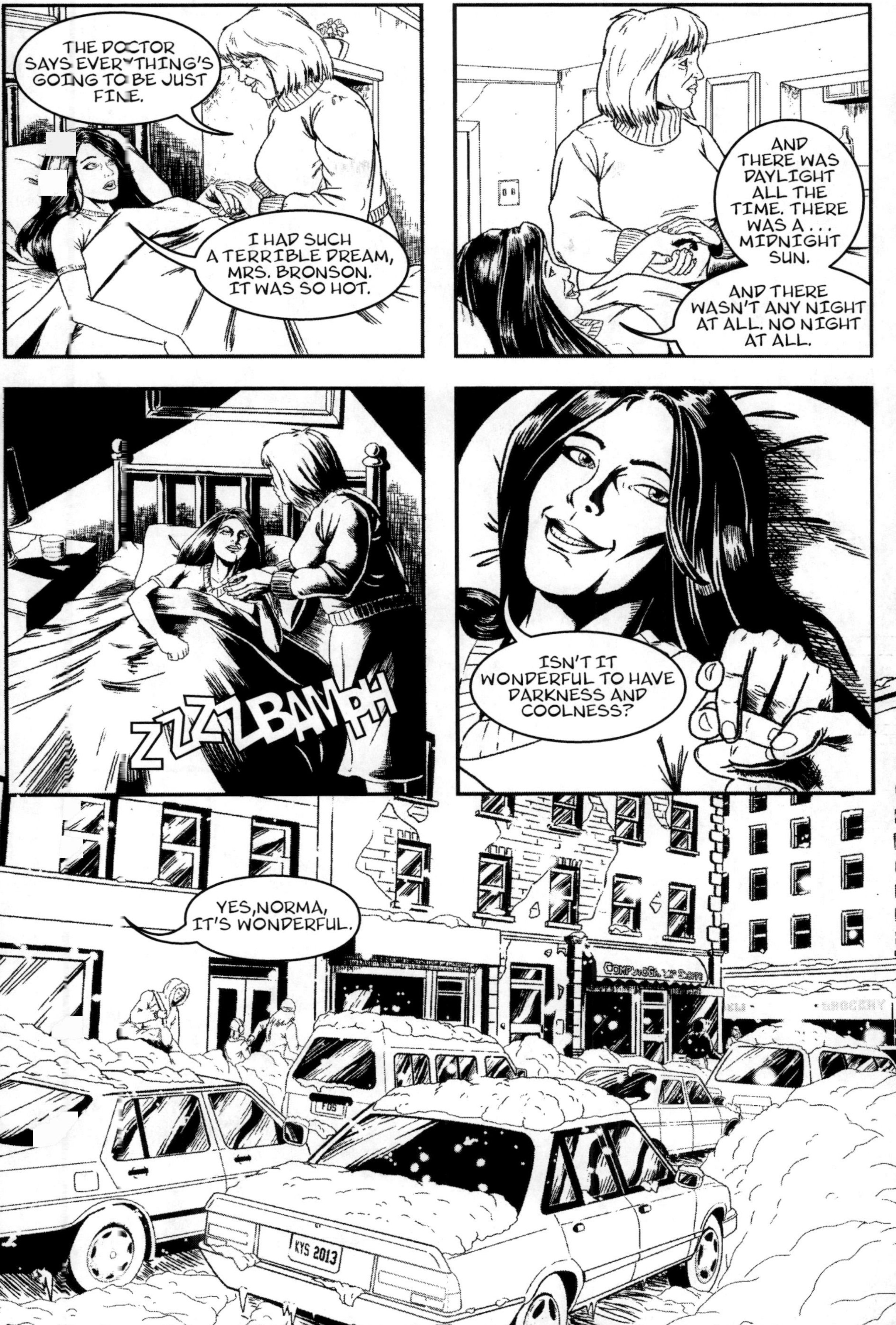
THE DOCTOR SAYS EVERYTHING'S GOING TO BE JUST FINE.
I HAD SUCH A TERRIBLE DREAM, MRS. BRONSON. IT WAS SO HOT.
AND THERE WAS DAYLIGHT ALL THE TIME. THERE WAS A . . . MIDNIGHT SUN.
AND THERE WASN'T ANY NIGHT AT ALL. NO NIGHT AT ALL.
ZZZZBAMPH
ISN'T IT WONDERFUL TO HAVE DARKNESS AND COOLNESS?
YES, NORMA, IT'S WONDERFUL.
KYS 2013

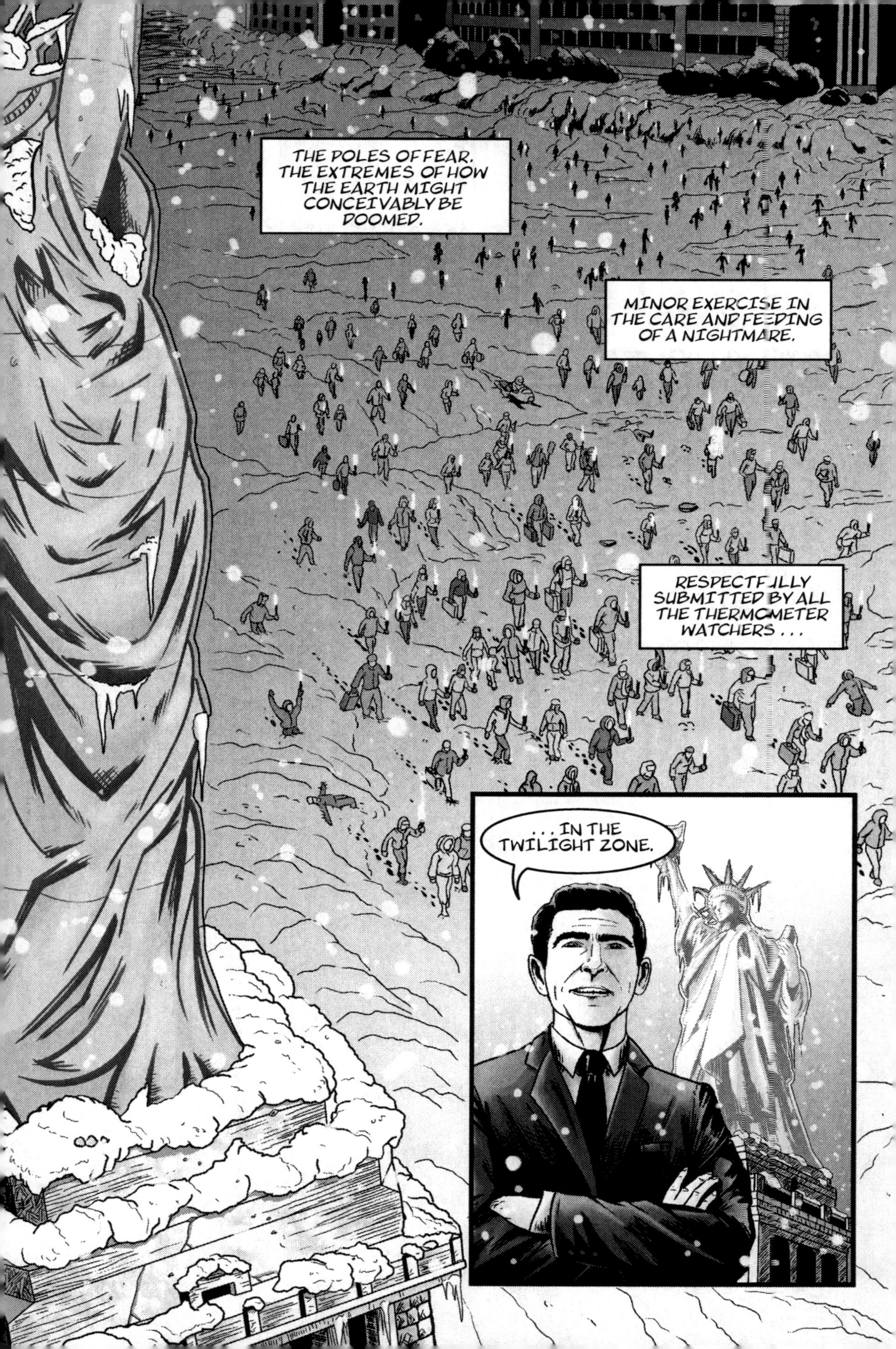
THE POLES OF FEAR. THE EXTREMES OF HOW THE EARTH MIGHT CONCEIVABLY BE DOOMED.
MINOR EXERCISE IN THE CARE AND FEEDING OF A NIGHTMARE.
RESPECTFULLY SUBMITTED BY ALL THE THERMOMETER WATCHERS . . .
. . . IN THE TWILIGHT ZONE.

The Midnight Sun

Season Three, Episode #10

Original Air Date: November 17, 1961

Written by Rod Serling

Cast

Narrator: Rod Serling

Norma: Lois Nettleton

Mrs. Bronson: Betty Garde*
*Also appeared in *The Odyssey of Flight 33* as Passenger

Intruder: Tom Reese

Mr. Shuster: Jason Wingreen*
*Also appeared in *A Stop at Willoughby* as Train Conductor
and *The Bard* as Director (uncredited)

Mrs. Shuster: Juney Ellis (as June Ellis)*
*Also appeared in *What You Need* as Woman on Street

Doctor: William Keene*
*Also appeared in *The Prime Mover* as Desk Clerk (uncredited)

Radio Announcer: Robert Stevenson (uncredited)*
*Also appeared in *Showdown with Rance McGrew* as TV Bartender (as Robert J. Stevenson)

Crew

Producer: Buck Houghton

Director: Anton Leader

Director of Photography: George T. Clemens

Music: Van Cleave

Film Editor: Jason H. Bernie

Production Note

The Midnight Sun aired within a year of the British movie *The Day the Earth Caught Fire*, which had a similar theme—and a much bigger budget. Serling had been battling with studio executives over the growing costs of producing the show, and he had to find creative ways on a shoestring budget to portray the end of the world. He had to cut two scenes from the episode—one with a refrigerator repairman and one with a police officer, which had already been cast. The scene with the police officer has been restored in Mark Kneece's adaptation. In addition, the episode was shot in the summer on a set without air conditioning. The director even had the heat turned up for key scenes to get the actors in the sweaty spirit of the story. And the melting paintings effect was accomplished by painting with wax on the surface of a hot plate, which was then turned on to melt the images.

ADAPTING STORIES FROM ROD SERLING'S

In terms of screenwriting adaptations it's trying to cut out stuff that's extraneous, without doing damage to the original piece, because you owe a debt of some respect to the original author.

—Rod Serling, 1975

At first, the idea sounded straightforward. Take an original *Twilight Zone* screenplay and adapt it into a graphic novel—break the visuals into panels, move the dialogue into balloons and captions. After all, Rod Serling himself was a fan of comics, and graphic novels are their visual and literary heirs. Serling collected Entertaining Comics titles such as *Tales from the Crypt* and *Weird Science*, the themes of which resonate in *The Twilight Zone*; even Serling's trademark narration could be considered an echo of the Crypt Keeper's introductions. Yet the more I considered the task of adapting the scripts, the more the gravity of what I was doing set in. I grew up watching *The Twilight Zone*, after all, as did so many Americans. The work required a certain reverential perspective, considering the show's iconic status, not to mention the quality of the original material.

In the 1950s the comics Serling had enjoyed were considered subversive, a threat to America's youth. Frederick Wertham published *Seduction of the Innocent* in 1954, excoriating comics in an atmosphere of public paranoia similar to a scene from *The Monsters Are Due on Maple Street*. A year later, a Senate committee was convened to investigate the pernicious influence of horror comics on America's youth, and the Comics Code Authority was established to censor comics' content. EC Comics went out of business as a direct result. In an interesting twist of fate, by the end of the decade *The Twilight Zone* was just beginning to find its television audience with stories that probably would not have made it past the comics censors. Recreating Serling's stories now, in graphic novel form, seems appropriate, emblematic of an era in which comics are finding a new readership, achieving new respect, and speaking to a new audience receptive to a more sophisticated message.

Serling's stories run the gamut from serious drama, filled with fantastic and frightening dilemmas of the human condition, to wry, tongue-in-cheek humor in a sci-fi wrapper. Selecting eight as graphic novel material meant making difficult choices. Serling was a prolific writer, creating more than half of *The Twilight Zone*'s 156 scripts. It was not only a question of which of these would work best in novelized format, but which ones, as a group, would come closest to capturing the essence of *The Twilight Zone*. The stories ultimately chosen for these books possess the strongest visual possibilities and reflect an effort to achieve a cross section of Serling's dramatic range.

As I began adapting the stories for artists, I immersed myself in the screenplays and watched each episode until I felt I had internalized not just the characters, the plot, and the point, but what I imagined to be something of the author himself. In the process, I felt a growing kinship with Serling. Parts of the screenplay were often deleted from the actual show. Lines, characters, even entire scenes were struck, sometimes for budgetary reasons, sometimes because of time constraints, sometimes perhaps because Serling himself may have anticipated problems with the scenes. The show usually had only a thirty-minute time slot. The deleted scenes, however, often add richness and complexity to the story, offering a glimmer into what Serling might have done were it not for the constraints of the television medium. Restoring scenes seemed to help push the story even harder. I felt as if I were developing Serling's original design, following the telling to its logical conclusion.

With each of these stories, I have aspired to take advantage of what the graphic novel format can do. Art and text draw the reader deeply into the narrative. The reader does not just hear, but ponders, actively bridging the gaps between the panels of art with his or her own imagination. The story doesn't just happen to the reader, but, in part, *is* the reader. In other words, *The Twilight Zone* episodes had to be recreated not just to fit into a graphic novel format but to belong to it.

As much as possible, I have endeavored to keep the intentions of the original story intact—that is the "debt of respect" owed to Serling—fully functional in a new medium. From some nearby fifth dimension, I hope Serling is smiling at the prospect of these books, pleased at the thought of a new generation arriving by way of a different avenue perhaps, but entering and being welcomed into the fold of "Zonies" around the world.

—Mark Kneece
Professor of Sequential Art, Savannah College of Art and Design

Acknowledgments

Our thanks go to Carol Serling for her time and consideration while reviewing the adaptation texts and illustrated pages, and also to John Lowe, chair of the Sequential Art Department at Savannah College of Art and Design, for his assistance in pairing the right artists with the right stories.

First published in the United States of America in 2009 by Walker Publishing Company, Inc.
Visit Walker & Company's Web site at www.walkeryoungreaders.com
Visit the Savannah College of Art and Design's Web Site at www.scad.edu

For information about permission to reproduce selections from this book, write to
Permissions, Walker & Company, 175 Fifth Avenue, New York, New York 10010

Library of Congress Cataloging-in-Publication Data
Kneece, Mark.
The midnight sun / adaptation from Rod Serling's original script by Mark Kneece ;
illustrated by Anthony Spay.
p.   cm.
"Rod Serling's the Twilight Zone."
Summary: New York City has become almost uninhabitable when continuous sunlight causes unbearable heat, rationing of water and electricity, and swarms of people leaving, looking for cooler weather further north.
ISBN-13: 978-0-8027-9720-9 • ISBN-10: 0-8027-9720-2 (hardcover)
ISBN-13: 978-0-8027-9721-6 • ISBN-10: 0-8027-9721-0 (paperback)
1. Graphic novels. [1. Graphic novels. 2. Climatic changes—Fiction. 3. Global warming—Fiction. 4. New York (N.Y.)—Fiction.
5. Science fiction.] I. Serling, Rod, 1924–1975. II. Spay, Anthony, ill. III. Twilight zone (Television program : 1959–1964) IV. Title.
PZ7.7.K65Mi 2009   741.5'973—dc22   2008038580

Packaged by Design Press, a division of Savannah College of Art and Design, Inc.
22 East Lathrop Street, Savannah, Georgia 31415

Adaptation from Rod Serling's original script by Mark Kneece
Illustrated by Anthony Spay
Lettering by Matthew Razzano and Mia Paluzzi
Series title treatment by Devin O'Bryan
Series copyediting by Kerri O'Hern
Series creative development by Anna Marlis Burgard and Emily Easton
Series art direction and design by Angela Rojas
Series project management by Angela Rojas and Melissa Kavonic
Creative consultant: Carol Serling

Photograph of Rod Serling © Bettmann/Corbis

"Fire and Ice" from THE POETRY OF ROBERT FROST edited by Edward Connery Lathem.
Copyright 1923, 1969 by Henry Holt and Company. Copyright 1951 by Robert Frost.
Reprinted by permission of Henry Holt and Company, LLC.

Printed in China
2 4 6 8 10 9 7 5 3 1 (hardcover)
2 4 6 8 10 9 7 5 3 1 (paperback)

All papers used by Walker & Company are natural, recyclable products
made from wood grown in well-managed forests. The manufacturing processes
conform to the environmental regulations of the country of origin.

Acknowledgments

Our thanks go to Carol Serling for her time and consideration while reviewing the adaptation texts and illustrated pages, and also to John Lowe, chair of the Sequential Art Department at Savannah College of Art and Design, for his assistance in pairing the right artists with the right stories.

Text copyright © 2009 by The Rod Serling Trust
Illustrations copyright © 2009 by Design Press, a division of Savannah College of Art and Design, Inc.
Introduction copyright © 2008 by Savannah College of Art and Design
"Adapting Stories from Rod Serling's *The Twilight Zone*" copyright © 2008 by Savannah College of Art and Design

First published in the United States of America in 2009 by Walker Publishing Company, Inc.
Visit Walker & Company's Web site at www.walkeryoungreaders.com
Visit the Savannah College of Art and Design's Web Site at www.scad.edu

For information about permission to reproduce selections from this book, write to
Permissions, Walker & Company, 175 Fifth Avenue, New York, New York 10010

Library of Congress Cataloging-in-Publication Data
Kneece, Mark.
Deaths-head revisited / adaptation from Rod Serling's original script by Mark Kneece ; illustrated by Chris Lie.
p.   cm.
"Rod Serling's the Twilight Zone."
Summary: A former Nazi concentration camp guard returns to Dachau to relive his memories of the war.
ISBN-13: 978-0-8027-9722-3 • ISBN-10: 0-8027-9722-9 (hardcover)
ISBN-13: 978-0-8027-9723-0 • ISBN-10: 0-8027-9723-7 (paperback)
1. Graphic novels. [1. Graphic novels. 2. Holocaust, Jewish (1939–1945)—Fiction. 3. Dachau (Concentration camp)—Fiction.
4. Germany—Fiction.] I. Serling, Rod, 1924–1975. II. Lie, Chris, ill. III. Twilight zone (Television program : 1959–1964) IV. Title.
PZ7.7.K65De 2009   741.5'973—dc22   2008038579

Packaged by Design Press, a division of Savannah College of Art and Design, Inc. ®
22 East Lathrop Street, Savannah, Georgia 31415

Adaptation from Rod Serling's original script by Mark Kneece
Illustrated by Chris Lie and Caravan Studio
Lettering by Thomas Zielonka
Series title treatment by Devin O'Bryan
Series copyediting by Kerri O'Hern
Series creative development by Anna Marlis Burgard and Emily Easton
Series art direction and design by Angela Rojas
Series project management by Angela Rojas and Melissa Kavonic
Creative consultant: Carol Serling

Photograph of Rod Serling © Bettmann/Corbis

Printed in China
2 4 6 8 10 9 7 5 3 1 (hardcover)
2 4 6 8 10 9 7 5 3 1 (paperback)

All papers used by Walker & Company are natural, recyclable products
made from wood grown in well-managed forests. The manufacturing processes
conform to the environmental regulations of the country of origin.

later, a Senate committee was convened to investigate the pernicious influence of horror comics on America's youth, and the Comics Code Authority was established to censor comics' content. EC Comics went out of business as a direct result. In an interesting twist of fate, by the end of the decade *The Twilight Zone* was just beginning to find its television audience with stories that probably would not have made it past the comics censors. Recreating Serling's stories now, in graphic novel form, seems appropriate, emblematic of an era in which comics are finding a new readership, achieving new respect, and speaking to a new audience receptive to a more sophisticated message.

Serling's stories run the gamut from serious drama, filled with fantastic and frightening dilemmas of the human condition, to wry, tongue-in-cheek humor in a sci-fi wrapper. Selecting eight as graphic novel material meant making difficult choices. Serling was a prolific writer, creating more than half of *The Twilight Zone*'s 156 scripts. It was not only a question of which of these would work best in novelized format, but which ones, as a group, would come closest to capturing the essence of *The Twilight Zone*. The stories ultimately chosen for these books possess the strongest visual possibilities and reflect an effort to achieve a cross section of Serling's dramatic range.

As I began adapting the stories for artists, I immersed myself in the screenplays and watched each episode until I felt I had internalized not just the characters, the plot, and the point, but what I imagined to be something of the author himself. In the process, I felt a growing kinship with Serling. Parts of the screenplay were often deleted from the actual show. Lines, characters, even entire scenes were struck, sometimes for budgetary reasons, sometimes because of time constraints, sometimes perhaps because Serling himself may have anticipated problems with the scenes. The show usually had only a thirty-minute time slot. The deleted scenes, however, often add richness and complexity to the story, offering a glimmer into what Serling might have done were it not for the constraints of the television medium. Restoring scenes seemed to help push the story even harder. I felt as if I were developing Serling's original design, following the telling to its logical conclusion.

With each of these stories, I have aspired to take advantage of what the graphic novel format can do. Art and text draw the reader deeply into the narrative. The reader does not just hear, but ponders actively bridging the gaps between the panels of art with his or her own imagination. The story doesn't just happen to the reader, but, in part, *is* the reader. In other words, *The Twilight Zone* episodes had to be recreated not just to fit into a graphic novel format but to belong to it.

As much as possible, I have endeavored to keep the intentions of the original story intact—that is the "debt of respect" owed to Serling—fully functional in a new medium. From some nearby fifth dimension, I hope Serling is smiling at the prospect of these books, pleased at the thought of a new generation arriving by way of a different avenue perhaps, but entering and being welcomed into the fold of "Zonies" around the world.

—Mark Kneece
Professor of Sequential Art, Savannah College of Art and Design

ADAPTING
STORIES FROM

In terms of screenwriting adaptations it's trying to cut out stuff that's extraneous, without doing damage to the original piece, because you owe a debt of some respect to the original author.

—Rod Serling, 1975

At first, the idea sounded straightforward. Take an original *Twilight Zone* screenplay and adapt it into a graphic novel—break the visuals into panels, move the dialogue into balloons and captions. After all, Rod Serling himself was a fan of comics, and graphic novels are their visual and literary heirs. Serling collected Entertaining Comics titles such as *Tales from the Crypt* and *Weird Science*, the themes of which resonate in *The Twilight Zone*; even Serling's trademark narration could be considered an echo of the Crypt Keeper's introductions. Yet the more I considered the task of adapting the scripts, the more the gravity of what I was doing set in. I grew up watching *The Twilight Zone*, after all, as did so many Americans. The work required a certain reverential perspective, considering the show's iconic status, not to mention the quality of the original material.

In the 1950s the comics Serling had enjoyed were considered subversive, a threat to America's youth. Frederick Wertham published *Seduction of the Innocent* in 1954, excoriating comics in an atmosphere of public paranoia similar to a scene from *The Monsters Are Due on Maple Street*. A year

Deaths-Head Revisited

Season Three, Episode #9

Original Air Date: November 10, 1961

Written by Rod Serling

Cast

Narrator: Rod Serling

Becker: Joseph Schildkraut*
*Also appeared in *The Trade-Ins* as John Holt

SS Captain Gunther Lutze: Oscar Beregi Jr.*
*Also appeared in *Mute* as Professor Karl Werner
and *The Rip Van Winkle Caper* as Farwell the Ringleader

Innkeeper: Kaaren Verne (as Karen Verne)

Taxi Driver: Robert Boon (as Robert Boone)*
*Also appeared in *Mute* as Holger Nielsen

Doctor: Ben Wright*
*Also appeared in *Dead Man's Shoes* as Chips
and *Judgment Night* as Captain Wilbur

Dachau Victim: Chuck Fox

Crew

Producer: Buck Houghton
Director: Don Medford
Director of Photography: Jack Swain
Film Editor: Bill Mosher

Production Note

Deaths-Head Revisited was inspired by the trial of Nazi war criminal Adolf Eichmann, which began in April 1961 and ended with his conviction on December 11, 1961, almost exactly one month after this episode aired. Considered by many to be the architect of the Final Solution, Eichmann escaped after the war and was found in Argentina by Israeli agents, who abducted him and brought him to Israel, where he was tried, convicted, and executed. So, like Lutze, Eichmann was put on trial and brought to justice by Jewish victims of the Holocaust. In another parallel to the Holocaust, two years before he appeared in this episode as Becker, Joseph Schildkraut played Anne Frank's father in the movie *The Diary of Anne Frank*.

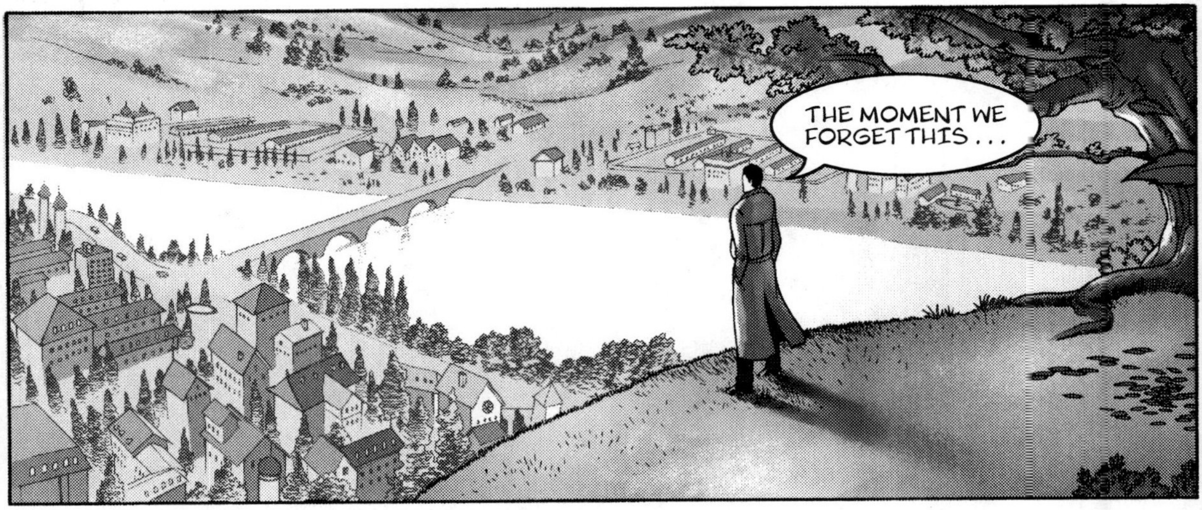
THE MOMENT WE FORGET THIS . . .

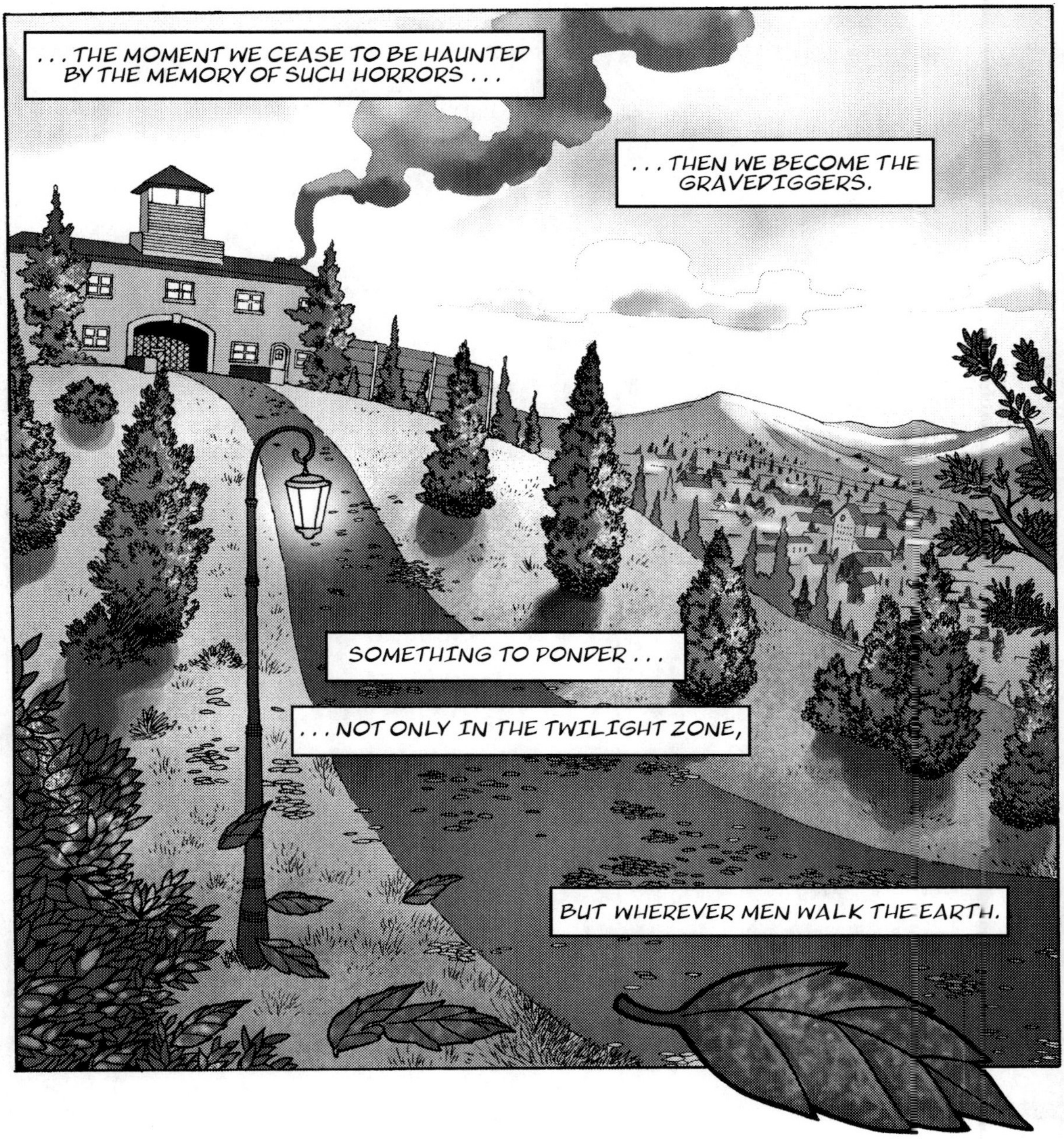
. . . THE MOMENT WE CEASE TO BE HAUNTED BY THE MEMORY OF SUCH HORRORS . . .
. . . THEN WE BECOME THE GRAVEDIGGERS.
SOMETHING TO PONDER . . .
. . . NOT ONLY IN THE TWILIGHT ZONE,
BUT WHEREVER MEN WALK THE EARTH.

ALL THE DACHAUS MUST REMAIN STANDING.

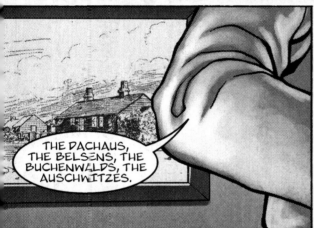

THE DACHAUS, THE BELSENS, THE BUCHENWALDS, THE AUSCHWITZES.

ALL OF THEM A MONUMENT TO A MOMENT IN TIME WHEN A FEW MEN DECIDED TO TURN THE EARTH INTO A GRAVEYARD.

INTO IT THEY SHOVELED ALL OF THEIR REASON, THEIR LOGIC, THEIR KNOWLEDGE, BUT WORST OF ALL, THEIR CONSCIENCE.

PAPA . . .

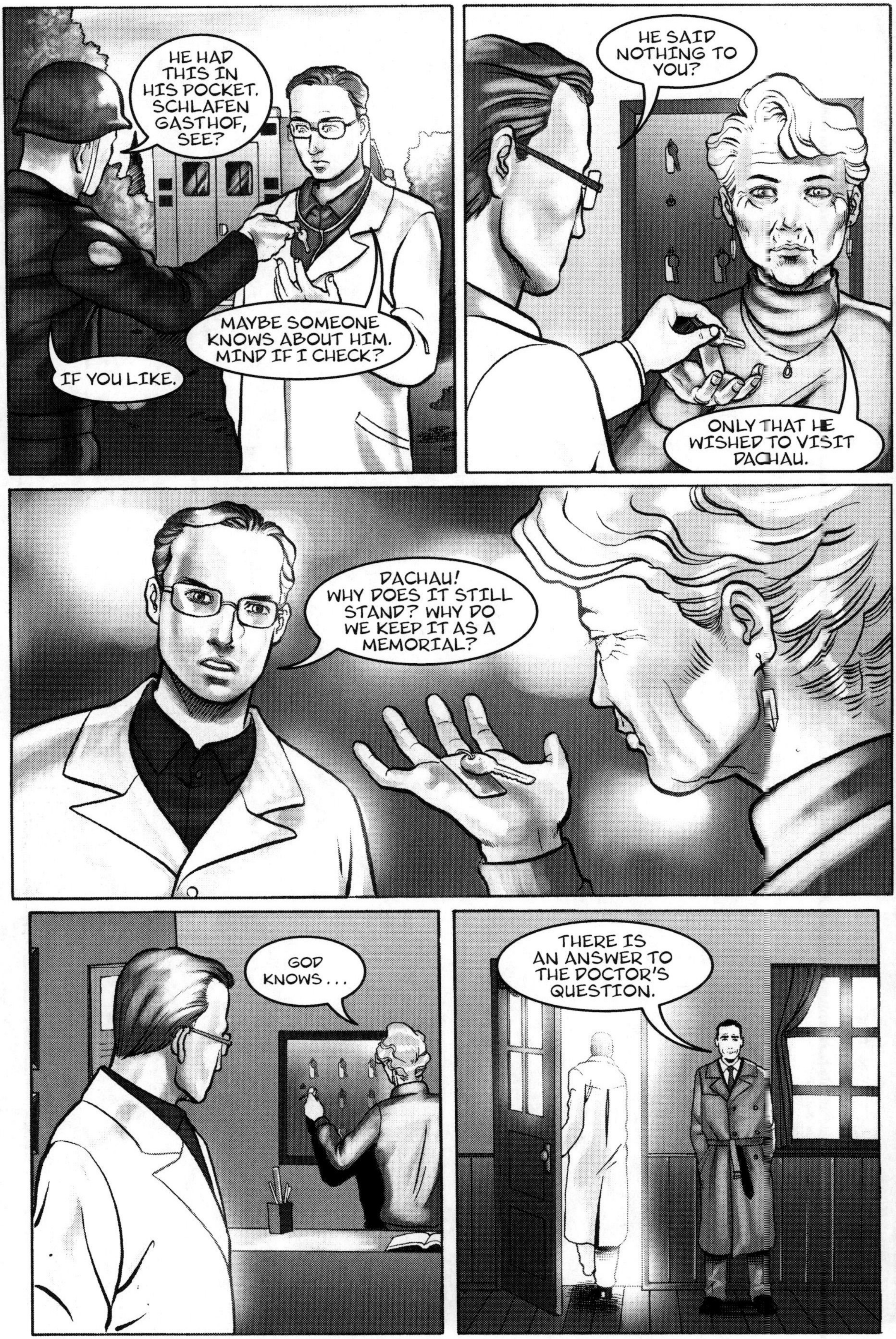
HE HAD THIS IN HIS POCKET. SCHLAFEN GASTHOF, SEE?
MAYBE SOMEONE KNOWS ABOUT HIM. MIND IF I CHECK?
IF YOU LIKE.
HE SAID NOTHING TO YOU?
ONLY THAT HE WISHED TO VISIT DACHAU.
DACHAU! WHY DOES IT STILL STAND? WHY DO WE KEEP IT AS A MEMORIAL?
GOD KNOWS . . .
THERE IS AN ANSWER TO THE DOCTOR'S QUESTION.

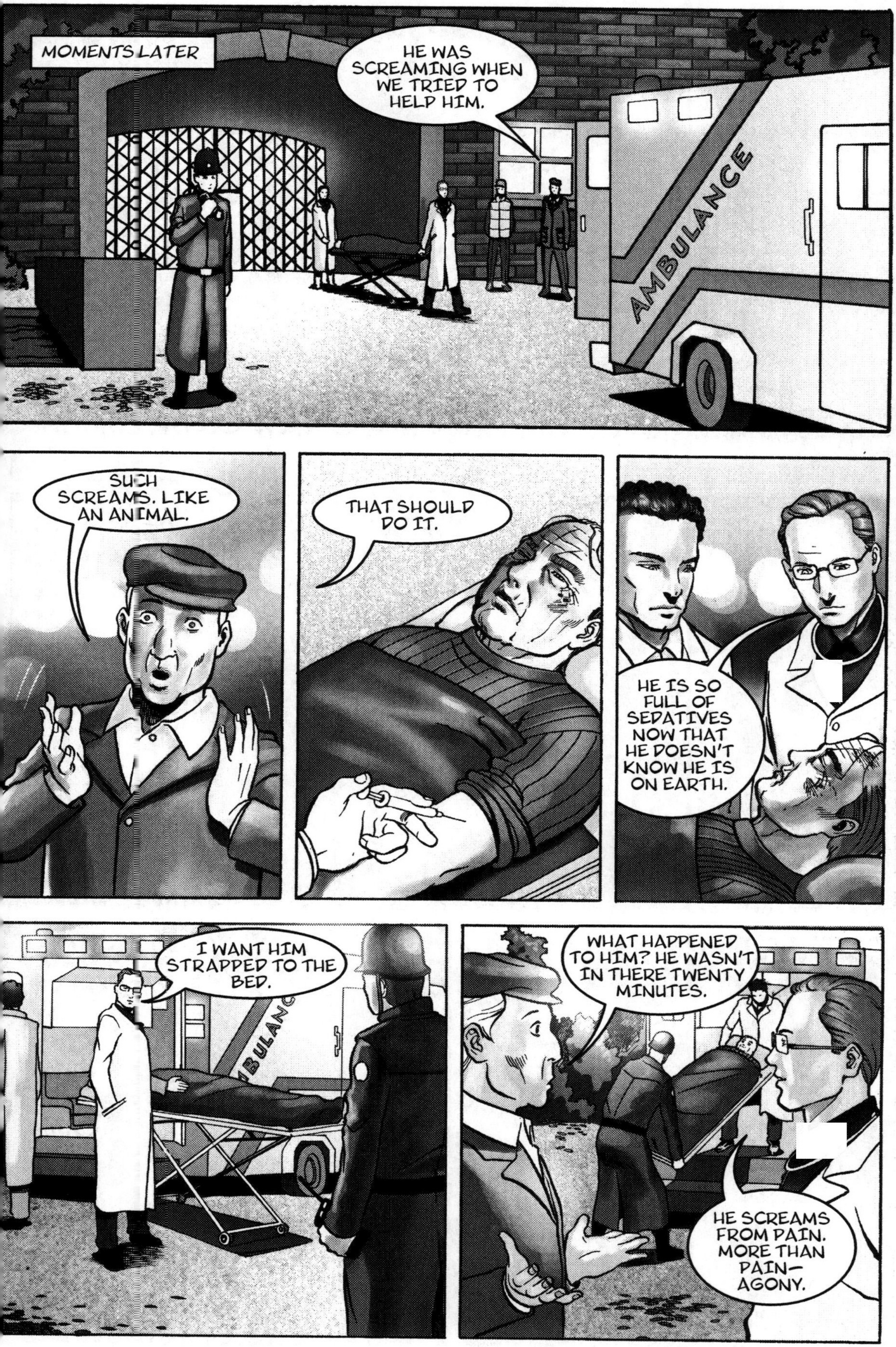
MOMENTS LATER
HE WAS SCREAMING WHEN WE TRIED TO HELP HIM.
SUCH SCREAMS. LIKE AN ANIMAL.
THAT SHOULD DO IT.
HE IS SO FULL OF SEDATIVES NOW THAT HE DOESN'T KNOW HE IS ON EARTH.
I WANT HIM STRAPPED TO THE BED.
AMBULANCE
WHAT HAPPENED TO HIM? HE WASN'T IN THERE TWENTY MINUTES.
HE SCREAMS FROM PAIN. MORE THAN PAIN—AGONY.

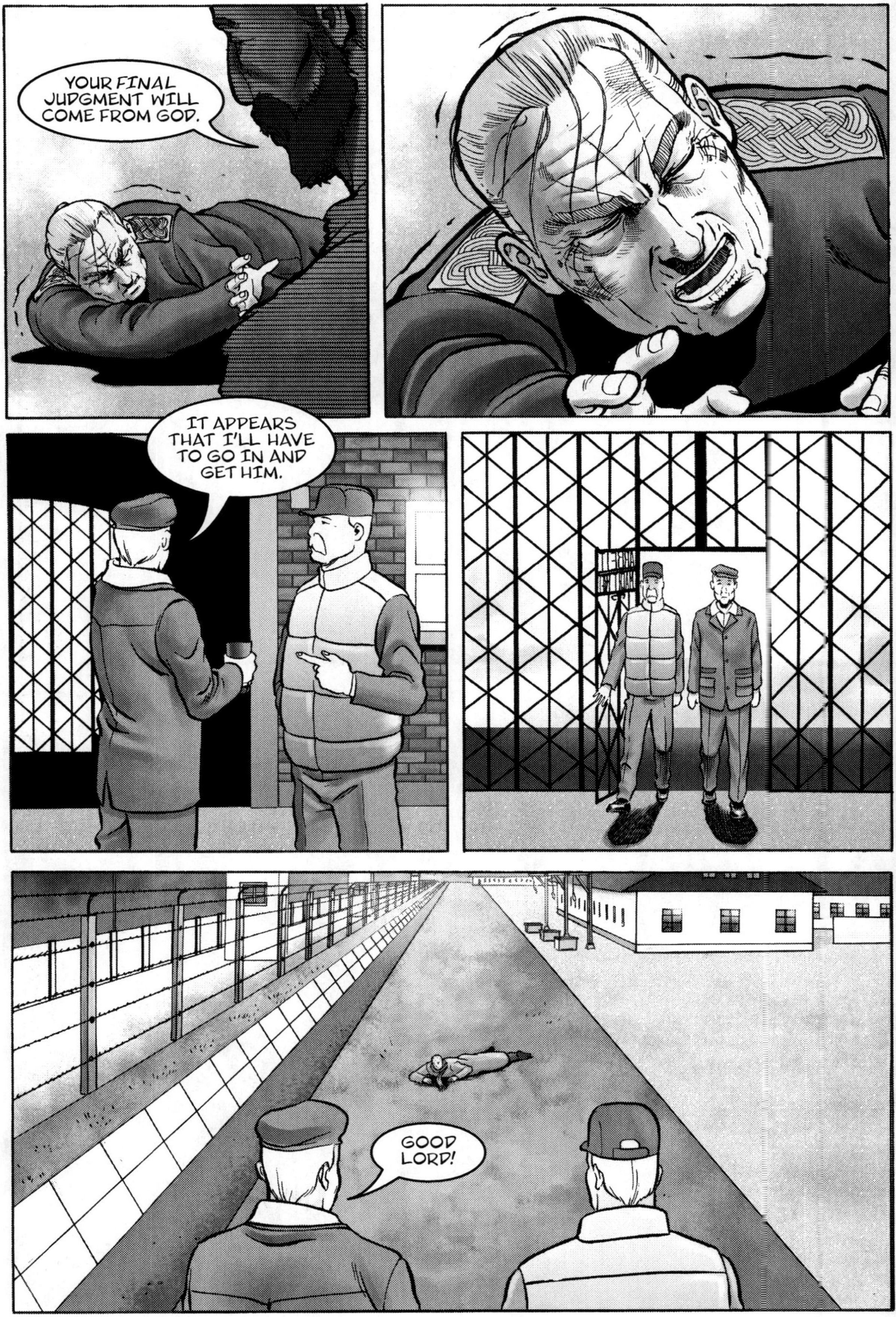
YOUR FINAL JUDGMENT WILL COME FROM GOD.
IT APPEARS THAT I'LL HAVE TO GO IN AND GET HIM.
GOOD LORD!

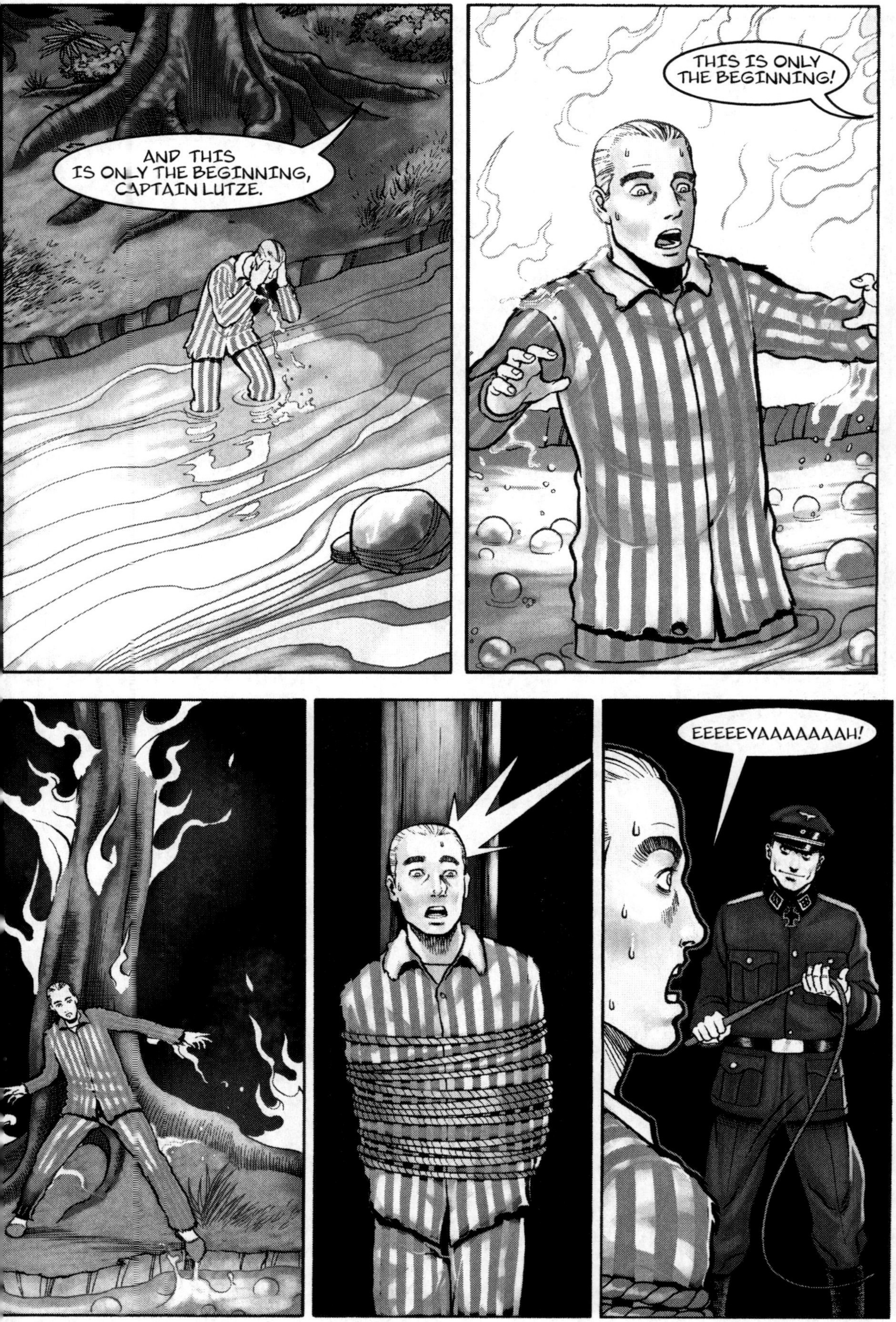
AND THIS IS ONLY THE BEGINNING, CAPTAIN LUTZE.
THIS IS ONLY THE BEGINNING!
EEEEEYAAAAAAAH!

AAAAAA . . .

AAAAA . . .
MMMMMMRRRNNNN . . .

CAPTAIN LUTZE . . .
IF YOU CAN STILL
REASON . . .

. . . IF THERE IS
ANY PORTION OF YOUR
MIND THAT CAN STILL
FUNCTION . . .

. . . TAKE THIS THOUGHT WITH
YOU. THIS IS NOT HATRED.

THIS IS
RETRIBUTION.
THIS IS NOT
REVENGE.

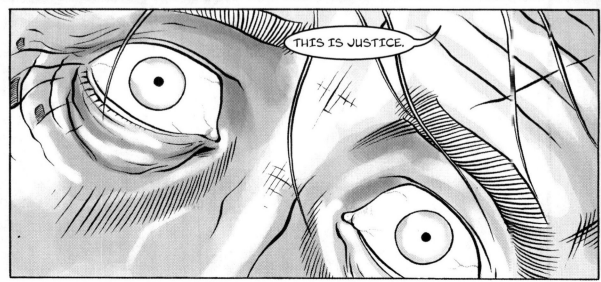

THIS IS JUSTICE.

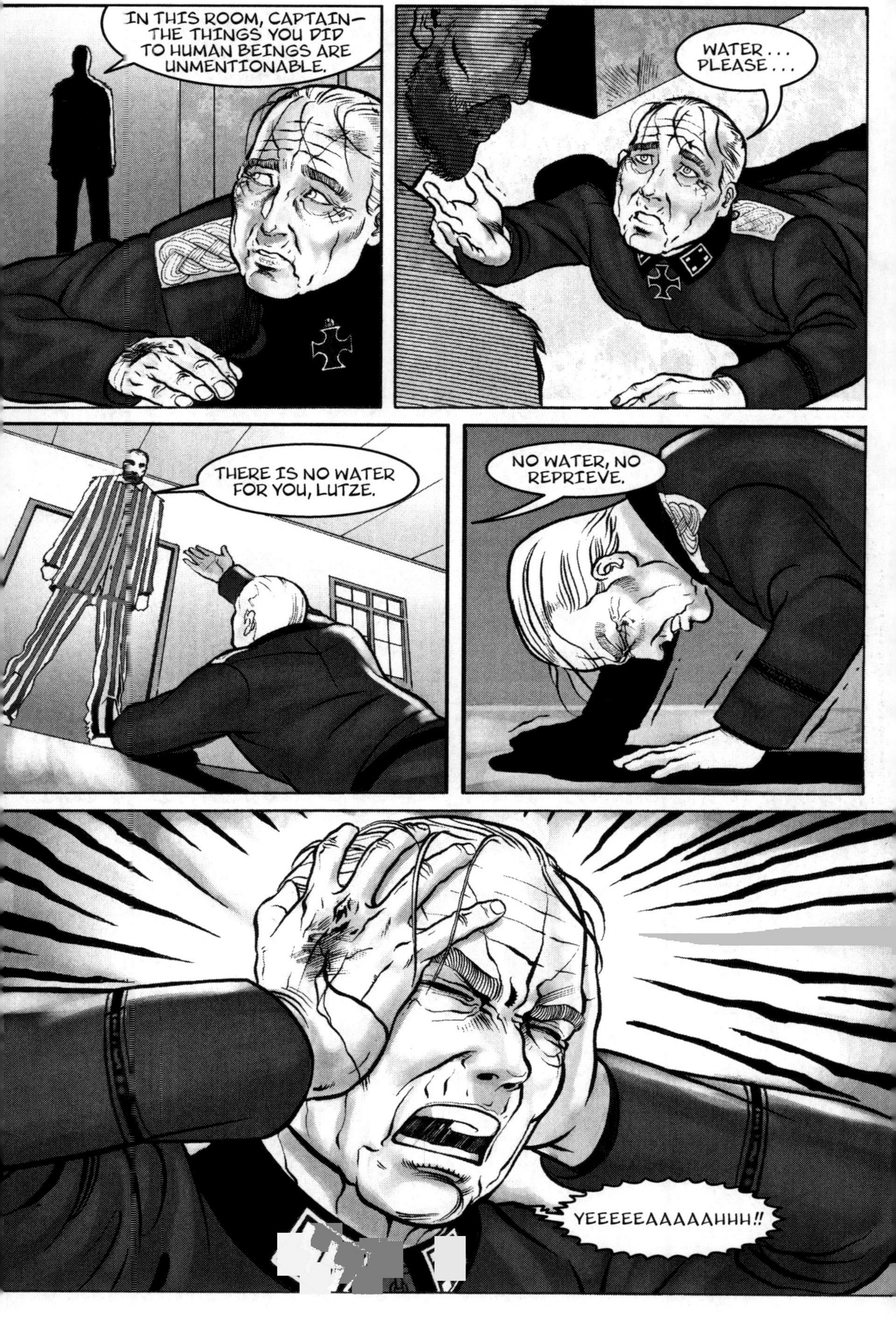
IN THIS ROOM, CAPTAIN— THE THINGS YOU DID TO HUMAN BEINGS ARE UNMENTIONABLE.
WATER... PLEASE...
THERE IS NO WATER FOR YOU, LUTZE.
NO WATER, NO REPRIEVE.
YEEEEEAAAAAHHH!!

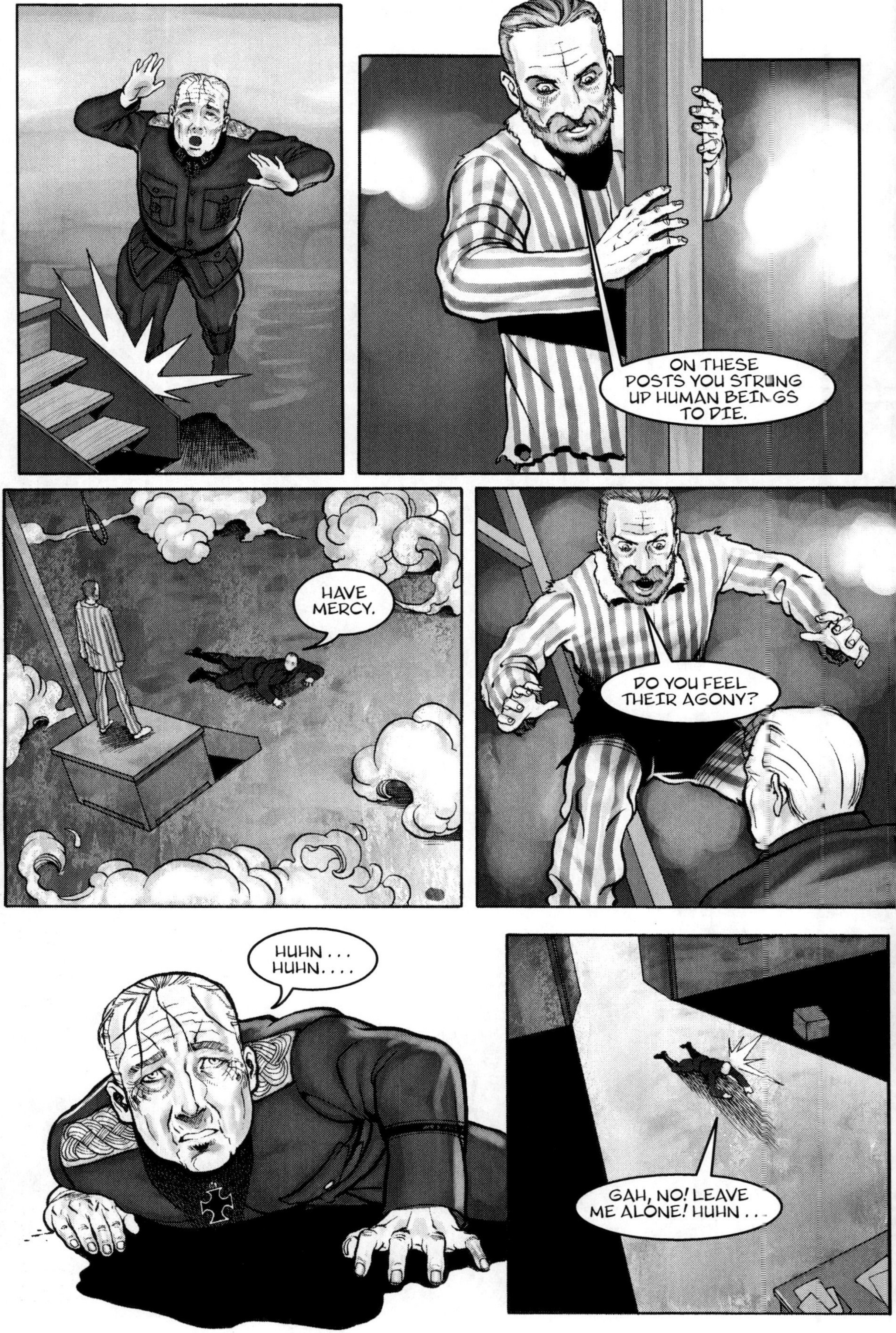

ON THESE POSTS YOU STRUNG UP HUMAN BEINGS TO DIE.
HAVE MERCY.
DO YOU FEEL THEIR AGONY?
HUHN . . . HUHN. . . .
GAH, NO! LEAVE ME ALONE! HUHN . . .

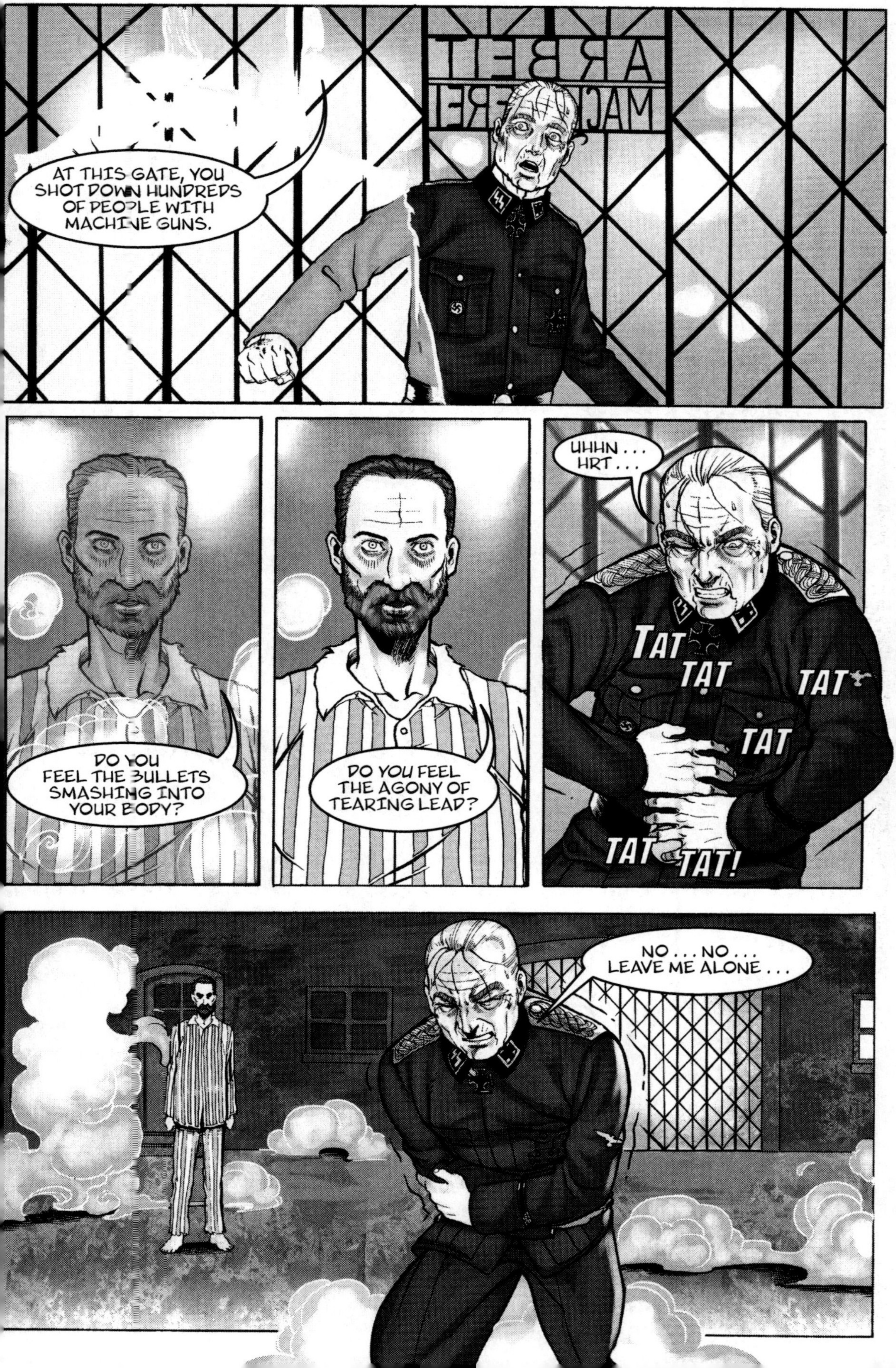
ARBEIT MACHT FREI
AT THIS GATE, YOU SHOT DOWN HUNDREDS OF PEOPLE WITH MACHINE GUNS.
DO YOU FEEL THE BULLETS SMASHING INTO YOUR BODY?
DO YOU FEEL THE AGONY OF TEARING LEAD?
UHHN . . . HRT . . .
TAT TAT TAT TAT TAT TAT!
NO . . . NO . . . LEAVE ME ALONE . . .

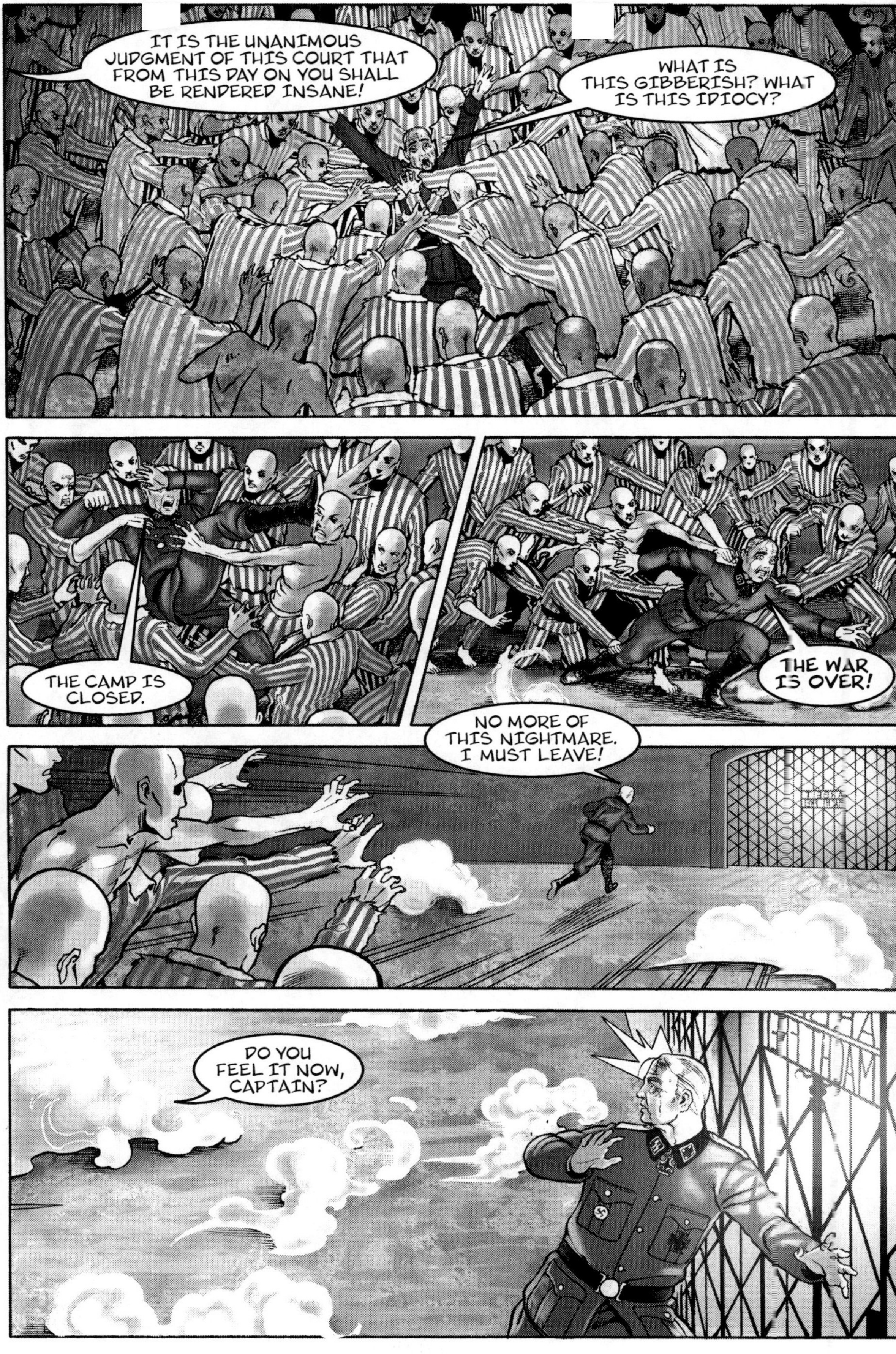
IT IS THE UNANIMOUS JUDGMENT OF THIS COURT THAT FROM THIS DAY ON YOU SHALL BE RENDERED INSANE!
WHAT IS THIS GIBBERISH? WHAT IS THIS IDIOCY?
THE CAMP IS CLOSED.
THE WAR IS OVER!
NO MORE OF THIS NIGHTMARE. I MUST LEAVE!
DO YOU FEEL IT NOW, CAPTAIN?

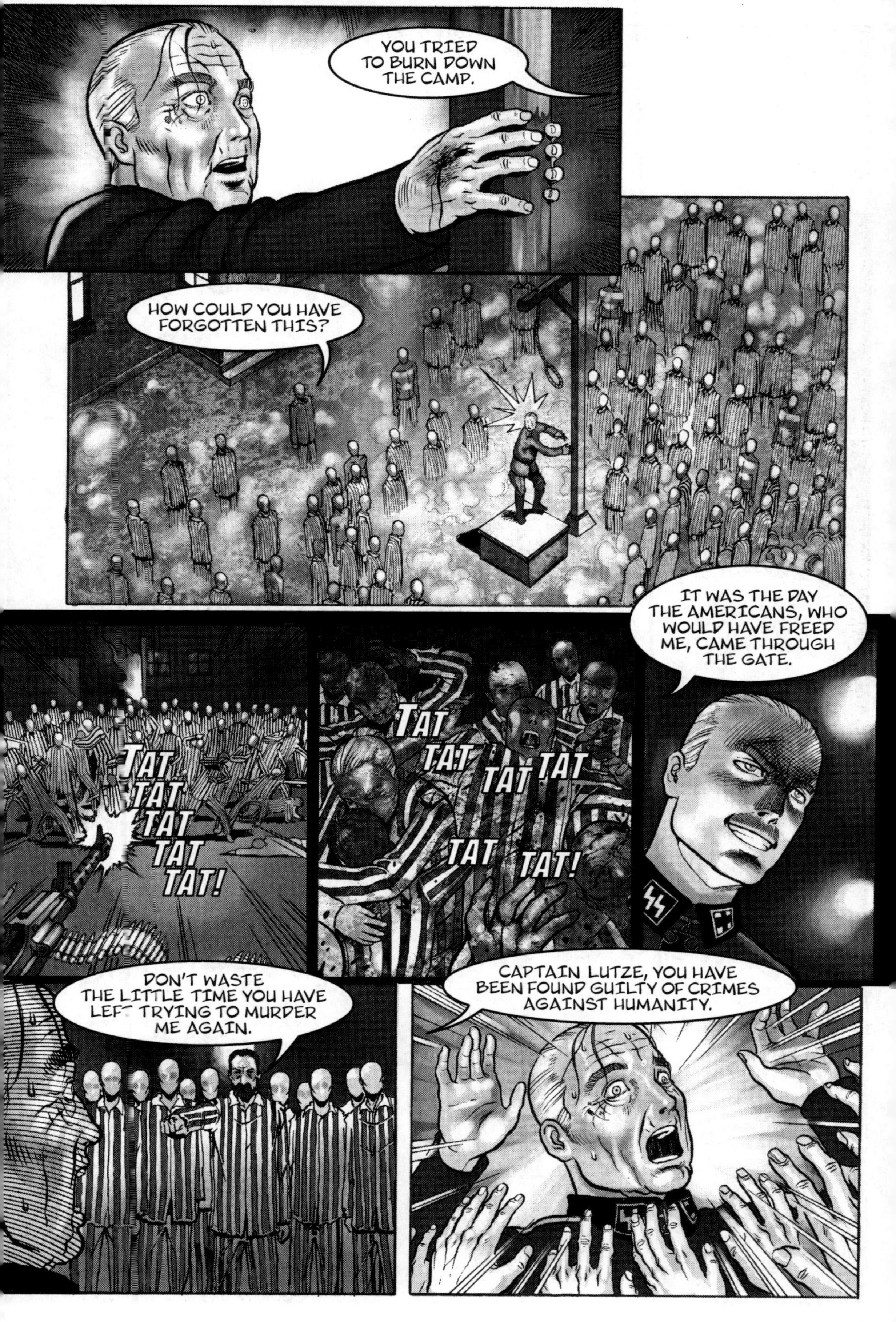
YOU TRIED TO BURN DOWN THE CAMP.
HOW COULD YOU HAVE FORGOTTEN THIS?
TAT TAT TAT TAT TAT!
TAT TAT TAT TAT TAT TAT!
IT WAS THE DAY THE AMERICANS, WHO WOULD HAVE FREED ME, CAME THROUGH THE GATE.
DON'T WASTE THE LITTLE TIME YOU HAVE LEFT TRYING TO MURDER ME AGAIN.
CAPTAIN LUTZE, YOU HAVE BEEN FOUND GUILTY OF CRIMES AGAINST HUMANITY.

SEWN TOGETHER WITH LITTLE THIN THREADS OF WISHFUL THINKING.

WHY DIDN'T I KILL YOU WHEN I HAD THE CHANCE?

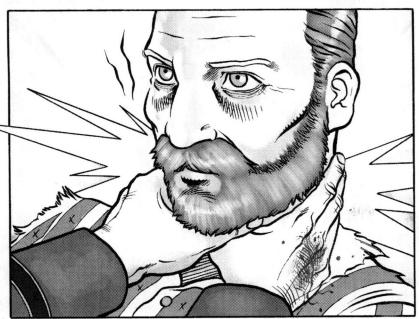

BECKER. BECKER, I DID KILL YOU. I KILLED YOU THE DAY...

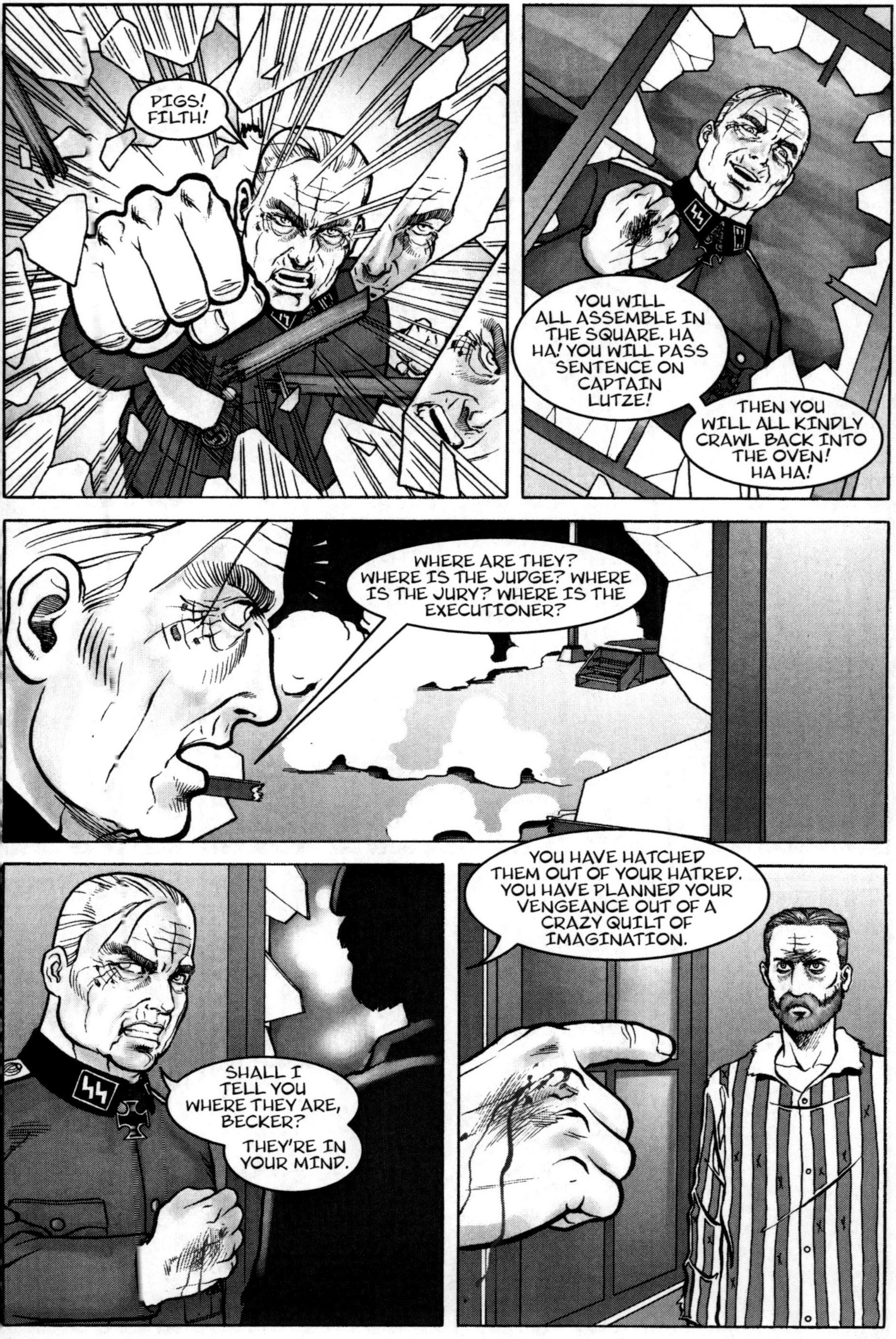
PIGS! FILTH!
YOU WILL ALL ASSEMBLE IN THE SQUARE. HA HA! YOU WILL PASS SENTENCE ON CAPTAIN LUTZE!
THEN YOU WILL ALL KINDLY CRAWL BACK INTO THE OVEN! HA HA!
WHERE ARE THEY? WHERE IS THE JUDGE? WHERE IS THE JURY? WHERE IS THE EXECUTIONER?
SHALL I TELL YOU WHERE THEY ARE, BECKER?
THEY'RE IN YOUR MIND.
YOU HAVE HATCHED THEM OUT OF YOUR HATRED. YOU HAVE PLANNED YOUR VENGEANCE OUT OF A CRAZY QUILT OF IMAGINATION.

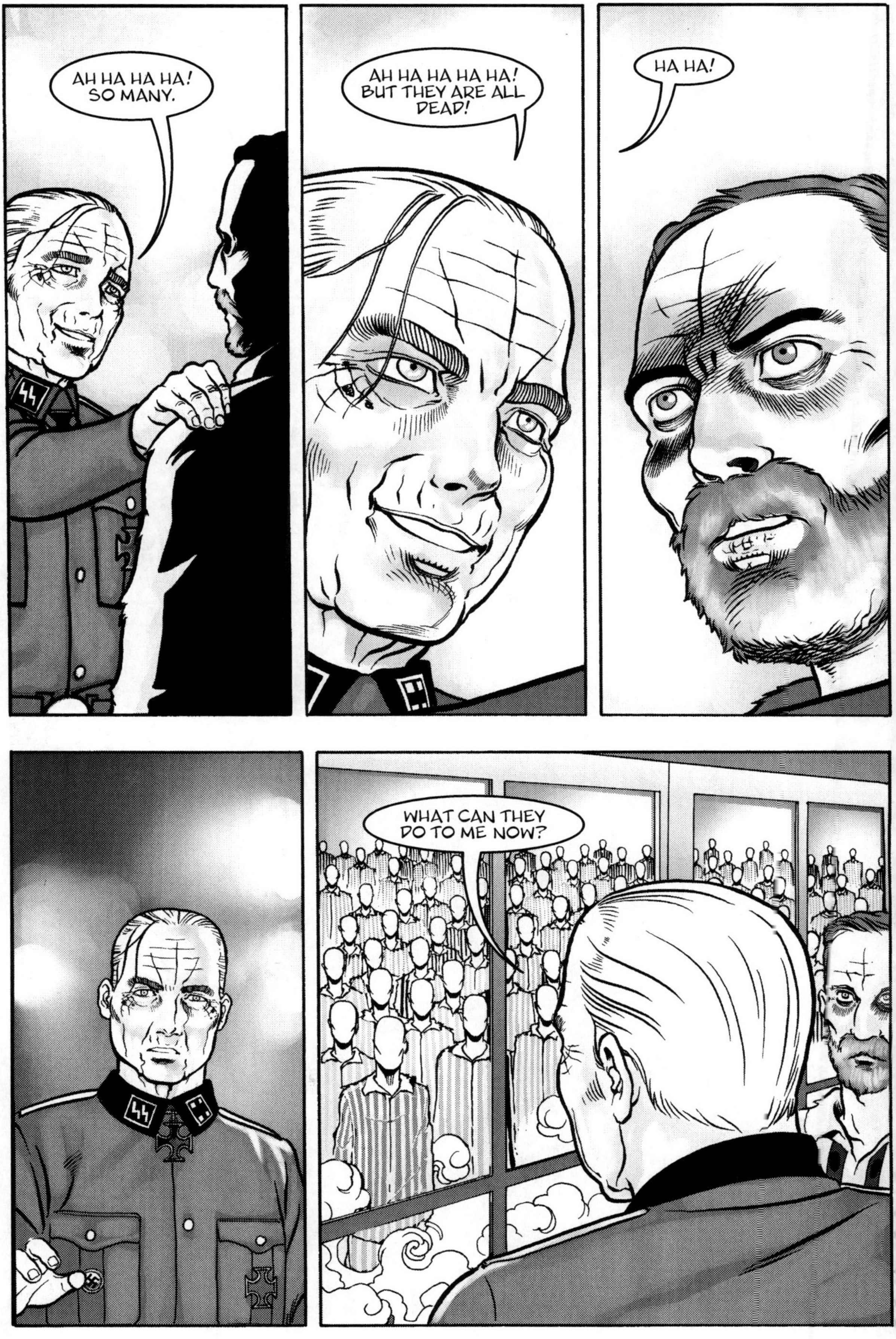
AH HA HA HA! SO MANY.
AH HA HA HA HA! BUT THEY ARE ALL DEAD!
HA HA!
WHAT CAN THEY DO TO ME NOW?

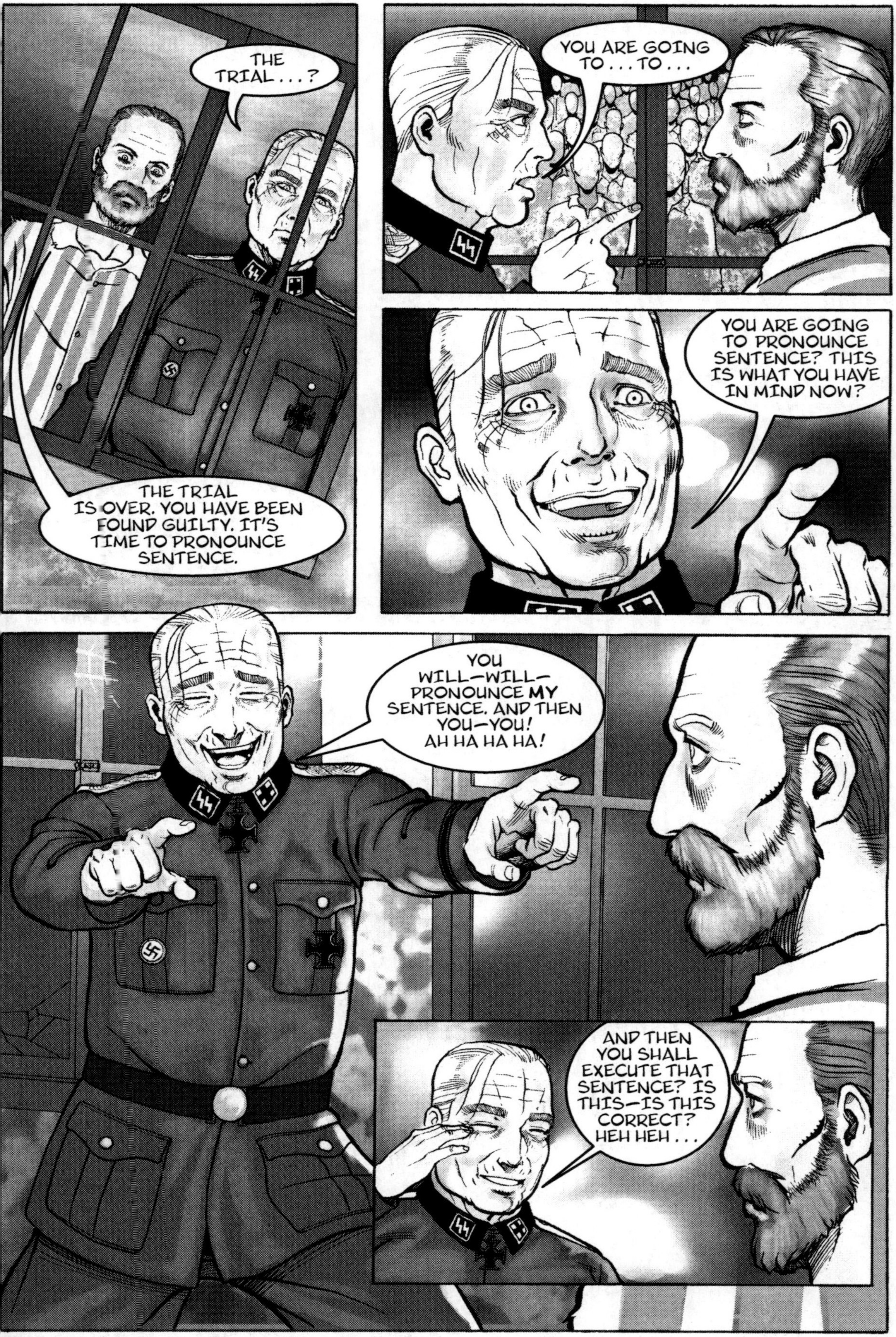
THE TRIAL . . . ?
THE TRIAL IS OVER. YOU HAVE BEEN FOUND GUILTY. IT'S TIME TO PRONOUNCE SENTENCE.
YOU ARE GOING TO . . . TO . . .
YOU ARE GOING TO PRONOUNCE SENTENCE? THIS IS WHAT YOU HAVE IN MIND NOW?
YOU WILL—WILL—PRONOUNCE MY SENTENCE. AND THEN YOU—YOU! AH HA HA HA!
AND THEN YOU SHALL EXECUTE THAT SENTENCE? IS THIS—IS THIS CORRECT? HEH HEH . . .

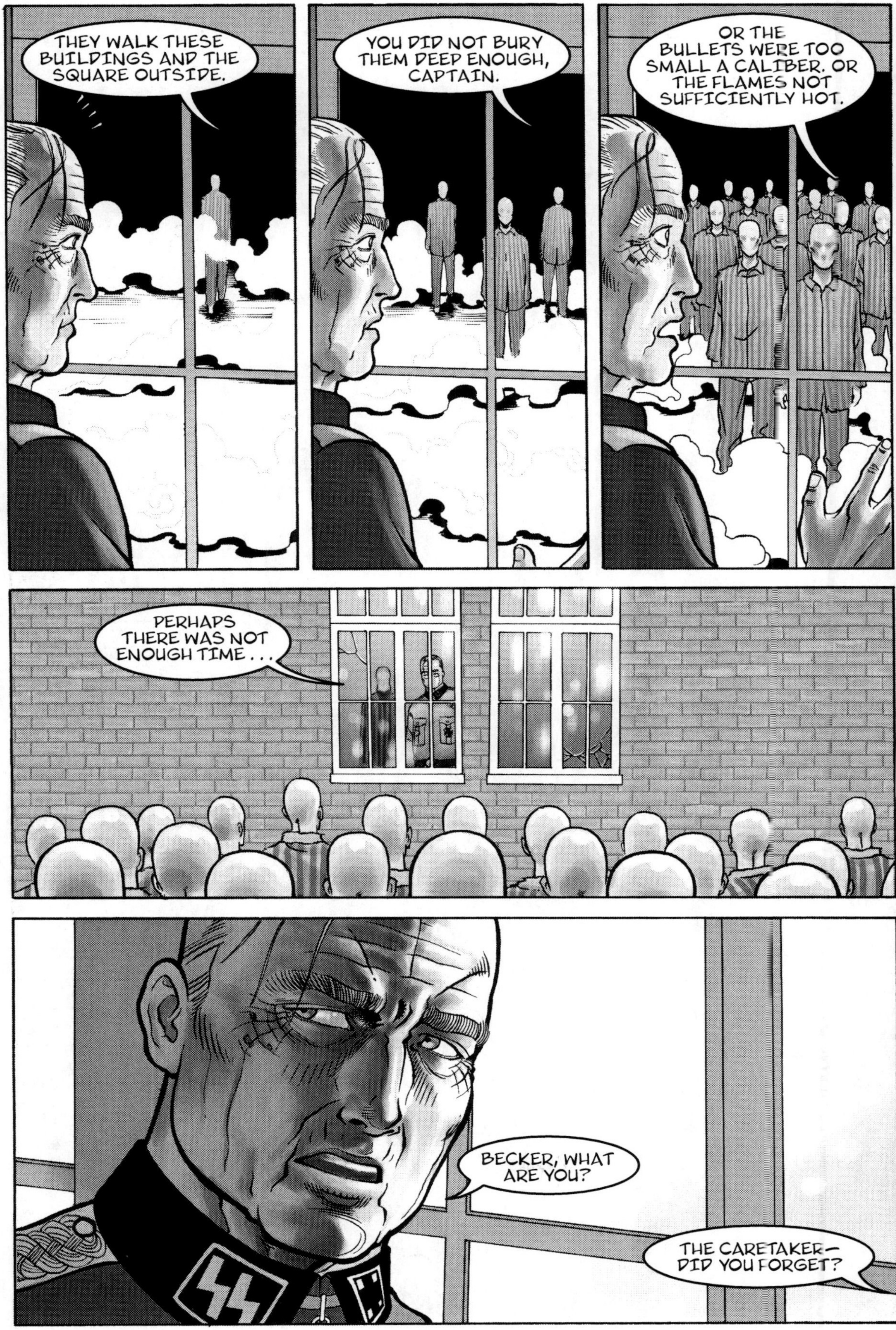
THEY WALK THESE BUILDINGS AND THE SQUARE OUTSIDE.
YOU DID NOT BURY THEM DEEP ENOUGH, CAPTAIN.
OR THE BULLETS WERE TOO SMALL A CALIBER. OR THE FLAMES NOT SUFFICIENTLY HOT.
PERHAPS THERE WAS NOT ENOUGH TIME . . .
BECKER, WHAT ARE YOU?
THE CARETAKER— DID YOU FORGET?

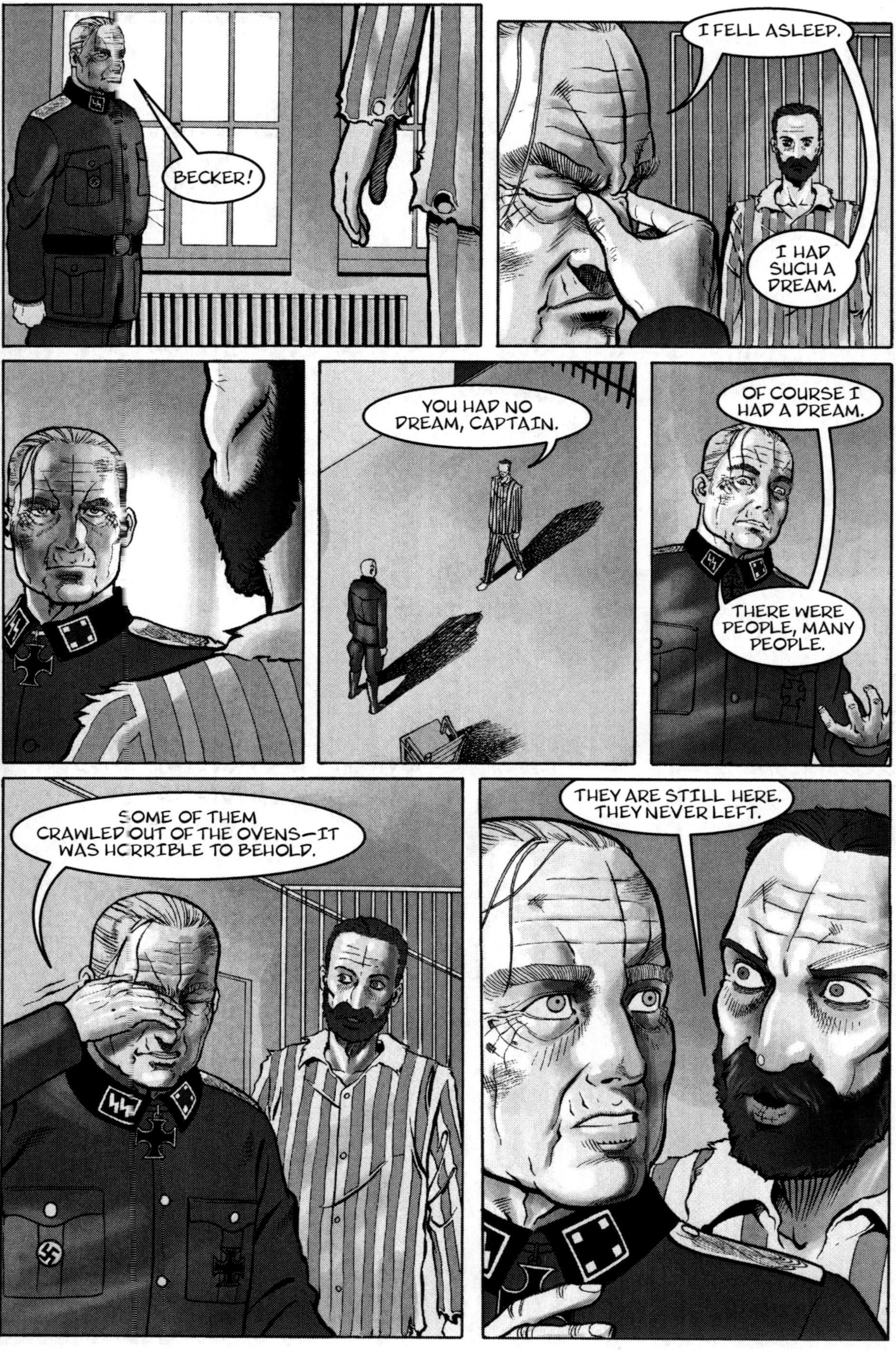
BECKER!
I FELL ASLEEP.
I HAD SUCH A DREAM.
YOU HAD NO DREAM, CAPTAIN.
OF COURSE I HAD A DREAM.
THERE WERE PEOPLE, MANY PEOPLE.
SOME OF THEM CRAWLED OUT OF THE OVENS—IT WAS HORRIBLE TO BEHOLD.
THEY ARE STILL HERE. THEY NEVER LEFT.

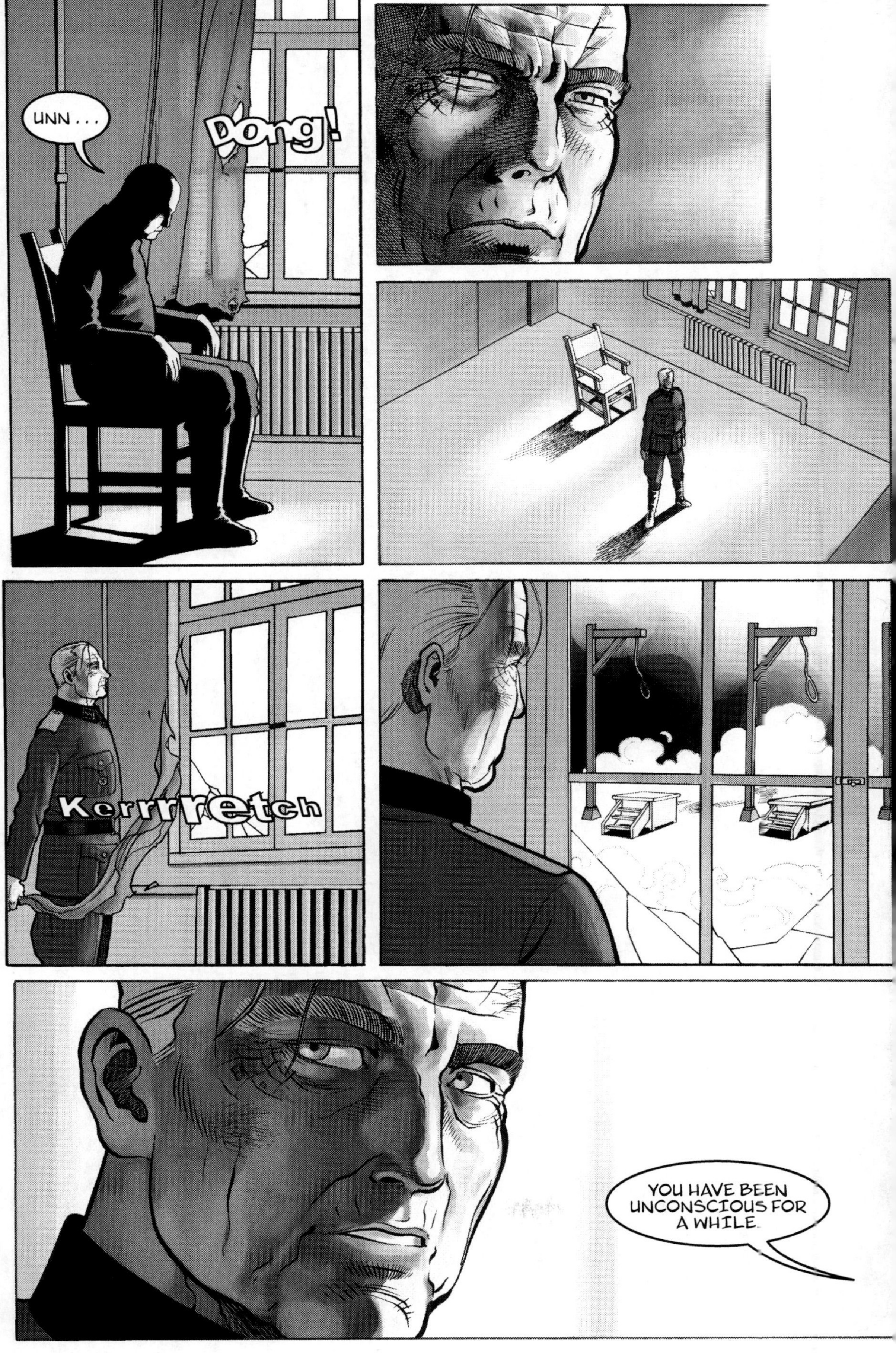
UNN . . .
Dong!
Kerrrretch
YOU HAVE BEEN UNCONSCIOUS FOR A WHILE.

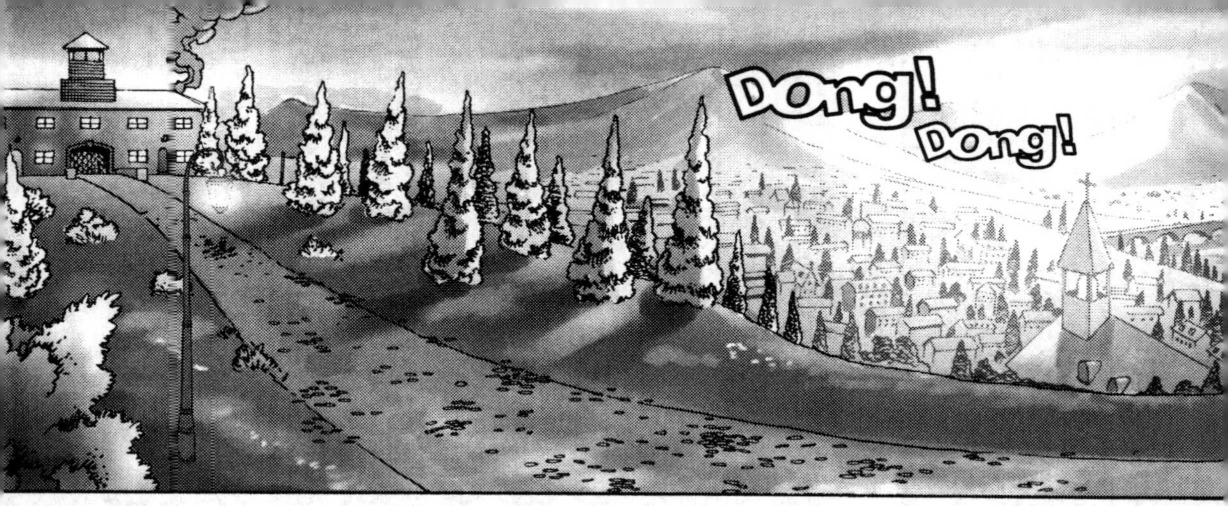
DONG!
DONG!

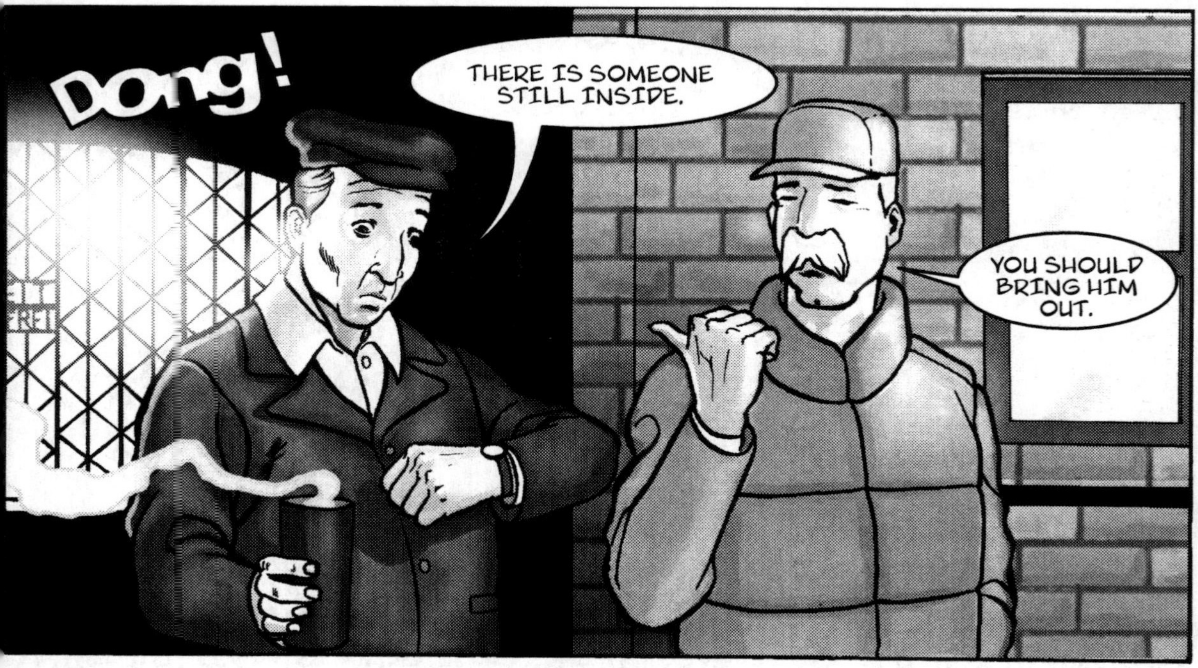
DONG!
THERE IS SOMEONE STILL INSIDE.
YOU SHOULD BRING HIM OUT.

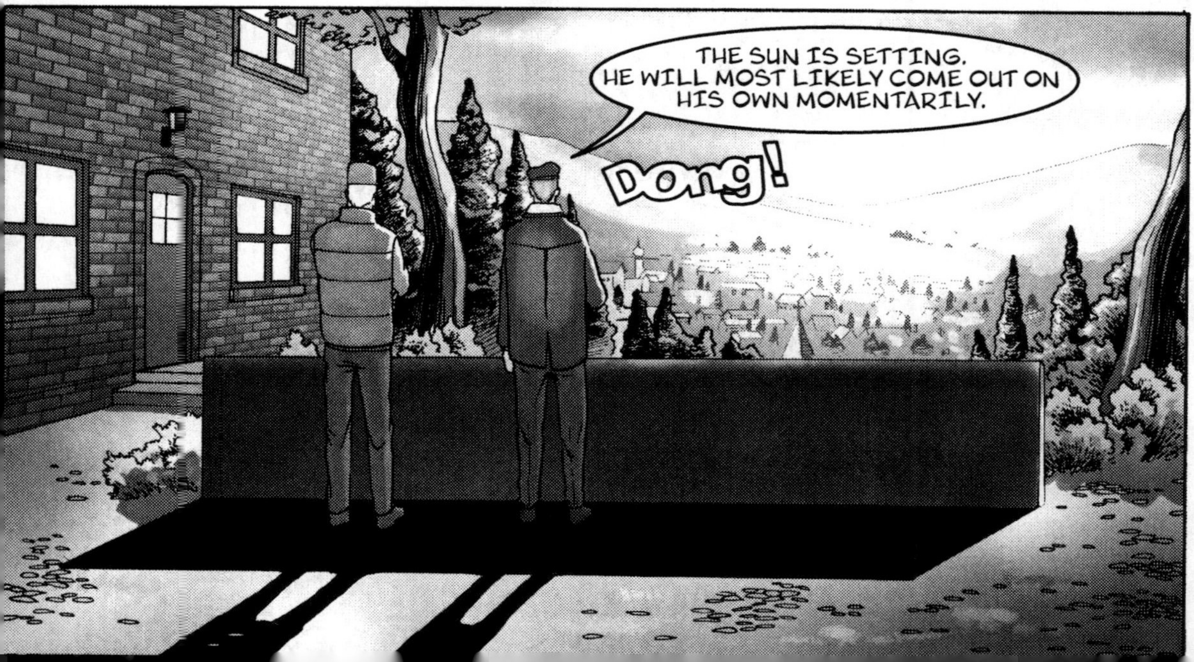
THE SUN IS SETTING. HE WILL MOST LIKELY COME OUT ON HIS OWN MOMENTARILY.
DONG!

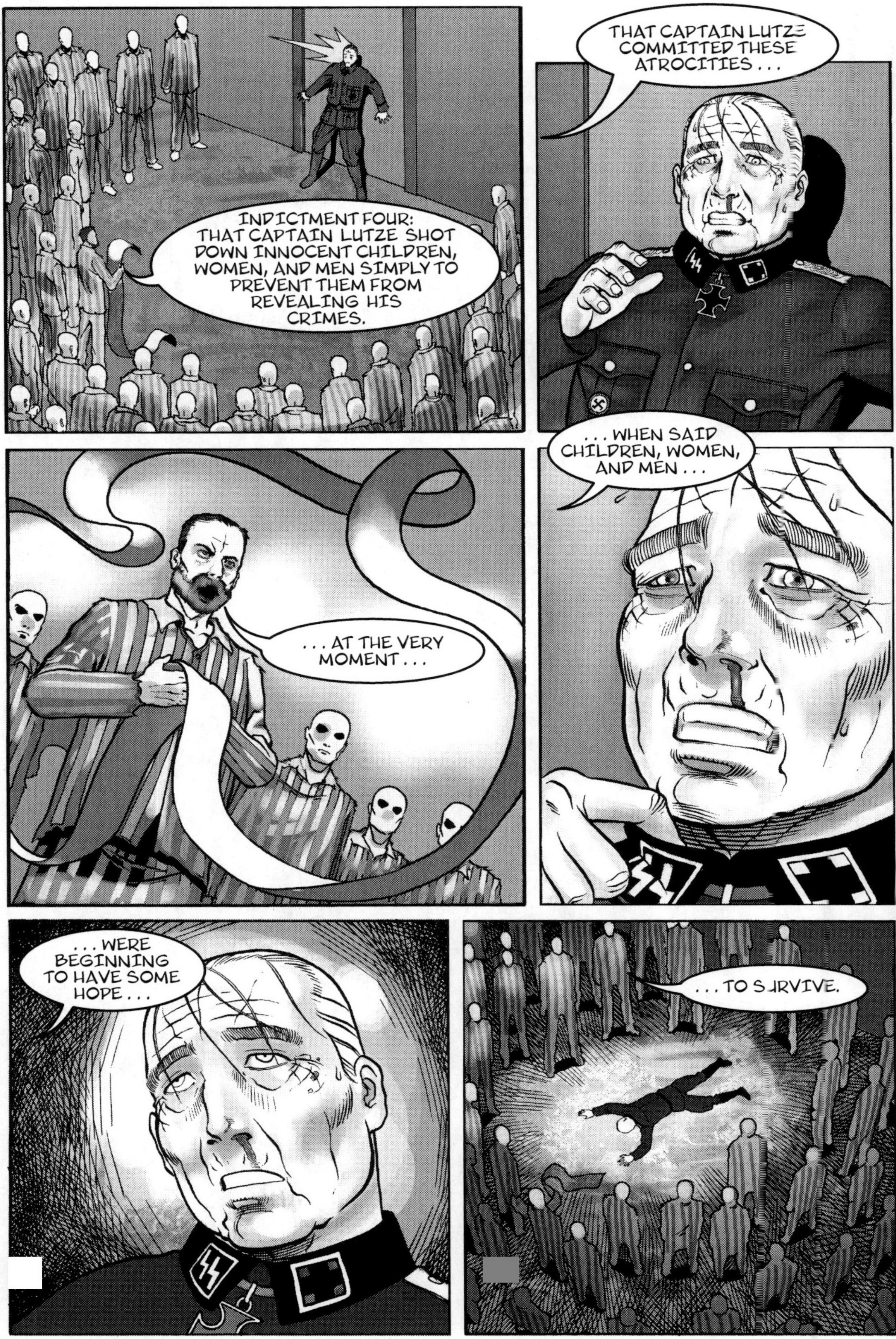
INDICTMENT FOUR: THAT CAPTAIN LUTZE SHOT DOWN INNOCENT CHILDREN, WOMEN, AND MEN SIMPLY TO PREVENT THEM FROM REVEALING HIS CRIMES.
THAT CAPTAIN LUTZE COMMITTED THESE ATROCITIES . . .
. . . AT THE VERY MOMENT . . .
. . . WHEN SAID CHILDREN, WOMEN, AND MEN . . .
. . . WERE BEGINNING TO HAVE SOME HOPE . . .
. . . TO SURVIVE.

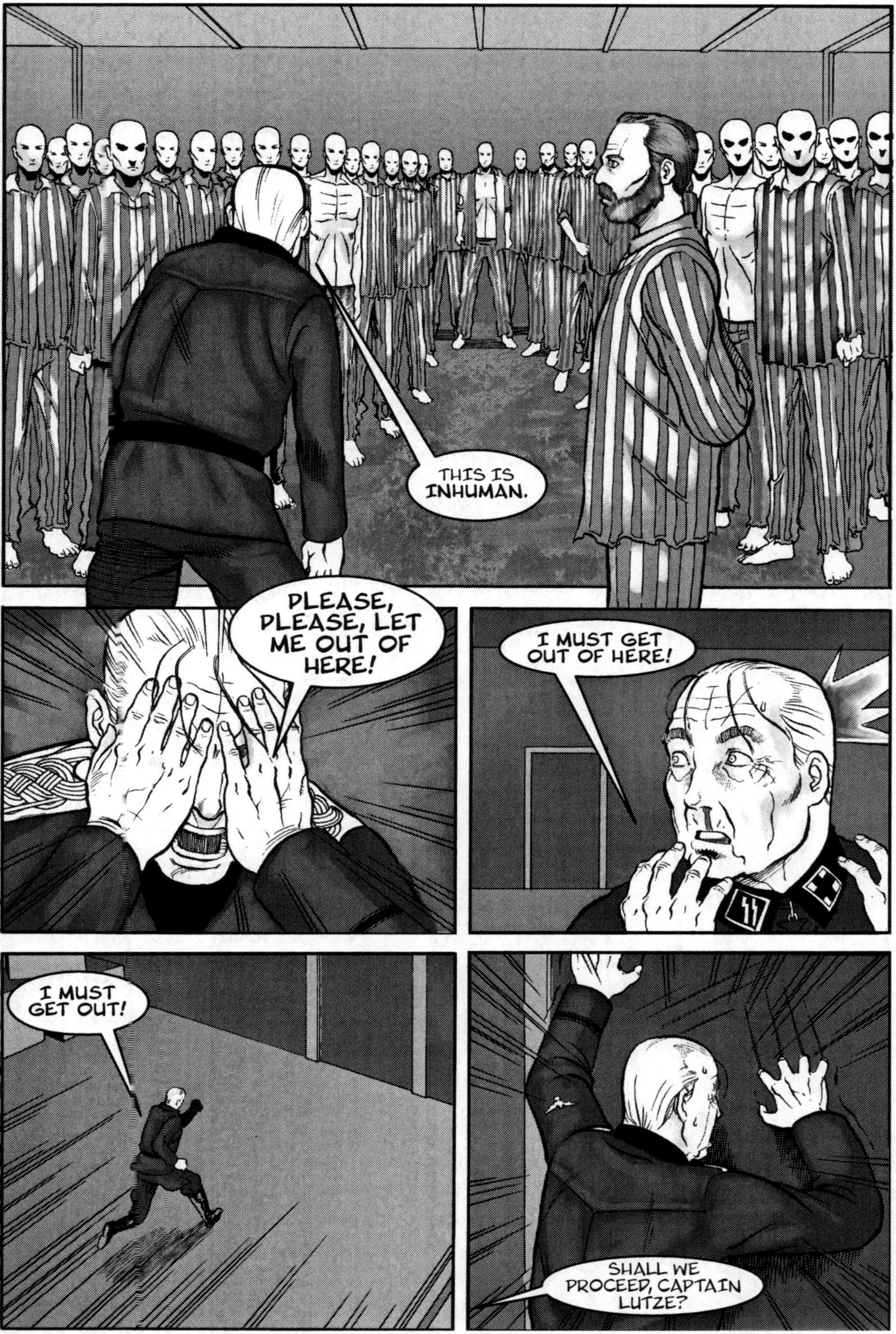
THIS IS INHUMAN.
PLEASE, PLEASE, LET ME OUT OF HERE!
I MUST GET OUT OF HERE!
I MUST GET OUT!
SHALL WE PROCEED, CAPTAIN LUTZE?

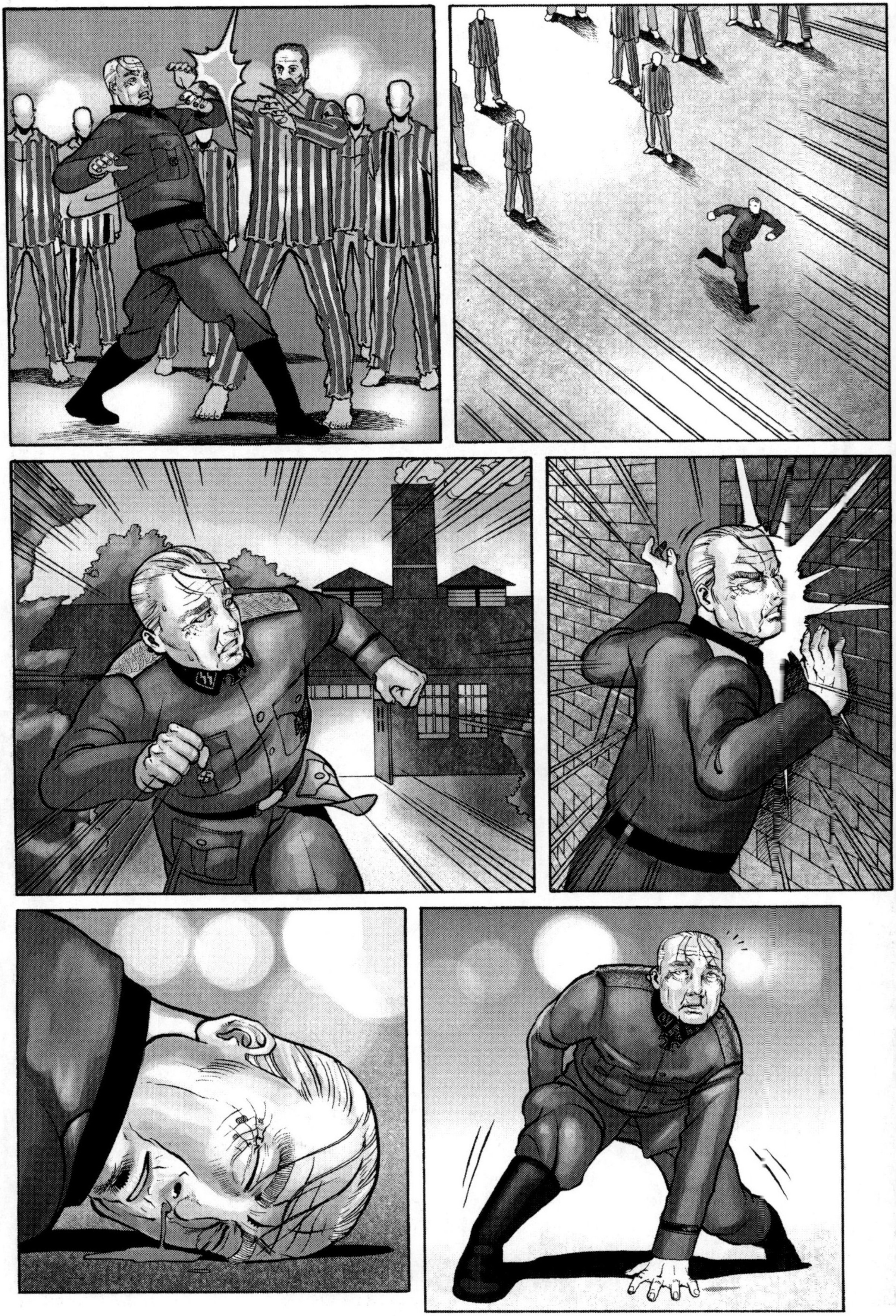

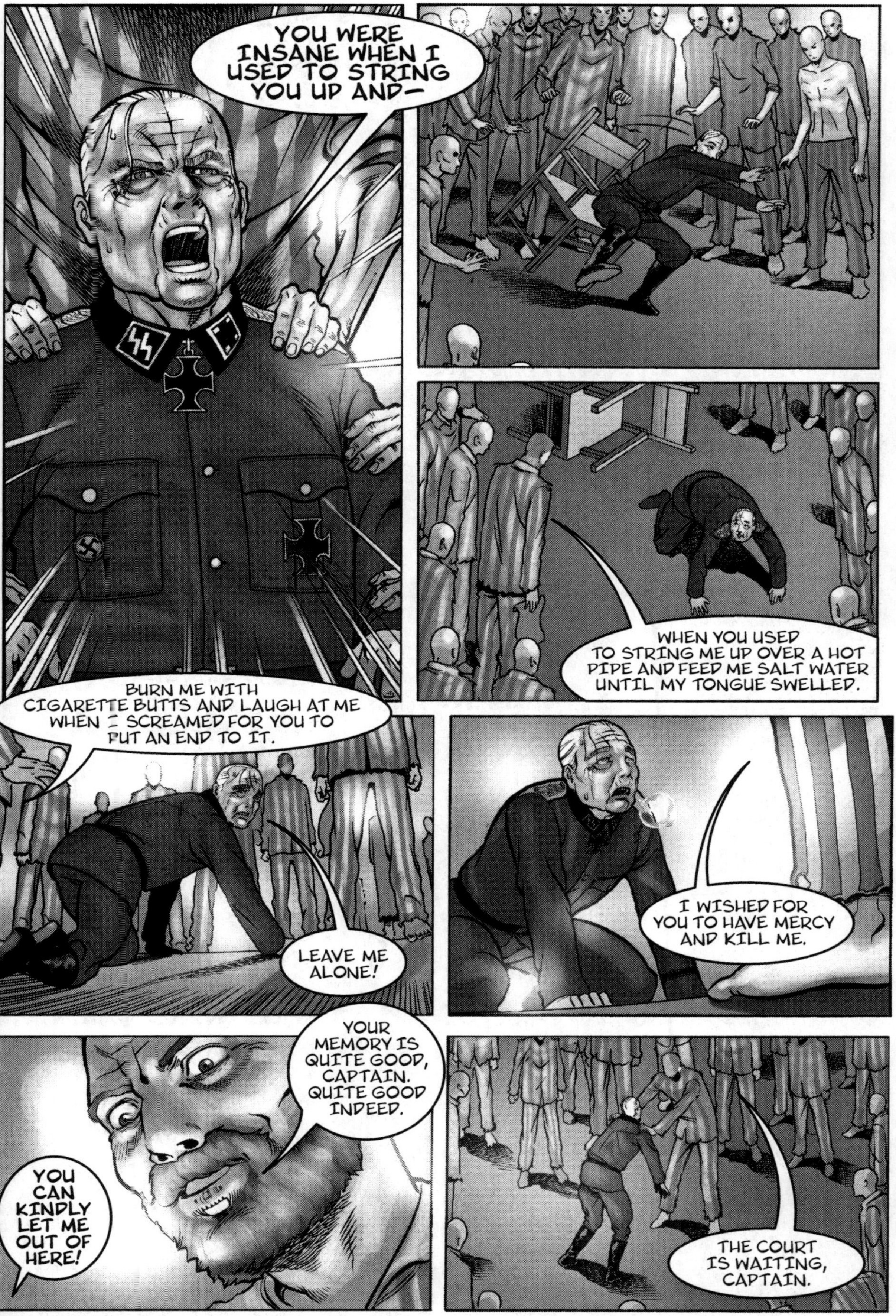
YOU WERE INSANE WHEN I USED TO STRING YOU UP AND—
WHEN YOU USED TO STRING ME UP OVER A HOT PIPE AND FEED ME SALT WATER UNTIL MY TONGUE SWELLED.
BURN ME WITH CIGARETTE BUTTS AND LAUGH AT ME WHEN I SCREAMED FOR YOU TO PUT AN END TO IT.
LEAVE ME ALONE!
I WISHED FOR YOU TO HAVE MERCY AND KILL ME.
YOUR MEMORY IS QUITE GOOD, CAPTAIN. QUITE GOOD INDEED.
YOU CAN KINDLY LET ME OUT OF HERE!
THE COURT IS WAITING, CAPTAIN.

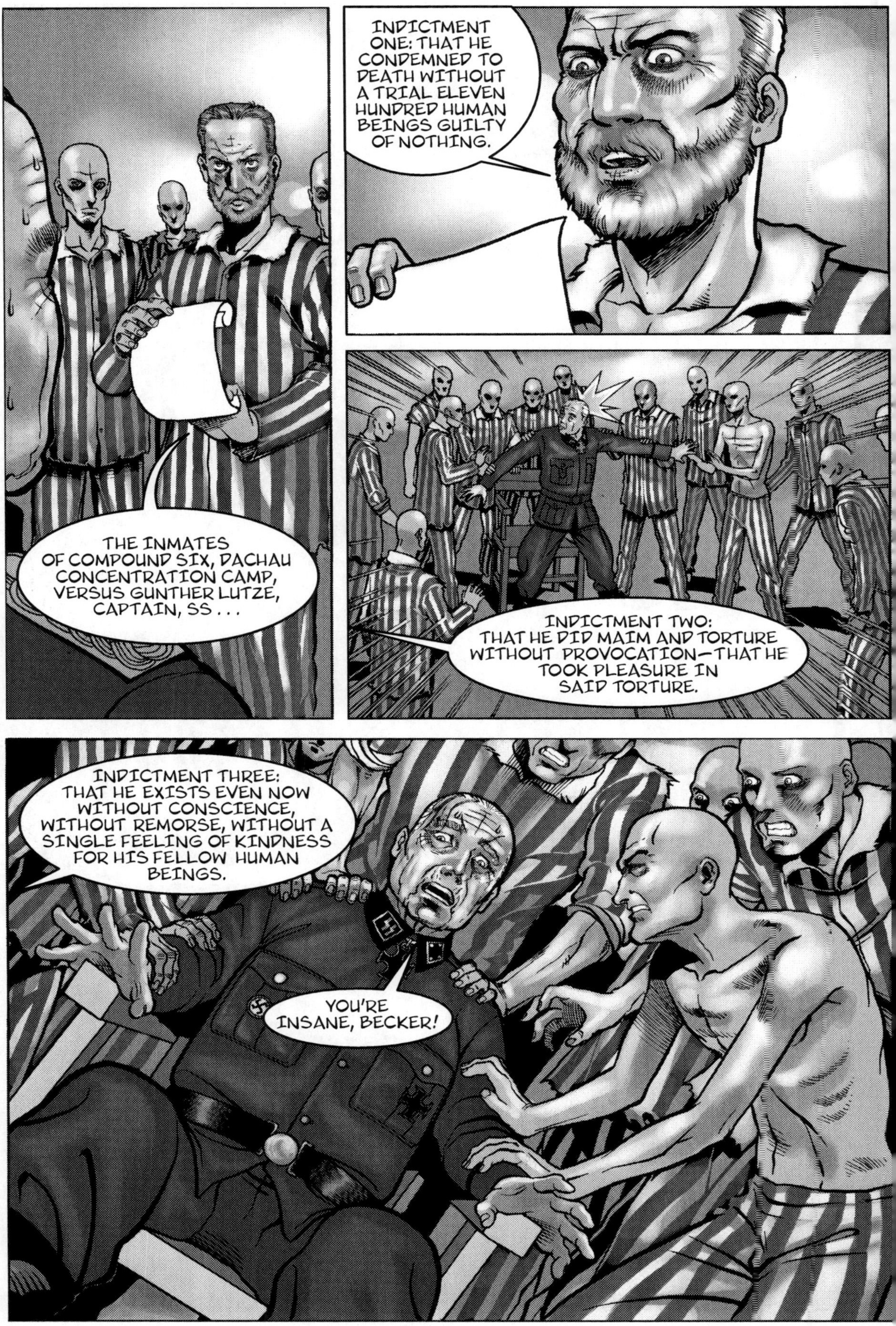
THE INMATES OF COMPOUND SIX, DACHAU CONCENTRATION CAMP, VERSUS GUNTHER LUTZE, CAPTAIN, SS . . .
INDICTMENT ONE: THAT HE CONDEMNED TO DEATH WITHOUT A TRIAL ELEVEN HUNDRED HUMAN BEINGS GUILTY OF NOTHING.
INDICTMENT TWO: THAT HE DID MAIM AND TORTURE WITHOUT PROVOCATION—THAT HE TOOK PLEASURE IN SAID TORTURE.
INDICTMENT THREE: THAT HE EXISTS EVEN NOW WITHOUT CONSCIENCE, WITHOUT REMORSE, WITHOUT A SINGLE FEELING OF KINDNESS FOR HIS FELLOW HUMAN BEINGS.
YOU'RE INSANE, BECKER!

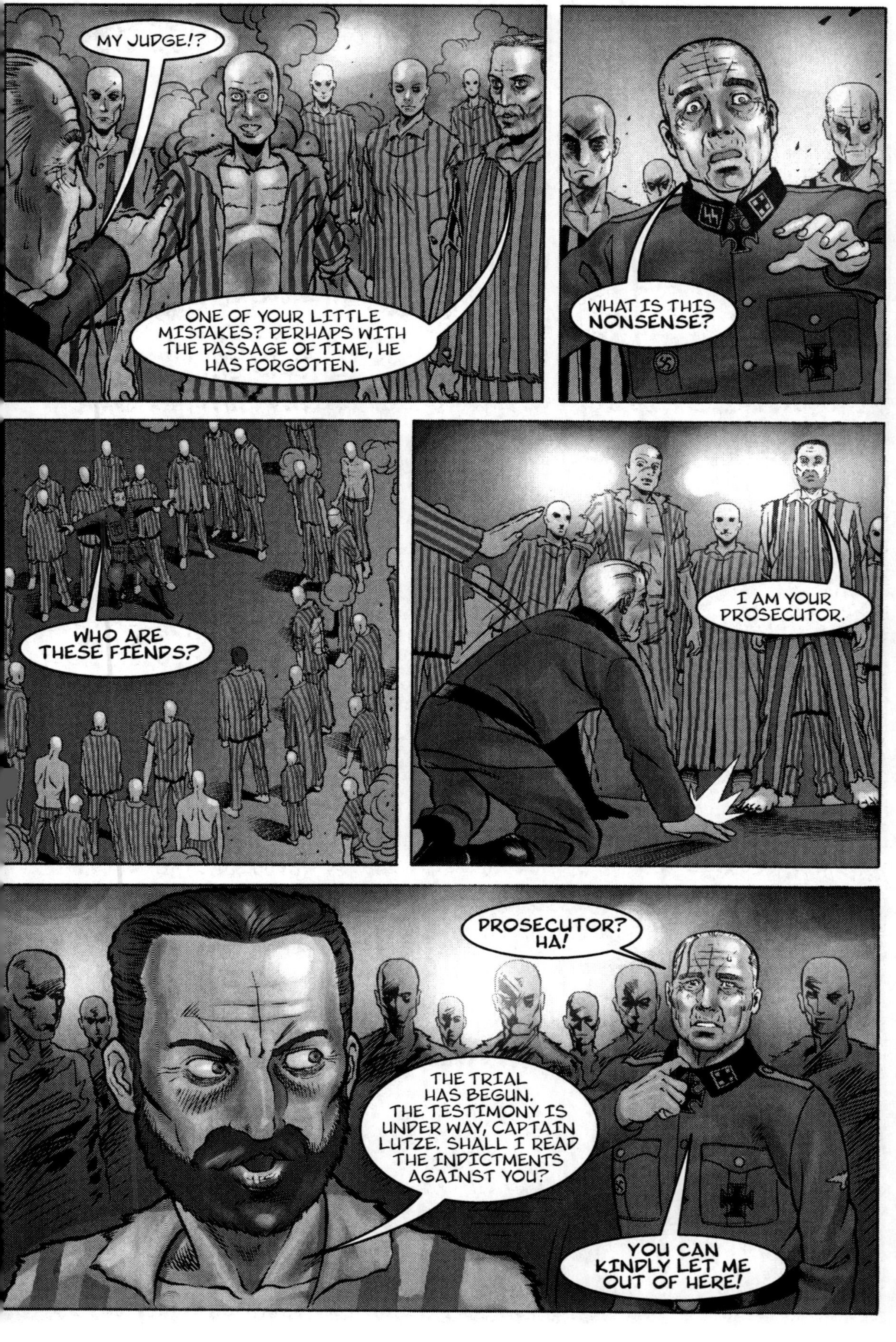
MY JUDGE!?
ONE OF YOUR LITTLE MISTAKES? PERHAPS WITH THE PASSAGE OF TIME, HE HAS FORGOTTEN.
WHAT IS THIS NONSENSE?
WHO ARE THESE FIENDS?
I AM YOUR PROSECUTOR.
PROSECUTOR? HA!
THE TRIAL HAS BEGUN. THE TESTIMONY IS UNDER WAY, CAPTAIN LUTZE. SHALL I READ THE INDICTMENTS AGAINST YOU?
YOU CAN KINDLY LET ME OUT OF HERE!

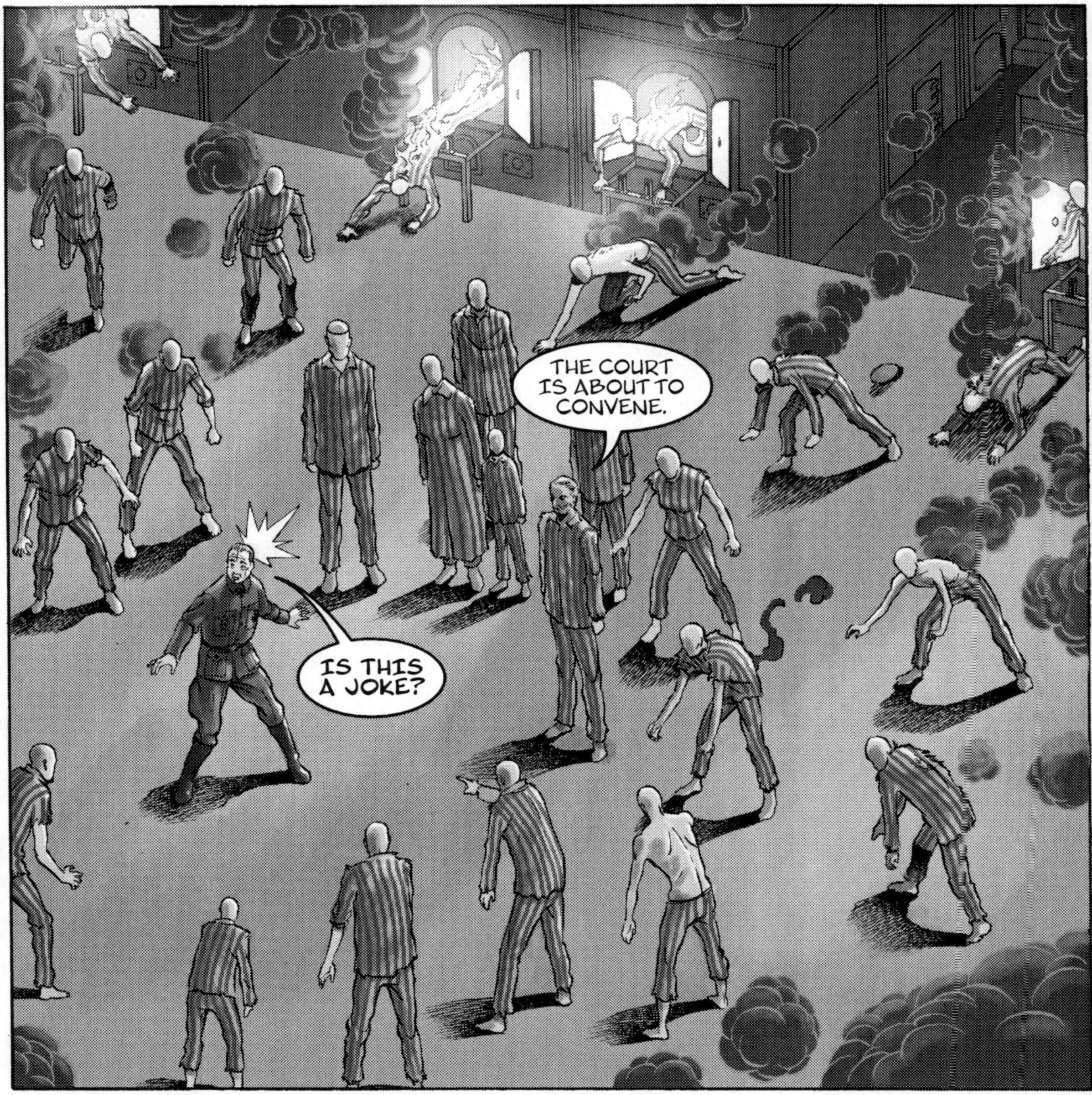
THE COURT IS ABOUT TO CONVENE.
IS THIS A JOKE?

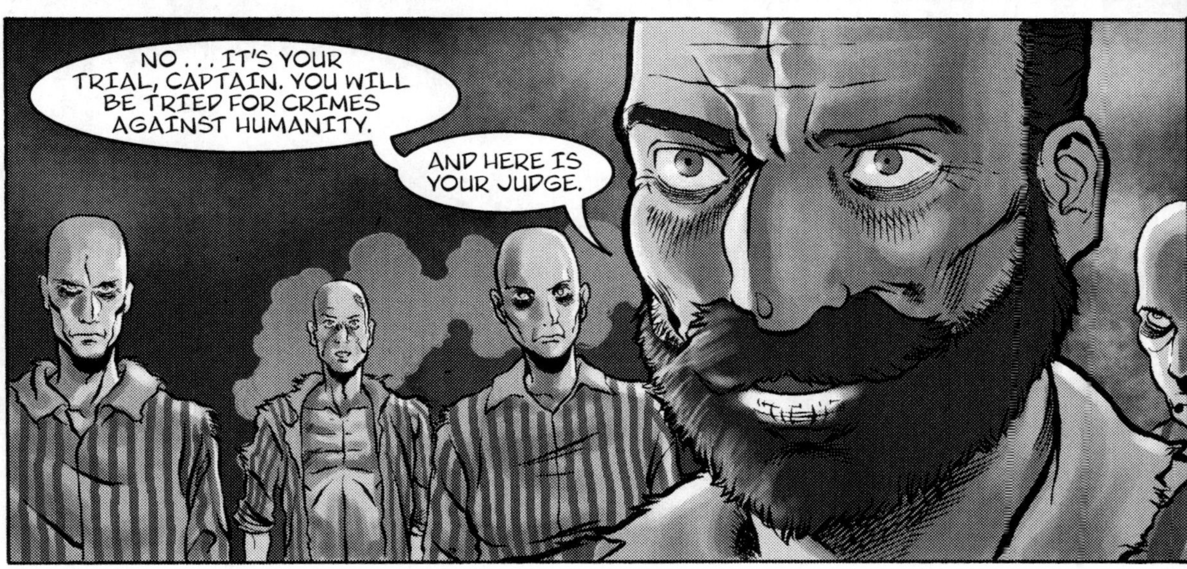
NO . . . IT'S YOUR TRIAL, CAPTAIN. YOU WILL BE TRIED FOR CRIMES AGAINST HUMANITY.
AND HERE IS YOUR JUDGE.

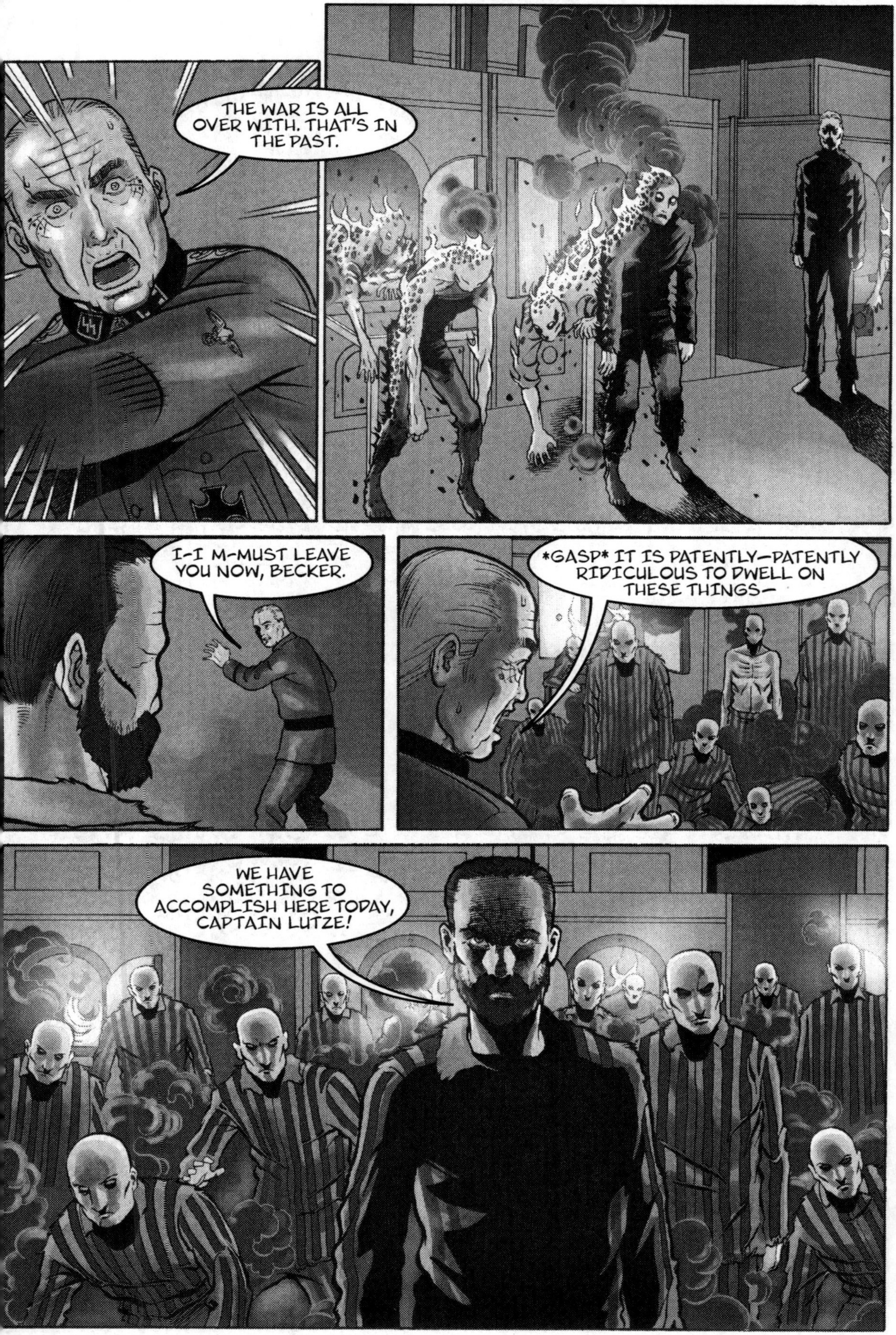
THE WAR IS ALL OVER WITH. THAT'S IN THE PAST.
I-I M-MUST LEAVE YOU NOW, BECKER.
GASP IT IS PATENTLY—PATENTLY RIDICULOUS TO DWELL ON THESE THINGS—
WE HAVE SOMETHING TO ACCOMPLISH HERE TODAY, CAPTAIN LUTZE!

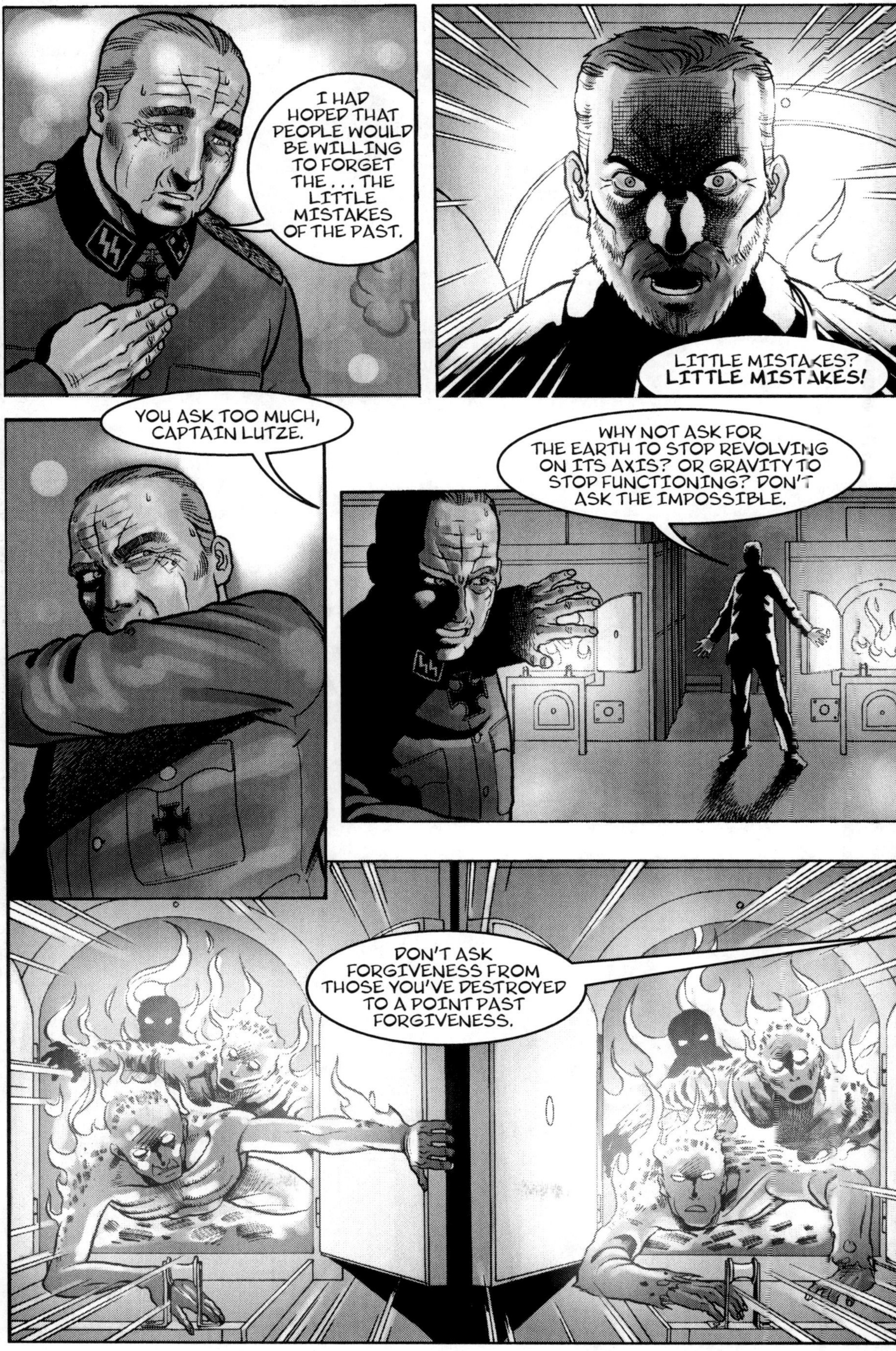
I HAD HOPED THAT PEOPLE WOULD BE WILLING TO FORGET THE . . . THE LITTLE MISTAKES OF THE PAST.
LITTLE MISTAKES? LITTLE MISTAKES!
YOU ASK TOO MUCH, CAPTAIN LUTZE.
WHY NOT ASK FOR THE EARTH TO STOP REVOLVING ON ITS AXIS? OR GRAVITY TO STOP FUNCTIONING? DON'T ASK THE IMPOSSIBLE.
DON'T ASK FORGIVENESS FROM THOSE YOU'VE DESTROYED TO A POINT PAST FORGIVENESS.

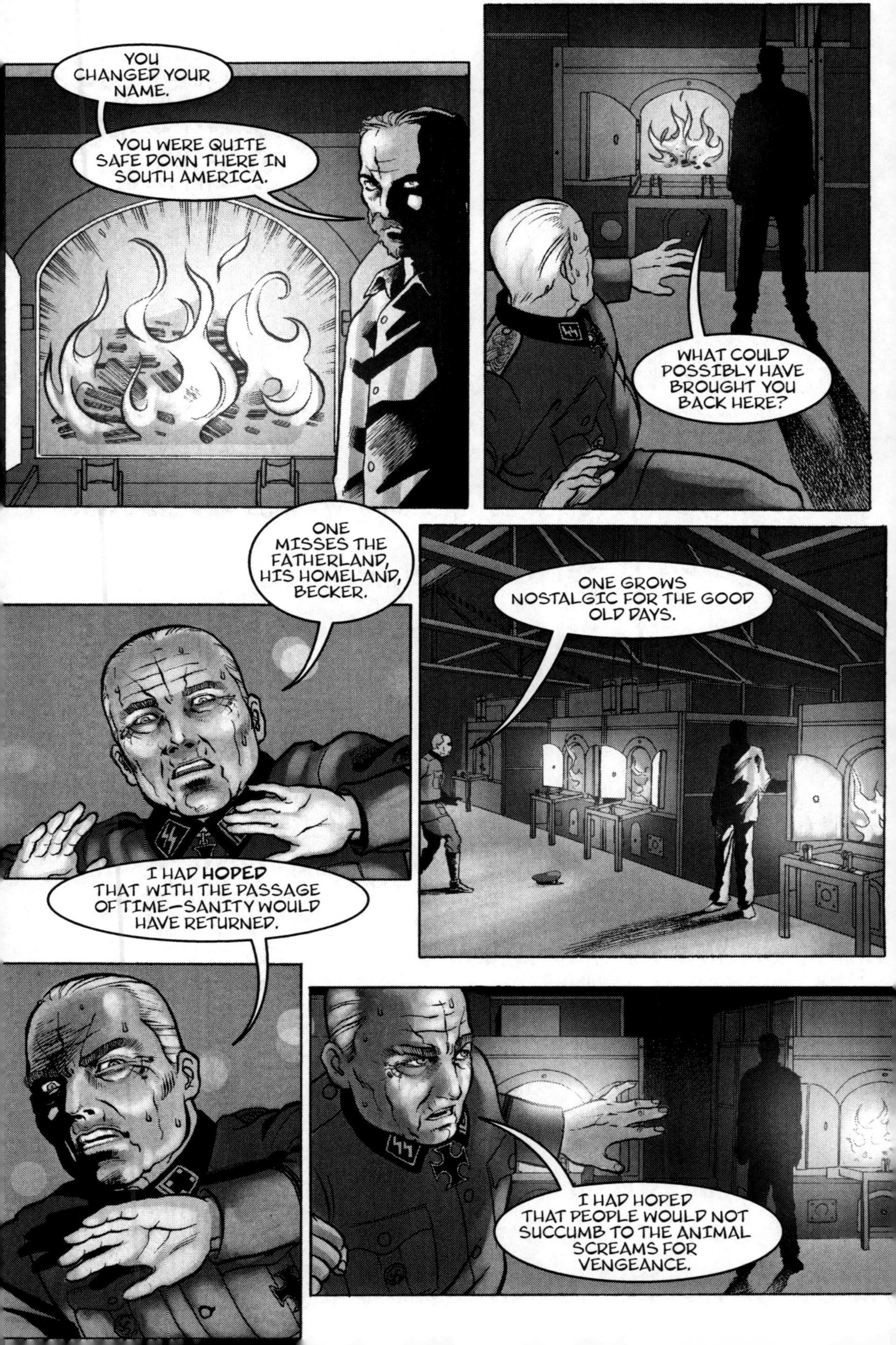
YOU CHANGED YOUR NAME.
YOU WERE QUITE SAFE DOWN THERE IN SOUTH AMERICA.
WHAT COULD POSSIBLY HAVE BROUGHT YOU BACK HERE?
ONE MISSES THE FATHERLAND, HIS HOMELAND, BECKER.
I HAD **HOPED** THAT WITH THE PASSAGE OF TIME—SANITY WOULD HAVE RETURNED.
ONE GROWS NOSTALGIC FOR THE GOOD OLD DAYS.
I HAD HOPED THAT PEOPLE WOULD NOT SUCCUMB TO THE ANIMAL SCREAMS FOR VENGEANCE.

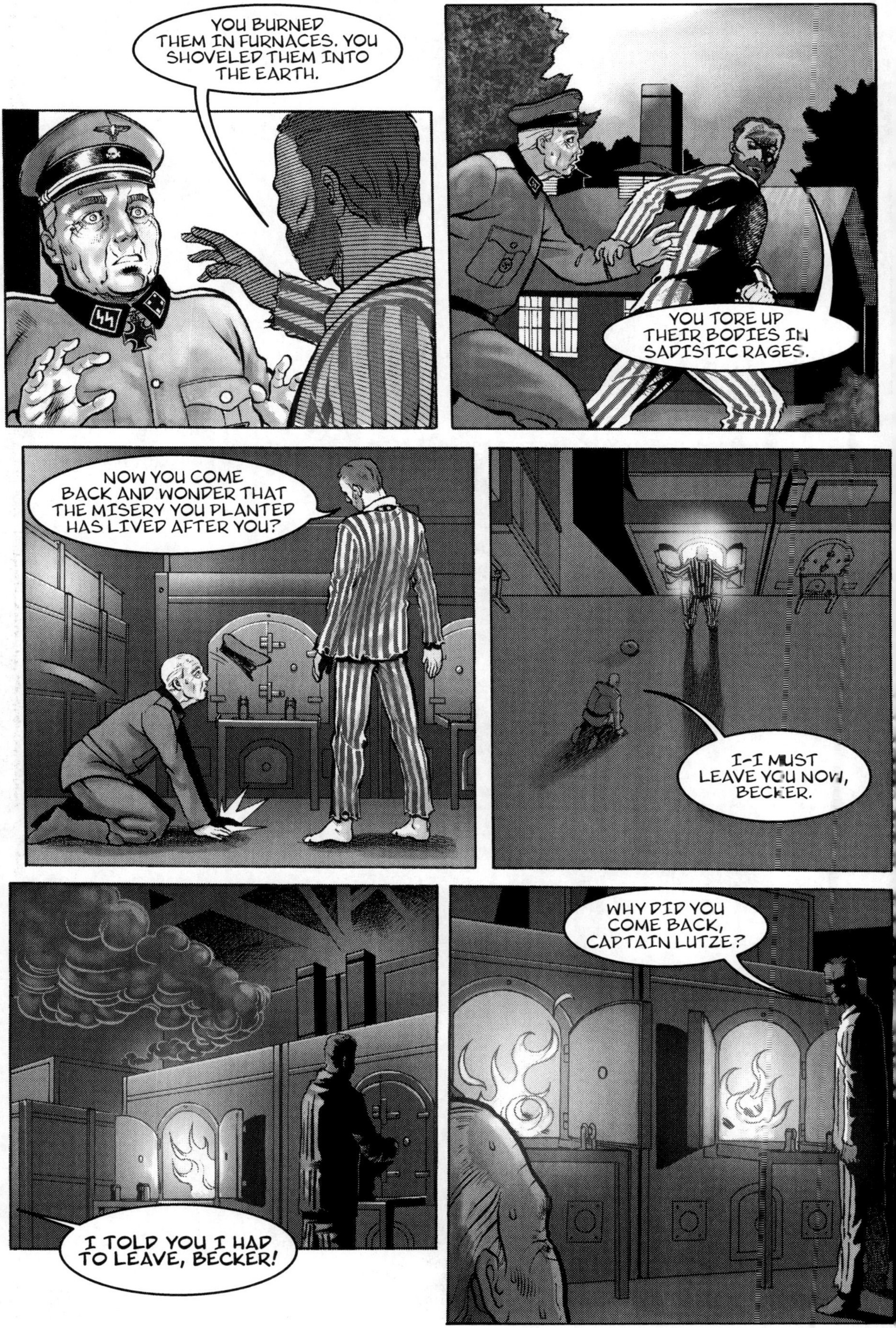
YOU BURNED THEM IN FURNACES. YOU SHOVELED THEM INTO THE EARTH.
YOU TORE UP THEIR BODIES IN SADISTIC RAGES.
NOW YOU COME BACK AND WONDER THAT THE MISERY YOU PLANTED HAS LIVED AFTER YOU?
I-I MUST LEAVE YOU NOW, BECKER.
I TOLD YOU I HAD TO LEAVE, BECKER!
WHY DID YOU COME BACK, CAPTAIN LUTZE?

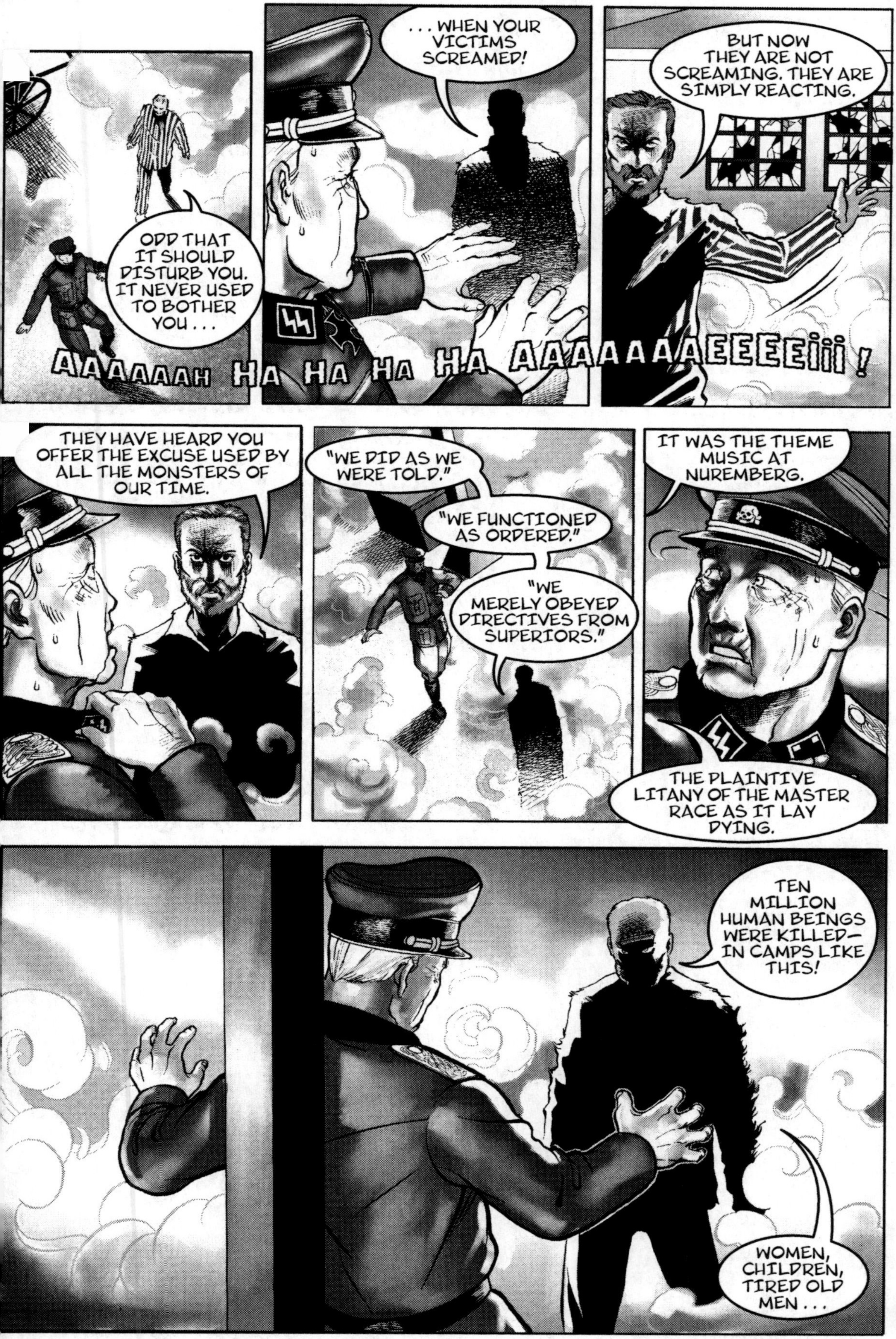
ODD THAT IT SHOULD DISTURB YOU. IT NEVER USED TO BOTHER YOU . . .
. . . WHEN YOUR VICTIMS SCREAMED!
BUT NOW THEY ARE NOT SCREAMING. THEY ARE SIMPLY REACTING.
AAAAAAAH HA HA HA HA AAAAAAAAEEEEEiii!
THEY HAVE HEARD YOU OFFER THE EXCUSE USED BY ALL THE MONSTERS OF OUR TIME.
"WE DID AS WE WERE TOLD."
"WE FUNCTIONED AS ORDERED."
"WE MERELY OBEYED DIRECTIVES FROM SUPERIORS."
IT WAS THE THEME MUSIC AT NUREMBERG.
THE PLAINTIVE LITANY OF THE MASTER RACE AS IT LAY DYING.
TEN MILLION HUMAN BEINGS WERE KILLED— IN CAMPS LIKE THIS!
WOMEN, CHILDREN, TIRED OLD MEN . . .

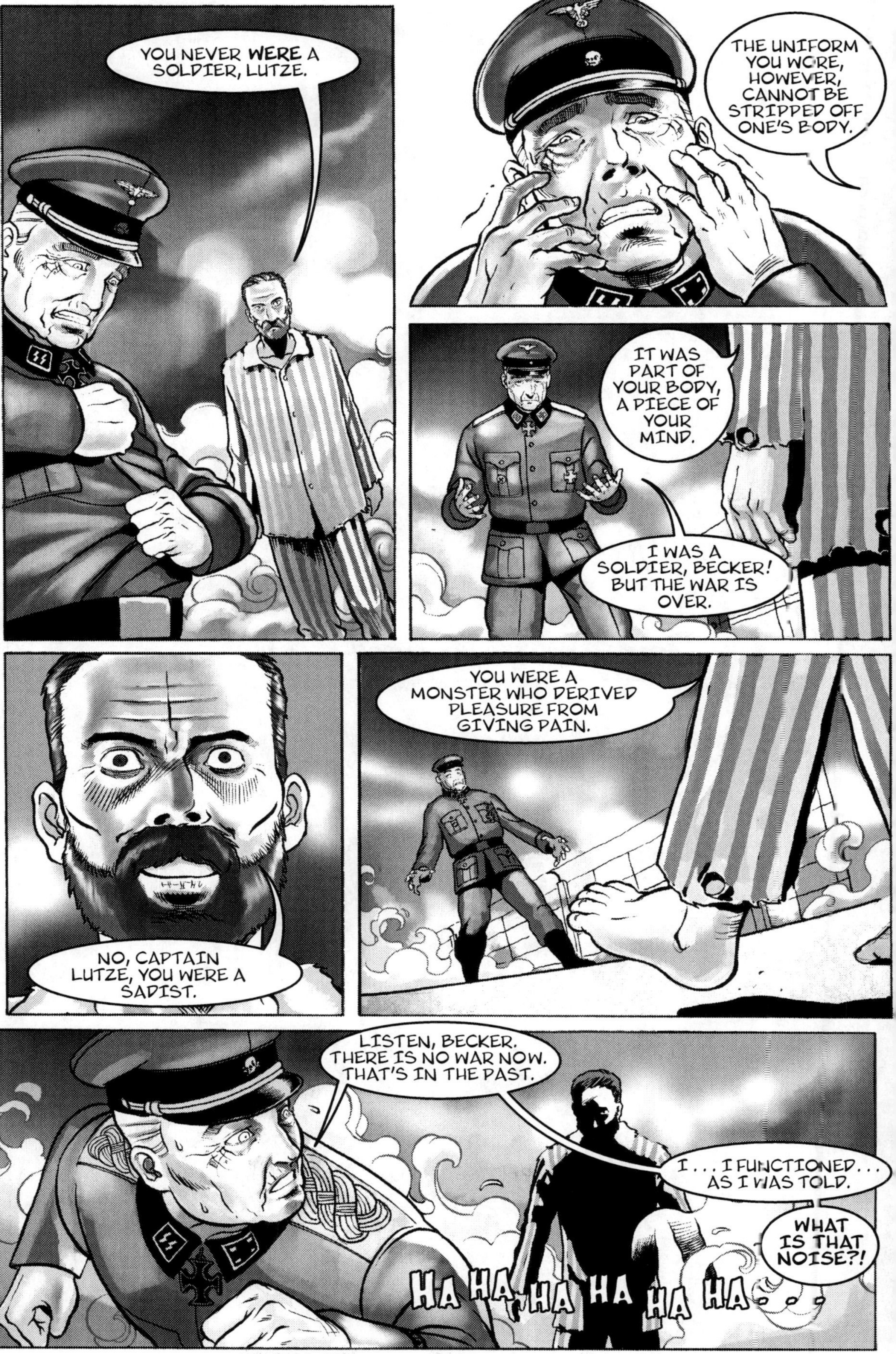
YOU NEVER **WERE** A SOLDIER, LUTZE.
THE UNIFORM YOU WORE, HOWEVER, CANNOT BE STRIPPED OFF ONE'S BODY.
IT WAS PART OF YOUR BODY, A PIECE OF YOUR MIND.
I WAS A SOLDIER, BECKER! BUT THE WAR IS OVER.
NO, CAPTAIN LUTZE, YOU WERE A SADIST.
YOU WERE A MONSTER WHO DERIVED PLEASURE FROM GIVING PAIN.
LISTEN, BECKER. THERE IS NO WAR NOW. THAT'S IN THE PAST.
I . . . I FUNCTIONED . . . AS I WAS TOLD.
WHAT IS THAT NOISE?!
HA HA HA HA HA HA HA . . .

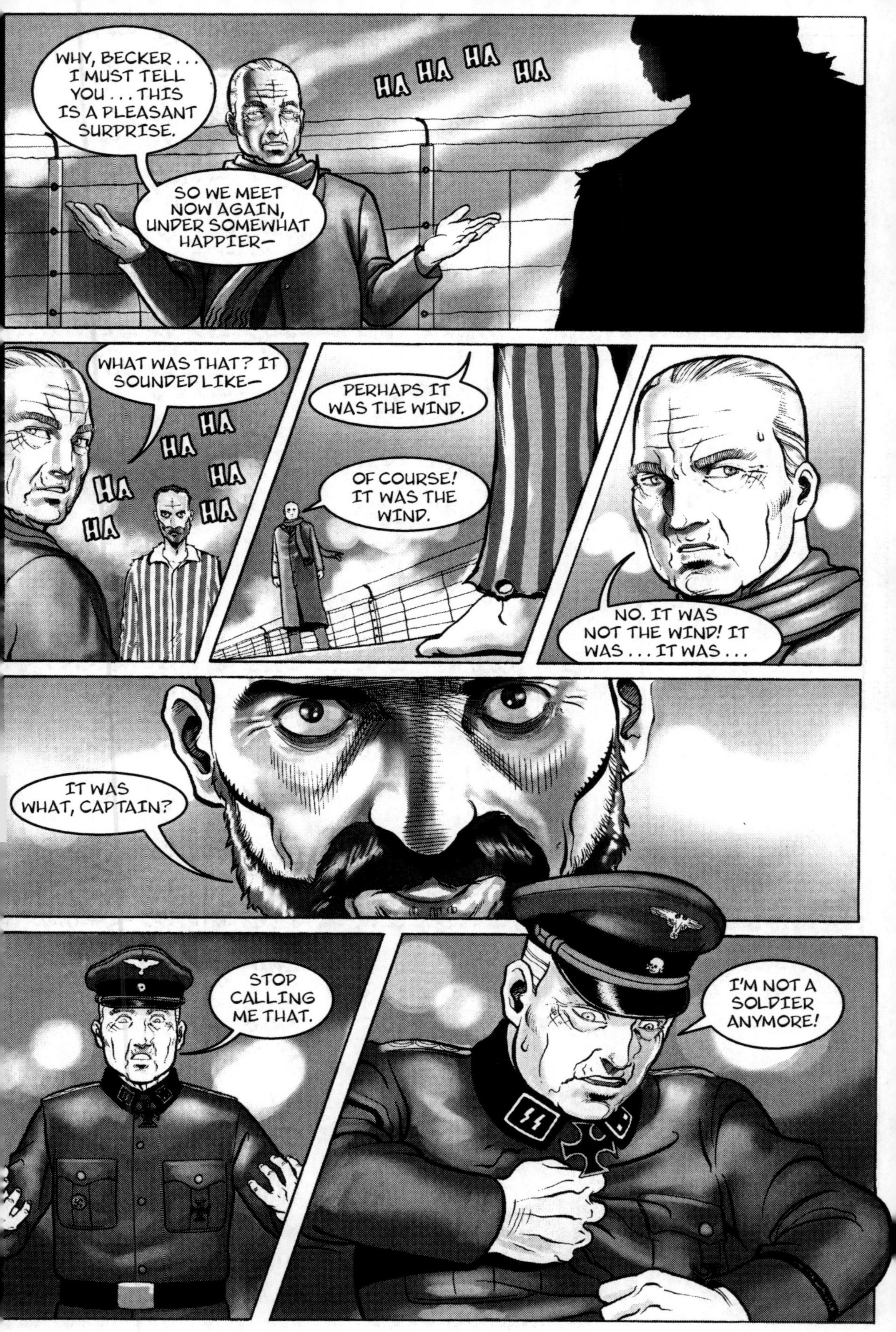
WHY, BECKER . . . I MUST TELL YOU . . . THIS IS A PLEASANT SURPRISE.
SO WE MEET NOW AGAIN, UNDER SOMEWHAT HAPPIER—
HA HA HA HA
WHAT WAS THAT? IT SOUNDED LIKE—
HA HA HA HA HA HA
PERHAPS IT WAS THE WIND.
OF COURSE! IT WAS THE WIND.
NO. IT WAS NOT THE WIND! IT WAS . . . IT WAS . . .
IT WAS WHAT, CAPTAIN?
STOP CALLING ME THAT.
I'M NOT A SOLDIER ANYMORE!

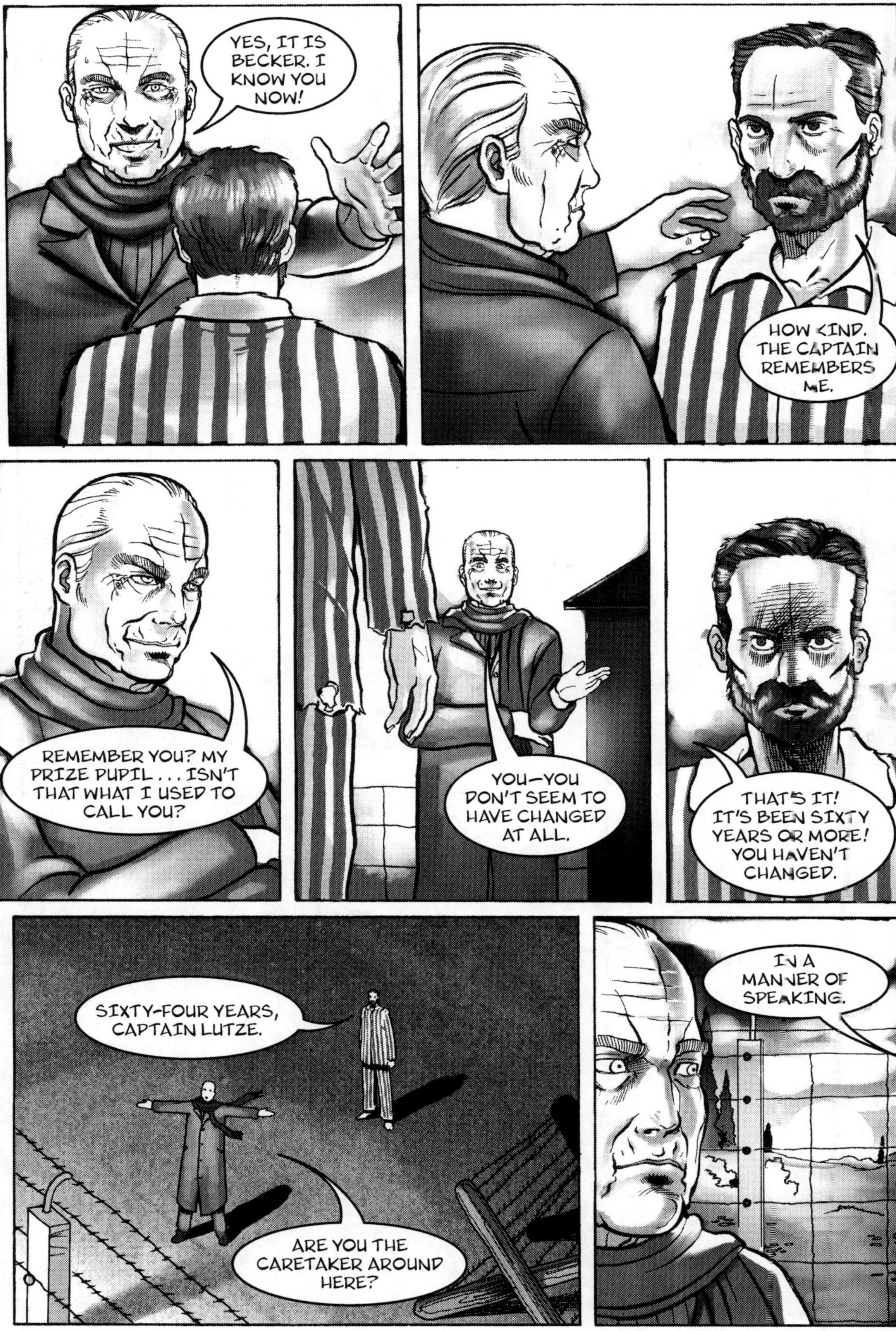
YES, IT IS BECKER. I KNOW YOU NOW!
HOW KIND. THE CAPTAIN REMEMBERS ME.
REMEMBER YOU? MY PRIZE PUPIL . . . ISN'T THAT WHAT I USED TO CALL YOU?
YOU—YOU DON'T SEEM TO HAVE CHANGED AT ALL.
THAT'S IT! IT'S BEEN SIXTY YEARS OR MORE! YOU HAVEN'T CHANGED.
SIXTY-FOUR YEARS, CAPTAIN LUTZE.
ARE YOU THE CARETAKER AROUND HERE?
IN A MANNER OF SPEAKING.

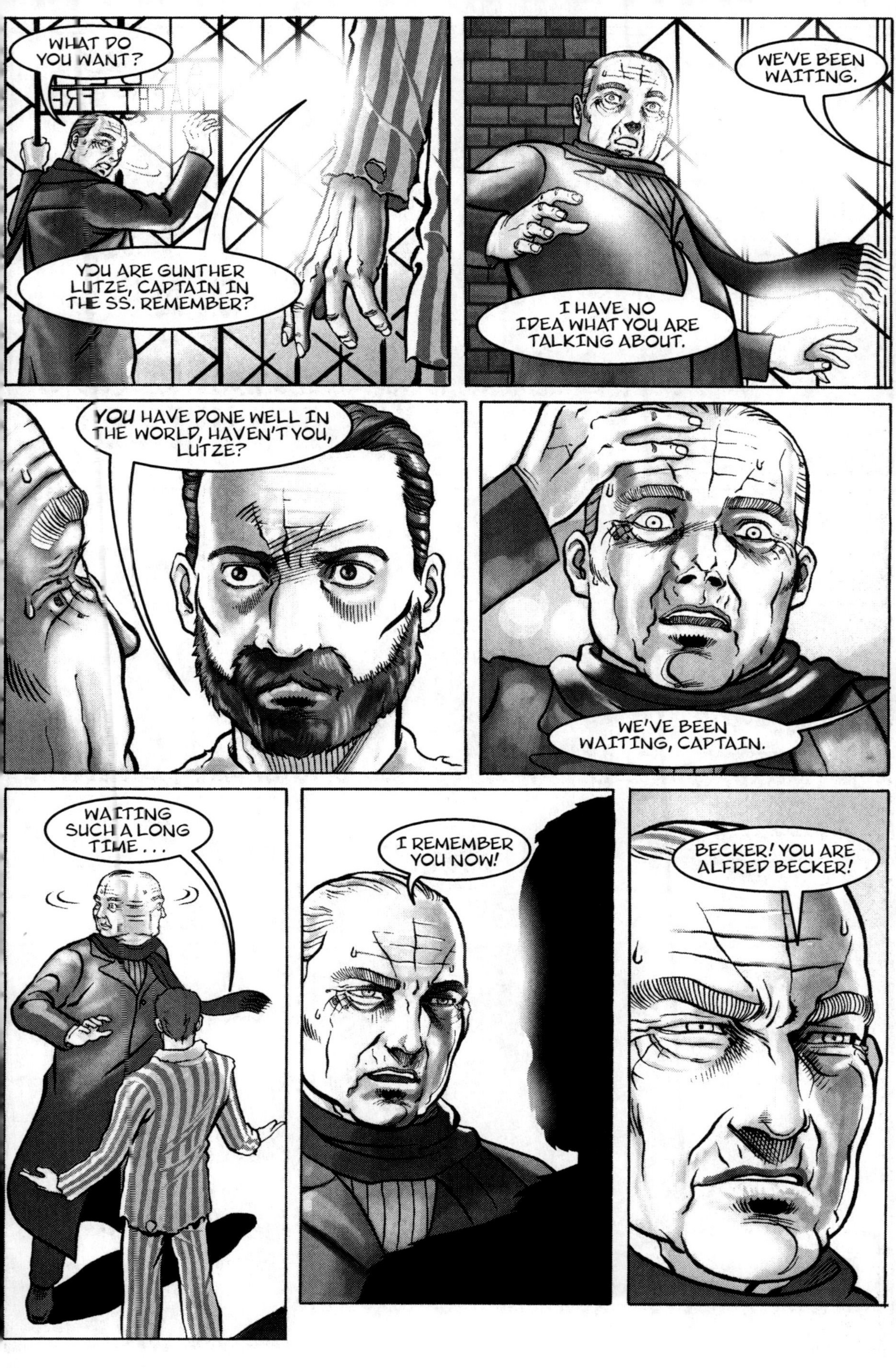
WHAT DO YOU WANT?
YOU ARE GUNTHER LUTZE, CAPTAIN IN THE SS. REMEMBER?
WE'VE BEEN WAITING.
I HAVE NO IDEA WHAT YOU ARE TALKING ABOUT.
YOU HAVE DONE WELL IN THE WORLD, HAVEN'T YOU, LUTZE?
WE'VE BEEN WAITING, CAPTAIN.
WAITING SUCH A LONG TIME . . .
I REMEMBER YOU NOW!
BECKER! YOU ARE ALFRED BECKER!

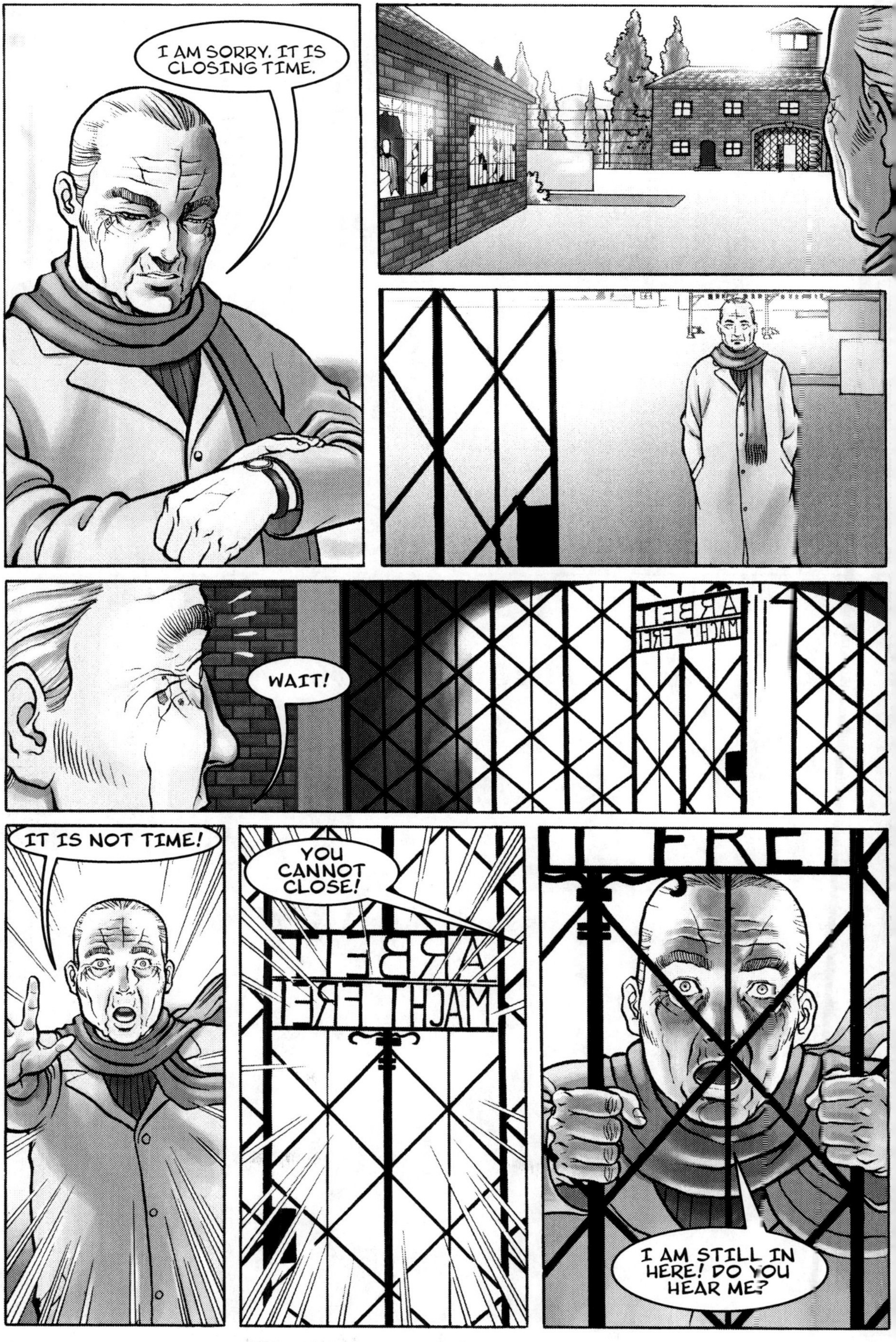
I AM SORRY. IT IS CLOSING TIME.
WAIT!
ARBEIT MACHT FREI
IT IS NOT TIME!
YOU CANNOT CLOSE!
ARBEIT MACHT FREI
FREI
I AM STILL IN HERE! DO YOU HEAR ME?

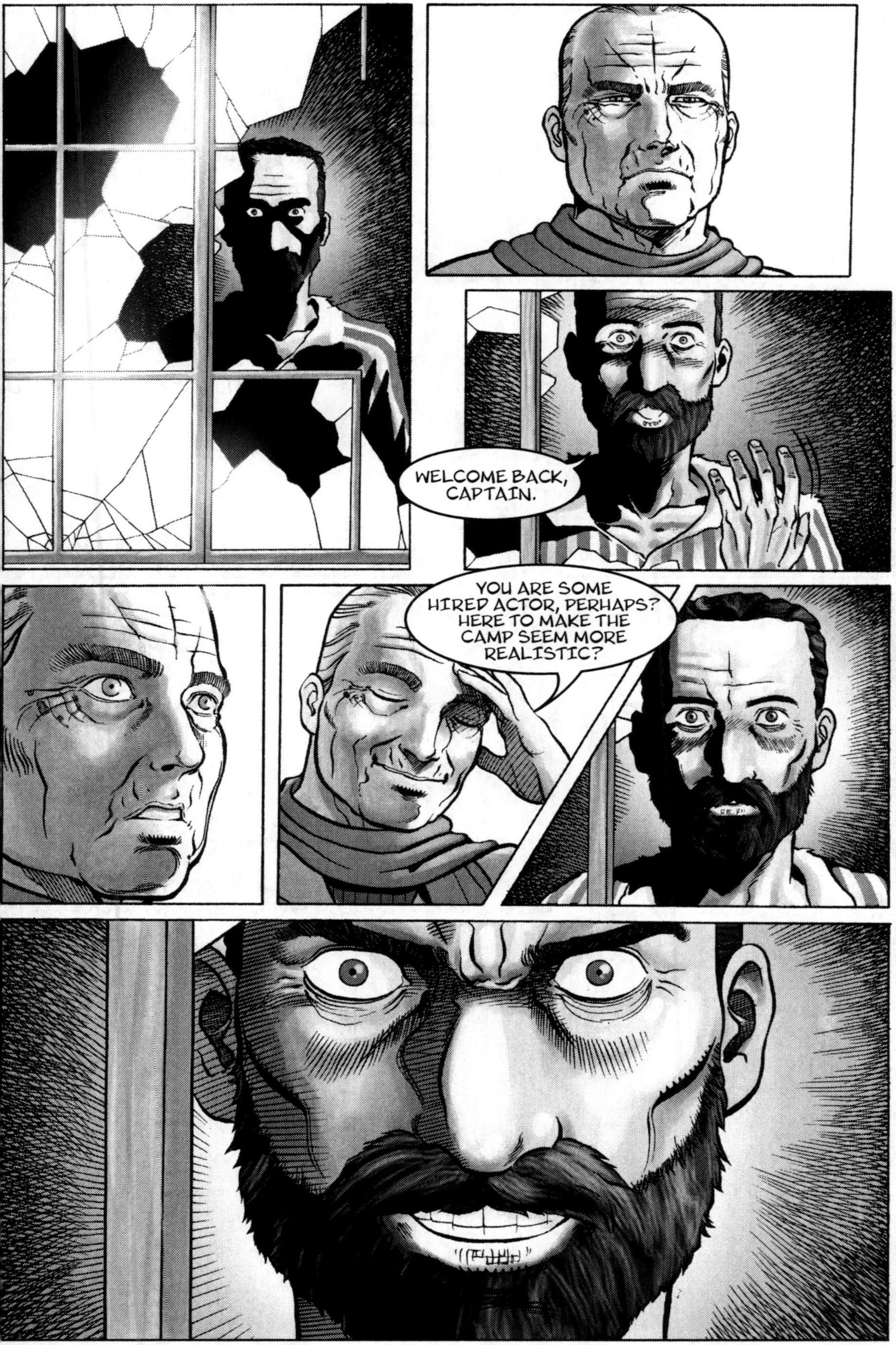
WELCOME BACK, CAPTAIN.
YOU ARE SOME HIRED ACTOR, PERHAPS? HERE TO MAKE THE CAMP SEEM MORE REALISTIC?

AND NOW IT IS CLOSING TIME AT FIVE...

...AND WALKING MAPS.

TENTION

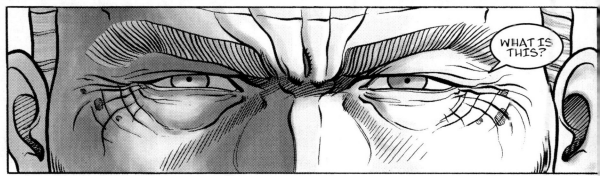

WHAT IS THIS?

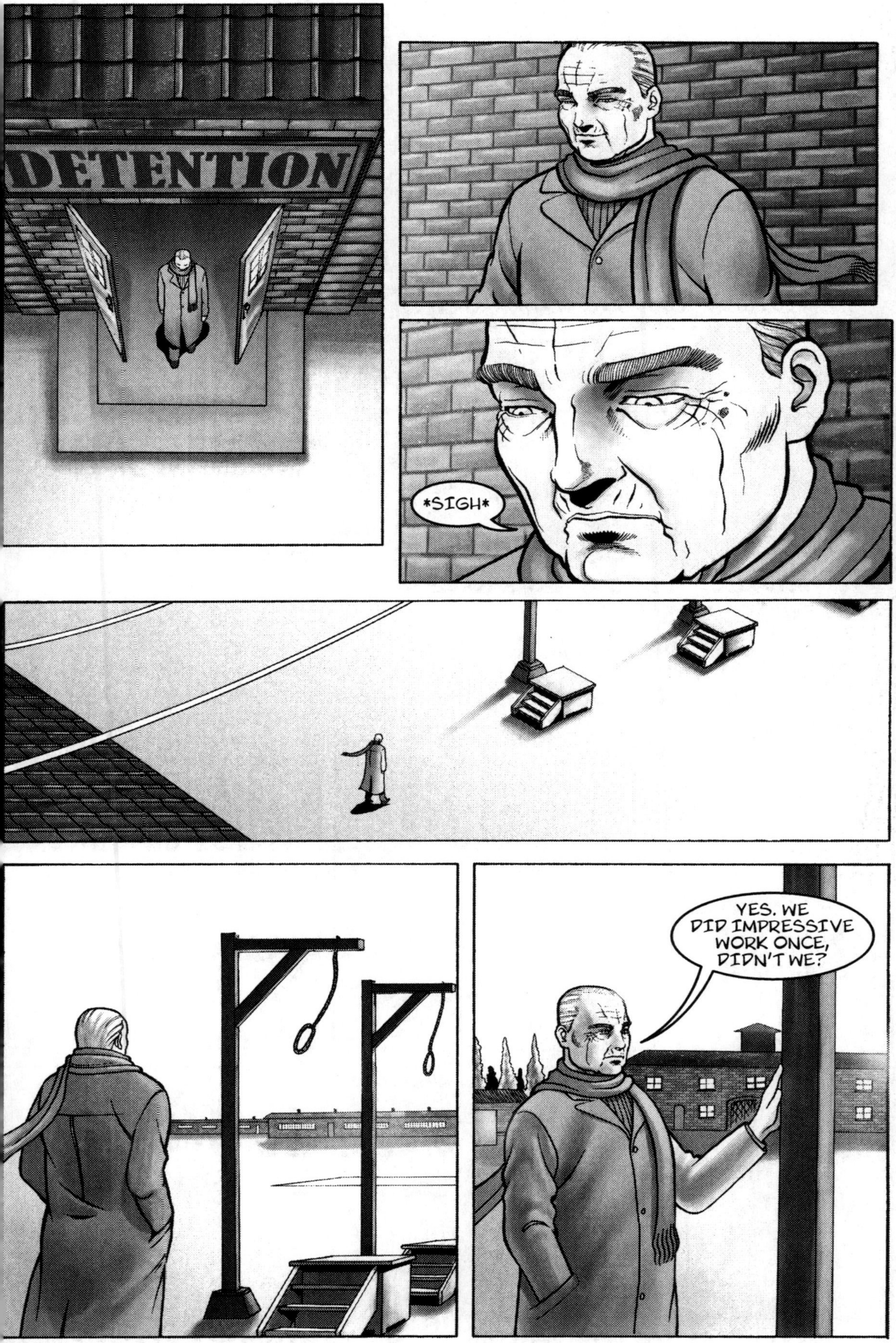
DETENTION
SIGH
YES. WE DID IMPRESSIVE WORK ONCE, DIDN'T WE?

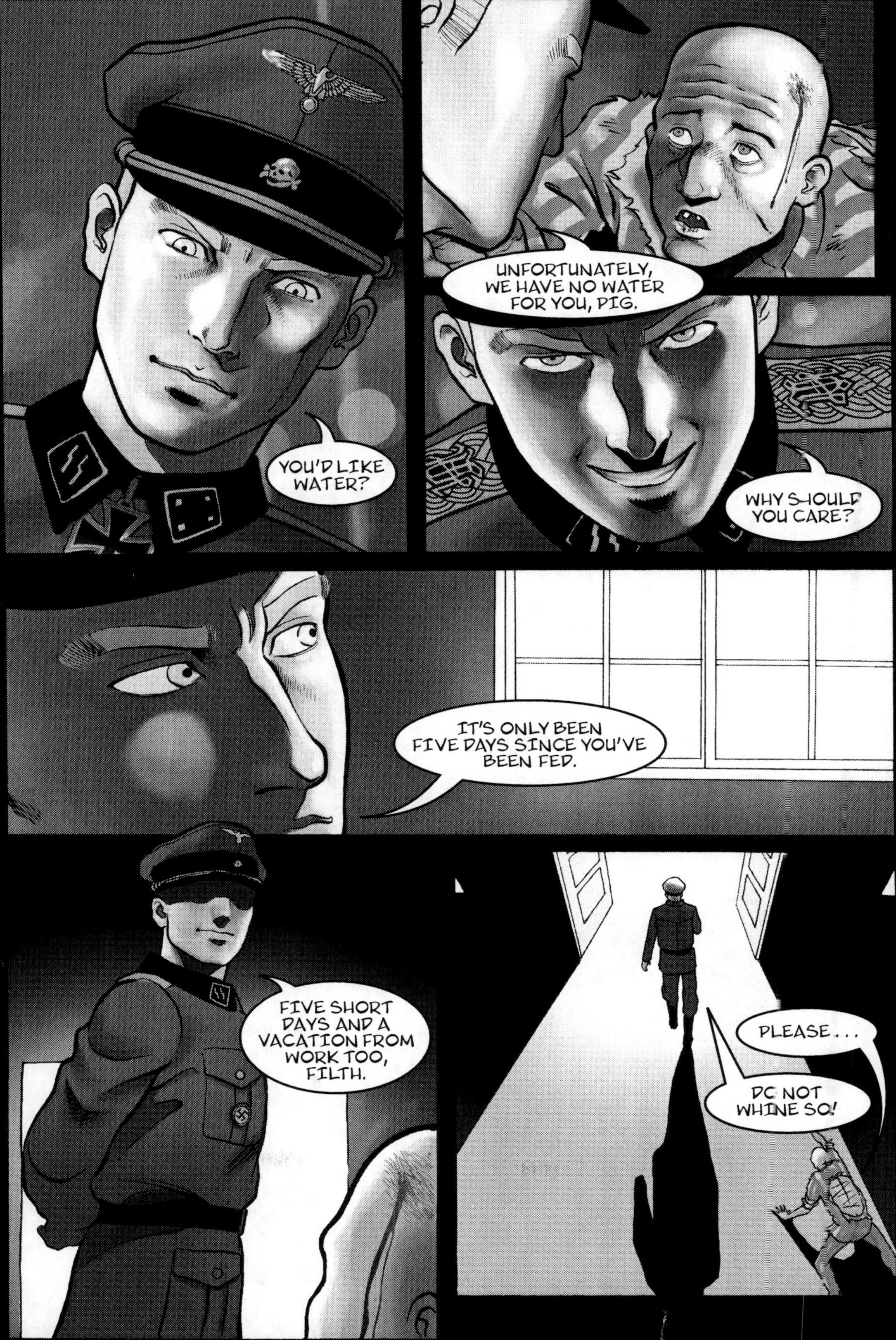
YOU'D LIKE WATER?
UNFORTUNATELY, WE HAVE NO WATER FOR YOU, PIG.
WHY SHOULD YOU CARE?
IT'S ONLY BEEN FIVE DAYS SINCE YOU'VE BEEN FED.
FIVE SHORT DAYS AND A VACATION FROM WORK TOO, FILTH.
PLEASE . . .
DO NOT WHINE SO!

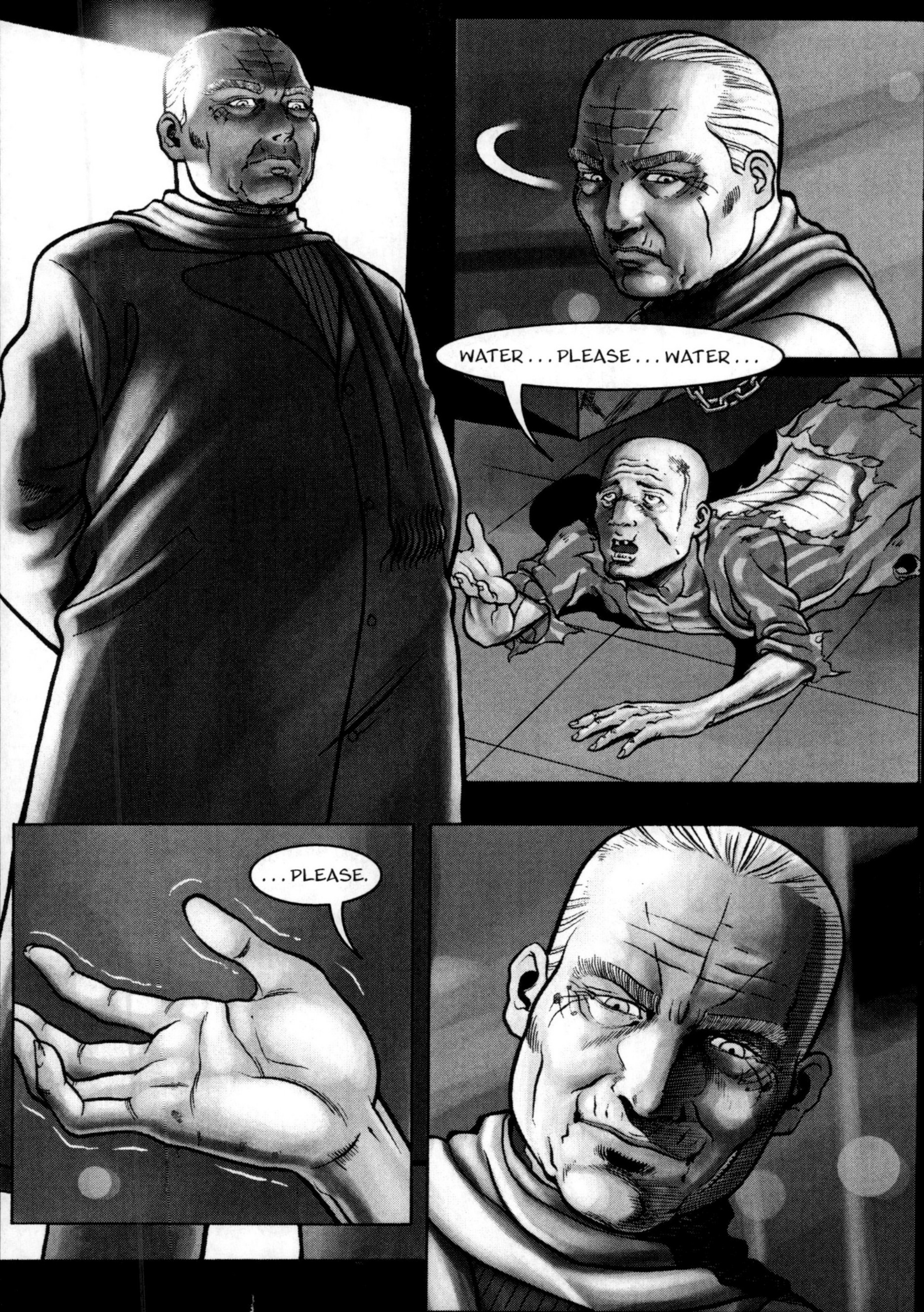
WATER . . . PLEASE . . . WATER . . .
. . . PLEASE.

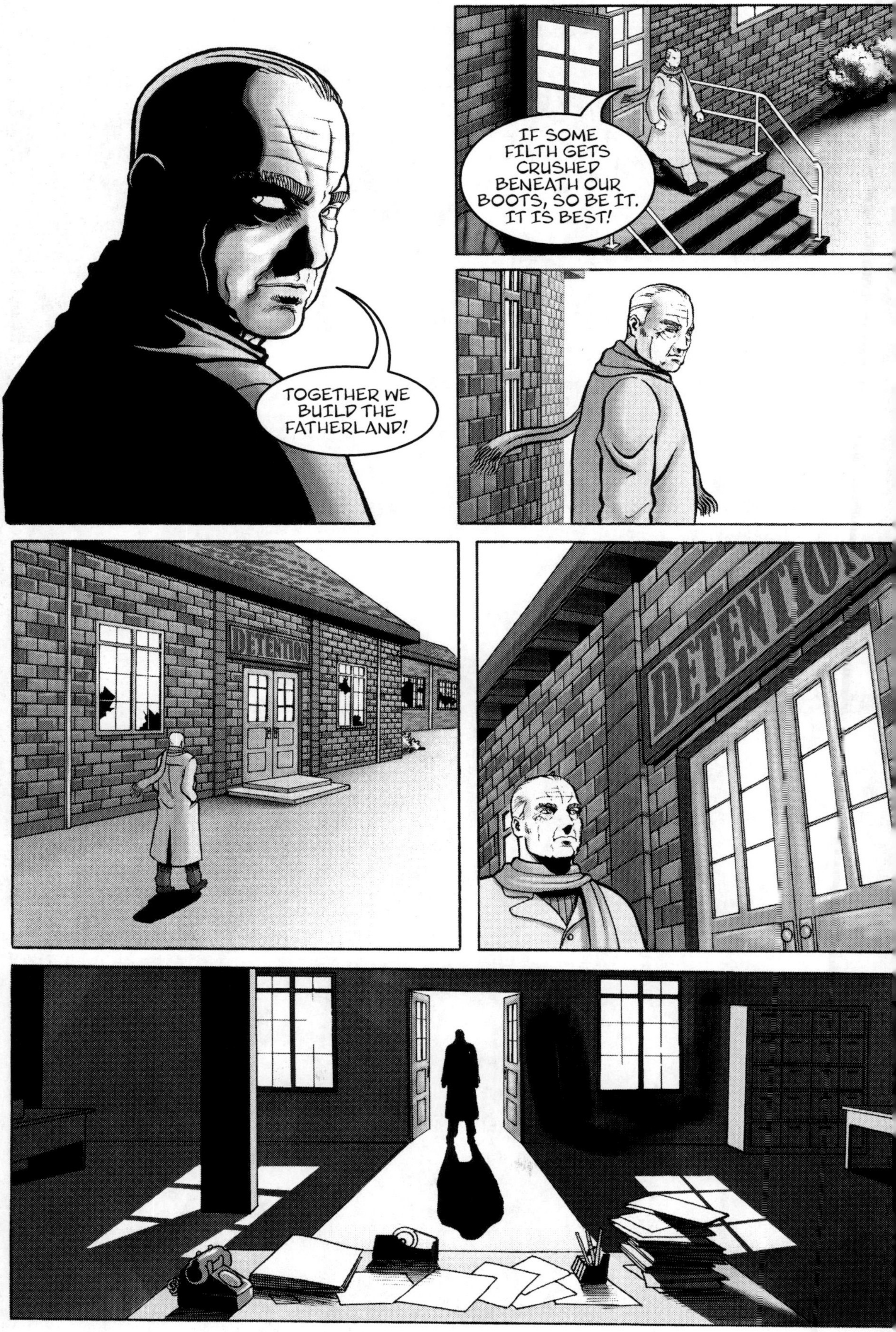
IF SOME FILTH GETS CRUSHED BENEATH OUR BOOTS, SO BE IT. IT IS BEST!
TOGETHER WE BUILD THE FATHERLAND!
DETENTION
DETENTION

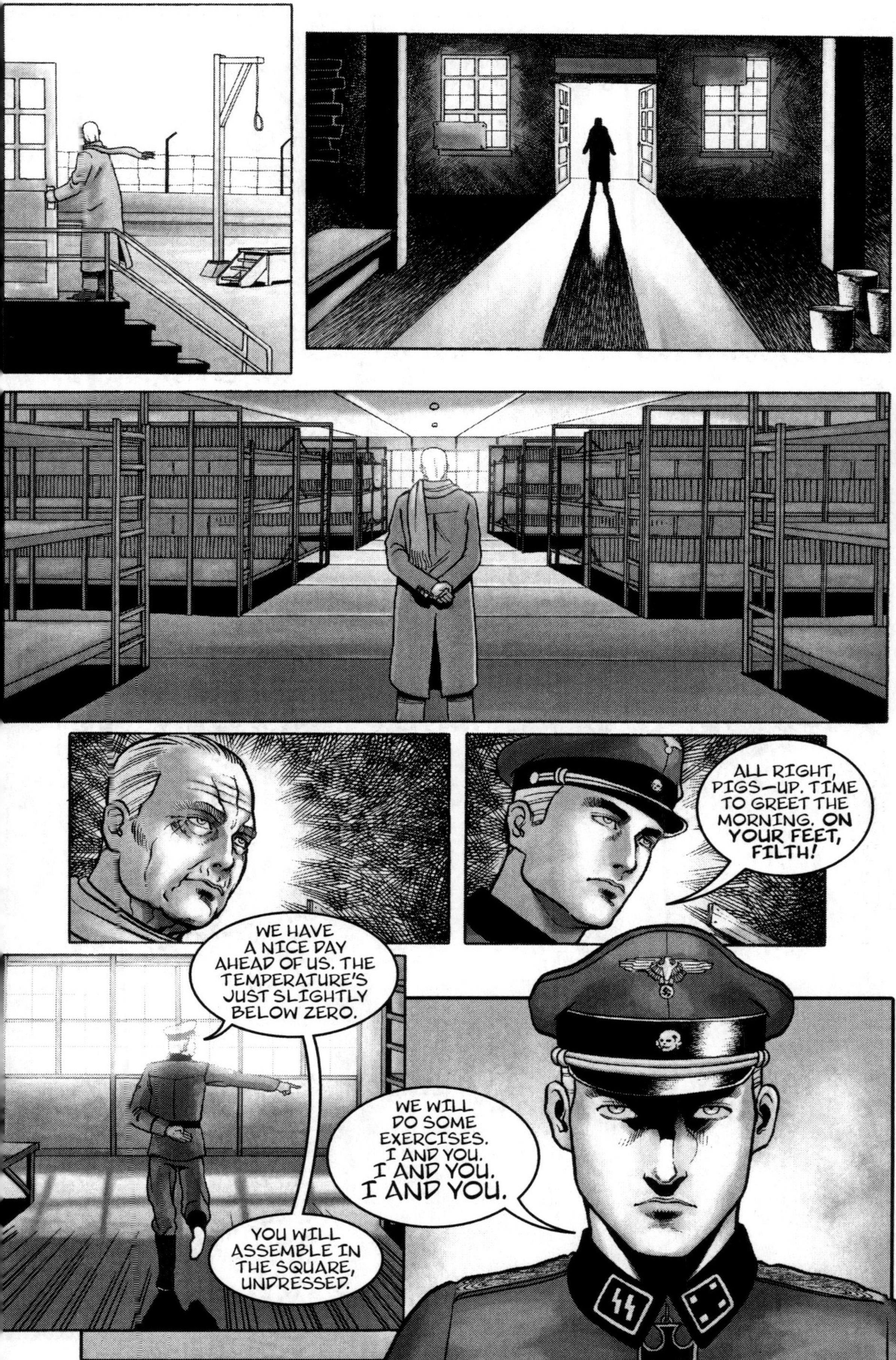
ALL RIGHT, PIGS—UP. TIME TO GREET THE MORNING. ON YOUR FEET, FILTH!
WE HAVE A NICE DAY AHEAD OF US. THE TEMPERATURE'S JUST SLIGHTLY BELOW ZERO.
YOU WILL ASSEMBLE IN THE SQUARE, UNDRESSED.
WE WILL DO SOME EXERCISES. I AND YOU. I AND YOU. I AND YOU.

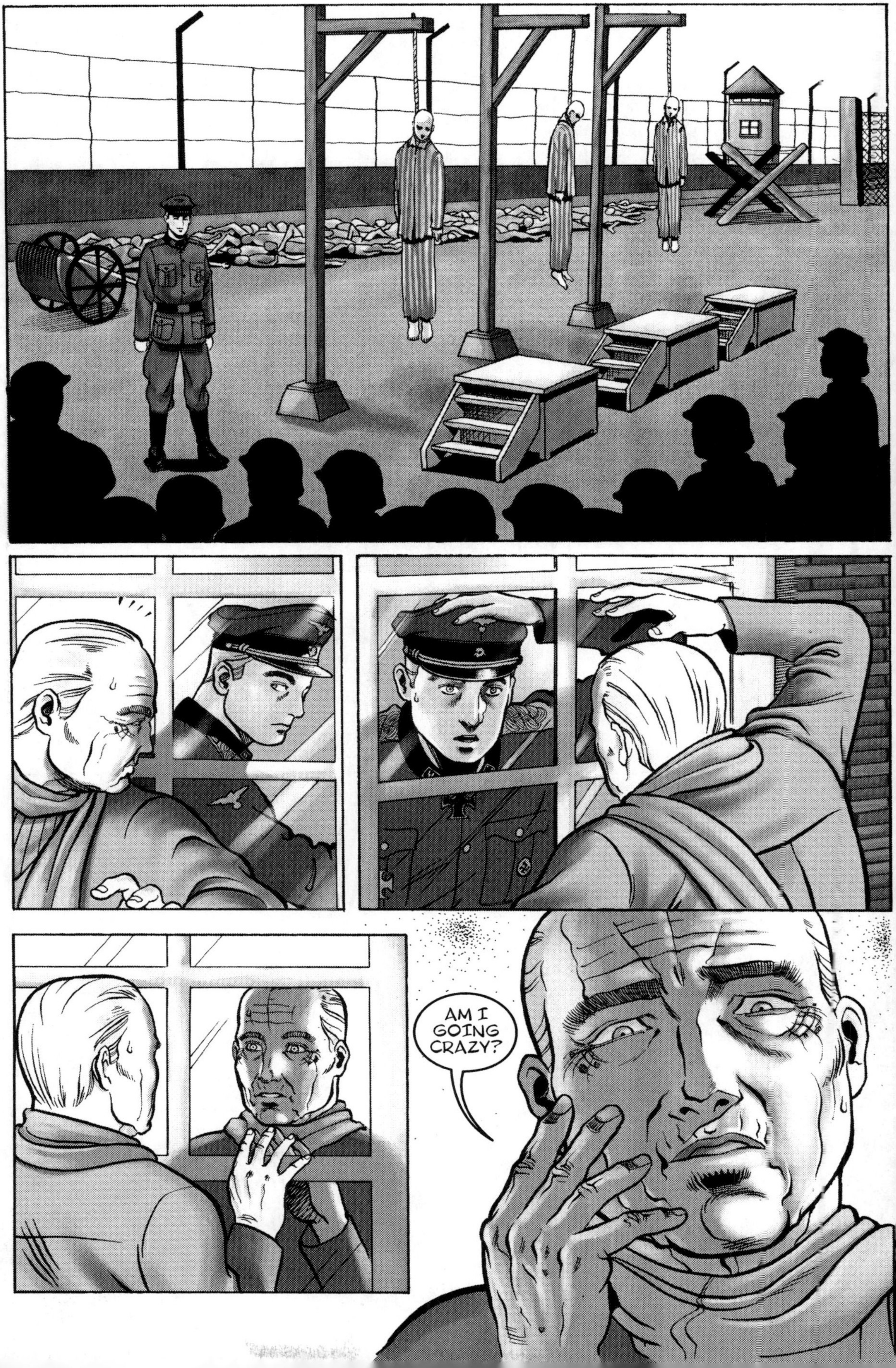
AM I GOING CRAZY?

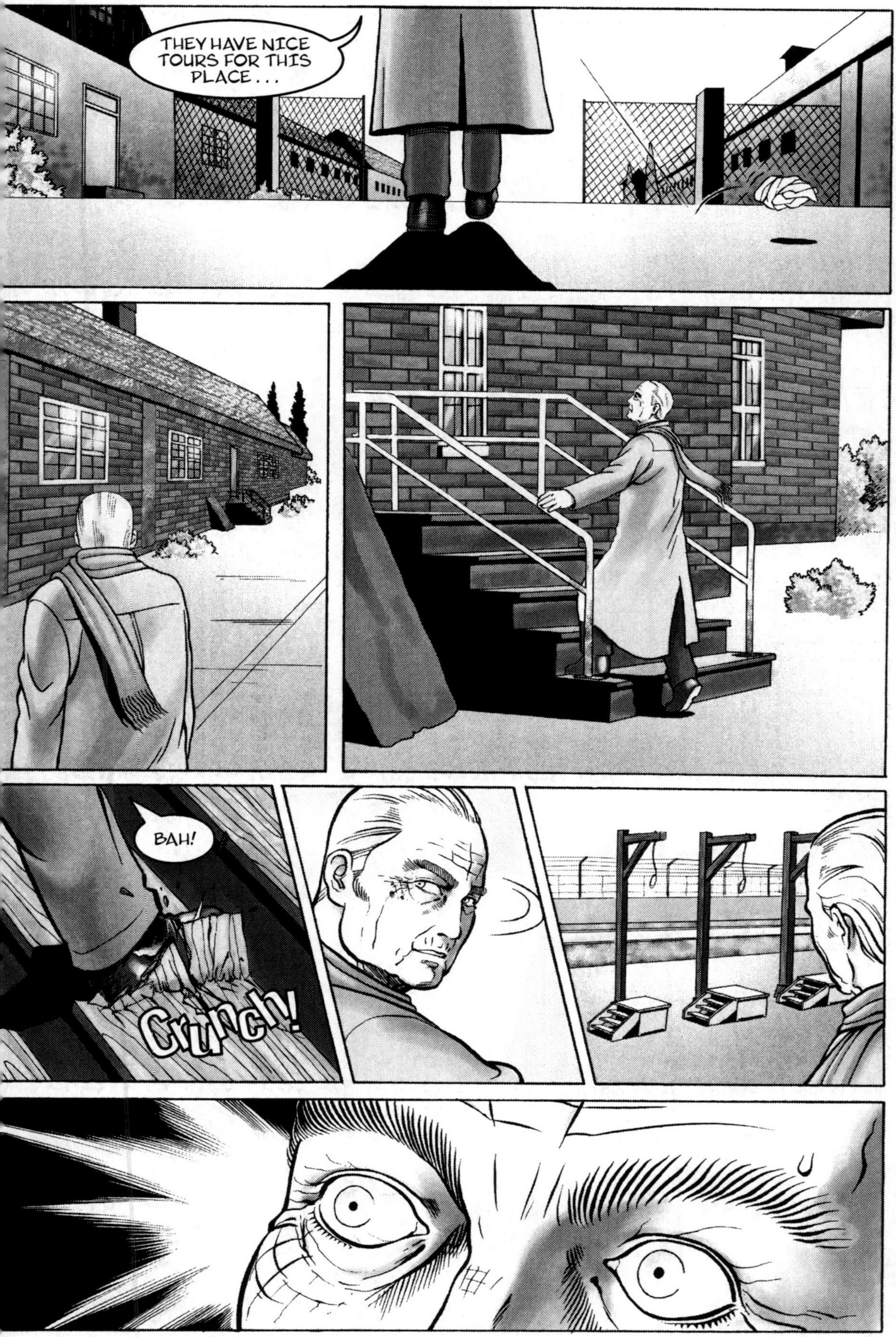
THEY HAVE NICE TOURS FOR THIS PLACE . . .
BAH!
Crunch!

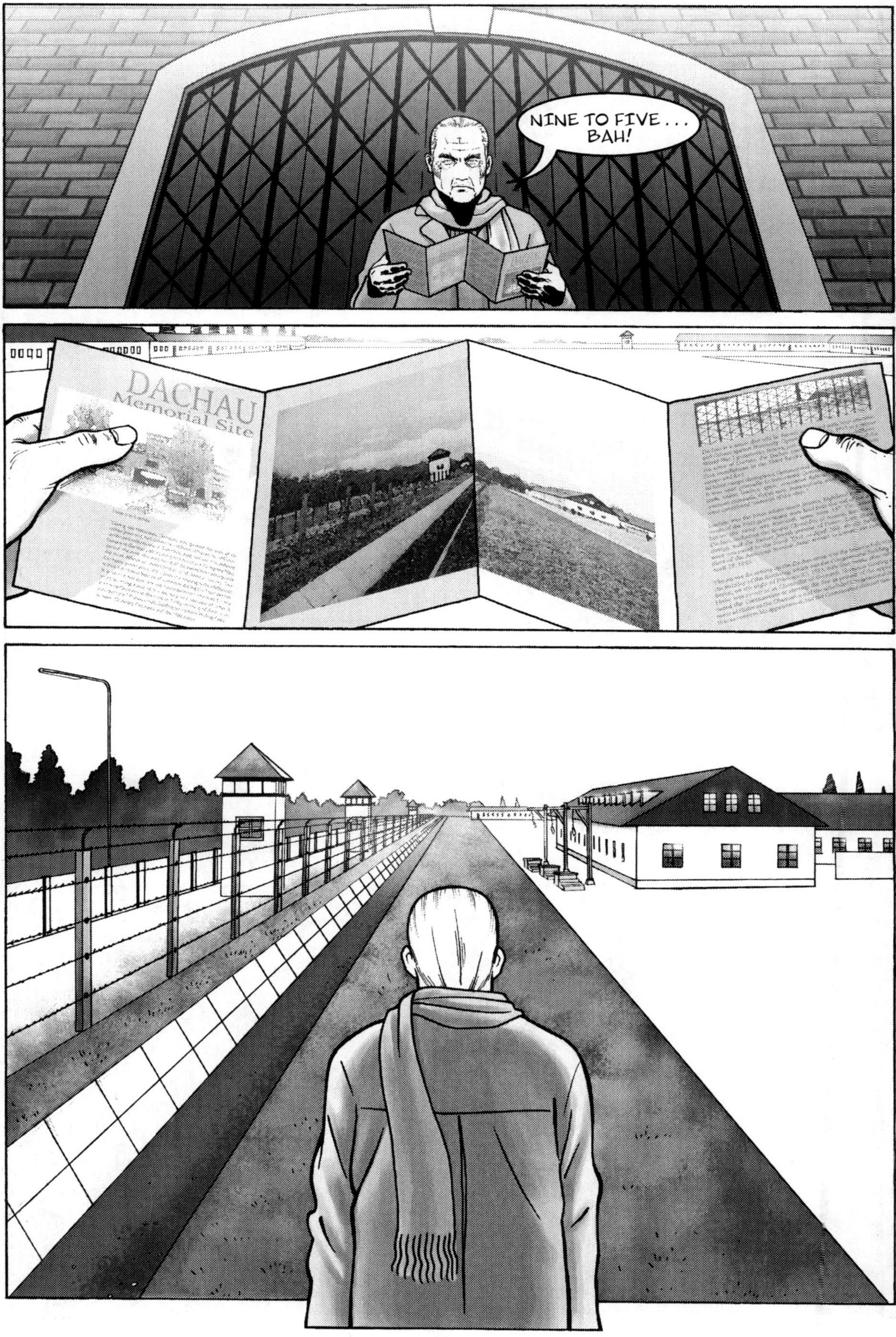
NINE TO FIVE . . . BAH!
DACHAU
Memorial Site

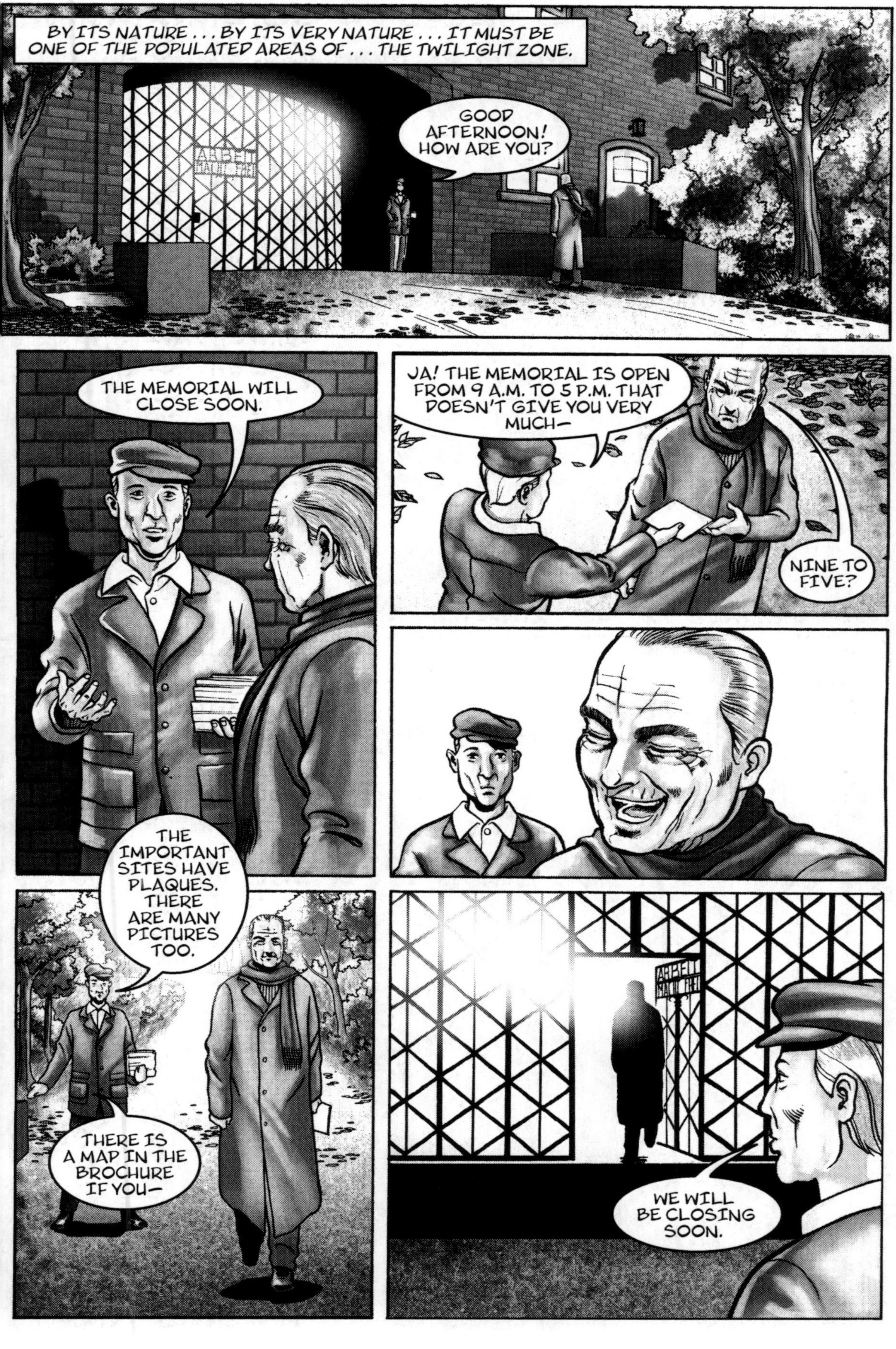
BY ITS NATURE . . . BY ITS VERY NATURE . . . IT MUST BE ONE OF THE POPULATED AREAS OF . . . THE TWILIGHT ZONE.
GOOD AFTERNOON! HOW ARE YOU?
THE MEMORIAL WILL CLOSE SOON.
JA! THE MEMORIAL IS OPEN FROM 9 A.M. TO 5 P.M. THAT DOESN'T GIVE YOU VERY MUCH—
NINE TO FIVE?
THE IMPORTANT SITES HAVE PLAQUES. THERE ARE MANY PICTURES TOO.
THERE IS A MAP IN THE BROCHURE IF YOU—
WE WILL BE CLOSING SOON.

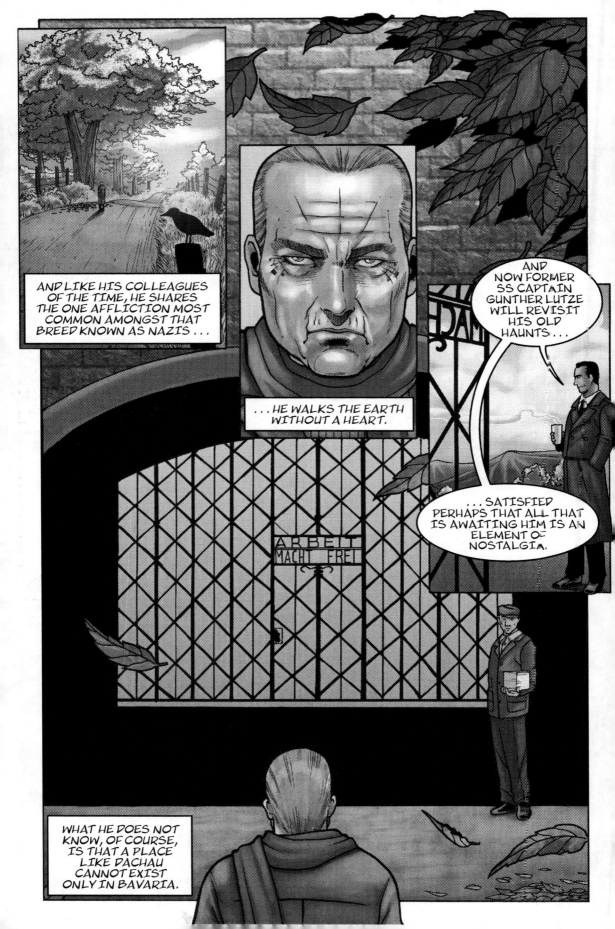

AND LIKE HIS COLLEAGUES OF THE TIME, HE SHARES THE ONE AFFLICTION MOST COMMON AMONGST THAT BREED KNOWN AS NAZIS...

...HE WALKS THE EARTH WITHOUT A HEART.

AND NOW FORMER SS CAPTAIN GUNTHER LUTZE WILL REVISIT HIS OLD HAUNTS...

...SATISFIED PERHAPS THAT ALL THAT IS AWAITING HIM IS AN ELEMENT OF NOSTALGIA.

WHAT HE DOES NOT KNOW, OF COURSE, IS THAT A PLACE LIKE DACHAU CANNOT EXIST ONLY IN BAVARIA.

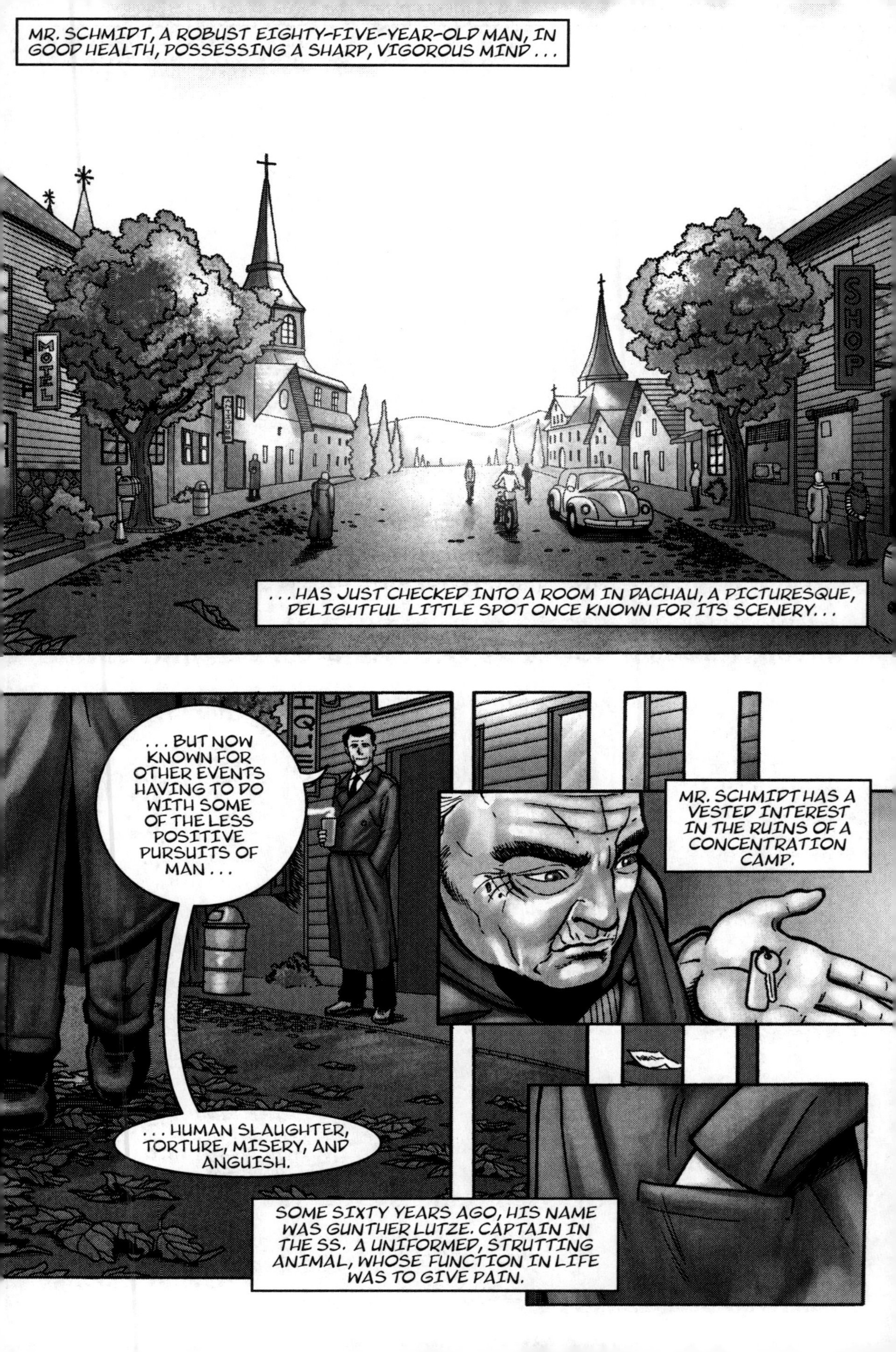
MR. SCHMIDT, A ROBUST EIGHTY-FIVE-YEAR-OLD MAN, IN GOOD HEALTH, POSSESSING A SHARP, VIGOROUS MIND . . .
MOTEL
SHOP
. . . HAS JUST CHECKED INTO A ROOM IN DACHAU, A PICTURESQUE, DELIGHTFUL LITTLE SPOT ONCE KNOWN FOR ITS SCENERY. . .
. . . BUT NOW KNOWN FOR OTHER EVENTS HAVING TO DO WITH SOME OF THE LESS POSITIVE PURSUITS OF MAN . . .
. . . HUMAN SLAUGHTER, TORTURE, MISERY, AND ANGUISH.
MR. SCHMIDT HAS A VESTED INTEREST IN THE RUINS OF A CONCENTRATION CAMP.
SOME SIXTY YEARS AGO, HIS NAME WAS GUNTHER LUTZE. CAPTAIN IN THE SS. A UNIFORMED, STRUTTING ANIMAL, WHOSE FUNCTION IN LIFE WAS TO GIVE PAIN.

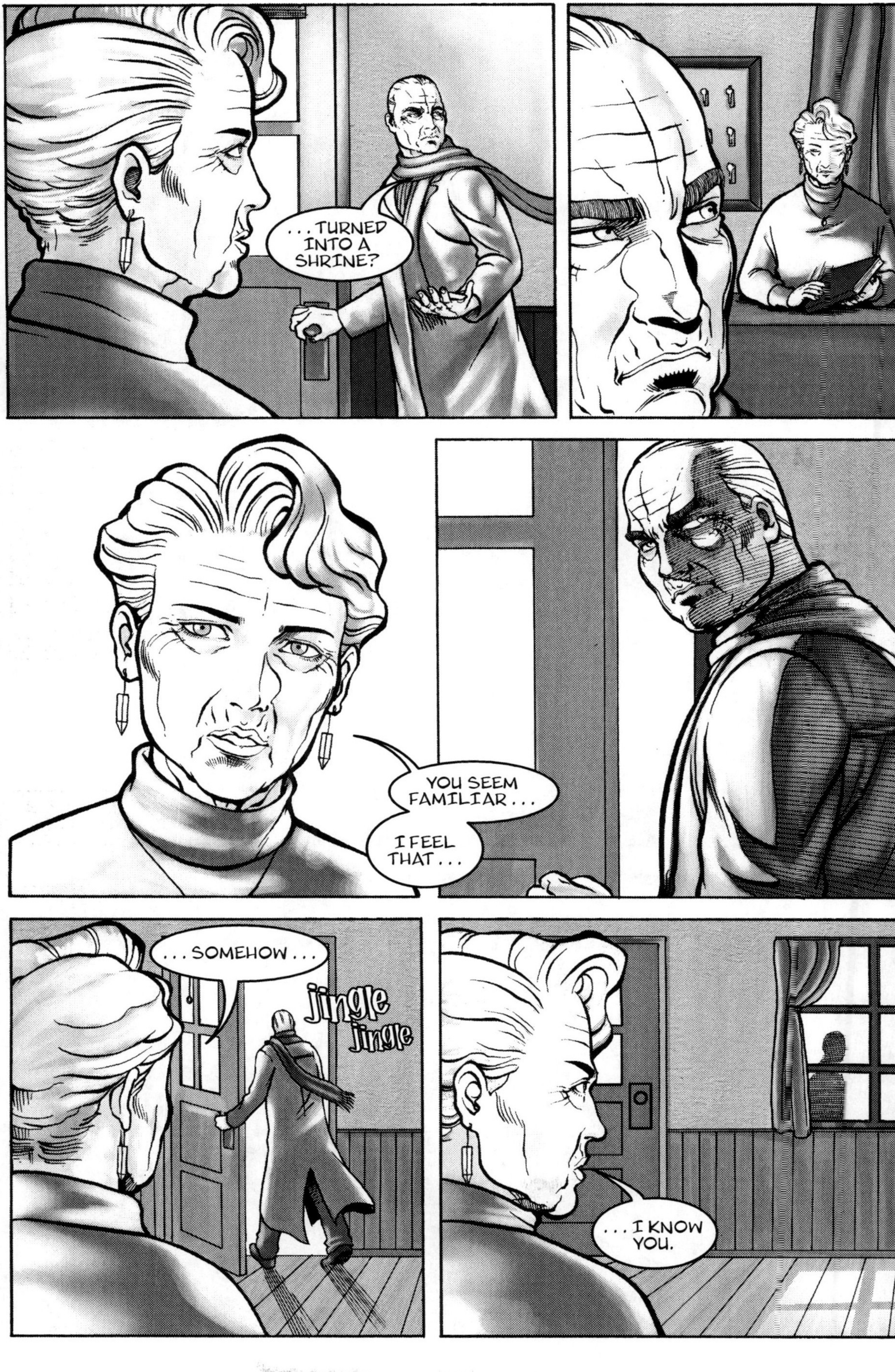
. . . TURNED INTO A SHRINE?
YOU SEEM FAMILIAR . . .
I FEEL THAT . . .
. . . SOMEHOW . . .
jingle jingle
. . . I KNOW YOU.

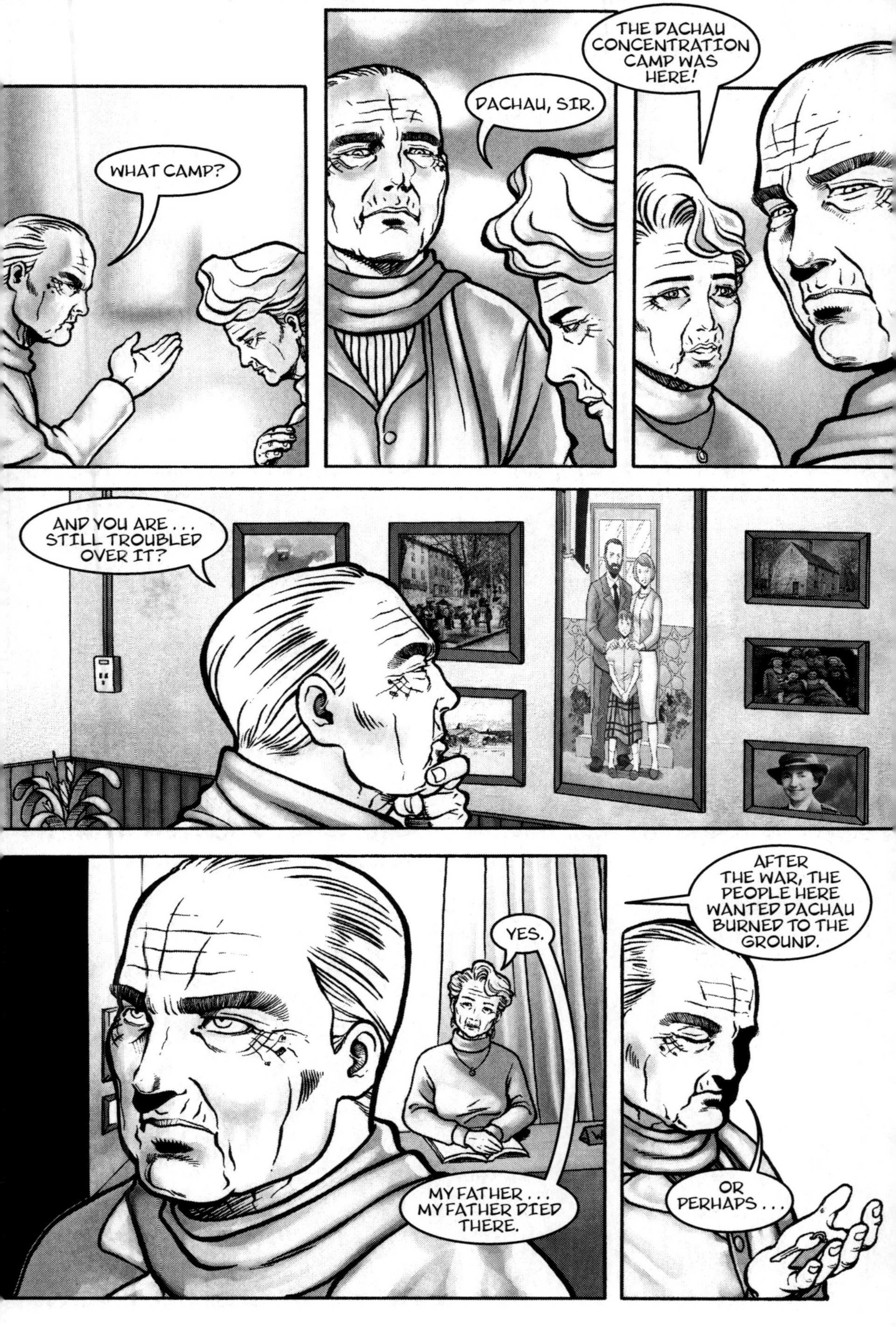
WHAT CAMP?
DACHAU, SIR.
THE DACHAU CONCENTRATION CAMP WAS HERE!
AND YOU ARE . . . STILL TROUBLED OVER IT?
YES.
MY FATHER . . . MY FATHER DIED THERE.
AFTER THE WAR, THE PEOPLE HERE WANTED DACHAU BURNED TO THE GROUND.
OR PERHAPS . . .

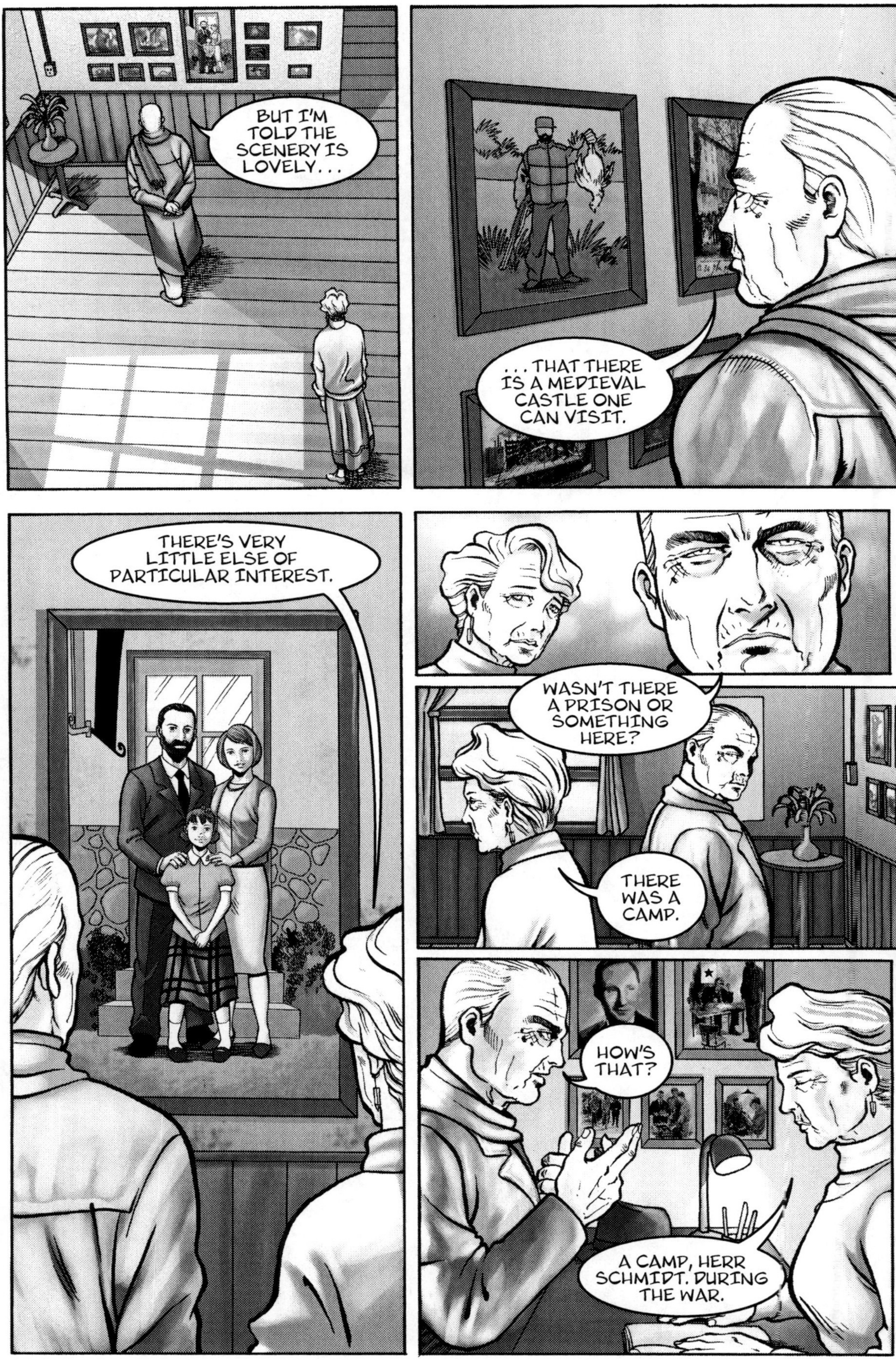
BUT I'M TOLD THE SCENERY IS LOVELY . . .
. . . THAT THERE IS A MEDIEVAL CASTLE ONE CAN VISIT.
THERE'S VERY LITTLE ELSE OF PARTICULAR INTEREST.
WASN'T THERE A PRISON OR SOMETHING HERE?
THERE WAS A CAMP.
HOW'S THAT?
A CAMP, HERR SCHMIDT. DURING THE WAR.

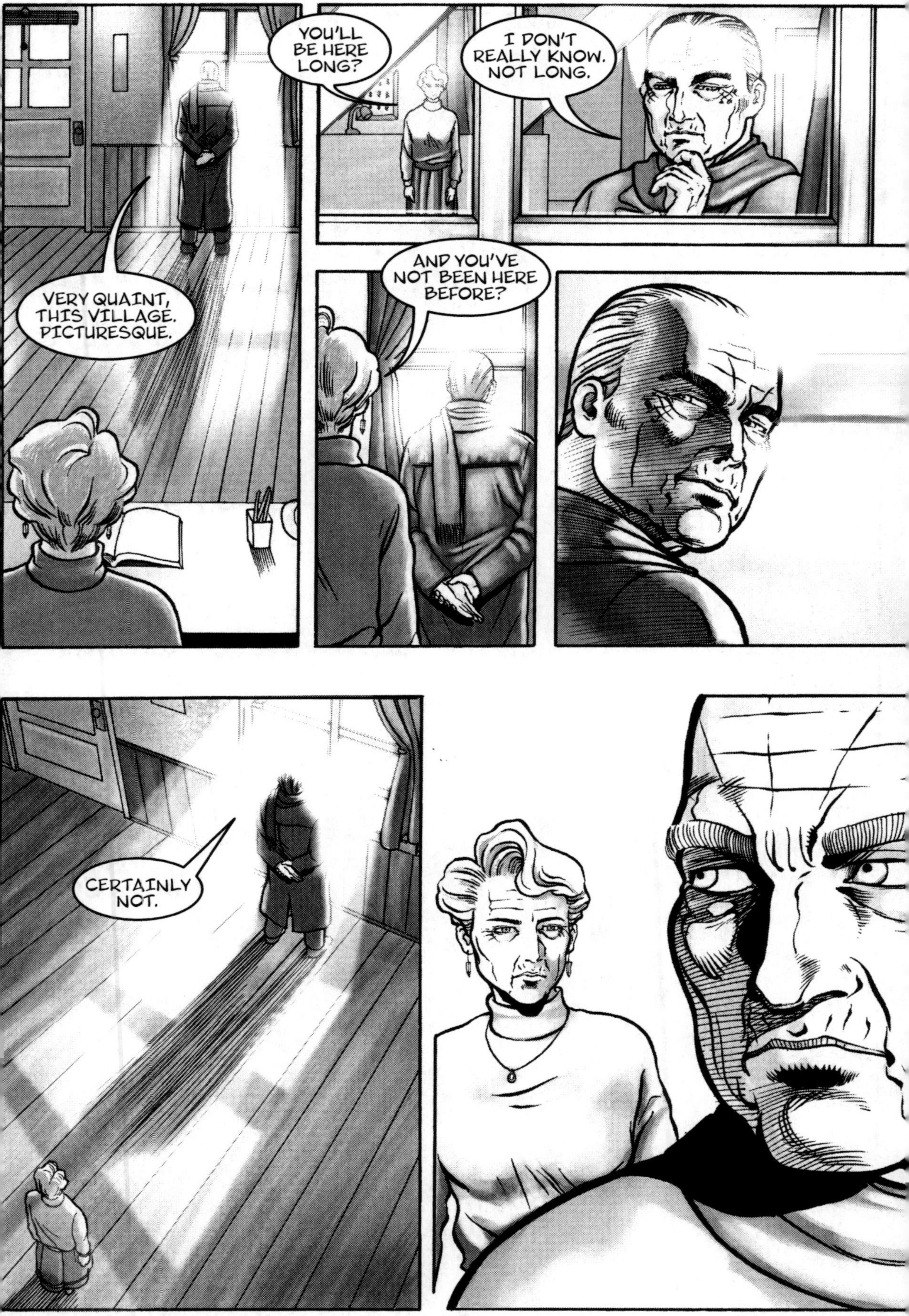
VERY QUAINT, THIS VILLAGE. PICTURESQUE.
YOU'LL BE HERE LONG?
I DON'T REALLY KNOW. NOT LONG.
AND YOU'VE NOT BEEN HERE BEFORE?
CERTAINLY NOT.

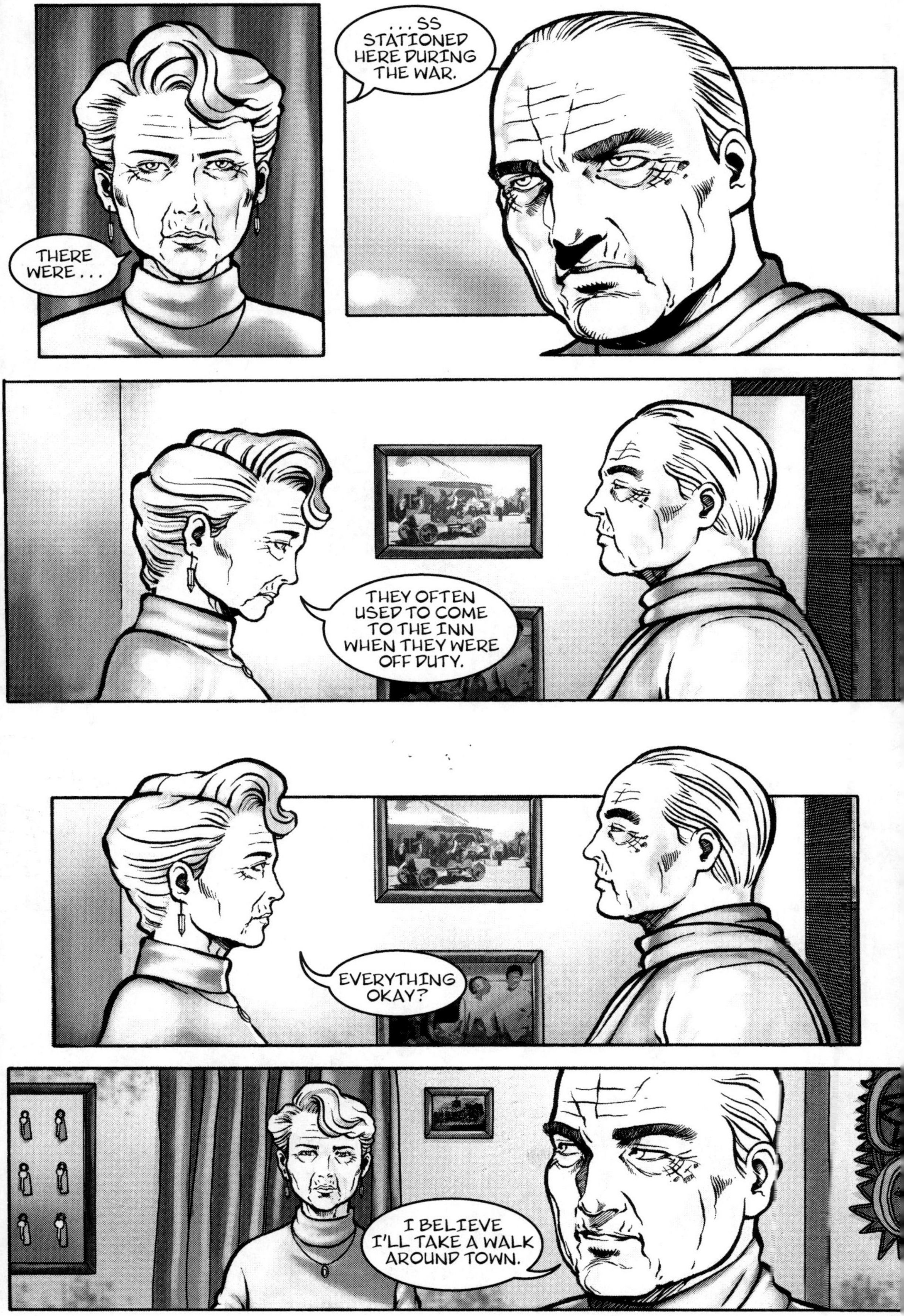
THERE WERE . . .
. . . SS STATIONED HERE DURING THE WAR.
THEY OFTEN USED TO COME TO THE INN WHEN THEY WERE OFF DUTY.
EVERYTHING OKAY?
I BELIEVE I'LL TAKE A WALK AROUND TOWN.

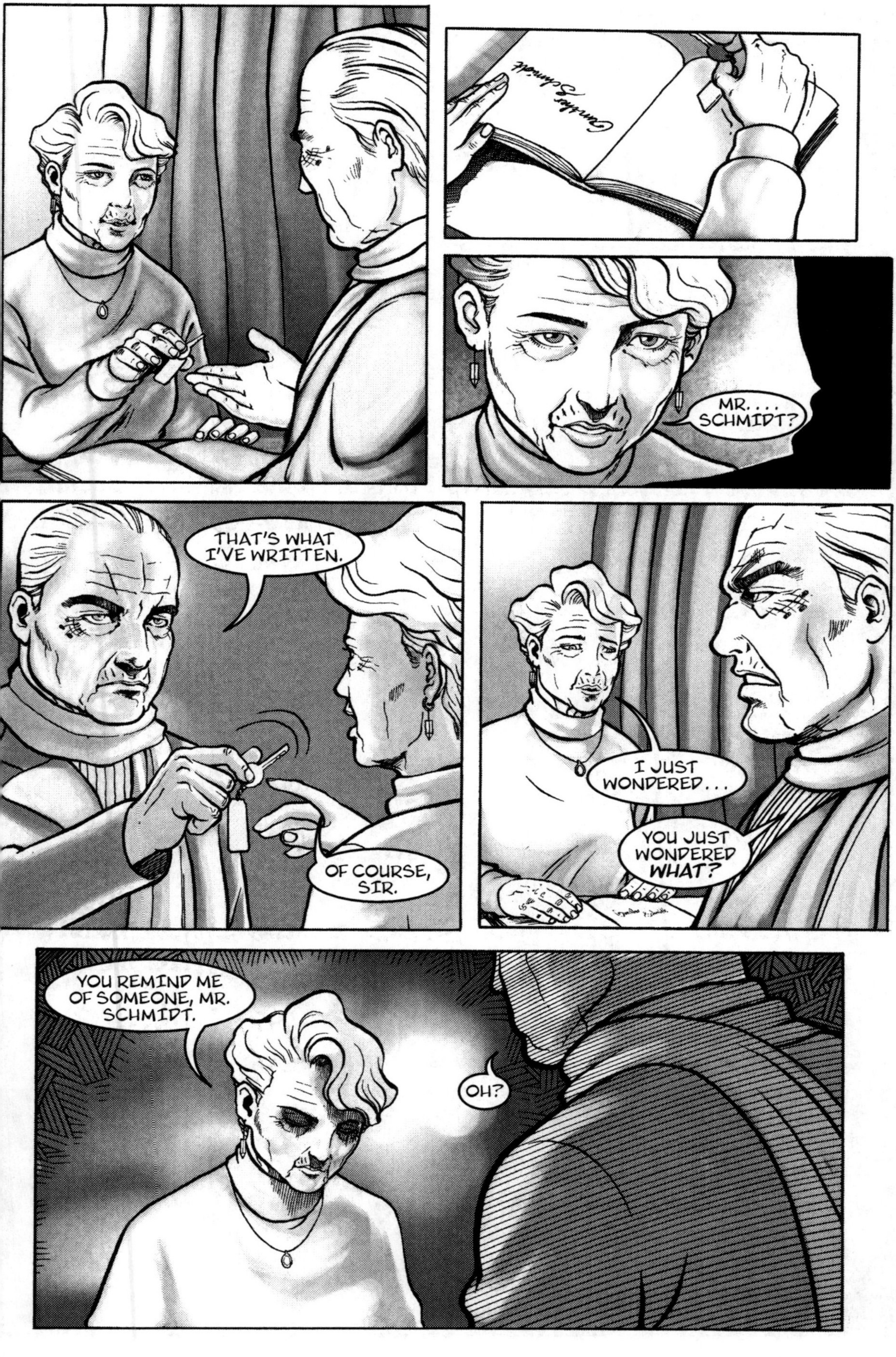
MR. . . . SCHMIDT?
THAT'S WHAT I'VE WRITTEN.
OF COURSE, SIR.
I JUST WONDERED . . .
YOU JUST WONDERED WHAT?
YOU REMIND ME OF SOMEONE, MR. SCHMIDT.
OH?

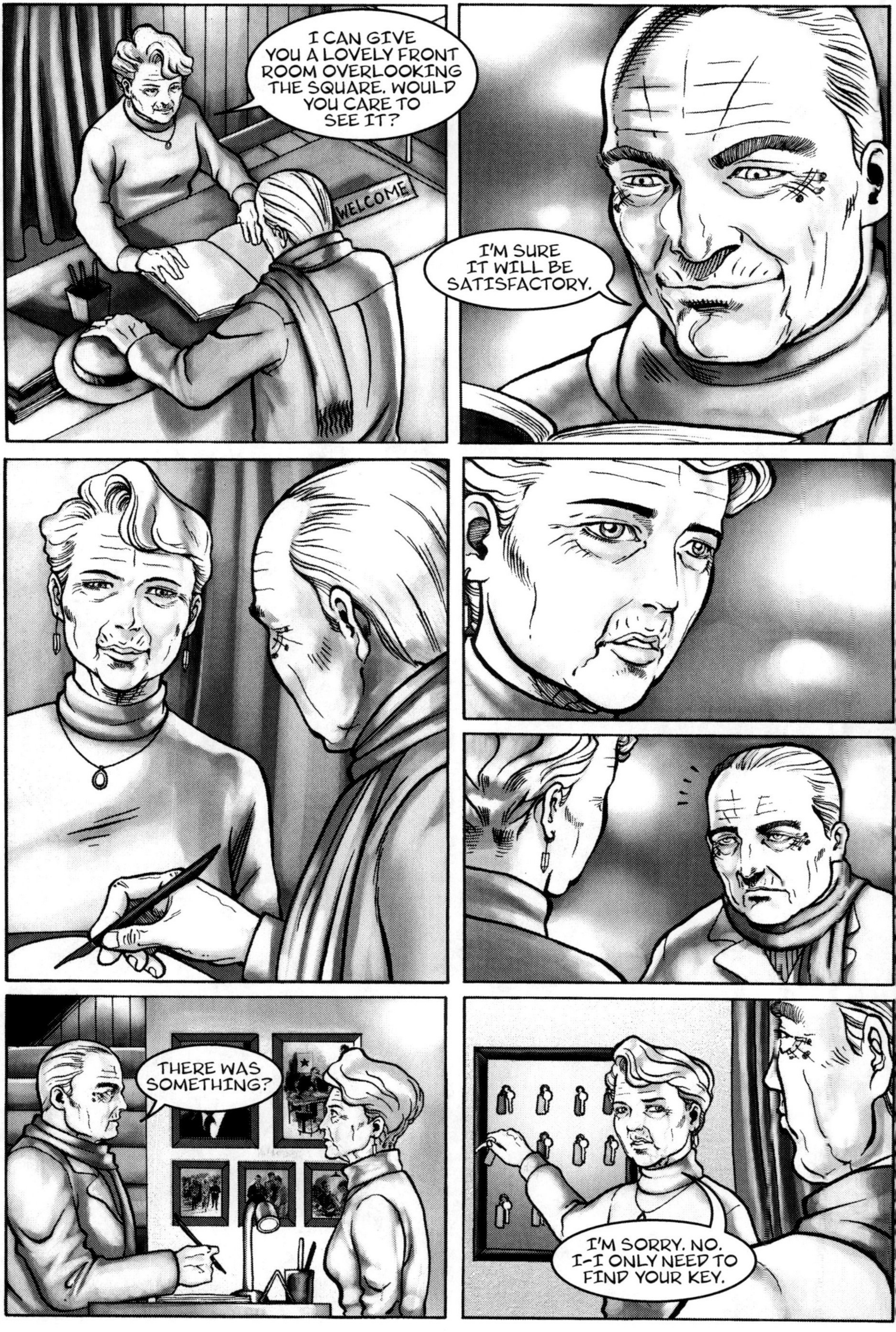
I CAN GIVE YOU A LOVELY FRONT ROOM OVERLOOKING THE SQUARE. WOULD YOU CARE TO SEE IT?
WELCOME
I'M SURE IT WILL BE SATISFACTORY.
THERE WAS SOMETHING?
I'M SORRY. NO. I-I ONLY NEED TO FIND YOUR KEY.

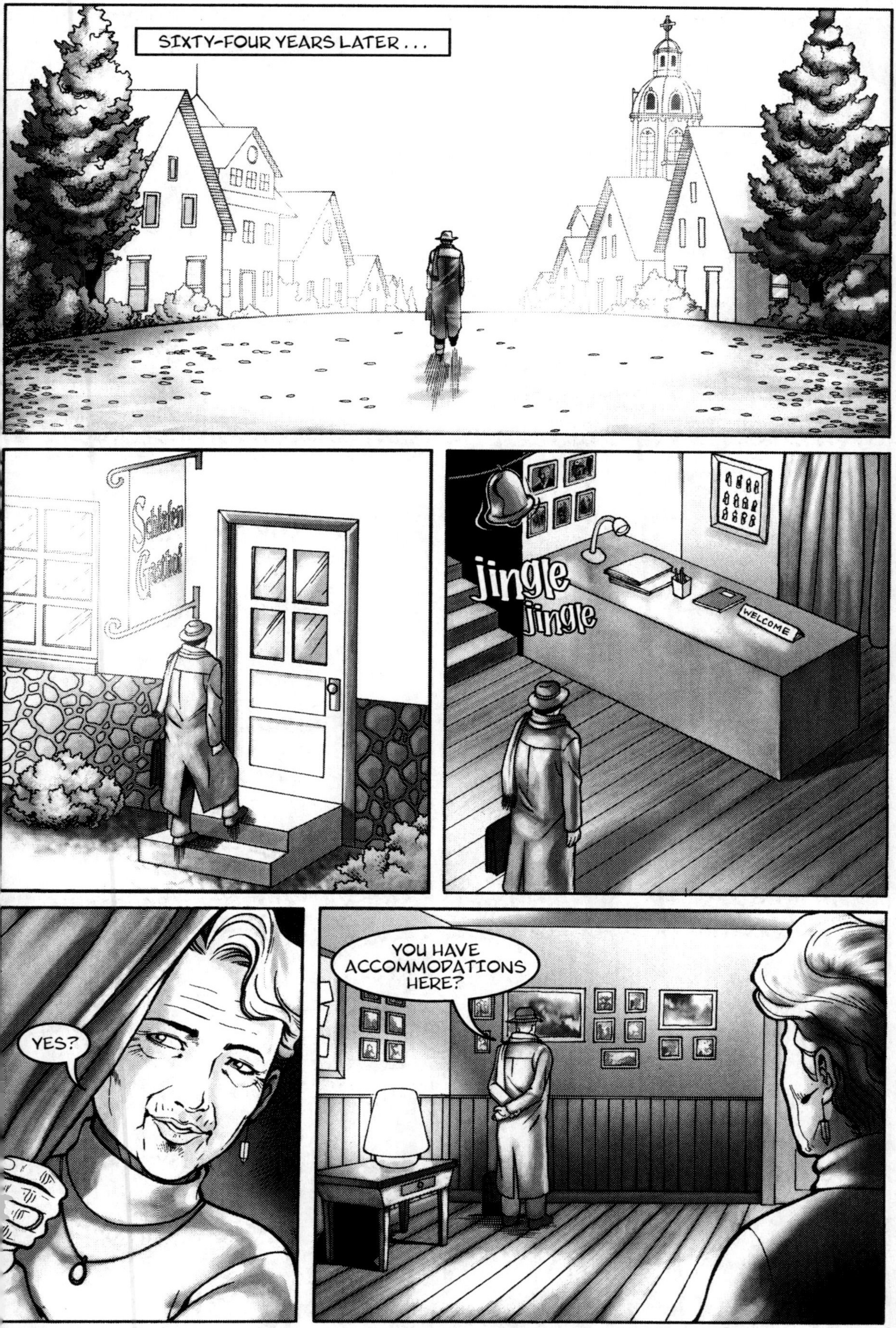
SIXTY-FOUR YEARS LATER . . .
Schlafen Gasthof
jingle
jingle
WELCOME
YES?
YOU HAVE ACCOMMODATIONS HERE?

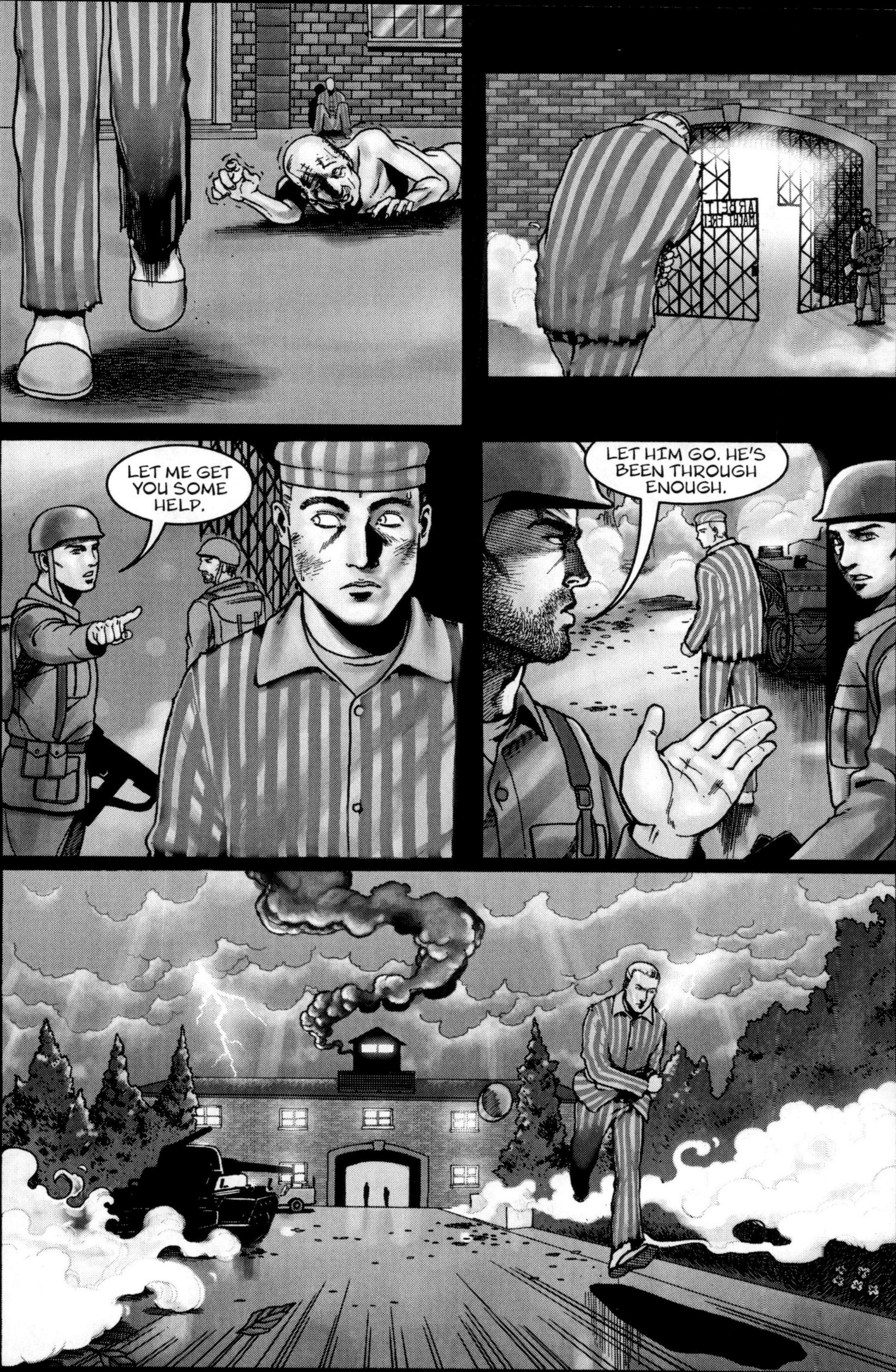
LET ME GET YOU SOME HELP.
LET HIM GO. HE'S BEEN THROUGH ENOUGH.

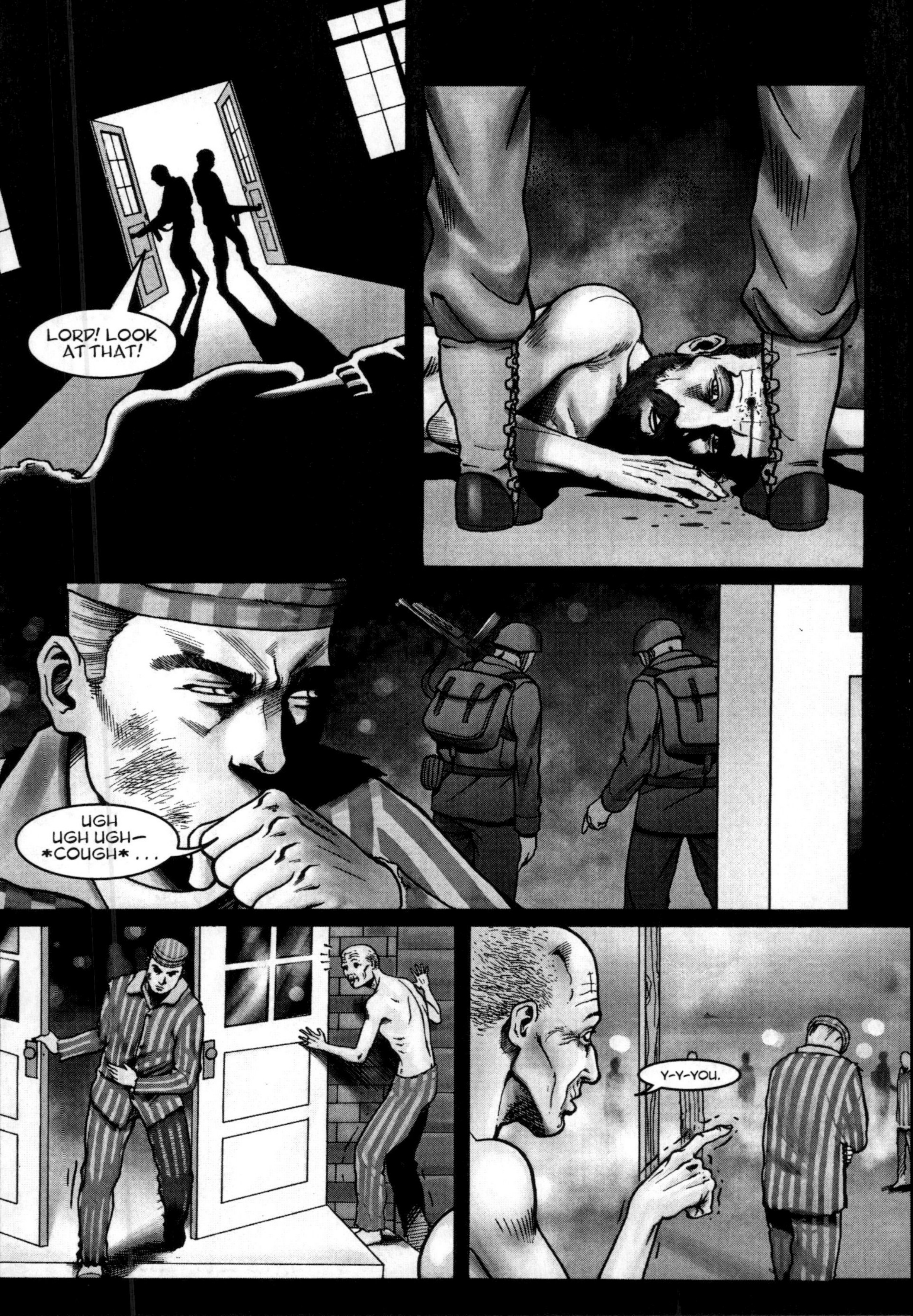
LORD! LOOK AT THAT!
UGH UGH UGH— *COUGH* . . .
Y-Y-YOU.

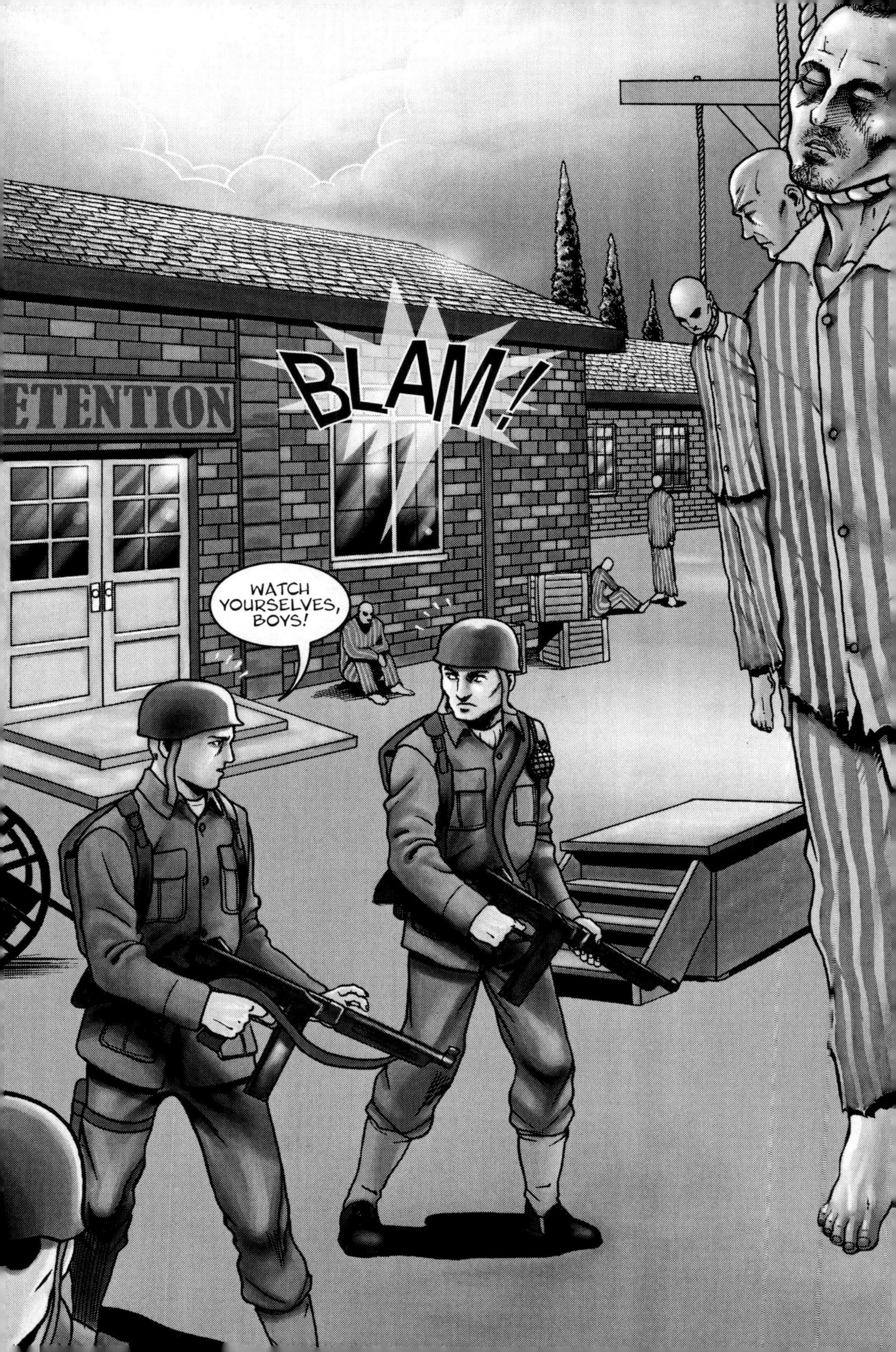

ETENTION
BLAM!
WATCH YOURSELVES, BOYS!

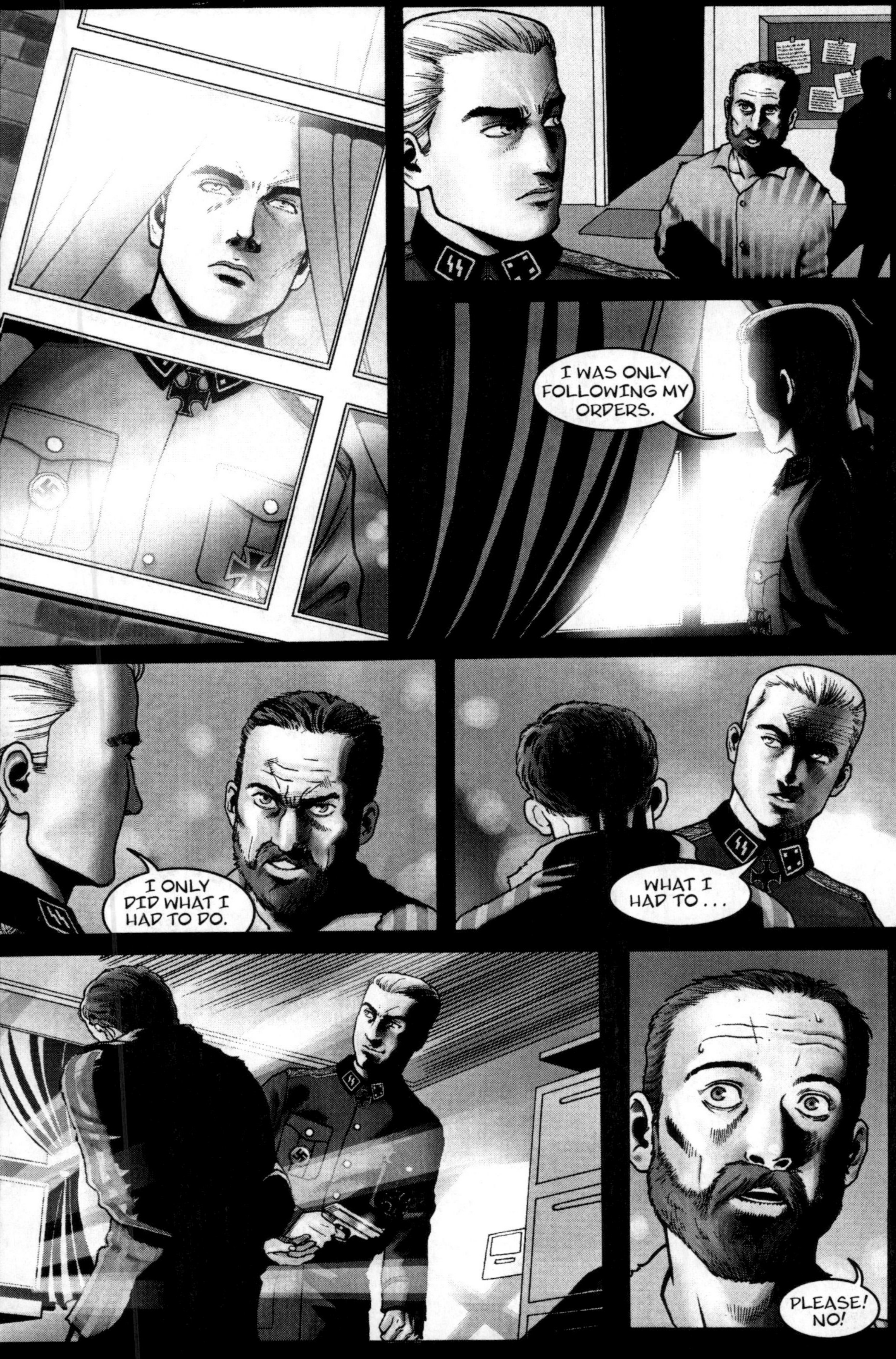
I WAS ONLY FOLLOWING MY ORDERS.
I ONLY DID WHAT I HAD TO DO.
WHAT I HAD TO . . .
PLEASE! NO!

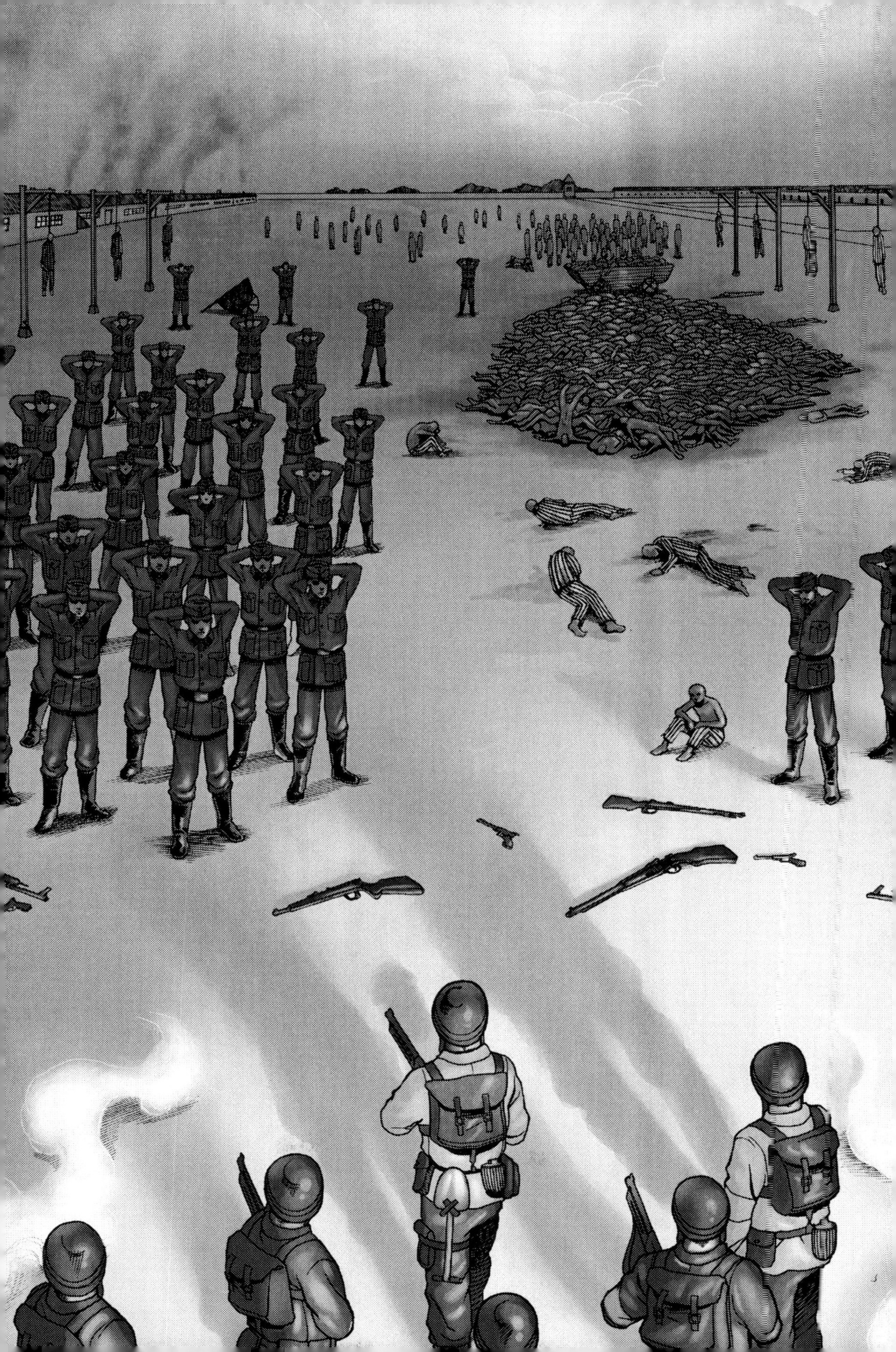

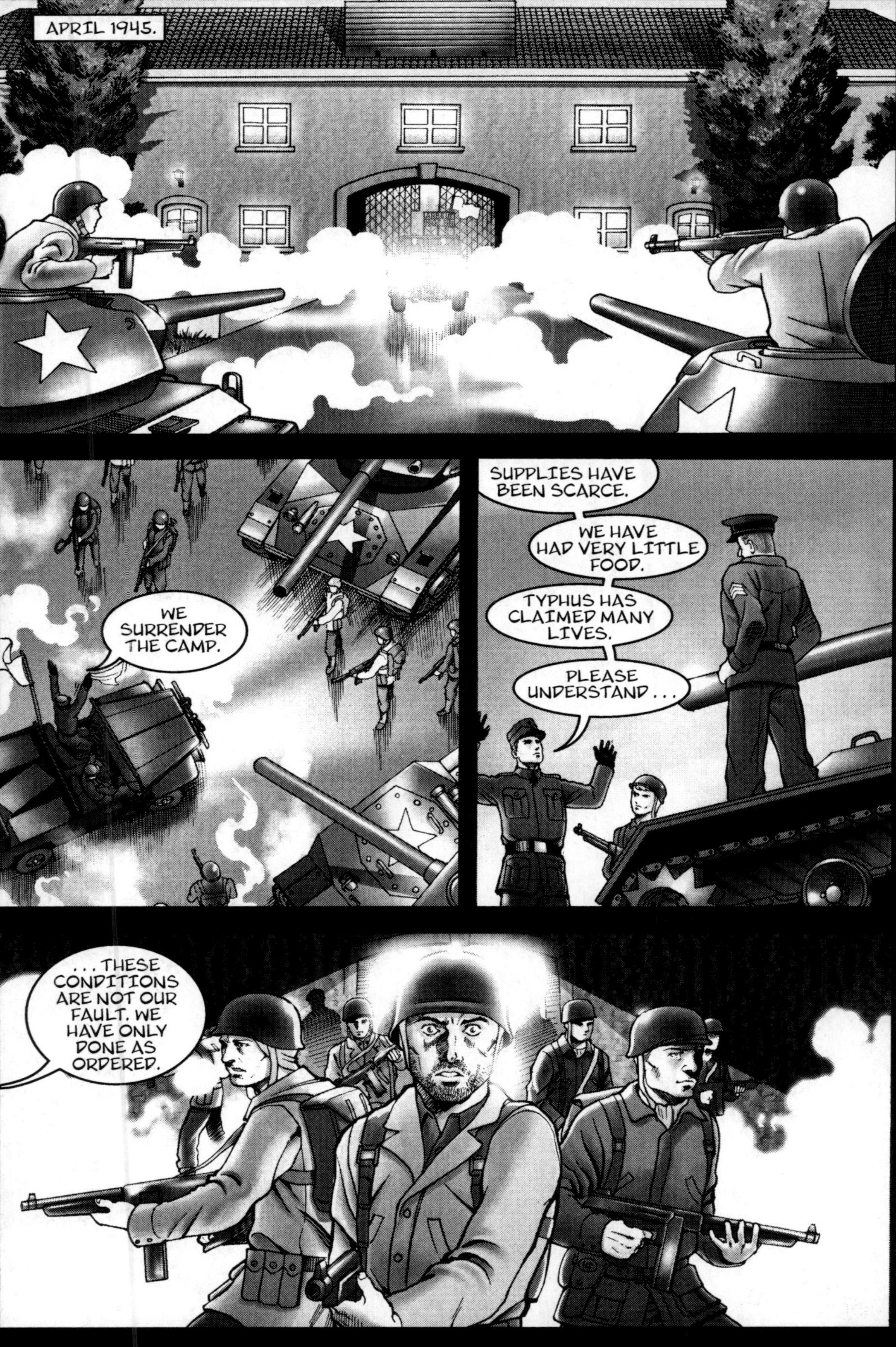
APRIL 1945.
WE SURRENDER THE CAMP.
SUPPLIES HAVE BEEN SCARCE.
WE HAVE HAD VERY LITTLE FOOD.
TYPHUS HAS CLAIMED MANY LIVES.
PLEASE UNDERSTAND . . .
. . . THESE CONDITIONS ARE NOT OUR FAULT. WE HAVE ONLY DONE AS ORDERED.

You're traveling through
another dimension,
a dimension not only of sight and sound
but of mind;
a journey into a wondrous land
whose boundaries
are that of imagination.
That's the signpost up ahead—
your next stop,
the Twilight Zone!

only the adoration of listeners and viewers but a host of prestigious awards, including a record-breaking six Emmy awards—two of them for his greatest achievement, *The Twilight Zone*.

The worlds and characters presented over the course of five seasons, beginning in October 1959, were like nothing audiences had seen before. Television, the new "must have" appliance for America's increasingly prosperous households, offered comedies such as *I Love Lucy* and *The Honeymooners*, news programs including Edward R. Murrow's *See It Now*, as well as Westerns, game shows, and soap operas. With a typewriter as his spade, Serling dug beneath the surface of the expected and planted the seeds of a more imaginative and thoughtful genre, writing more than half of the show's 156 episodes while producing and hosting all of them. He bravely took on themes of oppression, prejudice, and paranoia, all the while giving people what they needed at the end of the day: entertainment.

While he had his run-ins with censorship, Serling's clever use of other worlds and veiled scenarios generally protected him. As he explained, what he couldn't have a Republican or a Democrat espouse on the show, he could have an alien profess without offending the sponsors. This approach also allowed viewers to take away whatever message best suited them; the more reflective could consider the psychological and political implications, while others might be satisfied with simply enjoying the thrill of the surface story. So much more than mere science fiction or fantasy, Serling's scripts are parables that explore the multifaceted natures of hope, fear, humanity, loneliness, and self-delusion.

Half a century later, *The Twilight Zone* remains a part of our culture, routinely referenced in print and on television, having become a shorthand expression that succinctly describes the bizarre and unexpected. The original episodes are still aired on the SciFi Channel, both in late-night slots and as day-long marathons. The show was literally a Who's Who of Hollywood, helping to foster the careers of fledgling actors including Robert Redford, Ron Howard, Dennis Hopper, Charles Bronson, and William Shatner. It has also inspired countless authors and filmmakers, who have gone on to break through boundaries of their own.

In the fifty years since *The Twilight Zone* first aired, we've faced new enemies and have altered our definitions of happiness, but our core hopes and fears remain the same, as does our desire to be entertained. The stories are as compelling, and as telling, as ever. And now, in their newest incarnation, Serling's scripts serve as the basis for this graphic novel series, which honors the original text and even echoes the storyboarding of television, but offers a fresh interpretation, as seen through the eyes of a new generation of artists.

—Anna Marlis Burgard
Director of Industry Partnerships, Savannah College of Art and Design

There is a fifth dimension beyond that which is known to man. It is a dimension as vast as space and timeless as infinity. It is the middle ground between light and shadow, between science and superstition, and it lies between the pit of man's fears and the summit of his knowledge. This is the dimension of imagination. It is an area which we call the Twilight Zone.

America, between the 1950s and early 1960s, was itself in a sort of "twilight zone." Following the victories of World War II and the attending economic boom—but before the Civil Rights marches; the assassinations of John F. Kennedy, Martin Luther King, Jr., and Robert F. Kennedy; and the Vietnam War—we were wrapped in a gleaming package of shining chrome, white picket fences, and Hollywood glamour. But beneath this shimmering facade lay a turbulent core of racial inequality, sexual inequality, and the Cold War threat of nuclear attacks from the Soviet Union. We'd never been more affluent—or more frightened.

Enter Rodman Edward Serling of Binghamton, New York. Serling began writing in his teens for his high school newspaper; as a student at Antioch College, he was already selling scripts to radio programs. While serving as a paratrooper in the U.S. Army Eleventh Airborne (for which he earned a Purple Heart), he wrote for the Armed Services Radio. He went on to write for film and television, first in feature presentations for *Hallmark Hall of Fame* and *Playhouse 90*, including the lauded "Requiem for a Heavyweight," perhaps drawing inspiration from his own experiences as a Golden Gloves boxer. More than two hundred of his teleplays were produced. In all, his work would win not

ROD SERLING's THE TWILIGHT ZONE

DEATHS-HEAD REVISITED

Adaptation from Rod Serling's original script by

MARK KNEECE

Illustrated by

CHRIS LIE

WALKER & COMPANY
NEW YORK

Rod Serling's iconic episodes enter the Graphic Novel Zone with an inventive new series

One of most groundbreaking shows in the history of television, *The Twilight Zone* has become a permanent fixture in pop culture. This new graphic novel series reimagines the show's most enduring episodes, originally written by Serling himself, now adapted—from his original uncut scripts—for a new generation of fans.

Location: Dachau concentration camp years after World War II. A retired German SS captain returns to reminisce about his days in power. Until he finds himself at the mercy of those he tortured, on trial by those who died at his hands. Justice will finally be served . . . in the Twilight Zone.

Marketing
- Full-color shelf talker available
- Ongoing national media pitch
- Ongoing targeted science fiction/fantasy graphic novel pitch
- Online promotions
- Targeted educational mailing to graphic novel big mouths/bloggers
- YA Galley List serv offering

Let us know your thoughts on this title!
Please e-mail your comments to:
deb.shapiro@bloomsburyusa.com

Published by Walker Books
175 Fifth Avenue, New York, NY 10010
www.walkerbooks.com

ROD SERLING worked as a writer and producer throughout his career in television and has won the most Emmy awards for dramatic writing in the history of television. He wrote more than seventy-five episodes of the *Twilight Zone* series, for which he won three of his Emmys. He was also the show's creator, host, and narrator.

MARK KNEECE cowrote a story in *Alien World* in 1987 for Pacific Comics and discovered a talent for comics writing. He has written stories for numerous comics, including *Batman: Legends of the Dark*. In 1993, he came to Savannah College of Art and Design and helped found the sequential art department. Since then, he has taught comics writing as a professor of sequential art. He lives in Savannah, Georgia.

CHRIS LIE completed his MFA in Sequential Art at Savannah College of Art and Design. He has worked with several comic publishers on properties such as G.I. Joe, Transformers, Return to Labyrinth, Dungeons & Dragons, and Josie and the Pussycats. He founded Caravan Studio, a comic and illustration studio, where he works as art director. He lives in Jakarta, Indonesia.

WALKER BOOKS

SERIES: The Twilight Zone
TITLE: Deaths–Head Revisited
CREATED BY: Rod Serling
ADAPTED BY: Mark Kneece
ILLUSTRATED BY: Chris Lie
PB ISBN–13: 978-0-8027-9723-0
PB ISBN–10: 0-8027-9723-7
HC ISBN–13: 978-0-8027-9722-3
HC ISBN–10: 0-8027-9722-9
FORMAT: Paperback and hardcover graphic novel
TRIM: $6\frac{5}{8}$ x 10
PB PRICE: $9.99 U.S./$11.00 Can.
HC PRICE: $16.99 U.S./$18.50 Can.
PUB DATE: June 2009
PAGE COUNT: 72
AGES: 12 and up
GRADES: 7 and up

CONTACT: Deb Sh
(646) 438-6070
deb.shapiro@bloom

Please send

175 F
N